THE BEAR
HOUSE

THE BEAR HOUSE

MEAGHAN McISAAC

HOLIDAY HOUSE · NEW YORK

Library of Congress Cataloging-in-Publication Data

Names: McIsaac, Meaghan, author.
Title: The Bear House / Meaghan McIsaac.
Description: First edition. | New York : Holiday House, [2021] | Audience:
    Ages 10-14. | Audience: Grades 7-9. | Summary: "In a medieval world
    where the ruling houses are based on the constellations, betrayal,
    intrigue, and a king's murder force the royal sisters of the Bear House
    on the run"—Provided by publisher.
Identifiers: LCCN 2021001570 (print) | LCCN 2021001571 (ebook) | ISBN
    9780823446605 (hardcover) | ISBN 9780823450206 (ebook)
Subjects: CYAC: Fantasy. | Constellations—Fiction. | Kings, queens,
    rulers, etc.—Fiction.
Classification: LCC PZ7.M4786562 Be 2021 (print) | LCC PZ7.M4786562
    (ebook) | DDC [Fic]—dc23
LC record available at https://lccn.loc.gov/2021001570
LC ebook record available at https://lccn.loc.gov/2021001571

For Mae, for Henry,
And for you, dear reader

THE KINGDOMS OF

Celestial Sea

THE GOUGES

TAWNSHIRE

HEMOTH BEAR

LOURDES MANOR

KISHTOUL PASS

TAWNSHIRE TOWN

SHIVER WOODS

GREAT BEAR RIVER

WELLIN WOODS

DOWNSWIFT

HUNDFORD

HOUND

NORTH

W   E

S

ROARQUE

LION

TWIGATE

BLUE GIRAFFE

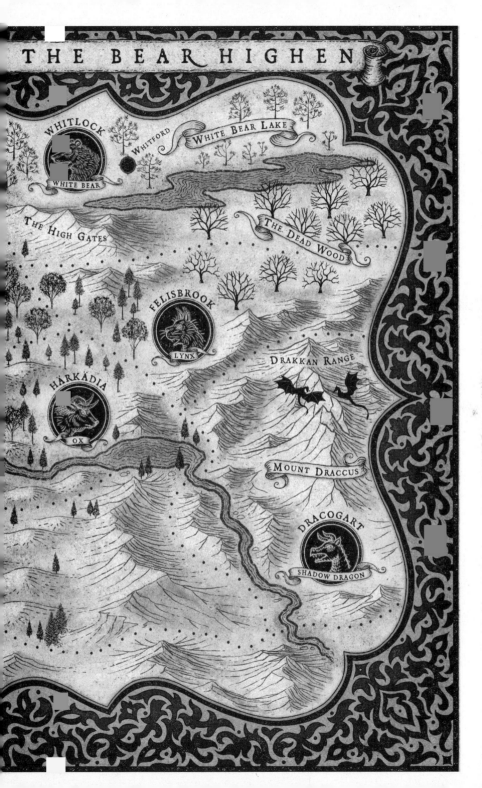

AT THE START OF ALL THINGS,
THERE WERE ONLY THE STARS.

Many different stars—light upon light upon light—but alone, they were not enough.

To cure their loneliness, their light combined, and of them were born the High Beasts, each belonging to their own quadrant of heaven.

To the skies of the South were born the High Fly, the Glimmer Snake, and more. And the stars of the South became known as the Waters.

To the skies of the East and West were born the Dust Ram, the White Bull, the Star Twins, the Prism Scorpion, and more. These traveled together, one after the other, a ring of High Beasts in a never-ending loop. These stars became the Ring.

To the skies of the North were born the White Bear, the Shadow Dragon, the Starhound, and more. But of them all, the stars loved the firstborn Bear best. And so the northern stars became the stars of the Great Bear.

When from the earth, Man emerged from the darkness, looking to the sky for guidance, the stars stretched out their light and sent these beasts to lead him, bringing them into the flesh.

And Man worshipped the stars, and he worshipped the beasts, and the beasts were sacred to him.

Thus, beneath the heavenly sea of the Waters, the Highen of the Waters was born.

Beneath the Ring's milky skies grew the Highen of the Ring.

And beneath the crisp, dark skies of the Great Bear, the mighty Bear Highen began.

—THE WRITINGS OF BERN,
On the Founding of Highens: The Fore, *Star Writ*

 PROLOGUE

THE Shadow Dragons were screaming. Their cries rose out of the dark, echoing over the peak of Mount Draccus.

Men had come for their eggs.

Quintin Wyvern crouched in the shadows of a rocky outcrop, watching the retrieval party approach the nests. The young prince had promised his father he would stay in the castle by his ailing mother's bedside. An outbreak of firelung had taken hold of the Kingdom of Dracogart, and Mother was just one of many fighting to survive. But that night, when the dragons began wailing, Lady Wyvern had squeezed Quintin's hand.

"Go," she told him, her breath ragged from the sickness. "Go and witness their sacrifice."

And so Quintin left her. He had followed hidden paths so as not to be seen, the mountain's breath thick and fetid and burning his lungs.

From his vantage point behind an outcrop of obsidian, Quintin saw the lights of the city of Dracogart below, saw the men in impressive armor walking up the main road, their horses sidestepping with nerves.

The mother dragons hissed at their approach, plumes of smoke billowing from their gaping mouths in warning. Only three eggs had been laid that year, each one a precious gift from the stars. They would take a further two years to hatch.

One of them would never get that chance.

There was a chirrup at his back, and Quintin startled. He turned and saw a Shadow Dragon, a juvenile female, crouched on the stones above him. She blinked at him, her yellow eyes anxious.

Umbra.

Quintin pressed a finger to his lips and turned back to watch the soldiers.

The mother dragons paced, encircling their nests. The light of the men's torches danced and glinted off their dark, stony scales.

Quintin knew they would not give up an egg without a fight. Shadow Dragons did not abide the laws of men.

And yet the law demanded an egg all the same. Word had reached Dracogart a week ago from the Major: the Kingdom of the Shadow Dragon must surrender one egg. And that egg would pay for the firelung cure that could only be found in the land of their enemies, the Ring Highen.

"We can't!" his mother had said, fuming, when she had still been well enough to stand. "There has to be another way!"

Chancellor Furia, King Wyvern's most trusted advisor, had agreed—even though Furia and Queen Wyvern rarely agreed on anything. "Sire, it is too sinful even to think of."

The eggs of the Shadow Dragon were sacred. Blessings from the holy stars themselves. How could Dracogart allow *anyone* to take what had been given by the stars?

"The Major was chosen to be Major because he is favored by the stars," King Wyvern told them. "If the Major believes this is the way to save our people, then we must trust that he is right."

Save the people, yes. *And more importantly now*, thought Quintin, *save Mother.* Her condition was worsening by the hour.

But still, he felt a nervousness in his gut. What if Father was wrong to allow this?

Umbra chirruped again, as if she could read his thoughts.

Quintin looked beyond Dracogart's rocky valley, over which the mountain's shadow fell—Father was out there, somewhere, hunting with his mount Draco, the largest dragon alive, the dragon-king of the Shadow Dragons. When the Major's men had left the castle for the mountain path to retrieve the egg, Father had left with Draco—the king of dragons would be angry to hear his wives so distressed, he'd said.

But Quintin knew the truth. Seeing the Major's men take an egg from the Shadow Dragons' nest was too painful for even his father to bear.

There were shouts from the men in armor, and when Quintin looked, one had approached the edge of the nest. The man held a spear, its tip fitted with a fat, dripping hearth weasel—as if a treat would be enough to trade a dragon for her child.

One of the mother dragons slunk toward him, a threatening hiss venting from her smoking maw. The fins at the edge of her jaw fluttered. She was eager to crunch bone.

"*Courage, men!*" shouted someone. "*Hold!*" cried another. And still more were roaring orders as the man in armor inched closer to the dragon.

Quintin held his breath. The young soldier stepped across the line on the ground where the rock had been scorched by dragon breath—the threshold of the nest.

"Too close," Quintin whispered.

The mother dragons reared up, all of them screaming in unison, black wings flapping. The foremost dragon lunged, her powerful jaws snapping with a thunderous clap just short of the young man's belly.

The dragons' screams built on one another, the noise folding onto itself, lifting with a ferocious desperation. They were screaming for Draco.

Draco, whose size and power would protect them all.

Draco, their king.

Quintin's eyes burned with tears. Draco was with his father. Draco would not save them.

And then a roar exploded from somewhere below the mountain. It was so loud and resonant, it was as if the earth itself had opened up.

Draco?

No. This roar was earthbound. Not of the sky.

Quintin heard Umbra screech and skitter away, scurrying back to her family, back into a nest farther up the mountain. She was only a little dragon, after all, even if she was Draco's daughter.

The mother dragons' mood shifted, their hissing and smoking replaced by a quiet, nervous chirping, tiny sparks spitting from the sides of their mouths. Quintin had never seen Shadow Dragons look like that—tails wrapped close to their sides, bellies pressed low to the ground, all huddled close together. They were frightened. Frightened of what was making its way up the mountain road.

A bear.

A bear unlike any Quintin had ever seen before.

The hulking beast stood heads above the horses, her girth so wide it took up the entire path. Her long, grizzled fur looked like fire, a bright amber color that gleamed in the torchlight. Her jaws looked powerful enough to crush iron, her paws big enough to shake the earth. There was no mistaking it—a Hemoth Bear.

She was Mizar. The mightiest creature in all of the Bear Highen.

And beside her stood a man, just as hulking and grizzled as she. The Bear Major himself: Jasper Lourdes.

They approached the nest, the dragons clustered together in a quaking mass. Mizar the Hemoth chuffed and snorted, her massive footfalls causing the very earth to shake.

Quintin watched as the Major placed a hand on the Hemoth's flank and the bear stopped. The Major continued to approach and, without hesitation, stepped over the nest's threshold. The dragons did not make a sound. He picked his way over rocks and boulders until he was standing above an egg, its black shell speckled with pinpricks of warm light.

One of the mothers, the one who had snapped at the soldier, whined with alarm, and the Hemoth roared again, dislodging rock and stone from the mountainside and sending it tumbling down. Quintin threw his hands over his head to protect himself from the stony shower; dust powdered his shoulders.

When the rumble faded to nothing, the dragons were silent again.

Major Jasper Lourdes bent down to the egg and took it gently in his hands.

Quintin longed to know how it felt. Warm, he imagined. Like the stones that lined the hearth fires in the castle.

Finally, delicately, the High King of the Bear Highen fit the egg into the crook of his arm, as if cradling a baby, and bowed to the frightened flock of dragons.

And just as suddenly as they'd arrived, the Major and the Hemoth left, disappearing down the mountain road with the Major's soldiers following behind.

Quintin was alone with the Shadow Dragons, trembling with his awe of the Hemoth Bear, and with fear and sadness for the egg the men had taken with them—the Shadow Dragon that would never be.

And the Great Bear Lord Tawn saw inside the heart of the human Dov, and saw in it that which pleased him: courage *to face whatever threat might meet him,* love *for all the On-High's children, and the* honor *to uphold the greatness of the stars* . . .

And so it was that the Great Bear Lord Tawn chose the human Dov to be protector of the realm.

And so it was that the Highen had its first Major and its first Hemoth Bear.

—THE WRITINGS OF BERN,
The Crowning of the First Major: The Age of Tawn, *Star Writ*

 ONE

BERNADINE Lourdes was pouting. The only daughter of the House of the White Bear was used to having her own way.

But this was *Aster* Lourdes's house—and she'd be damned by Tawn if she let her spoiled cousin dictate the afternoon.

"Pout all you want," Aster snapped, fishing through the drawers of her father's giant mahogany desk. "I told you, I've no interest in board games today."

The girls sat in the high-ceilinged study of Aster's father, where heavy, deep-red curtains framing the bay windows blocked the sunshine of another beautiful summer day. Bernadine sulked, a Crowns & Stones board across her lap. The periwinkle damask of her petticoat clashed with the rugged coldness of the room.

Aster loved this room. She loved the dimness; loved the musty smell of the old leather books in the towering shelves; loved the icy chill of the dark tiles under her feet, painted with depictions of Hemoth Bears from history. They reminded her of her family's importance to the Highen every time she took a step.

For Aster Lourdes was the daughter of the Bear Major, the ruler of all the Bear Highen—Jasper Lourdes, the Death Chaser.

Her fingers grazed the smooth, familiar handle of the object she was looking for, and she grinned. Her father's ivory quill knife. She pulled it out and placed it gently on the desktop.

Bernadine let out a huff, folding her arms and narrowing her eyes. "And *I* have no interest in your silly map."

"It's not silly, and it's not just any old map."

"It's boring."

"It's *not*. I'm making a *war map*."

Aster smoothed the giant map out on the surface of her father's desk. The parchment was wrinkled and bruised from constant folding and unfolding, its sides and corners fraying. No matter how lovingly she cared for her map, Aster could see she was loving it to death.

Picking up the quill knife, she resolved to be gentler, then set about her work, sharpening and shaping the tip of her quill. "Father and Uncle Bram plan to meet the enemy's forces near Kishtowel Pass, where the Great Bear River meets the Celestial Sea. I have to draw their route."

"You don't know that that's where they are. And it's *tool*."

"What?"

"*Tool*," Bernadine said again. "Look"—she hopped off the windowsill and stormed over, slamming her finger down on the name under Aster's quill—"K-i-s-h-t-o-u-l. It's pronounced Kish-*tool*. Not Kish-towel."

Aster slapped her cousin's hand away and made a mental note to remember Kish*tool*.

"I *do* know where they are," she insisted, hoping the mispronunciation would disappear from conversation.

"You know they *plan* to meet the Ring's forces at the pass, but that's all. There's no way to know where they are for certain—them *or* the Ring. Your map is probably all wrong."

"Of course they'll be there," said Aster, gritting her teeth and circling Kishtoul Pass to mark the end of her father's path.

In truth, she didn't know for certain. They hadn't heard from the Bear Highen's armies in a fortnight.

The day word reached her father that the Ring Highen had declared war, there had been shock and fear. The Major had just traded the Ring the egg of a Shadow Dragon—a deeply powerful and sacred object—for the venom of the Prism Scorpion to cure the firelung plaguing Dracogart. It was a mutually beneficial arrangement, one that promised friendship and peace after many centuries of rivalry—and often war. Two Highens, a sea apart, helping each other into a new age.

Certainly, there were voices that had cautioned against the trade. *Bah*, her father had said, waving an unconcerned hand, *men always have opinions on matters as delicate as this. All will be well.*

But now, with the egg delivered and the new alliance made, the Ring had the gall to attack? It was a baffling move, one her father and the other Heads of Houses were completely unprepared for. The Ring had attacked and burned several coastal cities quickly and mercilessly, and Father had had no choice but to answer.

Jasper Lourdes had mobilized his men. And as Minor of the Highen, first among the lesser kings and the Major's second, Uncle Bram had moved the White Bear's armies the very next day to join them. Both Aster's and Bernadine's father were at war.

"Fine. Do what you want," said Bernadine. "I'm going to try on some dresses."

"Which dresses do you think you're trying on?"

"Ursula's."

"You wouldn't dare!"

Bernadine peeked around the open door and looked back at Aster with a wrinkled brow. "Why wouldn't I?"

"Because Ursula will *kill* you if she catches you."

Bernadine waved an unconcerned hand. "She's outside. She'll never know."

Aster looked over to the window, the sunlight of a cloudless day fighting to invade the darkness of her father's office.

"She's harassing your bear boy again." Bernadine shrugged, slipping out the door. "She'll be at it all afternoon."

Aster winced as the door slammed shut, and, alone in the quiet, she sighed. Ursula, her big sister, had a wardrobe of at least two hundred dresses. Aster wouldn't see Bernadine again until dinner.

It was funny, really, how much Bernadine had changed since coming to live with the Major's family four years ago. Uncle Bram had sent her to Tawnshire from Whitlock after her mother, Aunt Gwynlin, became very sick. And when poor Aunt Gwynlin had died, Uncle Bram thought it best that Bernadine remain with her cousins, not only to keep her from the sadness of his empty house, but to have her brought up a proper lady at the Major's court. Whitlock was a cold wasteland compared to Tawnshire; Aster could still remember the Minor's little daughter arriving on horseback, wearing weasel furs and coveralls like a peasant. Not even a carriage! Just her own white horse and her father's soldiers to escort her. She had been a different girl then.

Aster stared at the handle of the quill blade in her hand: heavy ox bone, honey-stained, carved in the likeness of the Hemoth Bear. A simple instrument for a Major, humble, with no gemstones or precious metals. And yet the bear had been so carefully carved, with so much detail, that it was ornate in its own quiet way. It was a strange thing for a Major to have—traditionally, his quills were kept sharp by devoted attendants, and no Major bothered himself with such a small, tedious task. Perhaps that was why she liked it so much—because it made her father different. Keeper Rizlan had given it to him when he was a boy not much older than her. *To help with my studies,* her father had said.

Where was Father now? How long until he would send word?

She walked her fingers along the trail her father's armies had marched for the past month. From Tawnshire…southwest along the Great Bear River…and through the Wellin Woods, a dangerous forest of dark shadows and hungry wolves—or so her father always told her. She made a silent vow to see it someday.

Someday, when *she* would lead the Bear Highen's armies through the dangers of the Wellin Woods.

It could happen. It wouldn't, but it could. Ursula was the heir, the one expected to fill the role of Major, but sometimes Aster liked to dream it would be her.

The Lourdes had headed the House of the Hemoth Bear for centuries, and her own father was the younger of two brothers, whom no one expected to take the throne. And even though he had been chosen above her uncle by the Hemoth Bear, it had never divided the brothers, as some might expect. The White Bear, the second-most-powerful and -sacred of High Beasts, chose Uncle Bram, and the Lourdes brothers brought stability and prosperity to the Highen as no Major and his Minor had ever done before. They were a team, united by blood and purpose. If Aster became Major, she liked to imagine that Ursula would be just like Uncle Bram and serve as Minor, the Lourdes legacy continued.

But then, Aster doubted her big sister could even name the eight sacred High Beasts of the Highen, let alone their kingdoms. Aster closed her eyes and ran through them: Dracogart, the Kingdom of the Shadow Dragon; Hundford, the Kingdom of the Hounds; Felisbrook, the Kingdom of the Lynx; Roarque, the Kingdom of the Lion; Twigate, the Kingdom of the Blue Giraffe; Härkädia, the Kingdom of the Ox. And, of course, Whitlock, the Kingdom of the White Bear, where Bernadine and Uncle Bram reigned. And most importantly, there was Tawnshire, the Kingdom of the Hemoth Bear. Home.

A roar, furious and deep, suddenly shook the windowpane. Ursula's familiar high-pitched shriek rang out next, and Aster ran to the window.

There was her sister, racing across the front green away from the stables and the Bear Holding. Her usual train of six ladies-in-waiting was absent. What, Aster wondered, had her sister been up to that she had to leave her lady's maids behind?

"*Get it away from me!*" Ursula screamed, tripping over the front of her rose-colored dress and landing face-first in the grass.

Another loud roar—and then the large, round, shaggy form of Alcor, Mizar's cub, exploded out of the Bear Holding, his white teeth glinting in a terrifying snarl.

Ursula, Aster thought, finally understanding, *why can't you just keep your nose out of the Holding!*

Her big sister had been poking around the Bear Holding all season. Ursula had never shown any interest in Mizar or Alcor before—in fact, Aster had long suspected she was frightened of the monstrous war bears. It was a strange thing for her vain, cosseted sister to do, and Aster couldn't quite figure what had started it.

All she knew was this: it was a bad idea.

"*Bear boy!*" Ursula shrieked, Alcor closing the gap between them with raised hackles. The young bear was getting big. Aster couldn't believe how big. "*Bear boy! Bear boy!*"

Aster's eyes scanned the grounds, her heart beginning to race. Where were the Hermans, the Manor's guards?

Just steps away from Ursula, Alcor stretched out his long neck, flabby lips curling over razor teeth, and let out another roar. Aster's breath caught. She lifted a fist to the glass, about to bang on the pane—

And then she saw them: three Hermans, racing for Ursula, ready to throw themselves between her and Alcor.

But Alcor stopped. Just like that.

The bear sat back on his rump, gargantuan paws folded daintily in front of him. He'd forgotten Ursula completely. There was a sound, Aster noticed now, like a quacking, whining duck.

She unlatched the glass and leaned her head out the window. There: it was Devin, the bear boy, standing in the door of the Bear

Holding. He was blowing into what Aster knew to be his special kazoo.

The young bear—now more like a stuffed toy than a monster—leaned his head back as far as he could to see his kazoo-playing servant, then rolled happily in the grass, his fury completely dissolved.

Aster couldn't help but wrinkle her nose. She was relieved enough that Ursula was unharmed, but the fact remained—Alcor was shaping up to be a pretty lousy High Beast for the House of the Hemoth Bear. If it had been Mizar that Ursula had offended, her sister would have been flung in pieces all over the front green, the bear boy's kazoo only making matters worse.

The Hermans rushed to help Ursula to her feet.

"A monster!" she shrieked, pointing at the overgrown cub. "He's nothing but a killer!"

Aster rolled her eyes. He certainly was not. Not yet.

"That's what your father needs me to make him!" the boy bellowed back. Aster sat up. A servant, yelling at a daughter of the Major? That took a lot of nerve…or lack of brains.

Ursula straightened and stood in that dignified Lady-of-Lourdes pose she saved for visiting princes and dignitaries—proud and regal, like their father.

Aster watched as the bear boy's anger drained into his feet, his stiff, accusing posture dissolving into slumped shoulders and a drooping head.

"How dare you speak to me that way?" Ursula spat. "What will my father say when I tell him what an insolent wretch you are?" Ursula might have been beautiful, but at just sixteen she had a bite almost as powerful as Mizar's. "You are a servant of my house! *My* servant!"

"I am *Alcor's* servant!"

Aster watched the bear boy, surprised. He had always lived at the Manor, as far back as her memory would go. He'd grown up here, all thirteen years, just as she had. And in all that time, Aster had barely heard him speak. He was apprenticed to Master Rizlan, the High Keeper of the Hemoth Bears; maybe with all the talking Master Rizlan did around the Manor, there wasn't much left for the boy to say.

Ursula was less amused. "If you think for one minute that your first loyalties are to that—that—that—*animal* over there," she said, "you'd best think again! How dare you presume to put me and my family second to that beast?"

The boy said nothing, digging his knuckles into his eyes.

"Jumping Juniper Bears!" Startled, Aster whirled around to see Gatch, her nurse, standing in the door to the study. "Aster Lourdes! You're in your war formals!"

Aster gripped the leather pleats that made up the skirt of her war formals, twisting it to the side as though she could hide it behind her back. No use—she'd been caught. In her best dress for the festival season, without a festival in sight.

"I laid out your clothes for you this morning!" Gatch wrung her pudgy hands, storming over. "And you go and dig out your finest garment, *again*! Ohhhhh, your mother's gonna have a flying fit if she sees what I've let you do!"

Aster frowned, noticing the violet fabric of an evening gown draped across her nurse's arm. It was a fine frock, but nothing compared to the ornate stitching of her war formals. In the purple dress, she looked like a child. In the war formals, she looked like a queen.

Gatch grabbed Aster by the shoulders, turned her away from the window, and began undoing the back lacing of her dress. "I've been calling you for an hour! You should be nose-deep in your *Star Writ* studies by now. Not to mention how behind you are on your Roarsh lessons. I might've known you were up in this dank space! What in the name of Tawn do you get up to here all day?"

Aster pressed her palms against the dress's hardened leather breastplate, feeling the ridges of its embossed Hemoth Bear. Gatch was right, of course: her mother would be horrified to see her wearing something so precious outside the festival season. But it only came once a year, which—to Aster's mind—was entirely too infrequent.

"Honestly, Gatch, I do love this dress," Aster said, ignoring her nurse's question. "Please, can't you just pretend you didn't find me? I'll change before dinner!"

"Pretend you didn't find me, she says! Do you know how many stairs I've been climbing looking for you?"

Aster could guess. Gatch's brow was beaded with sweat and her palms were hot and wet as they lifted Aster's arms to the sky.

"Besides, yer mum's quite partial to the purple, as you well know, so's best to just—"

Another bellow from Alcor rattled the windows and cut Gatch off.

"What? What?" Gatch let go of Aster. "Stars above! What is Dev doing with that bear now?"

"It's not what the boy is doing." Aster sighed, watching Gatch wiggle up onto the bay window seat and peer out at the front green. "It's Ursula."

Gatch leaned out the window and screamed, *"Ursula Lourdes!"* The sound bored a hole through Aster's eardrums. "You get yerself back in this house and get to yer studies this instant! Leave the boy alone to do his blessed work, for the love of Tawn!"

Peeking over Gatch's shoulder, Aster could see her big sister, dagger eyes trained on them. She could have sworn Ursula's skin turned bright red to match her hair—hair like their father's. Aster bit back a snigger.

Gatch closed the window with a slam, so hard Aster worried she'd cracked the glass.

"Arms up," the woman said, tugging Aster's bodice up over her head, the leather and metal clinging to her skin, refusing to let go easily. "You'd think I've nothing better to do than chase you around all day. And at your age, no less."

Her age. Thirteen and nearly grown—this time next year she'd have no nurse, a retinue of lady's maids tittering behind her instead. What would that be like? Dainty young women who gossiped and whispered behind thin fingers. Not like old Gatch. Her nurse was crude and loud, big and determined and stubborn. Aster was very fond of her. Gatch was the only person besides Aster's father who could shut Ursula's mouth with a pointed finger, or silence Bernadine with a snap of her sharp tongue.

The idea of being without her struck Aster with a sudden pang of loss.

"There now," Gatch said, finishing up the laces on Aster's purple dress. The nurse gave one final tug. "Quite refined, if I do say so m'self. Now scoot. Yer mum'll be waiting on you to start supper."

"Oh, Gatch, don't say *mum.*"

Gatch let out one of her explosive laughs that always sounded more like a hacking cough. "Well, beg yer pardon, Miss Poppy Propriety." And with an affectionate tug of her hair, she sent Aster out the door.

It is, by my estimation, not the Major who receives the highest blessings from the On-High, nor is it even the mystical Oracle. It is the humble Keeper.

And because of the On-High's great blessings, it is the Keeper who is doomed to suffer most.

—THE WRITINGS OF THUBAN,
On the Mysteries of the On-High: The Star Majors, *Star Writ*

TWO

THE night air nipped at Dev's skin as he made his way to the back door of the kitchens. He was glad of the chill—it cooled his boiling blood.

The Lourdes girls would be the death of him, he was sure. Spoiled Aster and vain Ursula had been intolerable since the day he began his service at Lourdes Manor. Today had pinched the young Keeper's last nerve.

"Stupid, no-good, pampered princess *brats*!" he growled to himself.

The young Herman standing guard at the kitchen's servants' entrance cast a downward glance at him. Dev glared back, flinging open the rickety wooden door. A gust of warm, wet, savory air, the steam of a dozen cooking pots, dampened his face.

"Eh!" Gatch, the girls' nanny-woman, stood over a large wooden table. She held a bowl of oddgob, Chef Ingle's usual stew of leftovers. "What's all that about, little Dev?"

Little Dev. He was nearly fourteen, and taller than Gatch to boot. The *little* she insisted on was another irritating part of life at Lourdes Manor.

He ignored her and stormed up to the table—well, not even really a table. The servants of the Lourdes' house had no table. It was, in actuality, a counter, one the cooks used for chopping, and dicing, and rolling out dough. Dev always ate his dinner standing at that counter, the occasional piece of onion or carrot flying into his meal.

He slammed his fist down, and Cook Darby looked up from her creamed potatoes with a frown. Dev returned it. He'd dealt with enough attitude for one day.

"Well, well," said Gatch, shoving a spoonful of stew into her mouth. "Someone's in a right sour mood this evening."

"Chef Ingle," he barked, "can I get some oddgob here, or what?"

The wiry chef raised an eyebrow and looked at Gatch. Gatch just shook her head. Ingle grunted, but scooped a ladleful of stew into a wooden bowl.

Dev grabbed the hot bowl, burning both his hands, but he swallowed down the pain.

The crunchy, beady eyes of a particularly ugly crustacean stared up at him from the brown gravy. Binger heads. He *hated* binger heads.

He slammed his fist on the counter for the second time. "Turds of Tawn!"

"Jumpin'!" shouted Gatch. "A *very* sour mood!"

Dev shouldn't have been so blasphemous, especially as a Keeper. But he couldn't hold it in any longer. All he could hear was Ursula's voice in his head—her arrogant, nasal voice. "She called me her *servant*!"

"Who did?"

"Me!" he shouted. "Her *servant*!"

The kitchen went silent, save for a quiet bubbling. Gatch, Chef Ingle, and Cook Darby stopped what they were doing and stared at him, their old foreheads folded in half with worry. The other kitchen helpers looked anywhere but at Dev.

"Who did?" ventured Gatch finally.

Dev dropped his eyes to his bowl and shoved a crunchy, rubbery binger head into his mouth, his face suddenly red. Chewing would keep him from speaking; he'd already said too much. Keepers were supposed to be mild and forbearing and…well, all the things he wasn't being.

"You serve Alcor," said Ingle, a confused look on her face. "No other."

Dev shook his head.

"Is this about Lady Ursula?" Gatch asked quietly.

Dev kept chewing.

"Lady Ursula?" said Chef Ingle. "What *about* Lady Ursula?"

Dev sighed. He'd opened this door, he might as well go through. "She said I was *her servant*. As though I were nothing but a stableboy."

There was a simultaneous gasp from Ingle and Darby, Ingle dropping her soup ladle with a loud clatter onto the floor.

Dev winced. He shouldn't have spoken. Rizlan would not approve of him venting his frustration to half the Manor like this.

It wasn't as if Ursula could be changed. Very little about Lourdes Manor could be changed.

"That—that—*that girl!*" The scrawny chef fingered the bear pendant around her neck, her face contorted with fury. "Blasphemous! Disrespectful! Gatch, how *dare* she speak to a Keeper that way?"

Here it comes. Dev hated when Ingle got on about faith—about the Chosen Keepers and all that. Her piety sometimes embarrassed him. Yes, he had been selected at birth by the stars to be a Keeper of a High Beast—and not just any High Beast, but the most powerful and beloved of all the stars' children, the Hemoth Bear—but it was Master Rizlan, Mizar's Keeper, who led the faith at Lourdes Manor. Dev was only an apprentice, and truth be told, he studied scripture less than Riz would like.

Gatch nodded understandingly at him, a kind smile on his face. "Lady Ursula can be thoughtless at times." Dev didn't answer. "You have to understand, little Dev"—he shoved another disgusting binger into his mouth—"that she hasn't been raised with the same… vigilance to scripture as you."

"*No* vigilance, more like!" growled Ingle. "Imagine! A noble demanding service from a Keeper! It's disgusting! He was chosen! *Chosen!* This boy is a servant of the *Hemoth Bear*! Not of her spoiled behind!"

Exactly, Dev thought. He was *chosen* to dedicate his life to Tawn and his descendants. How could Ursula Lourdes not understand that? Sure, Dev spent his days shoveling bear dung, washing Alcor's stall, and studying scripture until he fell asleep on his books. But that was his duty. Keepers were not supposed to care for their own wealth and comfort. Keepers cared only for their Beasts.

Gatch put a hand on Dev's shoulder. "Ursula doesn't fully understand that you work for a Higher Power than her father. To her, *he* is the Highest Power."

That was ridiculous. A man with more power than the Hemoth Bear? More power than the On-High?

"If that mother of hers spent more time taking care of her spiritual well-being instead of indulging her *every selfish whim*—" shouted Ingle.

Everyone turned quickly to the kitchen door, terrified that Jasper Lourdes's wife would suddenly appear to punish them for speaking ill of her older daughter.

With a hand over her mouth, and in a hissing whisper, the chef finished: "—she wouldn't be the laughingstock of the Highen. Her *and* the little one."

Dev raised an eyebrow. As though the spoiled nature of Ursula and Aster were entirely the fault of Lady Lourdes. Dev knew the Lourdes better than he'd known any family of his own, and this was the truth: Jasper Lourdes adored his daughters. He adored them so much that he indulged them in everything. Oftentimes, that meant letting them neglect their *Star Writ* readings, or forgo a riding lesson, or sleep late—despite Lady Lourdes' objections.

And the lack of discipline in the Major's home was no secret to the Highen, either. Most people had a low opinion of the Major's daughters. No one believed Alcor would choose Ursula for Major when her father and Mizar came off the post. Not just because she was unprepared, but—these whispers were increasingly common in Tawnshire Town—because the On-High would reject her as punishment for Jasper's decision to hand a holy dragon egg to the Ring Highen, something no Major had ever done before. Did not the On-High entrust the Shadow Dragons to the *Bear Highen*, and the Bear Highen alone? Was it not sacrilege to trade their young like crops or cattle?

But if the girls weren't chosen to succeed Jasper, oh, what a disaster it would be. The Hemoth Bear had chosen a Lourdes for a millennium. It was a thing that kept Dev up at night—if Aster and Ursula proved to be the first Lourdes in a hundred generations to be unworthy of the Hemoth Bear, who *would* Alcor choose? What strange new lord or lady, Dev didn't like to wonder, would he and Alcor spend their lives alongside?

"Can we stop talking about this?" he grumbled.

He could feel the old women trading concerned looks over his head. Perfect. No doubt Gatch would talk to Master Rizlan about this when he returned from the front. Even if she didn't, Ingle and Darby were bound to gossip with every servant at the Manor; it was only a matter of time before Dev's complaint made its way to Lady Lourdes herself. Either way, when his mentor returned from battle, Dev would have to listen to another lesson on the importance of silence.

A wise Keeper uses his words sparingly, Riz always said. *Consider words your gold, young apprentice. To keep them behind closed lips is to stay a wealthy man.*

If that was true, then Riz was poor indeed.

He never chattered or gossiped. But he *did* lecture Dev nightly about the duties of a Keeper: offering counsel; divining prophecies;

fortelling the future; caring for the Highen's sacred beasts; and recording great events, that his writings might someday be added to the holy *Star Writ*. Most of their evenings lately, though, had been devoted to training Dev to open his mind to visions sent by the stars. Dev had yet to see anything, and he knew that Riz was getting frustrated. He should have seen *something* by now.

At least Dev wouldn't have to endure a lesson tonight. Though he missed Master Rizlan desperately, he had to admit that he liked having the Keepers' quarters all to himself.

Eager to enjoy some privacy, Dev lifted the hot stew of binger heads to his mouth and slurped up what was left. No time for chewing—an evening of peace and quiet was at the bottom of that bowl. With the last drop drunk, he slammed the bowl down and let out a belch.

And noticed everyone staring at him.

Including Lady Lourdes.

The Major's beautiful wife stood in the middle of the kitchen, staring down her nose at him. Her fancy gown glittering with precious Ursan amber was almost laughable, it was so out of place in the kitchen.

"I trust you enjoyed your meal, young Keeper." Her voice was rough, like the leathery bottoms of Alcor's paws. All that Celeste root she smoked had worn it out.

"Yes, my lady," he mumbled, adding a polite bow.

"I am pleased to hear it." She didn't look pleased. She looked downright disgusted, with frowning crimson-painted lips. Her dark eyes kept him frozen to the spot, afraid to move. He could feel his palms getting slick with sweat.

And then she blinked and turned to Ingle. In an instant, she'd forgotten Dev completely. "The girls are in low spirits tonight, Chef Ingle. They miss their father, and I fear they've grown restless. I've decided a change of menu is in order."

Ingle curtsied, so low she nearly fell over. "Of course, my lady. What did you have in mind?"

Dev fought the urge to shake his head. Ingle spoke the worst of Lady Lourdes, but she always bowed the lowest.

"Lamb pies." The words cracked from Lady Lourdes' mouth like the snap of a whip. "I don't care for them, but I do believe my Aster is fond of the ones you make. I should like an assortment of greens on the side, of course."

"Of course, my lady," said Ingle, already abandoning Darby's creamed potatoes.

Dev pursed his lips. He would have preferred those potatoes to Binger heads.

With a curt nod, Lady Lourdes left them, the train of her dress floating behind her, twinkling.

A change of menu, Dev thought. An entire meal tossed aside as though hundreds of Tawnshirians living a few hundred tail-lengths down the hillside in Tawnshire Town wouldn't have loved just a taste. It had been a very dry summer, and the yields of good Tawnshirian crops—lettuce, parsnips, chard, leeks, tomatoes—were low. The war was not good for business in the city, either. The unwanted potatoes was a true waste.

But creamed potatoes was a rich man's food, a king's food, not fit for the low and the humble. So Ingle had tossed it all, as was expected.

Dev left the counter and pushed open the kitchen door, the cool night meeting him with the refreshing smell of cherry trees from the Manor's orchards.

Ingle grabbed him by the shoulder. "Take this," she said, smiling and holding up a raw lamb shank wrapped in parchment. "For the little prince."

As inappropriate as Gatch's *little* was for Dev, Ingle's *little* was even more ill-fitting for Alcor. Alcor was certainly not *little*. Not anymore. But still, Ingle loved to sneak him treats. And Alcor was happy to eat them.

Dev nodded and took the shank.

The night's quiet and the chill of the wind surrounded him as he crossed the Manor's grounds. He let out a sigh of relief: the day was almost over. A quick stop in to Alcor with the shank, and then the hours were his. He'd curl up in front of the fire and watch the blaze until he fell asleep.

He could think of nothing he'd enjoy more than doing absolutely nothing at all.

Together, Mizar and her new Major drove back the Nightlocks from Tawnshire Town, back to their prison behind the moon.

Together, Mizar and her new Major saved the Highen's people from the greatest attack of Nightlocks since the beginning of the Age of the Lunar Offensive.

For this, the people of the Highen lovingly dubbed Mizar and Major Jasper Lourdes the Death Chasers.

—THE WRITINGS OF RIZLAN,
The Crowning of the Fifty-Third Major: The Lunar Offensive, *Star Writ*

THREE

ASTER looked down at her dinner: a perfectly golden pastry, glistening beside a bed of leafy greens. Lamb pie.

She eyed her mother, sitting at the head of the table. Lady Lourdes's long, slender fingers rapped the wood impatiently as she stared into the candle flames.

Ursula was late.

If their father were home, Ursula wouldn't *dare* be late. And even if she were, the dining hall wouldn't be so terribly quiet as it was now.

Aster's eyes passed over the heads of the servants and Herman guards standing against the far wall—the room felt so empty with all the courtiers and nobles missing from the Manor since Father had left to fight the Ring. Most had gone with him; others had returned to their own estates—with the Major gone, they found no reason to linger. Not that she missed them. They were all of them sniveling and insincere, and most of them insisted on calling her *little lady*, which bothered her no end. But the Manor without the court was a Manor without her father, and only reminded her of his absence.

Her gaze wandered to the stained-glass windows that lined the hall. The colors were ablaze—blues, purples, yellows, greens—and the amber fur of the Hemoth Bears in each pane was on fire with the light from the setting sun. When their father sat at the dinner table, the room echoed with his booming voice as he recounted the tales of each Bear and their Majors. Aster loved how her father told those stories.

And it made the quiet without him all the more unbearable.

Her eyes drifted to the mosaic on the ceiling: Father and Mizar saving the Highen from a host of Nightlocks. Aster's favorite story. The laughing nether demons glared down at her, fanged teeth and wagging tongues daring her to fight. They were the spirits of the condemned—sentenced to eternity behind the moon, banished for their crimes in life from the light of the stars, horribly twisted and changed. And hungry for the souls of others.

In the days when the Nightlocks descended on Tawnshire, all had cowered—but not Jasper Lourdes. That battle, forever captured in glittering glass and bone, took her father's status from Major to legend. *The Death Chaser.*

A chair squeaked. Aster looked over at Bernadine sitting on her right, fidgeting with her dress. It was a creamy silk gown, a gift from the House of the Lion. Aster watched her cousin try to adjust the neckline to fit her flat chest, but each attempt failed. After all, the gown was designed for someone older. The gown belonged to Ursula.

Lady Lourdes raised an eyebrow, appraising the soft fabric. "Why, Bernadine, is that a new dress?"

Bernadine's cheeks flushed red. She had never been a very good liar. Too honest for her own good.

Aster reached for her glass of water. "Did it come in the parcel your father sent to the Manor this morning?"

Bernadine blinked at her, not understanding.

"You wrote him how much you wanted a cream silk gown not long ago," Aster nudged. Honestly, would she have to do this completely by herself?

"Yes," her cousin agreed nervously, finally seeing the rescue Aster had handed her. "My father sent me this dress."

Lady Lourdes nodded. "He has good taste, that man. It's beautiful."

And just like that, Aster's mother forgot the dress completely, her fingers resuming their impatient rhythm on the table, her eyes narrowed on the door.

Bernadine smiled gratefully at Aster, who shrugged, folding and unfolding the napkin on her lap. *It's not Mother you need to worry about,* Aster thought. *It's Ursula.*

"Where *is* that girl?" Lady Lourdes growled. She snapped and pointed at one of the Hermans. "You there, find her."

The guard bowed and made a rush for the door—just as Ursula burst in, her six lady's maids in tow.

The girls had managed to put her back together after her run-in with Alcor. One of them was still fussing with Ursula's amber locks, which had been pinned high on her head and adorned with gold-plated flowers. Her dinner dress was one Aster had not seen before: a beautiful print of midnight-blue moon blossoms, embellished with delicate frost pearls that shone like starlight on fresh snow.

Fed up, Ursula smacked her maid's hand away. "Leave it." She waved the girls off, and each of them quickly took her place against the wall. With a confident grin, Ursula fluffed her hair one final time as she strode to the table and took her seat across from Aster.

"You're late," said Lady Lourdes.

"Am I?" Ursula smiled. "Forgive me, Mother, this dress has so many buttons."

Her lady's maids giggled, nodding to one another. Aster hated the way they were always laughing and whispering. Like everything Ursula said was marvelously clever.

"Is that gown also from the House of the White Bear?"

Ursula nodded. "Mmm, Uncle Bram sent it for me. Do you like it?"

Lady Lourdes did her best not to seem impressed. But their mother liked the dress very much indeed, Aster could tell. She watched as Lady Lourdes' eyes moved over the intricate pattern, admiring the precious frost pearls studding every inch of it.

Bernadine sat up, her eyes wide as she admired Ursula's new garment. "My father sent that dress for you? *My* father? For *you*? Are you sure?" Ursula shrugged, and Bernadine made a noise like a strangled cat. "He's only ever given me a *bracelet* of frost pearls before."

Frost pearls were infamously dangerous to collect. Hidden in the depths of frigid White Bear Lake in Whitlock, they could be harvested only on the night of the winter solstice. The blue oysters would yawn, and their pearls would catch the moonlight, glowing in the dark for whoever was daring enough to find them. Few divers were willing to risk their lives for frost pearls, and those who did sold each one for a small fortune. Why did Uncle Bram have to send something so extravagant?

"I thought I might wear it to the Festival," Ursula said. "To the Northern Crowning ball?"

Aster frowned. "The Northern Crowning ball? What do you mean you wish to wear it to the Northern Crowning ball?"

The Festival of Tawn was a yearly celebration in Tawnshire. When the time came for a new Major to be named in a Northern Crowning ceremony—the competition where the strongest candidate was chosen by the star-blessed Hemoth Bear—it was held at the Festival, and a magnificent ball followed to celebrate.

But the Northern Crowning only ever happened when the Highen had lost their Major. When a Major had died.

"You do know Father still *lives*, don't you?" Aster asked, her blood boiling.

"Honestly," laughed Ursula. "I don't mean that I expect the Northern Crowning to happen any day soon—Tawn forbid—I only meant that when it did—"

"You'll be an old hag by the next Northern Crowning!" Aster shouted.

The room went still, Aster's outburst echoing off the rafters.

All the eyes of the servants and guards fell on her. Her face burned.

"That's enough," Lady Lourdes said coldly, reaching for the long ivory pipe sitting beside her goblet. "Your uncle spoils you." Aster's nose tickled at the smell of the Celeste root's spicy smoke. "A fine gown for the Northern Crowning, yes…" Lady Lourdes blew a steady stream of blue smoke and considered the taste before adding, "…*if*, indeed, you are crowned."

Aster watched Ursula deflate, her eyes dropping to the cooling lamb pie in front of her.

Lady Lourdes placed her pipe gently back on the table and picked up her fork, breaking into the pie's flaky crust with a delicious-sounding crack.

But Aster couldn't bring herself to eat. Not with the subject of her father's death on the table.

Lady Lourdes lifted a piece of pie, no bigger than her thumbnail, to her mouth. "I'm told young Quintin of the House of the Shadow Dragons is quite well learned in botany and herbology. A healer's proclivity, they say. My, how focused a student he must be."

Ursula looked up, surprised. Her face began to redden.

"And, of course, there are all those brothers from the House of Hounds," said their mother. "Not scholars, I hear, but warriors all. They say those boys were practically born on horses."

Ursula sat there, silent, her mouth gaping but no words forming.

And Aster knew why. Riding was Ursula's talent—her only one, really.

Their father had had the girls trained in most forms of combat— swordplay, archery, strike combat, riding. They were capable enough if they were training to be soldiers, their sharps tutor liked to say, but she'd once overheard him tell their father that at the Northern Crowning they wouldn't stand a chance. At the time, Aster had been furious. The old goat was just a perfectionist, too hard on them, too strict. Now, she had to wonder if there was a reason for it.

The one place where everyone agreed Ursula had ability was on a horse. Riding was the event she hoped to excel in at the Northern Crowning, outmaneuvering everyone on her beautiful black jennet.

"You don't believe I will be the one," whispered Ursula. "You don't believe Alcor will choose me, do you, Mother?"

Aster watched their mother carefully, trying to read the thin red line of her painted lips. Was that what her mother believed? Did their father believe it too?

Lady Lourdes lifted her hand, and her manservant, Nash, stepped forward with a silver tray. On it was a small parchment. "A messenger arrived this morning with a letter."

A letter?

"Leave us," Lady Lourdes said, and with a wave the assembled staff were sent away. When they were alone, their mother opened the letter, her eyes never leaving Ursula. "He brought word from your father. Shall I read it to you?"

Aster's heart swelled. She'd waited so long for a letter from Father.

Her mother narrowed her eyes at Ursula before reading. "*The people of the Bear Highen are strong. I do not believe Mizar and I could hope to defeat an enemy so powerful as the Ring without the courage of the Bear Highen behind us. I am proud to call myself their Major. But I confess, after spending my days so close to the leaders of the other kingdoms, I find myself in doubt about Ursula's chances to succeed me.*

"*The Heads of Houses are fierce not only in battle but also in faith. And it is clear they have instilled an intense discipline in their children that we have not imposed on our girls. Have they even touched the* Star Writ *readings Keeper Rizlan assigned to them before my leavetaking?*"

Their mother peered over the paper and Ursula sighed. That was a no.

Aster felt her own cheeks getting warm. She'd not done her readings from Keeper Rizlan either.

"Have they so much as picked up a sword or strapped strike sharps to their hands since I left?"

Aster watched Ursula bite at her nail. Again, neither of them had done so.

"The Highen demands a leader worthy of the Hemoth Bear, be they warrior, philosopher, or scholar. A Major whose duty is to the Bear and to the Highen. As it stands, what kind of Major could we hope either of our girls would be?

"My deepest fear is that the answer will not satisfy the mighty Hemoth. My heart tells me that, when the time comes, neither of our daughters will be chosen for the crown."

Lady Lourdes placed the letter on the table beside Aster. Her father's familiar handwriting, as rough as he was, made her heart ache.

"Do you really want to see some Dragon boy crowned as Major?" their mother spat. "Or worse, one of those mongrels from the House of Hounds?"

"No!" Ursula snapped, the loudness of her voice not hiding the tremor beneath it.

"Do you have any understanding of how precarious our situation is? After this business with the blasted dragon egg, there are wolves waiting at your back! Have you any *idea* of the outrage that followed your father after he made the decision to deliver such a sacred item to our *enemy?*"

Aster heard in her mind her father's words about the voices of caution:...*men always have opinions on matters as delicate as this. All will be well.* He hadn't been worried about it all. But their mother, it seemed...

Aster watched her mother's eyes drift to the windows, her hand closing anxiously on her necklace. "Perhaps it is already too late. I blame myself, really. I let your father be so *easy* on you both, against my better judgment." She glanced sideways at Ursula and sighed. "I see so much of Leona in you."

Aster swallowed, waiting for her sister to explode.

Aunt Leona. Their mother's eldest sister.

It was not just a Major who could be chosen at a Northern Crowning, but the Head of any House in any kingdom, as new ones were needed. A Shadow Dragon chose the new King of Dracogart; a Starhound chose the new King of Hundford; and so on. Anyone could compete, but the thrones almost always stayed within the ancient families, passing from parent to child for centuries—unless a child was found wanting, and a High Beast rejected them.

Aunt Leona was supposed to become the Head of the House of the Lynx when their mother died. She had been raised to be the next Queen of Felisbrook.

But at the Northern Crowning, the High Beast chose another—a common man from the Felisbrook guard, Pan Leander.

And the entire family felt the shame of it.

But such a thing would not happen here, would it? Ursula was a *Lourdes*! The Hemoth Bear had chosen a Lourdes going back a hundred generations!

"In truth, I don't know that my heart could stand to see another member of my family bested at a Crowning."

"I am nothing like Leona," Ursula said quietly.

"Then show your father." Lady Lourdes wrapped her hand around Ursula's wrist, her knuckles turning white from the tightness of her grip. "Try harder, and be mindful of your duty. To the Hemoth Bear, to the Highen. Keep it in your heart, my darling, and never let it be forgotten."

Aster watched as tears dripped from her sister's eyes. And Aster felt her own eyes stinging. Their father was right. They weren't trying. Neither of them. She could feel her map, tucked up inside her stocking. How foolish, to spend the day dreaming of leading the

Highen armies. What good was dreaming if she couldn't do what a Major needed to do?

At least Ursula could ride a horse. What could Aster do?

The sudden bang of the dining hall doors loosened Lady Lourdes' grip. Nash was trying to hold back three imposing figures—soldiers.

"Just—just—just wait one moment," blundered Nash. "You can't come storming in like this!"

Their armor was filthy, caked with mud from being on the road. Aster could see the familiar tufts of orange that adorned their shoulders—Hermans. Her father's men-at-arms.

"It's all right," said Lady Lourdes, rising. "What is it?"

A woman barely older than Ursula stepped forward and nodded her head. "Lady Lourdes, I bring urgent news from the Major."

Aster stood up. *Urgent.*

She looked at her mother. Lady Lourdes was as unreadable as ever. But in the lines of her throat, Aster could see muscles tensing.

Something was wrong.

"Come with me," Lady Lourdes ordered the soldiers, the fabric of her dress billowing behind her as she marched for the door. Aster rose to follow, but her mother snapped her head back. "Finish your dinner."

And with another bang of the mighty dining hall doors, the three girls were left alone at the table.

Aster dropped into her seat, staring at her untouched pie. Their mother had just read a letter from their father that had arrived only that morning. What could have happened between then and now?

"Wh-What—" Bernadine tried. "What do you suppose has happened?" Her eyes were glossy, her chin quivering in that way it did whenever she was nervous. "Do you suppose Father and Uncle Jasper are all right?"

Ursula wiped her eyes and stood up. "I'm sure there's nothing to worry about, cousin."

"What makes you say that?" asked Aster. Because she was worried. Very worried.

"Because Father is the Major." Ursula pressed her hands against her cheeks and took a deep breath. Then she smoothed out the creases in her beautiful frost-pearl gown. "They do not call him the Death Chaser for nothing."

And with that, Ursula turned on her heels, heading for the door. Aster leapt up and rushed after her.

"Wait!" cried Bernadine. "Don't just leave me!"

Aster didn't listen, running to catch up to her sister as she left the dining hall and stormed toward the great hall. "Ursula, are you going to talk to Mother?"

"No."

Aster stopped. "Then where are you going?"

Ursula didn't answer. She didn't have to. Because as she hurried away, their father's words echoed in Aster's mind: *My heart tells me that, when the time comes, neither of our daughters will be chosen for the crown.*

There was only one place Ursula could be going.

…for no two Highens were ever greater friends than the Bear and the Ring.

—THE WRITINGS OF WIP,
On the Nature of the Ring: The Ring Wars, *Star Writ*

FOUR

ASTER hesitated. Should she really follow her sister?

Yes. What if she hurt herself bothering Alcor in his pen? Or worse?

So she hurried through the great hall of Lourdes Manor, Bernadine shouting after her.

"Aster!" Bernadine whined. "Please, wait for me!"

Aster stopped just short of the open doors, made of glossy, honeyed shiver oak. On the steps of the Manor stood a group of Hermans, huddled together and murmuring nervously to one another. It seemed that the arrival of the soldiers had unsettled everyone.

"Aster!"

One of the Hermans turned, and Aster pressed her back against a wall to keep from sight. She wasn't supposed to leave the Manor after dark. Her mother was very clear about that, and the guards knew it.

She whirled on Bernadine. "Shh! Shut up!"

Bernadine stopped, her cheeks flushed as she pulled up the bust of her stolen gown.

"Do you want the entire Manor to know what we're doing?" Aster hissed.

"What *are* we doing?"

"Going after Ursula."

"How?"

Aster peeked back toward the doors. The guards had returned to their conversation. Tawn knew how Ursula had managed to get by them unnoticed. Probably managed to sneak by while the men were engrossed in their conversation. Aster doubted she'd be so lucky, especially with Bernadine clamoring behind her—she'd be caught for sure. The front doors were too risky.

"The crawlway," she whispered, and hurried back the way they'd come, toward the grand staircase.

The Manor was riddled with secret passageways and hidden halls. They were for the Major's protection, but really, Aster had always found them chiefly useful for sneaking sweets with Bernadine. The cousins knew every inch of the Manor's hidden hall network, and after one fortuitous afternoon of exploration, they had discovered a damp passage – not even a passage really, more like a crumbling hole that was the result of a leak, or a cave in, or an animal. A result of time and accidents more than any purposeful design. However it came to be, it was just big enough to squeeze through and led the cousins outside the Manor, right beside the great hall's steps and straight into the juniper bushes. When she told her father what they'd found, he'd roared with laughter and dubbed it the Crafty Cousins' Crawlway, "a most mischievous little secret." And indeed, the secrecy of the crawlway was coming in handy tonight.

Aster opened a hidden panel beneath the stair and slipped into the crawlway, Bernadine behind her. As they crouched and crept forward, she heard Bernadine complaining, "This is going to ruin the dress! Whyever did we enjoy this filthy hole so much?"

"It was usually *your* idea to play in the crawlway, as I recall," said Aster.

When the girls emerged from the tunnel, the juniper bushes kept them hidden from the Hermans' view. The Manor's great green lawn stretched out before them, the grass swallowed by the night.

Far off, Aster saw her sister twinkling. She had never seen frost pearls at night before, but they lived up to their reputation, glinting in the dark like moonbeams off a pond.

"Where do you suppose she's going?" whispered Bernadine.

"I know exactly where she's headed—the Bear Holding. Come on."

With a deep breath, Aster ducked out of the bushes and across a gravel track, keeping one eye on the distracted guards. Bernadine followed, gathering up her skirts to keep them from dragging in the dirt.

The two girls hurried across the green, following the glowing frost pearls until they disappeared from sight. "Aster, what is she *doing*?" whispered Bernadine.

But there was no time to explain. Aster simply beckoned her to hurry.

The Bear Holding looked like any of the many stables on the Manor's grounds. Modest stone and plaster. Dark wooden beams, arcing and crisscrossing. Windows framed by posts. But one thing made the Bear Holding different: Ursan amber—polished, honey-colored stones the size of a soldier's shield adorning the doors and roof.

Ursula was already inside, Aster was sure. Uneasy *woof*s rumbled from within Alcor's stall—he was awake. And annoyed.

Bernadine took hold of Aster's hand. "What would Ursula come here for? Please tell me!"

Alcor's thunderous voice growled louder.

"For Ursula," muttered Aster, marching up to the Holding's main doors and hauling them open with a loud groan.

There was her sister. Standing in front of Alcor's stall.

Ursula had her arm held out to the massive Hemoth Bear, a cold lamb pie in her hand.

"What on earth do you think you're doing?" Aster rushed forward and grabbed the pie from her sister. "You know Father has ordered the Hemoth on a strict diet!"

Alcor huffed, steam exploding from his nostrils with a mighty snort.

"Be quiet," Ursula snapped. "Do you want to wake the bear boy?" She pointed to a staircase, filthy with dust and hay, that led up to the Keepers' quarters.

"Perhaps we should!" cried Aster.

In fact, it was a bluff. Aster knew too well that she would be in as much trouble for being in the Bear Holding as her sister.

Bernadine hugged the Holding's open door, half inside, half out. "Cousins," she said, one hand nervously fidgeting with her dress, "that Hemoth bear looks rather grumpy. I do think we should leave him to his rest."

Alcor growled, his snout crinkling just enough to show the points of his sharp white fangs.

"Too right, Bernadine," said Aster. "We should go back to the Manor and leave him be!"

Ursula snatched the pie back. "Don't you dare tell me what to do, little sister! This is none of your business. It's between me and Alcor!"

Aster reached for the pastry, but Ursula's arm was long. She held it just out of reach, using her free hand to keep Aster back.

"Between *you* and *Alcor*?" Aster snapped.

The bear let out a low groan, creeping closer to the edge of his stall.

"Don't you remember what happened earlier today?" Aster shouted. "Do you want that bear to gobble you up?"

Ursula grabbed hold of Aster's arm and twisted it back. Aster cried out, but she was not completely defenseless. Their strike tutor was the best in the Highen, and disobedient or not, she had learned from him. She lashed out with her other hand, blasting her palm into her big sister's ribs.

"*Aster!*" gasped Bernadine as Ursula coughed and sputtered, releasing Aster's arm.

"Count yourself lucky I am not wearing sharps," said Aster coolly.

Alcor poked his head out of his stall, sniffing intently at the air. And then he looked down.

Down at the lamb pie, lying in a clump of hay.

Aster lunged for it, but Ursula had recovered, and she snatched it up just before Aster could.

"Don't you give him that pie, Ursula!"

Alcor groaned, and Ursula's wild eyes flicked to the anxious bear. "Ursula—"

"I have to!" Ursula shouted. "I have to make him choose me! You heard Mother! You heard the letter! *He has to pick me!*"

Aster took a step back, suddenly a bit afraid of her big sister. She looked frantic, despairing. Certainly, their parents had been hard on Ursula, but this—she seemed positively *desperate*.

My deepest fear…, her father had written. *Neither of our daughters will be chosen for the crown.*

If Ursula failed to inherit Father's throne, the Lourdes' royal line would be broken. Aster was no more likely to be chosen as Major than her sister. Another family would become the House of the Hemoth Bear.

Had Ursula known their parents felt this way? Was that why she had spent the summer poking around the Bear Holding?

Alcor moaned, and Ursula turned back to the great Hemoth Bear. His massive head sniffed at the air, Ursula and the lamb pie just out of his reach. They stayed like that, bear and girl, staring at each other for the longest moment.

And then Ursula took a step forward.

"Ursula," whispered Bernadine nervously.

She was well within Alcor's reach now. The bear sniffed at the tears on her cheeks, and fear burned beneath Aster's skin as her sister placed a hand on the Hemoth's furry neck.

Aster waited for the explosion, for the earthshaking roar, for the flash of teeth. But the young bear was quiet, his muzzle brushing against Ursula's face as he nosed for the pie in her hand.

Ursula brought the morsel to his mouth. Alcor chomped loudly on the savory bite, not bothered by the girl stroking his mane. But how long would the young bear put up with that?

"Ursula," Aster breathed, holding her hand out for her sister.

Alcor's ears suddenly perked up, and Aster froze. But the bear's eyes weren't on her. They were on the open Holding door.

"What is it?" Ursula whispered to him.

Alcor's left ear twitched, listening.

And then voices rose in the night.

Shouts.

Screams.

"What is that?" gasped Bernadine.

Ursula stepped past Aster, standing in the doorway.

Aster could hear the voices, crying out in the dark—the shouts of guards, but others, too. Many others.

Ursula closed the door, stepped back, and pulled Bernadine away with her. She turned to Aster, fear in her eyes. "The Manor is under attack."

It is in these times of peace that the Bear Highen should take careful stock of its friends. For the gravest of dangers can be found lurking behind smiles.

—THE WRITINGS OF THUBAN,
On the Governance of Kings: The Star Majors, *Star Writ*

 FIVE

ICY dread seeped its way into Aster's bones. She couldn't move. Forgot how.

Who would dare attack the Manor of Major Jasper Lourdes?

The Ring.

Aster stood frozen with her sister and her cousin in the Bear Holding. She barely dared to breathe, the horribly intermingled sounds of angry and terrified screams echoing in the night air. Her mind raced, trying to make sense of it, trying to understand how the Ring could have gotten past her father's armies, how they could have come so deep into the Highen.

"They'll kill us," squeaked Bernadine. "All of us. The Ring can't let us live. We're the Major's kin!"

Aster looked to her older sister, who was staring at nothing, listening hard.

"Did you see them?" Aster whispered. "Is it the Ring?"

Ursula said nothing. Alcor *woof*ed quietly to himself as he began to pace his stall.

"Ursula?"

Nearby voices drifted on the breeze. Men's voices.

Ursula backed farther away from the door, trembling.

"We need to hide," she croaked.

The three girls stared at each other blankly. *Hide*, Ursula said. But where?

Suddenly, Ursula's sweaty palm clamped down on Aster's wrist, her other hand taking hold of Bernadine. Alcor began to moan.

Aster could hear the approaching men, louder now, and she felt cold blood pumping through her veins. *They're coming,* her heart told her. *The Ring.* And the girls were stuck—the daughters of the Major. *Trapped.*

Aster's vision blurred, and for a moment she could hardly stand. But Ursula's arm wrapped around her waist, hauling her along to the hay pile beneath the staircase. The girls crouched together in the fodder as the sound of feet on the gravel path outside sent Aster's heart pounding against her ribs.

"Help me," ordered Ursula, piling as much hay over them as she could.

Aster struggled to move her arms; her limbs tingled with so much terror that the muscles wouldn't obey. Somehow, though, the girls managed to bury themselves in dry, scratchy feed, and they lay as still as they could.

"...all purebred and imported from the Berenice region." The voice was clear, just beyond the doors. "Think I'll take m'self one. My old mare's on her last legs, after all. A Berenice stallion would do just fine, eh?"

Bernadine's bony shoulder rattled against Aster's, and Aster realized that her own body was shaking too. She looked over at Ursula, whose amber eyes were peering out between the slats in the steps.

"Eh?" said the man outside. "Reathin, you listenin'? I was saying, 'bout the mare—"

"Quiet." A second voice. Deep and cold. Aster closed her eyes, trying not to imagine the man who would match such a voice. "We're to recover the Hemoth. Not find you a horse you're not fit to ride."

Alcor.

Aster held her breath. The living symbol of the Bear House. The youngest descendant of the Great Lord Tawn. The favorite of the On-High. The highest of High Beasts.

They've come for Alcor.

"I'm only saying," said the other, "it's not as if the Lourdes have any use for 'em now."

Aster's heart seized in her chest. *Father. Mother.* Her eyes met Ursula's, and she felt her sister's trembling fingers close around her own.

Alcor moaned again, a frightened, hopeless sound, and Aster swallowed.

Silence.

Loaded, terrifying silence.

Aster squeezed her big sister's hand, unable to take her eyes off the Holding doors. She could feel the Ring there—its evil, its danger—just beyond the threshold.

And then a creak.

The door moved slightly, groaning against the effort, and a man stepped inside. His armored legs clanked as he moved.

Alcor began to spit. A quiet growl rumbled from somewhere deep inside him.

Aster's eyes moved up from the man's legs to the heavy brown leather of his tunic. A thick white pelt hung on his shoulders, the glint of an ornate breastplate peeking through.

Alcor's growls grew louder, more threatening. But the man did not look afraid. She could see his eyes beneath his thick, dark eyebrows, devouring every inch of the mighty young Hemoth.

The second man entered, taller but slighter than the first. He nearly fell back when he got his first look at Alcor. "Tawn be praised," he breathed.

Alcor released a roar so fierce the Holding shook, sending dust raining down on Aster's head.

Tawn be praised? she thought, confused. *The Ring don't worship Tawn.*

Aster caught sight of the slighter man's breastplate—the familiar curve of the lines carved there, the seven points representing the seven sacred lights in the heavens. The image of the White Bear.

It was the uniform of the Minor's men.

Beside her, Bernadine took a breath, but before she could call out, Aster smothered her mouth with her palm. Bernadine struggled, and Aster pressed harder; Ursula, too, held their cousin close, a finger to her lips for silence.

These men belonged to Uncle Bram.

Which meant Uncle Bram had betrayed the Major.

'Tis the lucky who slog,
In the cold wet bog,
Alongside the frogs for the berry,
'Tis the hardworking dog,
With his trousers a-sog,
Who will keep his beloved ones merry.

—HÄRKÄDIAN NURSERY RHYME

SIX

*D*EV snored, slouching comfortably in Keeper Rizlan's chair.

Keepers lived modestly, that was their duty. Three tunics washed by their own hands; a simple hard bed barely wide enough to turn on; one bowl and one spoon to eat only what their bodies needed. Simple possessions for a simple life.

But Rizlan had his chair, a gift from the Major. Polished oak with satin cushions. It was fit for the Major himself, but it was Rizlan's. His one piece of luxury, which he'd begged the Major again and again to take back.

Rizlan would tell Dev the story of this chair whenever Dev caught him enjoying a good sit—or whenever Dev tried to avoid a meditation lesson. The day Jasper Lourdes became Major, Rizlan had had a vision—one the Keepers of the other kingdoms did not have. He saw a horde of Nightlocks escaping their heavenly prison, their sights set on the Bear Highen. And because he saw them before they came, he was able to warn Jasper Lourdes. No Nightlock could stand before Jasper Lourdes' sword or the holy might of the Hemoth Bear. That was the night Major Lourdes and Mizar banished the Nightlocks back to the heavens. That was the night Major Lourdes and Mizar earned the nickname *the Death Chasers*. All thanks to Rizlan.

And his visions.

Which is why, my dear Devin, Rizlan liked to finish, *it is important you heed my lessons so that you may learn to have visions as I do.*

Yet try as he might, Dev couldn't seem to manage it. He'd never had a vision in his life.

You will yet, lad, Rizlan would say, reclining in his chair. *With a bit of effort on your part.*

But no amount of effort was working. Dev tried to study and meditate and pray as he should, and yet his mind remained empty. No foresight. No premonitions. Nothing at all.

For tonight, at least, he could forget all about it. And for tonight, the fine chair was Dev's.

He slept there, his tattered copy of the *Star Writ* slipping slowly off his chest. Embers spat and crackled in the fireplace, asking for another log that wouldn't come. The reading candles melted, wax dripping onto the warped floorboards. Finally, the last flame drowned in its own sweat, and Dev was left alone in the dark.

He was dreaming.

Dreaming of his mother.

More a memory than a dream, really. A series of moments strung together like beads. The golden strands of her summer-kissed hair tickling his cheek. The feeling of her hand rubbing his back in slow circles. The smoky-sweet smell of sap from the bog pines—the smell of the harvest. It was on her skin that night—the night the Keepers came for him.

The dream suddenly dissolved, winking out as he jerked from sleep—

—and fell out of Rizlan's chair. He lay frozen on the cold wooden floor of the Keepers' quarters, the damp sweat on his forehead cooling in the chill night air.

Dev rubbed his eyes with the heels of his palms.

That life was over now—he had left his mother and the harvests of Härkädia far behind and long ago. Tawn had chosen him. The Kingdom of the Hemoth Bear, Tawnshire, was his home now.

He picked up the *Star Writ* and found his page marker. He hadn't even come close to finishing the chapters Rizlan had left for him.

For a collection of the sacred histories and greatest battles of the High Beasts, the *Star Writ* was a frightfully dull read. It was the language that bothered Dev. Some of the entries were written centuries ago. People spoke differently then. Strangely. Hard to understand. Just another thing to add to the list Dev didn't do well as a Keeper-in-training. What good was he if he couldn't even make sense of the holy text?

He closed the massive book and placed it on the mantel beside his melted candles. One day, it would be his duty to add to the *Star Writ*'s pages with tales of Alcor and his Major. Dev yawned, silently wishing that that Major would not be Ursula Lourdes.

And then the floorboards shook beneath his feet from Alcor's mighty roar.

Dev's neck flashed with heat. *Ursula!* It wasn't enough that the Major's older daughter had to ruin his training sessions with the young bear—now she had to ruin his sleep, too?

He snatched his kazoo and threw open the door. His patience had run out. Ursula had to learn—she was *not* the Major, not yet, however much Jasper Lourdes and his pretty wife hoped she would be. Tonight he would teach her to remember that.

Dev barreled down the stairs, his tongue on fire with a venomous lecture for her.

But when he made it to the bottom, the words snuffed out to nothing. Because standing in front of Alcor's stall was not Ursula.

Two soldiers. The emblem of the White Bear on their breastplates.

"What are you doing here?" Dev asked, his voice cracking.

The slimmer soldier grinned. "Oi, the honorable Keeper. Come to give us your wisdom, have you?"

Alcor huffed nervously, shifting back and forth as the other soldier, his neck and shoulders as thick as an ox's, scowled at Dev.

And unsheathed his blade.

Alcor let out another earth-rattling roar, rising and pounding on his stall gate with his paws.

Dev tripped over himself as he ran back toward the stairs, the man thundering behind him. He threw himself up the steps two at a time, but he slipped and the soldier was on him in an instant.

And then, suddenly, the man was gone, tumbling down the stairs.

A slender arm, glittering with pearls, retreated through the slats in the steps. Someone was beneath him.

The skinny soldier ducked under the stairs and a scream—a scream Dev knew—pierced the air. Bernadine Lourdes was hauled out from the hay.

A second girl leapt from beneath the steps, throwing her tiny body onto the skinny soldier, beating him with her fists.

"Let her go!" she shouted in a voice accustomed to giving orders. *Aster Lourdes.*

The bigger man regained his footing, scrambling to pull the screaming Aster off his friend.

And then came Ursula, glinting and sparkling, with her arm wound back in first sharps position. "Must I strike you again?" she asked, her voice taut. She thrust her sharp-less palm forward, connecting with the slender soldier's lower back, and he buckled to his knees, howling from the force of it.

Alcor roared as the skinny man struggled to control Aster and Bernadine, shuffling farther back to avoid another blow from Ursula. She advanced on him. Dev could see the hesitation in her stance—it was not the stance of a confident sharps warrior.

They needed Alcor.

Dev tumbled down the stairs, dodging the big soldier groaning on the floor, and swooped around behind Ursula for Alcor's stall. Alcor snarled, his adolescent fangs looking decidedly adult as Dev's hand gripped the cold iron of the stall latch.

"Stop!"

Dev looked back to see the big soldier on his feet again—with Ursula gripped to his chest, his blade held menacingly at her throat. The skinny one laughed, holding a weeping Bernadine.

Dev's gut clenched. Aster was on the floor, gripping her face where one of the men must have struck her.

"If you release that bear," the big man said, pressing his sword harder against Ursula's throat, forcing her to cry out, "she bleeds."

Alcor bellowed.

Dev could feel the curve of the latch beneath his sweating palm. Should he pull it? He didn't *want* to release Alcor—he had worked with the young bear on battle training, yes, but these men were hardened soldiers. If Alcor hesitated, if he faltered, these men could hurt him. Dev wasn't sure the limited training he'd done with Alcor would be enough. In fact, he was sure it wouldn't be.

But Ursula . . .

He looked to Aster, and her eyes met his—fierce eyes. Eyes that told him not to listen. Eyes that ordered him to release Alcor. Eyes so powerful they could almost open the latch themselves.

Dev swallowed.

"Stop this!" screamed Bernadine. "Stop this, I command you at once! When my father finds out—"

The skinny man laughed as Bernadine tried to pry herself loose. "Your father will be right glad to see you, m'lady! He's got big plans for you. And for that nasty-lookin' Hemoth, of course. Ain't that right, Reathin?"

The big man, Reathin, said nothing, his eyes locked on Dev's, his blade on Ursula's throat, daring Dev to pull the latch.

"And for the lovely Miss Ursula, of course. Can't have you runnin' round, what with the Major's crown up for the taking now." The skinny man reached out a hand, fingering the neckline of Ursula's fine gown. She shuddered, and Dev felt his own skin prickle. "My, but the Minor's dress does look fine on you. *Impossible* to miss."

"Shut up, Vog," snapped Reathin. "Take the little Lady Bernadine to Minor Lourdes. Let him know we've found his bear and the Major's girls."

"Leave you by yourself? Why? Let's just be done with it!" insisted Vog. "Kill the Ursula girl now—she's the heir! That's what the Minor wants!"

Kill her? The Minor wants to kill *Ursula?*

Reathin's eyes never left Dev's. "Because the Keeper boy and I are at a bit of an impasse, you might notice."

Alcor huffed behind Dev. He could feel the Hemoth's hot, angry breath hitting the back of his neck. Could Alcor get to Ursula fast enough if he opened the stall? Get to her before this Reathin man had the chance to—to—

Dev's throat went dry, and he forced himself not to finish the thought.

"What about that one?" asked Vog, nodding at Aster, who was fuming from her spot on the ground. She was crouched like a cat, the scowl on her face almost as frightening as her father's.

"Take her with you. The Minor may still have a use for her," said Reathin. "The boy and I will keep Miss Ursula company. Won't we, boy?"

Dev said nothing, fighting the urge to swallow again and betray just how frightened he really was.

Ursula's eyes glistened with tears, and he wished he could read something there besides fear. What did she want him to do? Did she want him to release Alcor? To risk Reathin driving his blade into her throat? Risk the Minor's men harming the Hemoth cub?

Bernadine cried out as Vog dragged her by the arm. He reached down for Aster, who, to Dev's surprise, didn't struggle against him.

Had she given up? Was it wiser to surrender? Dev didn't know. He was a Keeper, a person of faith, not a warrior.

Vog hauled the two girls to the Holding's open door, and as they passed, Dev caught sight of Aster's face. There was something there, something that told Dev he was wrong. This wasn't surrender. There was a fight brewing inside her.

"Hurry up," snarled Vog, giving Aster a hard tug.

And then she lunged.

"Hold her!" shouted Reathin as Aster's hand came down on Dev's.

Down on the latch.

And pulled.

With the force of a thunderclap, Alcor threw open the stall, tossing Aster and Dev sideways.

Pain ignited in Dev's shoulder as his body slammed into the wall of the Holding. He fell to the floor, Aster's knees smashing into his gut as she landed on top of him. His ears rattled as Alcor's furious roaring buried the sounds of screams.

The helpless, high-pitched screams of Reathin and Vog.

But their screams didn't last long. And a hollow, empty quiet settled around him.

Aster's knees pressed harder into his stomach as she stood up. She reached down a hand for him, and, trembling, Dev accepted her hot, sweaty palm and was pulled back onto his feet.

The Holding had changed. All he could see was red—red, and Ursula and Alcor standing together over what was left of the Minor's Reathin and Vog.

The bright sap of the Ursan tree is sweet beyond sweet and a favorite treat of the Hemoth. But be cautious, for when it hardens, the amber is difficult to crack.

—THE WRITINGS OF BERN,
On Hemoth Bears: The Age of Tawn, *Star Writ*

SEVEN

"WE don't have much time," said Aster, stepping lightly over the particularly chunky bits of the detestable Reathin and Vog. "Surely other soldiers heard the commotion."

She stopped in front of what was left of big Reathin's torso, his blade stained red beside it.

"A-A-Alcor killed them," breathed Bernadine.

Aster looked back at her cousin, standing by the door with the bear boy. She was stiff as a board, gulping at the air like a frightened fish.

"Of course he did," said Aster. "He's a Hemoth Bear."

"*Killed* them," Bernadine said again. "Alcor *killed* them." She kept repeating it to herself, as if unable to think of anything else to say.

Aster glanced sideways at the massive Alcor, panting through a bloodstained maw. Mizar's offspring was indeed tremendous, and Aster wondered again how much the bear really cared for the company of little girls.

"He is trained, yes?" she said, turning to the bear boy. "He wouldn't…harm us?"

Before the boy could answer, Ursula interrupted. "He saved our lives, Aster."

"So did I," said Aster. "It was my idea to let him out, after all. Wasn't it?"

Alcor chuffed, sitting back on his haunches.

"He wouldn't." The bear boy's voice was weak and raspy, and Aster looked back at him. His wide eyes were locked on the skinny leg of Vog lying in the mud before him. "Alcor wouldn't hurt you."

Aster nodded. If the bear boy said so, then it must be true. The boy spent all day with the beast. Who else could better say what the bear would or would not do?

Aster turned back to the sword lying by the mangled corpse. A crude-looking weapon, she decided, nothing like the slender, graceful rapiers she and Ursula practiced with. A thick, double-edged blade, cruder and fatter than she would have liked, with a tapered tip—suited for stabbing and slashing, but not much else. Still, she bent down and gripped the handle, sticky with blood.

Heavy. Impossibly so.

"What are you going to do with that?"

Aster turned to see the bear boy looking at her, his eyes round as two full moons.

"We ought to defend ourselves, don't you agree?" she said.

"*You're* going to defend us?"

Her brow knotted. She would have liked to swing the blade, show him what she could do, but she didn't dare. The sword was more a club than anything, too heavy to lift above her head, and she'd look like a fool. If she'd had a choice, she would never have picked it.

"Yes, me," she said, wiping the blood off the handle with her skirt. "And Ursula, of course."

Aster's sister said nothing, her hand stroking Alcor's mane as he snorted quietly, licking the blood from his paws.

"Bear boy," said Aster. "Bring Alcor. We must go back and retrieve my mother."

"Your mother?" The boy looked at her as though she were mad, and Aster's eyes narrowed. The boy dropped his gaze to his feet. "F-Forgive me, m'lady. But I fear going back would be too dangerous."

"Perhaps for you, boy," she said. "But for the daughters of the Major, there is no danger too great to face. We must go back."

"The Major is dead," said Ursula.

Aster spun back toward her sister, a rush of anger searing her cheeks. "How *dare* you? How could you even *suggest* something so—"

Ursula's amber-colored eyes flashed. "You heard them! The Major's crown is up for the taking. That means he is *dead*. Uncle Bram betrayed Father! Betrayed us all!"

Aster stepped back. The wild look on her sister's face, the pain of her words, twisted Aster's stomach in knots so tight she thought she might be sick.

But Father is the Death Chaser, she thought. *Nothing can harm him.*

If Uncle Bram really *had* betrayed Father, though...her mind reeled.

No. It didn't make sense. A Major and a Minor were a united force. They always had been, for as long as the Lourdes had been Bear Lords—hundreds of years, a thousand, even. Uncle Bram had just thrown all that away? Why would he do something like that?

"And you?" growled Ursula, her ferocious gaze trained on Bernadine. "Did you know of this plot?"

Bernadine sniffled from her spot by the door. "Me?"

"He's your father." Ursula's stare was blazing. "Perhaps you helped him in this treachery."

"Ursula! Stop it!" said Aster. What could her sister be thinking? Bernadine had been with them the whole night. Been with them their whole childhood! She was practically their sister. Ursula *couldn't* believe Bernadine would betray Father like this—betray *them.*

Bernadine's eyes, swollen with tears, looked defiantly at Ursula. "It's not true. My father couldn't do this. He didn't do this."

"Stupid girl," said Ursula. "These are *his* men who've stormed your Major's house!"

Bernadine began to weep. "My father *loves* Uncle Jasper! Major and Minor—my father was devoted to yours. You cannot believe he would do this!"

Aster watched Ursula's lips tighten before she stormed over to the torso at Aster's feet, ripping off the breastplate with a sickening sound of *wet*.

"Believe it!" Ursula hurled the slimy piece of armor at Bernadine, who barely managed to duck out of the way. Her chest was rising and falling with furious breaths beneath her frost-pearl gown. "Because it's done!"

Bernadine stared down at the emblem of the White Bear adorning the intruder's breastplate—the mark of the Minor. The proof of his villainy was there, right there.

But still, Aster told herself, *Father is the fiercest warrior in the Highen, Mizar the strongest High Beast.*

They can't *be defeated.*

If Father had fallen to Uncle Bram, everything Aster knew, everything she believed about Father, about their family and the Highen—it would all be undone.

"The bear boy is right," said Ursula stonily. "It's too dangerous to go back for Mother. Since Uncle Bram has betrayed Father, he must want the Major's crown for himself. He will need us dead."

"But…" The bear boy lifted his head. "Only Alcor can chose the Major."

"Exactly. And Bram will want very few options for him to choose from," said Ursula, gripping one of the bloodied legs that had landed on the stairs. Tugging, she pulled a dagger from the soldier's boot. "My sister and I are nothing but an obstacle to his ambitions. Don't you understand? We must run—and we must take the Hemoth with us."

"Ursula," said Aster. "I will not leave Mother. We are her daughters. It's our duty to—"

"*My* duty is to the Hemoth Bear," Ursula snapped. "To the Highen.

Mother and Father said so themselves. We cannot risk delivering Alcor to Uncle Bram."

Yes, her parents had said that. But how could she leave without knowing what would happen to their mother? Was it not also her duty to defend her family?

Ursula pulled open the heavy doors of the Holding. "They're coming. We must move."

The boy was quick to follow, guiding Alcor over the threshold. "We'd best stick to the Shiver Woods," he said, motioning to the trees that grew behind the building.

Ursula nodded, beckoning Aster to follow.

"No!" said Aster. "We must go to the Manor! We must go back for Mother!"

The voices of more men were nearing now, shouting across the green. "Search the stables! The girls can't be hard to find!"

Ursula kicked a frustrated foot into the door. "You cannot defeat Uncle Bram's entire army all by yourself!"

"Not by myself!" said Aster. "With you!"

The sisters stared at each other for the longest moment, Aster searching Ursula's eyes for something. For the love of their mother, maybe. It was in her, wasn't it? She couldn't just leave Mother alone like this.

But Ursula's eyes remained hard. "As I said, I know my duty, sister," she said, her teeth gritted. "Mother knows it too."

Aster felt an ache in her throat.

Ursula would not go back for Mother.

The night surrounded her, dark and fearful, loud with the sounds of the Minor's men. How many? Twenty? Forty? A hundred?

Aster's grip loosened on her sword. Ursula was right. She could not go back on her own. She could not fight this army.

Ursula grabbed Aster by the wrist, marching her out into the night. Aster didn't resist. Instead, a shudder wormed its way up her legs, her spine, her neck. Would her father think her a coward for abandoning the Manor, abandoning their mother? *Duty*, her father always said. *You have a duty to the On-High.* Aster looked up at the stars that made up the great Hemoth in the sky. What did the Highest of High Beasts think when he looked down on her now?

"Wait!" The bear boy took off back into the Holding.

"What are you doing?" Ursula hissed after him.

Within moments he was back, a heavy book—the *Star Writ*—tucked up under his arm, and a sopping, bloodied cloak, taken from what was left of Reathin, held in his hands. He offered the cloak to Ursula. She frowned.

"Your dress," he said. "It's too easy to spot."

Aster looked over at the glinting frost pearls, bright as starflies. The boy was right.

A gift from the Minor. It arrived today.

Aster felt her cheeks flush with rage. To mark Ursula, she realized. So his men would know which girl was the heir to the Major.

Ursula's nose wrinkled at the red-soaked fabric, but she accepted. She slung the cape, heavy with blood, around her shoulders.

"Come on, then," she whispered, ducking between the Bear Holding and one of the horse stables, leading the way into the woods. Alcor snorted and heaved himself forward, his giant body brushing against the Holding as he followed Ursula, the bear boy at his heels.

Aster fell in behind them, stepping into the darkness of the trees. The Shiver Woods smelled like pine needles and juniper berries. She felt a flutter in her stomach; she'd never been in a forest at night.

The bear boy looked back over his shoulder, and Aster stiffened, wondering what exactly he thought he was looking at. But he wasn't looking at her, she realized. He was staring beyond her.

Bernadine. Where was Bernadine?

She turned back for her cousin. Bernadine stood in the shadow of the Bear Holding in her oversized dress, wringing her hands.

"Hurry up, will you?" whispered Aster.

Bernadine ignored her, craning her neck in the direction of the approaching voices.

Aster stomped an impatient foot. "Come on, I said!"

"My father," Bernadine whispered. "Do you really think he could be here? At the Manor?"

"Your father is a traitor," Ursula hissed. "Go back there and join him for all I care!"

"That's enough, Ursula!" snapped Aster.

Bernadine's mouth quivered, her face pained. Aster had seen her cousin look like that only once before—when Uncle Bram left her alone in Tawnshire all those years ago. Bernadine wasn't ready to accept the truth of this situation, just like she wasn't ready then. And Aster was angry at Uncle Bram for her. He hadn't just betrayed the Major—he'd betrayed Bernadine, too.

"We have to stick together now," said Aster.

"But he's my father!" Bernadine shook her head. "He couldn't have done this. Not without a reason!"

"Jealousy," said Ursula, turning her back on the two of them to head deeper into the trees.

The orange glow of torchlight lit the Holding behind Bernadine, men shouting as they caught sight of the bodies on the ground.

"Bernadine!" breathed Aster urgently. "Come now!"

"Run," whispered Bernadine, glancing at the Holding.

Aster stood there, dumbfounded. What did she mean, *run*?

Bernadine looked back to her. "Now, Aster! It's your only chance!"

Aster shook her head, marching back to Bernadine to drag her into the woods. She may have been forced to leave her mother, but she could at least control what happened to her cousin.

A pair of hands grabbed Aster by the arm. Ursula.

"She's made her choice," her big sister said. "These are *her* people. Let her go."

"But—" Aster watched through the branches as her cousin stepped out into the light of the torches, her hand held up in greeting to the Minor's men.

These are her people. Ursula's words echoed in Aster's mind.

Bernadine made her choice.

I fear the wolves, said the little cub to Mama Bear,
They're hungry and they're hunting in the forest just out there.
I fear the wind that brings the cold and shakes barren the trees,
I'm glad we're in our den, where nothing can harm me.
It's not the wolves, said Mama, or wind that you should fear.
It's the danger in the walls, that danger's much more near.
Listen, do you hear that? It's the rats, they're with us too.
If we forget they're in here, there's no telling what they'll do.

—TAWNSHIRIAN FOLK SONG,
recorded in the Writings of Drew the Dreamer

EIGHT

BERNADINE Lourdes walked, frightened and confused, at the center of a pack of the White Bear's soldiers—Frosmen, her people called them. They'd come here, to Tawnshire, and taken the Major's home.

But why? Her father's orders? Bernadine couldn't understand it.

A traitor. That was what Ursula had called her father.

But Ursula was wrong. She had to be. Ursula didn't know her father, not really, not the kind of man he was. Bernadine did. She knew he could explain everything. She would ask him, and he would answer. She needed him to.

As they approached the entrance to the Manor, Bernadine saw the bodies of four of the Major's guards, sprawled and crooked, on the steps. The youngest one, curly locks crusted with blood, stared up, empty-eyed, at the night sky. Bernadine had seen him standing guard by the door every day since she arrived at her uncle's home. Artie. His fellow Hermans called him Artie.

"M'lady!"

It was a voice she knew, echoing from within the foyer of the Manor.

Just inside the door was Hewitt Pire, the captain of her father's guard, smiling through an unshaven silver beard. His armor had lost its glint, tarnished with mud and Tawn-only-knew what else. His normally close-cropped gray hair had grown and was sticking out in all directions, scruffy and wild. "We've been looking all over for you, Princess!"

He crouched down, his face level with hers. Hewitt had met her at her height for as long as Bernadine could remember. And she'd always liked him for that.

But now his face looked different, beaded with sweat and brown, crusty droplets—dried blood.

She looked back at Artie, his vacant eyes forcing the breath from her lungs. Had her beloved Hewitt killed him?

"Oh, don't worry, little lady," said Hewitt, his large hand patting her shoulder as he stood up. "The dead can't hurt you."

She hadn't thought they could. But as Hewitt ushered her inside the Major's home, the click of his boots echoing off the walls, she wondered: Could Artie hear that clicking? Could he see them? Was he angry?

A shiver rippled through her, and for a moment, she thought Hewitt might be wrong about the dead.

"Your father will be so happy to see you," said Hewitt pleasantly.

"Where is he?" she asked, her heart aching with fear and worry and confusion and all manner of things she couldn't sort through without her father.

Hewitt smiled because he didn't have to answer. Bernadine could already hear her father's laughter, bouncing off the walls and making her chest swell with sunshine. That was what Minor Bram Lourdes' voice was to Bernadine. Sunshine.

Her feet quickened, pulling her ahead of Hewitt as she ran toward the sound.

Her father would explain this to her.

Her father would make everything right.

She followed his laughter to the dining hall, where his Frosmen were celebrating with casks of the Major's reserves. And there he was—Minor Bram Lourdes, standing on the table still set with the half-eaten lamb pies Bernadine had dined on with her cousins and aunt just hours ago. It had been months since her last visit with him, and since then he'd changed. *Thinner,* Bernadine thought. *Has he not been eating?*

Her father raised his mug, pointing it at a group of women kneeling on the floor before him.

"You're very funny, ladies," he said, smiling.

Bernadine's eyes moved over the women's faces—cooks and housekeepers whose names she'd never had reason to learn. But the one in the middle, with a split lip, Bernadine knew very well—Gatch, the nursemaid.

"You feed them, clean them, dress them," said her father, his tone light, jovial, as though they were old friends swapping tales in a tavern. "Your every waking moment is lived for the Major's daughters. Yet somehow, you can't think of a single place they might be hiding."

Bernadine had only ever known Gatch's face to wear a smile. Even when she was stern, her eyes were kind and bright. But now, Gatch's eyes were bladelike. Daggers. Aimed at her father.

"No ideas, then, eh?" The Minor hopped off the table, bending down to meet Gatch's face. "Shall I jog your memory?"

Her father raised his free hand, and a scream rose in Bernadine's throat. *"Father!"*

Her father spun, his eyes falling on her. Grinning, he dropped his mug on the floor with a loud thunk, wine spilling everywhere, and threw open his arms. "My Bernie Doll!"

He raced toward her, her sunny, loving father—the father she knew, the father she loved so dearly. But the man he'd been in the moment before, the man who raised his hand. Who had that been?

He lifted her off the floor as though she were nothing but air, scooping her into his arms and squeezing so tightly it was as if he'd never let her go. She squeezed back, burying her face in his shoulder.

Her nose wrinkled. Old sweat and thick, cloying body odor. That was not the smell of her father. Her father smelled of woodsmoke and cedar and fresh, clean snow.

This was wrong, all wrong. She pulled away.

Her father threw back his head and laughed, tweaking her nose. "Do I stink, love? Forgive an old soldier, won't you? We've had a hard few days on the road."

But why had her father *been* on the road?

Why was he *here*, and not with Uncle Jasper and the rest of the Highen's armies?

And where was Alurea, the White Bear, the High Beast of Whitford? Where was Iclyn, her Keeper? The White Bear was always with the Minor, just as the Hemoth Bear was always with the Major. They were bound in the same way. And yet Bernadine hadn't seen Alurea anywhere.

Before she could open her mouth, Hewitt spoke. "We found the princess outside the Bear Holding."

"Did you, now?" said her father, beaming. "Making friendly with the Hemoth, were you?" He laughed and shook her playfully. "That's my Bernie Doll."

Bernadine frowned. *No*, she thought. *No, I was not making friendly with the Hemoth. Why should I make friendly with it?*

His letters lately were forever asking about the frightening Alcor: what kind of treat was his favorite, how fast he was growing, how he liked best to be scratched. The questions always bothered Bernadine—not just because she couldn't answer them, but because they made up the bulk of her father's writing. Now she thought of it, he asked more questions about the bear than he asked about her.

"I'm afraid the Hemoth is gone, my lord," said Hewitt after another moment.

Bernadine watched her father's face darken. "What?"

"We found what was left of two of our men—they were torn to bloody pieces inside the animal's keep. Nothing else."

Bernadine's father dropped her on her feet, and he held her at arm's length. "My darling girl, were you hurt?" Frantically, he turned her sideways and around, checking every inch of her.

"We've searched the grounds," Hewitt went on. "There's no sign of the bear. The Keeper's apprentice seems to be missing as well."

Bernadine's father held her firmly by the arms, his concern giving way to something else—something fierce. "Tell me, Bernie Doll—did you see the Hemoth? Did you see Ursula?"

Bernadine bit her lip. What did her father want with them so badly?

Her father's icy gray eyes searched hers. And for the first time in her life she saw the eyes of a warrior there. Focused. Determined. Hard.

"Bernadine, this is very important." Her father's grip tightened. "Tell me, where have they gone?"

Bernadine's eyes dropped to her feet. That awful Vog man, what he'd said about Ursula, about her father wanting her cousin dead—it raced through her mind again and again.

"Will you hurt them?" she asked. Her voice was little more than a squeak.

There was quiet from her father, and she could feel him looking at Hewitt, deciding how best to answer. Finally, he sighed heavily and hugged her close. "Oh, my kind and gentle girl. You have your darling mother's nature, Tawn keep her star." He lifted her chin, and Bernadine was relieved to see that the eyes of her loving father had returned. "I will tell you something, Bernie Doll. You are the one who gives the orders here. If you order me not to harm your cousins"—he raised one hand, the other over his heart—"then I am bound to follow your command."

Bernadine stared at her father, his words not making sense. If *she* ordered him? Since when was she set above her father? And why should she *have* to order him? Shouldn't he not want to hurt them all on his own? Didn't he love them?

"Father, I don't understand. You would never harm Ursula or Aster—you couldn't." She swallowed. "Why have you come here? Did Uncle Jasper send you? Has something happened with the Ring?"

He pulled her close, stroking her hair. "Hush now, my doll. So many big questions. And none of them easy answers, I'm afraid." He brushed loose wisps of curly hair from her eyes. "Of course I do not wish to harm your cousins. They are but children. On their own in the dark." He stepped away from her, his hand rubbing his chin, worry lines crinkling his brow. "A dangerous situation for them. Especially with that Hemoth."

"Unpredictable beasts, Hemoths," agreed Hewitt.

Her father nodded grimly. "No telling what might happen."

Bernadine's mind filled with the memory of Alcor, tearing into the screaming Reathin and Vog. And the red. So much red.

Ursula and Aster were alone in the woods...alone with that monstrous bear. They *were* in danger. What if that bear did to them what he'd done to Reathin and Vog? They were her cousins, her kin—her sisters. How could Bernadine forgive herself if they died like those men had?

"They've gone into the Shiver Woods," she said suddenly.

Her father tapped her on the nose, a satisfied smile on his face. "That's my Bernie Doll."

He turned to Hewitt. The two men towered over her, and she suddenly felt alone, shut off in her world of the short and young.

"Take Farrst and Grieves and all their men," said her father. "Have them split into two groups and search the woods."

"Very good, my lord." Hewitt bowed and marched out of the dining hall, several Frosmen following.

A hunt had begun. She could tell.

But her father had promised he wouldn't harm them, hadn't

he? Bernadine's stomach fluttered with doubt. The man who made her the promise and the man who gave the orders to Hewitt—these were different men. Could one make a promise for the other?

"Father," she said, taking his hand. "I still don't understand. Why have you come? You're supposed to be fighting the Ring!"

Her father smiled down at her. "You are a charmingly curious child. But I'm afraid the answers are simply too...difficult...to understand."

"But I *want* the answers," she told him, careful not to whine. "Where is the White Bear? And her Keeper? Shouldn't they be with you?"

"Bernadine!" His voice rose to the ceiling, calling the attention of the Frosmen, and the room became quiet.

She stepped back. She'd upset him, though she didn't know how.

As quickly as his anger had come, it was gone, the hard lines of his face softening. He bent down before her, the weight of his giant, grown-up hands resting on her shoulders. "You must trust that what I do, I do for the good of the Highen. That what I do, I do for you, Bernie Doll."

Bernadine tried to nod, but she couldn't think how any of this was so. Of course she trusted her father. But...

"But what *are* you doing?"

The corner of her father's mouth pulled up in a proud half-grin, one wolflike tooth glinting like the frost pearls of their Whitlock home.

"Making you a Major."

And as the Shadow Dragon Calor bore down upon the city, it was Major Bram the Red who bowed humbly before the mighty Hemoth Bear Arnant, and asked of him the favor no Major had dared to ask before....

—THE WRITINGS OF BERN,
The Battle at Tawnshire: The Age of Tawn, *Star Writ*

NINE

ASTER did her best not to stumble, but the black was thick. The trees of the Shiver Woods blocked the starlight of the On-High so completely that she could barely make out the giant backside of Alcor, padding his way over the soft moss of the forest floor.

She could smell him, though. Like wet earth and a rancid chamber pot.

With a wrinkled nose, she let the young bear's stink and his incessant grumbling guide her through the darkness. Somewhere beside him was his boy, and in front, leading the way, was Ursula. Every few steps, the bottom of her blood-drenched cloak lifted just enough to show a glint of frost pearls underneath.

A gift from the enemy, thought Aster.

Enemy. The word startled her. *Uncle Bram, an enemy.*

Her father had always lovingly called her uncle a clown, and he was. He was good at making his nieces laugh whenever the family came together to celebrate the Festival of Tawn. *Uncle Bram—our enemy.* The idea was absurd. She'd laugh if she weren't so angry.

The group walked in silence, save for the unhappy noises coming from Alcor, but Aster barely noticed. Her mind was alive, a torrent of ideas and plans and strategies to find her way back to the Manor and rescue her mother.

And what of Bernadine? She would need rescuing too, if Aster did indeed find her way back. Or would Bernadine stand by Uncle

Bram? *She's made her choice,* Ursula had said. But did her cousin really know what that choice meant?

"I can't see anything," came Ursula's voice from up ahead. "You're sure this is the way, bear boy?"

"Yes."

A long silence followed as the Lourdes sisters waited for him to say more.

"And you're sure it's safe there?" pressed Ursula. "In the Oracle House, I mean."

"Yes. Of course."

More silence. Aster didn't care for the way the boy said *of course,* as though Ursula's questions were foolish, as if they should already know the Oracle House would be safe. How should they know that?

Aster knew little about the Oracles of Berenice, and what she did know, she couldn't really make sense of. They were special, that much she remembered, each born with the mark of the Great Lady Berenice—red eyes, eyes like fire. Keeper Rizlan said they were blessed, because the marks meant they could hear the voices of the stars. *How* they heard the stars, Aster couldn't begin to guess at. With their ears? Why shouldn't everyone hear the stars if the stars had something to say?

Aster tilted her face to the treetops, catching only the slightest glimmer of stars through the thick, leafy branches. If the On-High were watching her now, what were the Oracles being told?

Alcor let out a low moan, and Aster heard the ground beneath him crunch as the Hemoth sat back on his haunches. The bear repeated the same pathetic sound, a *bope bope bope.*

"Can't you control that bear?" hissed Aster. "It's a wonder all of Tawnshire doesn't know where we are with that noise!"

"He's frightened," said the boy, stroking the beast's neck.

"Frightened?" scoffed Aster. "*He's* frightened? He's a Hemoth Bear!"

Aster could just make out the silhouette of the boy as he whirled to face her. "He's not used to this!" he said. "Being up so late. Not getting a snack. His whole schedule is off."

His schedule. His snack. As if he were one of the lapdogs the House ladies carried around at Highen balls.

"Father and Mizar didn't eat for a week during the war on the Nightlocks," she reminded him tersely.

She could feel the heat of the boy's glare through the dark. "Well, Alcor is not Mizar."

The bear resumed his *bope bope bope* noises, and the boy responded by clicking his tongue again and again, like a mother tutting a fussy baby. It was all rather embarrassing, for a supposedly mighty Hemoth, but it seemed to work well enough. At least the boy hadn't used that awful kazoo of his. With one last groan, Alcor hoisted himself back to his feet and began to walk again.

"Bear boy," said Ursula, "what makes you so sure the Oracles will take us in?"

"If we ask," he explained, "they are bound. Whosoever seeks refuge with the Oracles shall receive it. It is the law of the stars."

"But we need to hide more than anything. What if they...talk?" Aster asked. "Tell someone we're there?"

"They can't," said the boy, stopping dead. "That would be against the the will of the On-High. It's here, in the *Star Writ*. Don't you read?" Aster could see him balancing the massive tome on his knee, hear the flipping of pages.

"Oh, don't look it up," she groaned. "I'm not about to stop and read in the dark now, am I?"

There was a heavy thud as he slammed the book closed. "Then I'll tell you what it says. It says the Oracles of Berenice hear the voices of the On-High. And the On-High decreed in the Age of Fyrn that anyone seeking protection *need only ask*, and the On-High would grant it *through* the Oracles of Berenice, and the Oracles of

Berenice would do *nothing* to endanger those in their care. Babies know that!"

"You dare condescend to me?" demanded Aster, hackles rising.

"Be quiet," snapped Ursula. "Both of you."

But Aster would not. Not after the way he had spoken to her. "You would lecture *me*? A daughter of the Major? You are not a Keeper yet, bear boy."

"I have a name and it is *not* Bear Boy!"

She knew the boy's name. Dev—that was what Keeper Rizlan called him. But some nasty little part of her heart, the part that liked to win, *needed* to win, rose up with a laugh. "You really think someone like me has any need for the name of someone like you?"

"That's *it!*" With a *ker-thunk*, the boy slammed the *Star Writ* to the ground. Alcor growled and Aster stepped back as the boy stormed toward her in the dark. "I've had enough of your spoiled, arrogant, ignorant princess *tripe!*"

Aster lifted the point of her sword, the weight of it straining her already tired muscles. The boy stopped dead as the tip pressed against his chest. "You will keep your distance, *bear boy.*"

"I said stop!" Ursula stepped between the boy and the sword tip. "The bear boy—er, Dev—is right, Aster."

Aster let the sword tip drop. "Right? Did you hear what he called me?"

"I heard him. But he's *right* to lecture us on the *Star Writ*. We don't know about the Oracles. We don't know about anything. We are completely unprepared for what is happening and it's our own fault." Ursula swallowed, the same pain Aster had seen when Mother read the letter returning to her eyes. She looked at the bear boy. "Teach us what you know, Dev, and we will listen. And be grateful."

The bear boy gaped at Ursula, just as surprised as Aster.

What was Ursula suggesting? That this was all *their* fault somehow? Because they didn't read Keeper Rizlan's assigned passages?

My deepest fear…Her father's words from her mother's lips.

"Shh." Ursula snapped her head to the side suddenly, forgetting Aster and the bear boy completely. "There's someone out there."

Aster followed her gaze into the trees. Distantly, she could see the flickering of torchlight between trunks. And there were voices, soldiers' voices, and the whinnies of nervous horses.

"They can smell him," whispered the bear boy. "Their horses smell Alcor."

Aster's grip on her blade tightened. She looked up at Ursula.

Alcor moaned quietly, and the horses spat and stomped their worry. Horses that Aster could just make out behind the pines, each of them bearing one of Uncle Bram's men on its back. There were Frosmen on foot, too, hacking at branches, searching the shadows of the trees.

Beyond them, no more than an orange glow against the sky, she could see the dim light of Tawnshire Town. The Minor's men were blocking the way into the capital.

They meant to capture them like rabbits run to ground.

Aster brought her hand to her hilt and lifted her blade, poised for another fight.

"Are you mad?" The bear boy grabbed her firmly by the elbow. "There's too many of them!"

"What do you propose, then?" she hissed, wrenching herself free of his grip. "Are there any better ideas in your precious *Star Writ*?"

Ursula frowned as she watched the soldiers through the branches. "Dev is right. There are too many."

Aster caught the faint lines of a smug smile on the bear boy's face. Her knuckles began to ache from the grip on her sword. "So? Shall we sit here and wait for them to find us, then?"

Ursula ignored the question, turning back to the boy. "How far to the Oracles?"

"The city center," he said.

"How far *exactly*!" she snapped.

The boy stumbled back. "I—I—I don't know exactly! Three hundred tail-lengths?"

The Manor's massive grounds from east to west were an even hundred, end to end. *Three times that length?* thought Aster. Might as well be a million for all the good it did them.

Alcor began his anxious *bope bope bope* again as he watched his boy walk back to retrieve the *Star Writ* from the dirt. Her sister's eyes followed the frightened beast.

"We'll never get Alcor that far without being seen," said Ursula. Tawnshire Town was entirely more city than it was town. The capital of Tawnshire. The beating heart of the Highen itself. It was dense. It was cramped. And there were eyes everywhere.

Aster watched the torchlight flicker closer, the speech of men and the snorting of horses growing louder. She looked back at Alcor, Dev's hand stroking his furry neck. There was nowhere to hide. The bear was simply too big.

"Perhaps we should make a run for it."

Ursula shook her head immediately. "We can't outrun those horses."

"No," agreed Aster. "*We* can't." She turned. "Bear boy—" He glared, and Aster sighed. "Fine then, *Dev*. Has Alcor ever let you ride him?"

Dev stiffened, clutching the *Star Writ* to his chest. "No! Alcor is a High Beast, not a mule! Who would even dare—"

"Bram the Red," whispered Aster.

Ursula's eyes grew wide with recognition. "The eighth Major."

Aster nodded. "Just like in the Dragon Wars."

A grin spread across her sister's lips. "Father's favorite story."

Aster felt a sudden rush of pride. It *was* her father's favorite tale—the one where Major Bram the Red defeated the rampaging dragon Calor. The Major rode his mighty Hemoth against Calor, the Red Flame, saving Tawnshire from fire and brimstone.

And Ursula was a magnificent rider. If anyone could do what Bram the Red had done, Aster was sure it would be Ursula.

"Alcor will never allow it," said Dev, his disapproval obvious. "He doesn't like things on his back. Your father wanted him to wear the colors of Tawn at last year's Festival. Alcor shredded them."

Aster shrugged. "Well, let's see, shall we?"

She lunged for Alcor—too busy trying to prove herself right to really consider what it was she was about to do—and launched herself onto the Hemoth's back.

And immediately regretted it.

The bear bellowed in annoyance, tossing Aster with no more effort than she might flick a fly. With a painful thud, she landed on her side, palms screaming from the needles and twigs embedding themselves in the flesh.

Behind her, the boy snickered, and a heat rushed to Aster's cheeks. She scrambled to her feet, ready to rebuke him for his insolence, but stopped at the sound of shouting men.

The soldiers had heard Alcor's roar.

"Fools!" Ursula hissed, and Aster felt her insides wither.

Her sister moved toward the angry bear as the darkness around them receded in the advancing torchlight. Aster could see the shadows of the soldiers closing in—they'd be on them any moment.

Ursula got down on one knee, her arms held open to the mighty Hemoth. "Please, Alcor," she whispered, "descendant of the Great Lord Tawn. We humbly beg you this one favor."

The bear was still.

And the voices were louder now, clear and close.

Aster looked anxiously to Dev, his wide eyes meeting hers. *What do we do?*

As if reading her mind, Dev dropped to his knees before Alcor. "Please, Alcor," he repeated. "We've no right to ask it, but we beg you, grant us this privilege."

The bear shifted his weight, dancing nervously before Ursula and Dev.

"Here!" a soldier shouted. "Over here! It's them!"

The surge in her stomach sent Aster to her knees. "Please, Alcor!" she screamed.

A thunder—so fierce and loud it deafened them—exploded from the Hemoth Bear's throat, rumbling the ground.

Aster cowered.

"Hurry!" Ursula shouted over the screeching of terrified horses. "Get up!"

Aster looked up from her spot on the forest floor into the ferociously snarling face of Alcor, his white fangs gleaming in the firelight. She flinched back, nearly crying out.

But Ursula sat astride the growling bear's back, her arm outstretched, the boy struggling to climb up behind her, his left arm useless as it held tight to the *Star Writ*. "Aster!"

The pounding of hooves rose up around them as the Minor's men burst into their patch of forest, swords drawn.

Aster scrambled to her feet as Alcor let out another blast. She reached up for her sister's hand, the boy grabbing hold of the other. Her arms trembled from the strain, nearly ripping free of the sockets, but they pulled her up astride Alcor between them.

Surrounded.

Ten soldiers, six on horseback, all with their blades drawn.

And it was quiet, save for the snorting of skittish horses.

Alcor *woof*ed heavily, and Aster suddenly became aware of the power beneath her. Her legs could feel the Hemoth's muscles, tense and hot through a layer of thick orange fur. His heart thumped a fast, battle-ready rhythm. She was atop a Hemoth. Just like Bram the Red.

She looked defiantly into the stunned faces of the soldiers, swords glinting in the flames.

The eldest of the group, silver-haired and weatherworn, tried to wipe the surprise from his face. "Come down off there," he commanded, a tremor rattling his gravelly voice.

Aster glanced up at the side of her sister's face—and saw Ursula's jaw tighten.

"You will come down!" the man shouted, and Alcor began to tremble. "In the name of the Minor!"

The tremble grew into a quake, and Alcor released another blast of sound, sending the horses up on their hind legs. The soldiers began to shout and break formation, trying vainly to regain control of the terrified creatures.

And Alcor lunged, his mighty body surging forward with such force that they were all almost thrown from his back. Aster gripped tight to her sister's waist as they charged through the forest. Branches splintered into nothing but dust in Alcor's wake, the forest itself bowing to the might of the Hemoth.

Before too long, they exploded from the darkness onto the lamplit streets of Tawnshire Town—the angry cries of the Minor's men following them all the way.

Eyes that are red,
   See the day you'll be dead,
      And they can tell the stars when you're bad,

But voices and visions?
   I've made my decision—
      The Oracles, they're all a bit mad.

—HUNDFORDIAN FOLK SONG

TEN

THE bear barreled through the streets of Tawnshire Town.

Dev could barely hang on. His body flopped like a fish—he clung desperately to Alcor's fur with one hand, the *Star Writ* in his other. He'd never ridden a horse, never mind a creature as mighty as a Hemoth. Every stride of the bear threatened to pitch the young Keeper off, his white-knuckled grip the only thing keeping him astride.

The clack of horseshoes on cobbles told him the Minor's men were close behind, their angry cries echoing off the plaster walls of Tawnshire Town's tightly packed taverns and shops.

Could Alcor outrun a horse? The bear had never had much cause to run fast at all. Dev squeezed his eyes shut and prayed that the On-High granted the young Hemoth speed.

"*Yah!*" bellowed Ursula, her body low against Alcor, her arm coming down with a blasphemous smack to the bear's side.

Abhorrent!

Profane!

Sacrilege!

"*Alcor is not a—*" Before Dev could say *mule*, his balance shifted, his bottom slid out from under him, and he toppled backward. Frantically, his flailing arm grabbed for the nearest lifeline—the hair of Aster Lourdes.

She shrieked, her head wrenching back, but he managed to grab hold of her waist with his other arm, hand still clasping the sacred book. He pulled himself back to safety, clinging to her, his legs pressing hard around Alcor.

"Stay *low*, you oaf!" Aster shouted. "Like this!"

The two Lourdes girls were bowed so low their stomachs were practically pressed against Alcor's back. Dev did as she said, but still he clung to her waist, not trusting himself not to slip again.

Ursula's arm came up, but this time Dev said nothing, silently begging the On-High's forgiveness as the princess's hand came down with another blasphemous smack.

"Where now, Dev?" Ursula called.

Where now? Where were they? Streetlamps and candlelit windows whooshed by in a sickening blur, Aster's hair whipping Dev's face. He couldn't tell what street they were on, couldn't recognize Tawnshire Town at all—everything looked different from the back of a charging Hemoth.

"Bear boy!" bellowed Aster. "Where do we go?"

With a ferocious snarl, Alcor came to a sliding halt, only barely stopping before colliding with a row of bakeshops.

The screams of horses called Dev's attention back to the advancing men. One soldier, the silver-haired one, pulled ahead of the pack, waving his sword above his head. Teeth bared, he roared like a Shadow Dragon swooping for the kill.

The soldier's sword came down, and Dev quailed, expecting to feel the bite of the cold blade.

Instead, there was a loud clank of metal.

"*Bear boy!*" Aster screamed, forcing Dev to open his eyes.

Aster held her stolen sword up, blocking the man's strike, and Ursula lashed out with her foot, kicking wildly at him. Alcor shifted and *woof*ed, not sure where to go.

Which way to go? Bakeshops. Rizlan let him buy a honey cake every Festival here. Parade Street. The dancers and performers would make their way through, following the river to Blue Marble Bridge.

The man struck again, and again Aster blocked—but only just barely, his blade ripping into her skirts. *"Dev!"*

"That way!" he cried, pointing to the right. "The bridge! That way!"

Ursula raised her leg high, and her foot connected with the man's gut, doubling him over. But the rest of the Minor's men had caught up, and all of their swords were brandished high.

Dev's stomach jumped into his throat. "Go, Alcor! *Go right!*" His own fist pummeled the sacred Hemoth as Alcor tore off down Parade Street.

"There! There!" he screamed, the blue glint of precious Twigatian stone coming into view. Blue Marble Bridge. The bear was across in three strides, but the Minor's soldiers kept pace, the silver-haired man pulling up on their right.

"Faster, Ursula!" Aster screamed.

But there was no going faster. Alcor was at his limit. Dev could hear it in the bear's snorting breaths, feel it in the strain of his muscles.

The silver-haired man struck out with his blade, slicing the Hemoth's leg so that Alcor bellowed in pain. But the bear kept on, not stopping for his wound. The bear was running for the lights.

Dev could see them now, his heart swelling at the tiny dots of white flickering in the windows of the Oracle House. "It's there!" he cried, pointing at the towering wooden building leaning precariously over the center square.

But the silver-haired soldier knew where they were going and drove ahead of the charging Hemoth, racing for the steps of the Oracle House.

Panic seized Dev's throat. "He'll block the bell!"

Aster shouted over her shoulder. "The what?"

"The bell! We need to ring the bell for sanctuary!" He pointed at the thick woven rope hanging to the left of the House's doors. The silver-haired soldier was already at the steps, rounding his horse and stopping. "He won't let us get to the bell!"

More of the Minor's soldiers passed by them, flying for the steps as Alcor slowed to a hobble. The bear moaned, crying in that way Dev had come to know as tears. Alcor tossed his head, trying to look over his shoulders at Dev. He was in pain, and he was frightened. Dev slipped off the limping bear, tripping as his feet met cobble, and rushed to stroke his nose.

Alcor had been injured tonight. The most blessed of the On-High's children, stabbed on Dev's watch. He should have seen it coming, should have had a vision—he should have warned everyone!

But he hadn't seen it coming. He was useless as a Keeper. This was all his fault.

Ursula and Aster dismounted with more grace, facing the wall of the Minor's men with their chins held high and defiant, each so much like Lady Lourdes.

"Stand aside." Ursula's demand was met with a smattering of chuckles. "You will let us pass," she insisted.

One of the men sneered, his eyes devouring the young princess in a way that turned Dev's stomach. "Afraid you're due back at the Manor, m'lady."

Aster stepped forward, sword battle-ready. "You will let us pass or answer for your treason against Jasper Lourdes, the Death Chaser!"

More laughter from the men, but the silver-haired soldier who led them did not smile.

Dev wanted to yank Aster back, to shout at her and Ursula, *Who do you think you are? You're the Major's daughters, not the Major himself!* To these men, the reign of Jasper Lourdes was over. To these men, the Lourdes girls were nothing but spoiled children.

The silver-haired man pulled his sword and advanced, frowning. "Enough of this running around. You children have sinned against the Great Lord Tawn, riding his son like a pony for your games."

"You dare speak of sin to us?"

"Aster," Ursula warned. But the youngest daughter of Jasper Lourdes would not be easily silenced, Dev knew that much.

"What of *your* sins, Frosman?" Aster trembled with rage as she stared down the old soldier, her voice shaking with emotion. "You've betrayed your Major!"

"The Major is dead."

Whatever boldness had swollen Aster's insides, Dev saw it deflate at the mention of her father's death, shrinking like a leaf over a candle flame. She looked small, Dev thought. Ever so much smaller than the soldier. Not a princess now. Just a little girl standing in front of an army. A little girl who'd only just realized that her father wouldn't be coming to save her.

Dev felt his own insides wither just a little. He'd half-believed Aster when she insisted her father still lived. But he didn't, and fear came in an icy rush across Dev's neck.

Beyond the girl and the soldier, the lights of the Oracle House flickered. Hundreds of candles in glass jars sat on the sills of the many windows that dotted its six stories. The flames were pure white, unmoved by the wind, swelling and waning in unison.

Starlight.

Dev glanced up at the night sky, the On-High staring down between black clouds. The *Star Writ* felt heavy in his hand.

Who holds the On-High's favor this night? Whose sin has offended the stars more?

There was a loud groan as the doors to the Oracle House opened.

Two white-haired figures stood there. Two women, their skin as pale as the moon. He watched their eyes—red as dragon fire—fall on Alcor, and both made the sign of the On-High: hand to the heart, to the lips, and skyward. Dev could see the brass cones dangling from a red cord around their necks—ear trumpets. To help them hear the voices of the stars.

Oracles.

"Blessed Ears!" shouted Dev. "Oracles of the On-High! Please! Grant us Haven!"

The women said nothing. The younger of the two looked at the bell rope dangling uselessly beside the door. The rope Dev had no hope of ringing—not with Frosmen in his way.

"Shouting does you no good, boy," said the silver-haired man. "Only the bell can give you sanctuary." Moving like lightning, he grabbed Aster by the arm, and she cried out as he wrenched her blade from her grip.

"Daughters of the Major," said the older of the two Oracles.

"Seeking asylum from the Minor," said the younger.

"Curious," they said together.

The women descended the steps, moving with a floating, confident grace, their red robes billowing behind them. The Frosmen turned to one another, and they shifted on their feet, instinctively clearing the women's way.

Dev wasn't surprised to see the men so unnerved. It wasn't often one found oneself in the presence of Oracles.

Oracles sealed themselves off in their Houses, rarely leaving or interacting with the outside. They spent their time with their ears pressed to their brass trumpets, listening to the On-High, not daring to miss a word. They were a mystery to the world they shut out, and that made them strange—and frightening. Even Dev found himself uncomfortable.

The silver-haired man was no exception. He held tighter to Aster as though the Oracles might rip her away from him. Dev wished they would. But the Oracles paid no attention to the girl in the man's rough arms.

Their eyes were for Alcor.

They floated over to Dev and the Hemoth, dropping to their knees before the bear.

"Tawn be praised," whispered the younger, while the older clutched her trumpet to her chest. Quietly, she repeated the oath of the Oracles in fast whispers—*My heart, my voice, I give you.*

"The bear is to be returned to the Manor," proclaimed the old soldier. "I am Captain Hewitt Pire, and I have orders to see he is brought to his rightful home."

"Orders," said the older, casting her eyes up at the sky.

"Not the Major's orders," agreed the younger, helping her companion to her feet.

"What mortal man can command the descendant of the Great Lord Tawn?" the older asked the younger. "Even the Major does not command the bear."

The way they spoke was odd, Dev thought. As though Captain Hewitt Pire weren't there at all—only the words he spoke, lingering on the night air around them.

The younger answered her companion's question. "Aye. The descendant of the Great Lord Tawn bows to no mortal man, sister."

"Mortal man bows to Him," the old sister said.

"Mortal man bows," agreed the younger.

Dev watched the captain's men whispering to one another, nervously glancing between the Oracle women and the windows of the House. Dev could see the jars of starflame, and he knew the Frosmen had the same questions he did: Were the On-High speaking now? Could the women hear their voices?

"Mortal man," said Captain Pire, his voice razor-thin, "can bow to Tawn's son at the Manor where the bear belongs."

The older Oracle cocked her head to the side in thought. "Yet the bear is here."

"And?" snapped Captain Hewitt Pire, stepping toward the women.

Dev saw Aster wince as the captain yanked her arm. And her

eyes caught his. They flicked left, then back to him. Was she trying to tell him something?

"The bear is here," said the older Oracle. "Does he not belong wherever he brings himself?"

"The *children* brought him here," growled the captain. "And they will be reprimanded for it."

The younger Oracle ignored the captain, turning to her companion. "If the children brought the bear, then surely the bear had wished to be brought."

The older nodded. "Surely the bear had wished to be brought." The old woman's red eyes snapped suddenly to Dev, and he jumped. "Keeper?"

He felt her gaze taking all of him in and appraising who and what he was. Keeper. Yes. Well, almost. Or maybe not. He was a poor student of scripture. He could be rash and impatient. And, worst of all, he hadn't foreseen the threat. What sort of Keeper couldn't see what would come?

"Wait just a minute," said the captain. "This *boy* is not a Keeper. He is just an apprentice."

Dev flushed, embarrassed. Yes, just an apprentice. One who obviously had no hope of filling his master's shoes.

"The boy keeps the bear, does he not?" asked the younger Oracle.

"Both young," said the older Oracle, "boy and bear."

"A young Keeper for a young bear."

The women looked Dev over and nodded, satisfied with their assessment.

But the Frosman was not satisfied. "What gibberish is this?"

The younger turned to face the old man while her companion continued to watch Dev. Her red eyes moved sideways, just the same as Aster's had.

He followed her gaze to where the soldiers stood, huddled

together, eyes fixed on their captain. So fixed that they had ignored a gap in their formation—a path running between the group, through which the two women had passed moments before.

"The Minor has ordered the bear returned to the Manor," the captain was saying. "And so the bear will go."

The old woman turned back to the captain. "Which bear?"

"The White Bear, of course," the younger told her.

"*This* bear!" shouted Captain Hewitt Pire.

"But this is the Hemoth Bear," said the younger.

The older nodded. "The Minor is bound to the White Bear."

"Not the Hemoth Bear."

"Indeed. Let the Minor attend to the White Bear only."

Yes, thought Dev. *Where are the White Bear and her Keeper?*

The captain's frown deepened. "We are here for the Hemoth."

"Where is the White Bear, Captain?" the younger demanded, and at that, the Oracles raised their trumpets to their ears. "Where is the High Beast of Whitford?"

Aster caught Dev's eye again, and she looked toward the path, the clear way to the bell. But the men—they would lunge for him. He'd never make it.

"The White Bear." The older Oracle's voice had changed. Rounder somehow, resonant, like an echo through a cave. "Alurea, Daughter of Eira."

The younger Oracle spoke with the same resonance. "Her name, Frosman."

"*Speak the White Bear's name!*" the two cried together, their voices booming, merging, until Dev felt the air around them straining as if the world might pull apart.

The stars were speaking. Only the Oracles could hear the words, but Dev could feel it in his bones.

And so could the others. The Frosmen shifted fearfully, eyes wide, weapons drawn.

Captain Hewitt Pire opened his mouth to speak…but said nothing. He tried again, but again he choked on the name. *Alurea.*

The Oracles moved toward him, speaking together so that Dev's brain hummed with the sound. *"You will not speak her name?"*

The captain stumbled back, holding Aster like a shield between him and the women.

"Woe to you, who cannot speak her name," they moaned. *"Killer of the White Bear."*

Killer.

Killer of a High Beast?

Bile rose in Dev's throat.

Together, the Oracles dropped their trumpets and reached their arms toward the holy lights of the House. The men clumped tighter together, murmuring and shifting as they turned to look—all of them—at what the women stretched for. *"Speak the White Bear's name before the On-High!"*

And Dev ran.

He bolted for the bell rope as fast as his legs would carry him, the Frosmen shouting at his back. He flew up the steps—but a hand grabbed him by the ankle. Captain Pire. Impossibly fast and strong for an old warrior.

Dev fell, and he lost hold of the *Star Writ*, his palms ripping open on the stone.

There was no thought. Just wild, animal terror driving his arms and legs to flail. His foot wrenched free of the man's grip, and he clambered up another step. But Pire was fast, getting hold of him again.

Dev stretched out with his fingers, the bell rope mere inches beyond his reach. But the Frosman dragged him back, the stair coming up to slam Dev's chin.

And then he saw the *Star Writ*, lying open where he'd dropped it—right beside him.

So he grabbed the mighty tome and brought it down hard on Pire's head.

The old man's grip relaxed instantly, and Dev kicked free and scrambled back to the rope, pulling down with all his weight. The bell rang out clear and loud across the square, and Alcor roared.

"We seek the sanctuary of the On-High!" Dev screamed. "Protection for me, Dev, Keeper of the Hemoth, and for my friends, Ursula and Aster Lourdes, daughters of Major Jasper Lourdes! But mostly"—he huffed and puffed, trying to regain his breath—"for Alcor, son of Mizar and descendant of the Great Lord Tawn!"

No sooner did the echo of his words fade than he felt a strain in the world again. As if the air around him were suddenly heavier. Thicker. And a light—white mixed with hues of pink and purple and blue—colored the edges of his vision.

His body glowed with starlight.

Dev gasped and looked toward Aster and Ursula. The Frosmen were cringing away from them, horrified by the bright light rising up around the Major's daughters.

And Alcor—he shook out his orange fur as the light engulfed him, luminous and radiant in the On-High's glow.

Sanctuary.

The younger of the Oracles opened her arms. "So you have asked it."

The older nodded. "So it is granted."

Granted. Dev watched the glittering light wind around his arm. *Sanctuary.* He'd done it. They were in the On-High's keeping now.

He looked out on the Minor's men staring up at him. The Oracles were leading Alcor, Aster, and Ursula up the steps, but Captain Pire groaned and stumbled to his feet.

"Stop them, you fools!" he bellowed at his men. "By order of the Minor! You must stop them!"

"But sir," said one of his men. "Haven!"

"Dragon spit!" Pire hissed. "Stop them!"

Dev held his breath. These men, the Minor's men—their sins were grave and numerous. After killing High Beasts and Majors, what did they care for Haven?

A group of four, five—then six—stepped from formation, advancing on Aster and Ursula and Alcor. One of the men in front grabbed Aster by the arm, and Alcor roared, rattling the Oracle House's wooden frame.

A blast of light erupted where the soldier's hand touched Aster's skin, and he was thrown thirty tail-lengths, hurtling over the heads of his fellow Frosmen toward the far side of the square, bouncing off the wall of a candle shop and landing in a groaning, broken heap.

"Courage, men!" bellowed Pire. "Seize them!"

But the Frosmen wouldn't dare, stepping back to give Aster and Ursula a wide berth.

The younger Oracle stood beside the fuming captain and bent down for Dev's copy of the *Star Writ*. "Be careful, Hewitt Pire."

"The On-High already have a tally of your mighty sins," said the older. "Is it wise to anger them further? On the steps of their own House?"

Captain Hewitt Pire's mouth pursed, rage flaring his nostrils. He scowled at Dev, at the Major's daughters, at Alcor, all of them glowing with Haven's mark. Dev watched him thinking, calculating the next tactical move.

But there was none. His men would not chance the On-High's power, not with it glowing so blatantly before them, not when it could throw them into stone and glass and shatter them.

The old soldier's eyes darted to the flames in the windows.

Never had Dev seen a man look upon starlight in that way—with a deep, wretched fear, almost a hatred. Only a man who committed terrible, terrible sins could look upon the glorious light of the On-High with such furious dread.

Dev shuddered to think of the sins of Captain Hewitt Pire. Murderer. Traitor. Killer of the White Bear, a High Beast. Servant of the Minor who had destroyed the Major and the mighty Mizar.

And what of Rizlan? Had Captain Hewitt Pire and his Minor destroyed him, too? Dev's throat tightened.

A gentle hand came to rest on his shoulder, and Dev looked up into the red eyes of the younger Oracle. "You dropped this, young Keeper," she said, holding out his copy of the *Star Writ*. "Its pages will need your quill."

Dev took the book and hugged it to his chest. Need his quill? The pages of the *Star Writ* could only be filled by Rizlan's. Dev swallowed the lump in his throat, and it sank into his gut like a cold, hard stone.

Unless, he realized, Rizlan was gone.

Then the duty fell to Dev.

What was most striking about Lady Bernadine, the only child of Bram Lourdes, was not her simple clothes or her wild untamed hair. It was her hardness—she was like the icy sea cliffs of her Whitlock home. How she would adapt to palace life in Tawnshire, I could only imagine.

—THE WRITINGS OF RIZLAN,
The Brothers Lourdes: The Lunar Offensive, *Star Writ*

ELEVEN

BERNADINE sat at a window, staring up at the On-High, at the constellation of the White Bear, where her mother's soul watched over her.

Long ago she'd picked the star at the end of the tail, the brightest, as her mother's star. And when Eira, the first White Bear, called Bernadine's soul home, her star would burn bright beside her mother's.

Of course, she couldn't know for *certain* which star belonged to her mother. But Bernadine liked to believe it was that one. And on nights when she felt anxious or alone, nights like tonight, Bernadine looked to her mother for guidance.

"Oh, Mother," she whispered. "I don't understand what Father has done. Make me a Major?" A chill ran through her. *In Eira's name, why?*

She glanced at the moon. Bright. Pale. Full. The door to death was closed completely, the Nightlocks safely trapped behind it. Why, then, had so much trouble befallen her family this night? So much bedevilment? Misery hung heavy over everything, like a mist.

No one in the Highen wanted to see Bernadine Lourdes as Major, least of all Bernadine Lourdes herself. She didn't even want to be Minor.

Bernadine had always known her father couldn't be Minor forever. But when the time came for him to be replaced, she dearly hoped that the White Bear would choose another. High Beasts, of course, almost always chose the next Head of House from the same family, but only if a candidate had proved their worth. Bernadine knew herself. She had no illusions that she was suited to life as a fierce and cunning Minor. The Lourdes had held both Major and Minor houses for centuries, but she simply was not made for it.

When the time came for a new Minor to be chosen, she had always hoped to stand aside and let the young warriors of Whitlock enter the selection circle at the Northern Crowning. She'd imagined the ceremony more times than she cared to admit:

The White Bear would choose the bravest young warrior of Whitlock, with a handsome face and a dimple on his left cheek. Bernadine would congratulate him with a ladylike bow. She would have a red-painted smile, just the kind the lady's maids painted on Ursula—a red-painted smile that would seem both elegant and mysterious. And the new Minor would love her instantly. And they would be wed.

That way, the Lourdes legacy would remain intact: Bernadine would be keeping the rule of Whitlock in the family. Simple. Romantic. Perfect.

A silly fantasy, maybe, but still it was what she wanted. Bernadine always pictured herself as a queen consort, just like her dear Aunt Luella, the Lady Lourdes. Never as the leader of an army, let alone the leader of the entire Highen.

What could her father be *thinking*?

And besides, she thought, her breath making little fog circles on the cool glass, Uncle Jasper wished for *Ursula* to succeed him as Major. Surely Uncle Jasper would not like to hear his brother speak of Bernadine inheriting the crown. (Not to mention the other Heads of Houses, who all had high hopes for their *own* children.)

Bernadine frowned at the Frosmen singing and drinking on the steps of the Manor beneath her window. Others teased and whipped the beautiful Berenice stallions, riding them clumsily across the green. Surely Uncle Jasper wouldn't be pleased by this, either.

Nor would Uncle Jasper be pleased to find Bernadine occupying his wife's chambers. Bernadine turned around, pressing her back against the cold glass and surveying the ornate bedroom. Aunt Luella's. Soft periwinkle walls, decorated with gold trim. A high ceiling painted like the night sky, the On-High and the High Beasts lovingly detailed in gilt. Flowered curtains. Gold furniture with plush pink cushions.

There was a tea set decorated with purple ferns—particular to Felisbrook—on the table where Aunt Luella would sit and gossip with the ladies of the Highen's houses when they came to the Manor. There was a red-sand pottery box, too, filled with saltwater taffies from Roarque.

Bernadine's chest tightened.

She remembered the day she first came to the Manor. Remembered how overwhelmingly big the grand whitestone building had looked to her Whitlock eyes, with its elegant stained-glass windows and golden turrets. Remembered how exhausted and cold she'd been from her long journey on horseback, and how worried about her ailing mother. Remembered how Aster and Ursula had laughed at her Whitlock clothes—a cloak of fox fur, coveralls stitched by Captain Hewitt's wife that were more comfortable for riding. She'd looked so wild, so filthy and crass next to her pretty cousins and sophisticated aunt. Bernadine remembered how she had cried when they laughed, and how Aunt Luella had admonished the girls for it. Then Aunt Luella brought Bernadine to her apartments. She wiped her tears and they drank juniper tea from the tea set with purple ferns, nibbling on taffies from the Kingdom of the Lion. And when her father came to the Manor to tell Bernadine that her mother had died, it was Aunt Luella who held her—here in this room—and rocked her back and forth and stroked her hair until she'd exhausted all her tears.

Her eyes flicked nervously to the chandelier above her. On each golden candleholder was wrought the visage of the Lynx, the

High Beast of Felisbrook. Every bit of this room was made for Lady Lourdes. Her mark was on all of it.

The air suddenly felt thin, claustrophobic. Frantically, Bernadine pulled at the latch on the window and greedily gulped down the crisp night air.

A gentle knock echoed through the room.

She looked over her shoulder as her guard, a Frosman named Neva, hurried to answer the door. Why Bernadine *needed* a guard, she didn't understand.

With her head hung low and her mouth heavy at the corners, the Manor's head cook, Darby, shuffled quietly into the room. In her hands she held a silver tray, balancing a silver mug.

"I'm not thirsty," Bernadine said.

"But my lady," said Neva, "warm milk and honey will help you sleep."

Sleep? How could she be expected to sleep on a night like this?

Darby placed the tray and mug gently on the table, beside the beautiful tea set. Her eyes met Bernadine's, and though she quickly looked down, Bernadine had seen it. *Hate.* It flashed in the old Tawnshirian cook's eyes like a flame and twisted Bernadine's Whitlock stomach in knots.

"I wish to sleep in my quarters," said Bernadine.

Neva tilted her head, confused. "These *are* your quarters, my lady."

"My *real* quarters!" Bernadine snapped. "These chambers belong to Lady Lourdes!"

"I—I fear," Neva stammered, "that your old quarters have been given to Captain Pire."

Hewitt? He'd been given her rooms?

Bernadine sat back on the window bench. Why would Hewitt even *need* his own quarters? How long were her father's men planning on staying at the Manor?

"Oh, my lady." Neva took a step toward Bernadine, a gentle smile on her face. "These chambers are meant for a queen! You *belong* here."

At that, Darby snorted.

Neva's head snapped toward the cook, her gentle smile gone. "How dare you?" she growled, before she lunged and struck the old woman.

"Stop!" cried Bernadine, horrified.

The guard froze, that maddeningly confused expression on her face. She was gripping Darby by her arm, ready to slap her again.

Bernadine trembled, but stood defiant. "Let go of her, Neva."

After a moment, Neva did as she was told, releasing Darby with a rough push. Darby scowled at them both, rubbing her cheek where Bernadine was sure Neva had left a bruise.

"Thank you, Darby," said Bernadine, trying to keep her voice steady. "You are dismissed."

The old cook's eyes flashed again, and Bernadine felt like hiding beneath the bed. What had overcome Neva? And what had she, Bernadine, done to incur such wrath from Darby?

The room, of course. This Tawnshirian room, lovingly decorated for a graceful Felisbrook bride—not a little girl from Whitlock. She felt like an intruder, a thief, sitting in her aunt's chambers. And Darby, she realized, thought the same thing.

When the cook had gone, Bernadine addressed Neva. "Where is Lady Lourdes? Where is my aunt?"

"I'm afraid I'm not entirely sure, my lady. Last I saw of her, she and your father were having words."

"May I see her?"

"I don't think your father would like that, my lady," said Neva. "He's asked that you be kept here. For your own protection."

"Protection from *what*?"

"Any who might try to harm you, of course."

Bernadine bristled, annoyed that Neva seemed to know something she didn't. "Who wishes to harm me?"

"My lady," said Neva, "this is an unfriendly place for us."

"It has been plenty friendly to me!" Bernadine shouted.

Neva wore her face of pure confusion again, and Bernadine couldn't stand to look at it.

"Leave me!" she ordered.

"But my lady, my orders are to stand watch—"

"Then stand watch outside! I wish to be alone!"

Neva's mouth clamped shut, and she took a step back from Bernadine. She looked toward the door, then back at the girl, and Bernadine could see the struggle in her mind between orders from her father and orders from Bernadine herself.

Bernadine's eyes narrowed. "I said *go.*"

With a tiny bow, the nervous Frosman marched herself out, the door closing with a quiet click and plunging Bernadine into silence.

Though it wasn't silent at all, really. Alone, without Neva or Darby, the voices of Aunt Luella's chambers hissed and growled at Bernadine: the chandelier lynx, the teacups, the High Beasts on the ceiling, all of them whispering.

Imposter.

Liar.

Thief.

Bernadine leapt from her seat, her hands over her ears. "Stop it!"

But they wouldn't stop. She knew they couldn't. Because she didn't belong.

She had to leave. But how? Neva stood just beyond the doors.

Bernadine's eyes found the red-sand pottery, and a memory turned over in her mind. It was the eve of the Festival of Tawn, and the Heads of Houses and their retinues had come to Tawnshire. The Major and his wife were hosting a ball; Ursula had just turned twelve and was allowed to attend. Bernadine and Aster were left upstairs to entertain themselves. Gatch had fallen asleep, and the girls were on the brink of boredom…until Aster remembered the gift the Head of the Lion House had brought for her mother: saltwater taffy, Lady Lourdes' favorite treat. He brought it every year.

"Come on, then," Aster had whispered. "If we can't enjoy the party, we should at least enjoy the sweets."

"How?" Bernadine asked. "There are Hermans in the hallways. Someone will see us and tell!"

"No one will see us." Aster grinned, reached for a painting of Hemoth cubs, and—Bernadine remembered her surprise—swung the painting open, revealing a dark corridor where a wall should be. A secret passage.

"It leads to Mother's room," Aster had explained. "There are passages all through the Manor. Legend has it they were built by Dov the Brave for his family's safety. But I find they are most useful for mischief."

Alone now, Bernadine's eyes flicked to her aunt's lush, red-blanketed bed, and to the wall-hanging beside it—High Beast Kerrwick, the first sacred Lynx, embroidered in pink silk and gold.

She ripped the hanging aside and pressed and prodded at the wall, her fingers catching on what she knew was the seam of the entryway. She pulled with all her might, and the door came free, the heavy stone scraping along the floor.

Bernadine stopped. She waited for Neva to burst into the room, alerted by the sound of the secret door. But she didn't. All Bernadine could hear was the whooping of the Frosmen out on the green.

Before she ducked into the passageway, she hesitated, eyes landing again on the red-sand pottery beside the tea set. The girls had fought, she remembered; after they snuck into Aunt Luella's chambers, they fell into an argument over who should have what color. The shouting grew so loud, it woke Gatch, who caught them—neither girl got to have a sweet. Bernadine had wanted blue.

She tiptoed to the box, just as she had four years before, and peeked in at the little colored squares. Three blue, two pink, one orange.

Orange, Bernadine knew, was Aunt Luella's favorite.

She grabbed the orange and one of the blues and hurried back to the secret door, closing it carefully behind her.

The passage was dark, but surprisingly warm. She could go left, to the Major's study; straight, which led down and outdoors; or right, to Aster's rooms. If Hewitt had been given Bernadine's quarters, then perhaps Aunt Luella had been taken to Aster's.

Bernadine stayed right, tiptoeing down the narrow hallway, careful not to make a sound.

At the end of the darkness she could make out slits of light in the shape of a portrait—Aster's Hemoth cub painting. The door was high, and a pair of ancient, musty wooden steps offered just enough lift to reach the handle.

She pressed her ear to the door: shuffling, the click of heels, a whiff of Celeste root.

"Aunt Luella?" she whispered, pushing open the door. As she stepped over the threshold, she stumbled, tumbling forward onto Aster's bed.

"In Tawn's name!"

Bernadine looked up from her spot on the bed to see her aunt, regal as ever, staring down her nose.

"What on *earth*, girl?" she demanded.

"Aunt Luella!" Bernadine rolled off the bed, relieved to see Lady Lourdes still looking very ladylike. "I'm so glad I found you!"

Lady Lourdes' eyes fell on the blue and orange taffies lying beside Bernadine on the bed. "I see you've made yourself quite at home in my chambers."

"No, no, Aunt Luella," she said, snapping them up. "I don't want to be in there. Please, by all means, take back your rooms!"

Bernadine offered up the orange taffy, but Lady Lourdes slapped it away. Bernadine watched the little orange square ping off her cousin's wardrobe.

"Take back my rooms?" Lady Lourdes sneered, cold as ice. "Foolish girl. Do you really think I have any control over where I go and what I do now?"

"Of course!" Bernadine cried. "Father wouldn't—"

"Your father," her aunt spat, "has made me a prisoner in my own home. He holds me captive while he pillages my husband's lands! The lands of the brother he *murdered*!"

"Murdered?" Bernadine gasped. Aunt Luella thought Father had murdered Uncle Jasper? Absurd! But before she could protest, her aunt stepped menacingly toward her, hands stiff like claws, seeming ready to scratch out her eyes.

"Your hideous father drove my children out of their home, to flee into a world they are not *ready*—"

Lady Lourdes' voice broke then. Her head dropped into her chest, and her taut hands clutched tightly to her skirts. She collapsed in the chair by the wardrobe.

Bernadine's knees felt unsteady. What had made her aunt think such awful things? What terrible person would feed her such impossible lies? "Aunt Luella, you've made a mistake. He couldn't—"

"And it's all because of you." The Major's wife shook her head. "What is that song the Lynx people sing? '*Oh so wise is the White Bear, true, be wary ye their cunning, too.*' To think I took pity on you, the girl who would destroy my family."

Bernadine's stomach clenched. *Destroy?* But she was part of this family!

"The girl," her aunt said, "who would steal the Highen for herself."

Steal the Highen?

"No," Bernadine said pleadingly. "No, Aunt Luella, you don't understand—"

"Oh, I understand." Her aunt rose to her feet, her red-painted lips set in a furious thin line. "And I understand that the Great Lord Tawn and his fellow High Beasts will bring a reckoning upon you and your father too terrible to comprehend. The On-High have no mercy for men like him. No mercy for murderers! For fratricide! For astrocide!"

Astrocide? The killing of a High Beast? "How could you say something like that!"

"Because it's the truth!" Lady Lourdes shouted. "And nothing, Bernadine Lourdes, will save you from the On-High's wrath!"

Bernadine's blood turned to ice, her heart pounding in her chest. Voices rose by the door—Frosmen.

"In here!" her aunt cried. "Intruder! Come quick!"

Shaking with fright, Bernadine clambered onto the bed as the locks in Aster's door clicked open. Her fingers pulled at the edges of the painting, trying to force it loose, but four gruff hands seized her by the arms.

"Let me go!" she shrieked. The Frosmen ignored her, dragging her back to the door.

Aunt Luella turned her back. "Get this child out of my sight."

"Auntie, please!" she wailed as the men pulled her into the hall, slamming the door and locking Lady Lourdes back inside. Their fingers dug into her arm, bruising her skin, and she wriggled and writhed. "Take your hands off of me! When I tell Father about this—"

"Your father has been informed," said one of the men, his voice like gravel.

Bernadine stopped, the fight evaporating from her limbs. "He knows?"

"He waits for you in the drawing room."

The White Bear has a mouth of forty-two razor-sharp teeth that can crush a man's bones to pulp or tear the belly from a blubbery seal. But that same mouth cradles its young so gently, the infant cub can be carried for miles without waking.

—THE WRITINGS OF BERN,
On White Bears: The Fore, *Star Writ*

# TWELVE

BERNADINE stood before the massive doors. The unmistakable azure of blue palmwood marked them as the entrance to the drawing room. The Frosman on her left, holding tightly to her arm, knocked three times.

Her father's voice answered—low, quiet. Sad. "Come in."

The Frosman pushed open the door, and Bernadine saw him: he was leaning against the gilded fireplace, orange flames silhouetting his exhausted frame as his head hung low. So unlike the silly heart she loved. And her heart ached for him.

Oddly, on the mantel, a dark, shimmering orb was glinting by the light of the fire.

No. Not an orb. An egg.

Black as night and flecked with golden light. A Shadow Dragon's egg.

Bernadine's stomach sank—it was the egg Uncle Jasper was supposed to take to the Ring Highen.

Without turning around, her father waved his hand. "Leave us."

The Frosmen obeyed, and with the bang of the heavy blue-palm door, Bernadine stood alone with Minor Bram Lourdes.

The fire spat and crackled, punctuating the heavy silence that hung between daughter and father. Silence was unlike them. And Bernadine felt a pain at the back of her throat, a pain that begged to be cried away. They had always spoken, Bernadine and her father. Why did he not speak now? Why could she not find words?

Astrocide. It was the only word in her head, tumbling around and around, over and over.

But she couldn't speak it. Not to him. It was too heinous. Too perverse.

And she was afraid.

No, she decided, it was up to him to break the silence.

"I asked," he said finally, his voice dry, "that you stay in your room." He turned then, his wet, tired eyes finding hers. "And yet you left anyway. Why, Bernie?"

The question wasn't an angry one. He wasn't cross. He was sad. Hurt. Like he truly didn't understand why she would disobey his order.

"I..." Why had she disobeyed? She suddenly couldn't remember. She had to see Aunt Luella. Why? Because of the room. She'd been left in Aunt Luella's room. "I wanted Aunt Luella to take back her chambers. Why would you give me her chambers?"

"Because they are no longer her chambers," he said. "Luella Lourdes is no longer the Lady of this House."

Bernadine's fingers fidgeted in front of her, entwining and unwinding in a nervous dance. No longer Lady of the House? Did he expect Bernadine to take Aunt Luella's place? How? Why?

"Father..." Her voice broke. "What have you done? Aunt Luella spoke of...terrible things."

He moved away from the fireplace, grabbing the back of a large upholstered chair and turning it to face her. He sat down, his elbows on his knees and his chin resting on his folded fingers, watching Bernadine thoughtfully. Every moment he didn't speak, didn't tell her Aunt Luella was wrong, made her more afraid.

"Father!" she said, moving toward him. "She thinks you are responsible for Uncle Jasper's death. She even..." Bernadine looked behind her, afraid someone might be lurking in the shadows of the room. But there was no one else to hear her. "Father, she spoke of *astrocide!*"

Bernadine watched her father's head drop, watched him rub his forehead with his fingers. She waited, wanting him to deny it, wanting him to explain why Aunt Luella would think something so wrong.

But he said nothing.

"Where is Uncle Jasper?" she demanded. "And Mizar the Hemoth Bear? Where is the White Bear, Alurea? And Keeper Iclyn? How can you be here without them?"

He did not look up.

"Father...did you hurt them?"

"Bernie Doll," he said quietly, "my kind, innocent princess. Pure as the Whitlock snows."

"No!" said Bernadine, so loud and so sudden her father was forced to meet her eyes. "Don't talk to me like I am just a child. I want you to answer me! Did you do what Aunt Luella says you did?"

The grey of his irises glowed silver in the firelight. He nodded once, barely, and spoke. "I did."

She felt a swell of vomit and clung to the wall, afraid she'd lose her balance.

"Why? Father, I can't—" The sunshine of her life. He'd killed Uncle Jasper. Killed High Beasts. All to make her a Major? The On-High would damn them both, all to put her on a throne she never wanted? "Tell me you did not do this for me! I don't *want* this!"

Her father watched her, motionless, from his chair. "Not just for you, Bernie Doll."

Her lungs ached for breath, but she couldn't get enough; her eyes burned with tears, but they wouldn't fall. She thought she might throw up. She didn't know him, this man sitting before her. Couldn't recognize him. "I will *not* be your Major!" she wailed. "How could you do this to me? To us? To my cousins?"

What was the point of even asking her father to explain himself? No explanation could justify astrocide. Aunt Luella was right. The On-High's reckoning would be terrible. And they would never find their place among the stars.

Bernadine crumpled to the floor, weeping into her skirts. She would never see her mother again.

"Do you remember how it came to pass that your uncle, my little brother, was chosen as Major?" the Minor asked quietly.

Bernadine looked up, bleary-eyed. "What?"

"After the death of our father, old Major Carmick, the Highen expected that *I* would be the one chosen as Major. I was older, after all—more thoughtful, more tempered. Until the Nightlocks attacked…and the Great Bear chose Jasper."

"Yes. Mizar chose Uncle Jasper." Was that what this was all about? What this all came down to? The day Mizar chose Uncle Jasper over her father?

He waved his hand, as if swatting away the memory. "I was jealous of Jasper at first, but when the White Bear named me Minor and I came to Whitlock, I realized that the On-High had a different destiny for me." He crouched down before Bernadine, and she recoiled. "Bernie," he said softly, "can you guess what my destiny was?"

All the frightened girl could do was shake her head.

"It was your mother," he said. "Your beautiful, generous mother, who gave me you, my Bernie Doll."

"Then why did you ruin our chance to see her again?" cried Bernadine. "The On-High will never forgive you for this. They won't let us join her in the stars. Our spirits will be locked behind the moon as Nightlocks! You've robbed me of my mother!"

"No," her father snapped, getting to his feet. "Your uncle robbed you of your mother. Robbed me of my wife! He could have saved her and *he didn't*!"

He paced the room, furious steps, and Bernadine feared he was looking for something to break. She'd never seen him so angry.

"But," she said, "Mother was ill. The Heart Frost took her…"

"It didn't have to!" He grabbed hold of the chair, and Bernadine expected he might throw it, but he stopped. A heavy breath escaped him as he stared into the flames. "What do you remember of the days of your mother's illness, Bernie?"

Those days, Bernadine thought, had been the most confusing of her life. What did she remember? Everything and nothing. Bits and pieces, really. The smell of her mother's room, faint with lemon from the snowdrop flowers used by the doctor in her medicine. The grave faces around the Manor. The wailing of the peasants who cried beyond the gates. The rich red wood of the Crowns & Stones game Lady Pire tried to distract her with. The silly song her father would sing her before bed to make her smile.

Claire the Hare,
Who didn't know where
She left her favorite bonnet.
She looked up and down
And all around
And saw she'd sat upon it.

And she remembered that every night after the song, he would take her to see her mother. And Bernadine would kiss her mother's cheek.

She could never forget the feeling of her mother's skin when she was sick. Icy and wet. As though she'd just come from a swim in White Bear Lake.

Her father watched her expectantly.

"I don't know, Father," she said. "I don't remember much. The White Bear fell ill, and so did Mother. The doctors came and their medicines couldn't help her."

"Yes. Gwynlin died. And the White Bear?" asked her father.

"Alurea?" She didn't understand. He knew what had happened. "She survived the illness. She beat the Heart Frost."

"How?"

Bernadine had never given much thought to how. Alurea was a High Beast. A mighty White Bear. "Her bear-heart was stronger than Mother's."

Her father shook his head. "No. It wasn't."

Bernadine waited for her father to say more, but he didn't. He seemed to be waiting. Waiting for her to figure something out. How had the White Bear survived the Heart Frost that killed her mother? If the Bear's heart wasn't stronger than her mother's human one, what could have saved her?

"Medicine?" Bernadine asked. "Did a doctor have better medicine for bears?"

"No," said her father. "The doctors had no medicine that could help your mother or Alurea. There is only one thing that can cure Heart Frost. Do you know what that is?"

Bernadine could barely shake her head. A cure?

He walked to the fireplace, his hand running along the mantel before stopping at the egg. "It is the yolk of a Shadow Dragon's egg."

Her mother could have been cured by the egg of the Shadow Dragon? The Kingdom of Dracogart had a whole *flock* of Shadow Dragons living in the peaks above the city. She would have climbed a mountain herself if it meant she could have saved her mother.

"The House of the Shadow Dragons," she began. "Could you not have asked them—"

"I asked, Bernadine," said her father. "I begged. I begged them for the egg that would save my darling Gwynlin and her beloved White Bear. But the Head of the House of Shadow Dragons refused."

An angry tremor shook her voice. "Why would he do that?"

"Because the egg of the Shadow Dragon would hatch someday.

It would become a High Beast. To crack the egg and eat the yolk was tantamount to astrocide, as far as he and the Highen were concerned."

There was that word again, and Bernadine hated it even more. "But Uncle Jasper. He is Major. Did he see it that way? He could have ordered the Dragon House to hand over the eggs...couldn't he?"

"Yes, he had that power. And I begged him to command Dragg Wyvern to give me two eggs for your mother and the White Bear." He paused. "Jasper summoned the Heads of Houses to Tawnshire, to beseech the House of Shadow Dragons to save the White Bear and your mother. I stayed in Whitlock, waiting by your mother's bed while they argued her final days away."

Her father stared into the flames, seeing some memory she couldn't there in the fireplace.

"My brother arrived on the eighteenth day. And he brought with him an egg." He turned to Bernadine then, his eyes wet. "One single egg. Very few eggs had been laid that year. To break two would have threatened the Dragons' lineage. So Jasper forced them to give up just the one. And I could only watch while my brother, the great Death Chaser, gave the precious egg to that mindless, savage animal instead of your mother."

"Alurea?" Bernadine's stomach churned. "Uncle Jasper gave the egg to the White Bear?"

But of course he had. Alurea was a High Beast—she was sacred. Uncle Jasper had had no other choice...had he?

"The Oracles said the On-High had decreed that it was the White Bear who should take the egg," her father continued. A grunt, almost a laugh, escaped him. "And I accepted it. I accepted the will of the On-High and my brother, because I was the Minor! It was my sacred duty to serve them both. I swallowed my grief and my pain and I continued like the good soldier I was...

"And then the Heart Frost came for the High King of the Ring."

The trade, Bernadine remembered. Before Uncle Jasper left,

the trade with the Ring was all anyone could talk about. One single Shadow Dragon egg in exchange for the venom of the Prism Scorpion.

"The Shadow Dragon's egg," she said, understanding, "it was for the High King of the Ring? To cure him of Heart Frost?"

Her father nodded grimly. "My brother, he went to the Oracles… and they agreed that he should give this man the egg. But why now? Why could he sacrifice a Shadow Dragon for a mortal life *now*, when he could not do it for my Gwynlin? What was the reason for this naked, gutless hypocrisy?"

Bernadine's heart hammered in her chest. "What did he say?"

"He said it was because *one egg for the lives of many is a better deal than for the life of one.*" Her father's jaw set as he bit back his rage. "My wife. Your mother. To Jasper, to the On-High, she was *only one.* She devoted her life to the On-High, to their High Beasts, and still they saw her as worthless. As nobody. And I knew then that the On-High care nothing for us."

How could the On-High not care? They watch over us from the time we are born! That was what her mother had always told her.

Her mother, Bernadine realized, whom the On-High chose to die.

Her father stepped out from behind his chair. "They don't care what we do or how we worship."

Her mother would be horrified by talk like this. Her mother, the most devout servant of the On-High, a pious believer—

—and still the stars had abandoned her.

Her father's warm, callused hands took gentle hold of hers. "To get what you want," he said, "you must take it by force, just like the Major took Mizar for his battle with the Nightlocks. It was *power* that he seized that day, Bernadine. And he used that power to save a bear over your mother. She died because I had no power to stop it."

He pulled Bernadine to her feet, his strong hands supporting her because her legs would not stand on their own. "And what I want is for you to have this power. To chart the course of your own life. To choose the egg for yourself should you ever need it."

She clung to his arms as her legs locked, holding her up as if he had somehow transferred his strength to her—her heartbroken father. He had not betrayed Uncle Jasper. It was Uncle Jasper who had betrayed him.

His grip tightened. "You, Bernadine Lourdes, will never have to bow to anyone."

And the On-High breathed as one, and from their breath sprang the High Beasts—Hemoth, White Bear, Starhound, Shadow Dragon, Lion, Blue Giraffe, Lynx, and Ox. And the sacred animals looked upon one another and loved each other from the start. "We are family," said the Hemoth Bear. "We are the On-High's children. And we shall care for one another." And the On-High were glad.

—THE WRITINGS OF BERN,
The Arrival of the Beasts: The Fore, *Star Writ*

 THIRTEEN

THE doors to the Oracle House closed with a bang, and Aster found herself staring into a flock of crimson-hooded creatures.

She'd never seen Oracles before. And looking at them now, she wished it could have stayed that way. They had pale faces and fiery eyes, and they looked very much like birds—blank-faced, quizzical, heads cocked sideways as they stared. They didn't seem surprised to see the daughters of the Major. In fact, it appeared to Aster that they hadn't taken much notice of the girls at all.

Their eyes, again, were for Alcor.

"Hemoth Bear," muttered one.

"Highest of High Beasts," whispered another.

Then all of them made the sign of the On-High—hand to the heart, the lips, and the sky—and bowed before the bear. As though the bear had any notion that all this reverence was for him.

Aster looked at her sister, who stood at her side, her hands balled into fists. Ursula's chest rose and fell quickly, her teeth locked in what looked like a painful grimace.

"Ursula?"

But her sister didn't answer. Aster followed her glossy gaze to the far wall beyond the genuflecting Oracles.

Along the floors—and on tables and desks and chairs and windows—were jars. Simple jars, the same Chef Ingle might use to keep preserves. And inside, Aster could see that each contained a single flame with no candle. It just floated in empty space, white and still. There were so many, and they were everywhere, Aster realized, along the rafters, in alcoves, on the many windowsills that climbed up and up to the large round opening in the roof that let them see the stars. Everywhere a jar could be placed, a single flame twinkled, their combined light bathing the whole House in an eerie silver glow.

A wail echoed through the chamber suddenly. It was Ursula—the dam had broken. She crouched, hunched, the bloodstained cloak heavy on her delicate shoulders.

"Ursula!" cried Aster, pulling the wet, filthy cloak off her sister and tossing it aside. The frost pearls on her gown winked and danced in the light of the Oracle House, and Aster could hear the startled gasps of the red-eyed audience.

"What do we do now?" Ursula asked, collapsing on the stone floor of the Oracle House as though her legs were ribbon. She didn't seem to be asking Aster, but rather posing the question to the world, as if the walls themselves would whisper the answer.

"Father will come," Aster said, sitting beside her helplessly. "He will come with Mizar and he will—"

"Father will come?" Ursula whispered. "*Father will come!* Have you not understood anything? Father is dead! He's gone! He's not coming for us, Aster."

Aster flinched away from her sister, the words like sharps. She'd heard Captain Hewitt Pire, and had even let herself believe him for a moment, but…"That Frosman was trying to scare us," she insisted. "Father is the Death Chaser—"

"Aster!" Ursula shouted. "Father was not a god. He could die just like anyone else. And he has."

"You don't know that," Aster said quietly.

One of the oldest Oracles, the one who had helped them escape the Minor's men, padded over to the girls. "Girls born of the Major," she said in an imposing voice, speaking to the room. "Fatherless daughters now."

Ursula looked up at the Oracle, eyes swollen and cheeks stained with tears. "You know, don't you? The On-High told you of Father's death."

The old woman joined Aster and her sister on the floor, ancient bones shakily lowering her to brittle knees. Her wrinkled hand reached for Ursula's face, and she smiled a sad leathery smile. "The On-High have seen it."

"The On-High have told us," agreed the younger one, standing beside them.

"The On-High told you?" asked Aster. These Oracles and their magic! Aster didn't understand it. Wasn't sure she even believed it. Stars speaking to people? Why would the stars speak of their father to these women and not *her*? "What exactly did they tell you? What did they see?"

The old woman wrapped her fingers around the ear trumpet dangling from her neck. She closed her eyes and listened. "The Major answered the Ring King's call."

A voice from the crowd of gathered Oracles, an older man, spoke. "A call for help, an egg for poison milk."

"And the liar saw his opening," said the woman beside him. "And became the falsest of emissaries."

"Uncle Bram?" asked Aster slowly. *He* went as ambassador to the Ring. *He* secured the deal for the egg.

"He went," agreed the old Oracle. "And returned with lies. Returned with a trick on his lips."

Aster remembered the days that had surrounded the negotiations with the Ring. She had only half paid attention to the tense discussions between her parents, to the whispers among the servants, to the hushed conversations between the lords and ladies at court. Mother was angry at Father for agreeing to give up the egg, she knew that much. The servants had hinted at their disapproval too.

But Father had made up his mind. It was agreed that the Minor would return to the Ring Highen with the Shadow Dragon's egg, exchanging it for the Prism Scorpion's venom. It was the only way to cure the firelung. It would take a month for the Minor to travel to the Ring and back, including to Dracogart with the cure.

But everything had gone wrong when soldiers from the Ring landed on the Highen's shores, attacking the Minor and stealing the egg.

Attacking the Minor....

"Uncle Bram lied about the attack," Ursula said. "The negotiations for the egg were real. But the Ring never came to the Highen's shores, did they?"

The old woman nodded.

"Uncle Bram lied to Father?" said Aster. "Why? Why would he do that?"

"So the older brother could ambush the younger. On the shores of the Celestial Sea, the liar's armies waited. And both Major and Bear fell victim to the Minor's blade."

Ambush. Father and Mizar were ambushed?

The Minor deceived the Highen's armies so he could take the Major by surprise on the edge of the Celestial Sea...and...and...It was all too much to make sense of—their silly uncle, the man who taught them to stick spoons to their noses, orchestrated all of this?

"Uncle Bram killed Father?" Aster breathed, barely daring to say the words loudly enough for anyone to hear.

"He did," said the old Oracle.

No, Aster thought, the crushing weight of it straining her ribs, the ache so bad she was sure they would break. The Oracles were certain. Ursula was certain. But Major Jasper Lourdes was the Death Chaser!

Why did no one remember that? Why didn't Ursula remember it? How could they believe that someone like Uncle Bram, a fool, could get the better of their father?

And yet Uncle Bram was here. In Tawnshire. With his Frosmen. And Father was nowhere.

"But *why*?" Aster said. "*Why* would Uncle Bram want to hurt Father?"

Ursula sighed and pushed herself up from the floor. "For the Highen, Aster. He wants control of the Highen."

"But he can't!" she cried, her voice getting away from her and echoing through the House. "No one can be Major unless the Hemoth Bear chooses them! Uncle Bram has already been claimed by the White Bear. The Hemoth Bear couldn't choose him even if it wanted to!"

"Not him," said the old Oracle.

"The daughter," said the younger one. "In two months' time. At the Festival of Tawn, there will be a Northern Crowning."

"Bernadine?" whispered Aster. Uncle Bram meant for the Hemoth Bear to choose *Bernadine*?

"That's why he's so desperate to get his hands on Alcor," agreed Ursula. "He needs time to build a bond between the bear and Bernadine before the Crowning, to ensure she's chosen."

All of this—Aster's mind struggled to understand—was to make Bernadine a Major? Her father had died so the Highen could be led by the girl in coveralls from Whitlock?

"Uncle Bram will be back," said Ursula, staring into the jars of flame, frost pearls mirroring their glint. "He'll be back to take Alcor by force."

Dev threw a protective arm in front of Alcor. "He can't take Alcor," he said. "Haven!"

Ursula rose and turned to face him, her back straight and her jaw set. How much she looked like their father, Aster realized.

Commanding. A leader. "Uncle Bram murdered the Major. He committed astrocide when he killed Mizar and the others. And if the Ring is still waiting across the sea to receive the Shadow Dragon's egg, he may have started a war. Ignoring the laws of Haven would be the least of his sins—especially now the starfire has faded from us. A simple word won't stop him."

Murdered. Aster turned the idea over again and again in her mind. Her father, *murdered.*

No. It didn't fit him. He must have had some idea. Must have had an inkling that Uncle Bram schemed to betray him. Wherever her father was, Aster decided, it was not with the On-High, no matter *what* these Oracles said. She had to believe he was alive somewhere.

But still. He was not here. So it fell to them.

"What can we do?" she asked.

"We must get word to the other Heads of Houses," said Ursula. "We must call for aid."

"But the Heads of Houses," said Dev, stroking Alcor's mane, "did they not all go to help the Major in the war against the Ring?"

Yes, Aster knew. Her father had called on all of the Heads of Houses and their armies to fight a Ring that was not, in fact, attacking. Where were they now?

"Only three Heads of Houses survive," said the old woman. "The Ox and the Lynx, who helped your uncle in his treachery. And the Blue Giraffe, who is only four years of age."

"The Lynx?" gasped Aster. Their mother's homeland.

Ursula bit her lip, her skin like night snow in the glow of the pearls. "Pan Leander has been against Mother's family since he became Head of the House of the Lynx instead of Aunt Leona. I'm not surprised he'd want to see Father and Mother gone. And us gone too."

"But the Ox?" Aster asked.

Ursula shook her head. "I've no idea why they would align themselves with Uncle Bram. But that's not the question we need to be asking right now. The question is, if Uncle Bram has done away with all of the Heads of Houses, who is caring for the kingdoms?"

The old woman grunted as she tried to get to her feet, her younger companion rushing to help. "Traditionally, the Major says who cares," she said, breathless.

"It is simple, children," explained the younger one. "A Head who goes to war will leave their kingdom in trust to a steward, or to one of their blood—their child, perhaps. But if a Head of House should *die*, the Major may choose another guardian to serve the kingdom until that kingdom's High Beast has the chance to choose a new Head at the Northern Crowning."

"And when there is no Major?" asked Ursula.

The younger Oracle's eyes flicked nervously to the older, and the older's head hung low. "The Minor chooses."

Aster's gut twisted. "Are you saying Uncle Bram has the power to choose the leaders of the Highen? When *he* killed the Heads of Houses?"

The Oracles looked at each other, unsure how to answer, which told Aster everything she needed to know.

Yes. The power was all Uncle Bram's.

Before the Oracles could say anything more, Ursula's voice snapped through the room like lightning. "He shall not have that power! Not after the crimes he has committed."

"But what can we do?" Aster asked. "He is still the Minor."

"We must send word to the other kingdoms," said Ursula. "Before Uncle Bram can put his sympathizers into power."

"Send word to *who*?"

"To the children of the Heads of Houses. They are in the same position we are. Uncle Bram stole their parents from them, stole their futures. They will stand with us against him, I know it."

Aster wasn't so sure. After all, most of the children of the Heads of Houses wanted to be Major themselves. Why, those boys from the House of Hounds spent their entire lives training for what they hoped would be the day the Hemoth Bear chose *them*. Why should they help the old Major's children—their rivals?

"How are we even to contact them?" asked Aster. "We can't leave the Oracle House."

Ursula said nothing, her eyes unfocused as she thought.

"The stars."

Aster turned to see the bear boy, his hand motioning to the jars of white flame. "We can send a message through the stars, can't we?"

"The stars?" she said, but Dev ignored her. He was watching the Oracles, his eyes wide with hope.

The old Oracle smiled, clutching her ear trumpet to her chest. "The On-High will listen. The On-High will speak. Before the sun rises, the Children of Kings will hear of your plight. They will know the terrible fate of their Major."

Terrible fate, thought Aster, watching as the assemblage of Oracles scattered about the room, all of them kneeling before a different flame-cradling jar. *A terrible fate witnessed by the On-High and whispered to the Oracles.* Aster's eyes followed the old woman, watched as she made that servile salute before a cluster of jars. Then the old woman raised the brass trumpet around her neck and held it to her ear.

The trumpets let the Oracles hear the voices of the stars. The stars said they saw her father's death. Her father, *the Death Chaser*. It just wasn't possible. If he had died, surely Aster would have felt it the moment his spirit was taken back by Tawn. She would have felt a giant gaping hole in her heart, the place where she kept her love for him. She could feel it now, full and complete.

Aster's gaze roamed over the other Oracles, holding similar trumpets, mumbling to themselves and waiting for the voices of the On-High.

If the stars can speak, Aster thought, *then it follows that the stars can also lie.*

A Shadow Dragon's wings do not reach maturity until approximately their fiftieth year. A notable exception would be Draconis, the first Shadow Dragon, who is said to have flown as a hatchling. Indeed, never underestimate the Shadow Dragon, for its strength and courage continue to surprise.

—THE WRITINGS OF BERN,
On Shadow Dragons: The Fore, *Star Writ*

FOURTEEN

THE fire had grown tired.

Quintin Wyvern watched the flames dip lazily in the obsidian fireplace from his spot beside his mother's bed. Broken lungs held the once-proud queen hostage in her own room. As they did every night, her teeth began to chatter. Despite the piled furs and blankets and scalecoat covering his mother's body, she was shivering.

Rubbing the sleep from his eyes, Quintin got to his feet to stoke the little fire. He grabbed the bellows, pulling open its handles and letting the leather bag fill with air. He smiled, remembering what his mother used to tell him when he was little: *If you'd been born a dragon, you'd have lungs just like the bellows. Let the bellows be your dragon lungs. Breathe deep, Quintin, breathe deep...* He did, sucking in the smoky hearth air just like the bellows. *And release the fire!* He exhaled, squeezing the handles of the bellows together at the same time. The fire growled back to life, its flames devouring the oxygen.

"Much better," he said with a nod. "How's that feel now, Mum?"

His mother lay there, the same as before—eyes closed, teeth chattering.

She was often cold now. Another symptom of *pneumopyrosis*— that was what Physician Scaleg called his mother's sickness. Everyone else called it firelung, a terrible disease that only seemed to attack the people of the Dragon. Quintin had once asked Physician Scaleg what caused it, but the old man simply shrugged and said that no one knew.

Maybe no one knew for *certain*, but the people of Dracogart had their theories.

Keeper Aden, the dragonminder, had once told Quintin that before the people of Dracogart were human, they were dragons. (And that the people of Tawnshire were once bears, eons and eons ago, and the people of Hundford once hounds, and on and on and on.) Over time, by the will of the stars, the dragons' bodies changed into the bodies of the people. But Aden said it was important to remember that the dragon was a creature of flame, its insides burning with a power and a strength. Some people, like Quintin's mother, inherited so much of this power, this strength, that their feeble human form could only contain it for so long—eventually, the dragon spirit grew hot again, and their lungs burned away inside like paper. It came in waves, firelung, as the dragon blood rose and fell throughout the generations, and sometimes it was a plague.

Quintin accepted this theory. He had always liked the idea that some part of the mighty Shadow Dragon was alive inside his people.

But as he looked at his mother now—at her thin, frail body beneath the piles of coverings, the soft brown skin of her face marred by black veins—he saw no sign of power. No strength. Just a withering body, burning up from the inside out.

"Where is Scaleg?" he murmured. He'd been waiting for the master physician for over an hour to administer his mother's tonic. He was late, and Mother was getting colder.

He went to the window, restless, and looked out over Dracogart. The city was barely visible at night; were it not for the soft yellow lights glowing in the many windows, he might not have been able to see it at all from his mother's balcony. Streets of obsidian cobbles; piazzas studded with fountains; elaborate balustrades with stone carved shadow dragon guardians watching over rich men's homes, simple charcoal painted dragons over doors of the less wealthy—all of the city spread out below him. It sat square in the shadow of Mount Draccus, the towering black mountain that was home to the Shadow Dragons.

And home to Quintin's family. Castle Wyvern was a large, forbidding keep carved into the living stone of the mountain, just below the High Beasts' nests.

He watched the Shade Guards standing by the palace gates, their breath like smoke as they laughed together in the dark. Beyond the gates, he saw no sign of the physician's cart.

A woman stood on the palace steps too—Chancellor Furia.

Quintin's nose wrinkled. He rather disliked the chancellor; she'd become quite a nuisance in his father's absence. Quintin himself being too young to watch over Dracogart in Father's stead, the king had turned to Furia, naming her steward—a title and powers she was all too happy to take full advantage of. Quintin could hear her now, admonishing the guards for chatting while on duty.

His mother groaned quietly and shifted beneath her blankets. Her forehead wrinkled, and she grimaced, but then lay as still as before.

Quintin tried not to wonder about the pain she was in. How much longer could she last without her evening tonic?

Or—more frighteningly—how much longer could she last without the venom of the Prism Scorpion the Ring had promised?

A broken promise, Quintin thought bitterly. And a broken kingdom would follow, if the sick of Dracogart weren't saved.

But it wouldn't do to dwell on what-ifs. His father—with the whole of the Highen's armies—would triumph over the Ring. And when they did, his father would return. And when he did, he would bring the Prism Scorpion's venom. And everyone who was sick would be made well again.

Including his mother.

If she could just hold on.

Something flickered in the sky—bright yellow, not unlike the windows of Dracogart—and disappeared.

Not a star, he was sure. The mists had sunk low from the mountains, blocking the lights of the On-High. This was something else.

He straightened, squinting into the night. A Shadow Dragon, probably, out for an evening hunt. He liked to imagine it might be Umbra, daughter of Draco, the King of Shadow Dragons.

"Are you out there, Princess?" Quintin whispered.

Umbra was only fourteen—the same age as Quintin. They were born the same year, same month, same week, same day. His mother called it a sign from the On-High—a sign that Quintin and Umbra would be the greatest rulers in the history of Dracogart. But Umbra was still a baby by dragon standards—most dragons didn't fly until their fiftieth year; any earlier would be a miracle.

A miracle, Quintin thought sadly. That was something he could use.

The light exploded again, bigger than before—closer.

And then he was sure. Dragonfire.

There—a massive dragon. As big as Draco!

How could that be? Most Shadow Dragons were no bigger than a carriage. That was why Draco was the king of them all—he was four stories tall. But Draco was with Quintin's father and their army, fighting with Major Jasper Lourdes against the Ring. How could there *possibly* be another dragon in Dracogart as big as him?

A deep, haunting cry carried across the mist, and with it came another blast of fire, so bright and close it illuminated the dragon's face. But even if it hadn't, the cry was one Quintin knew well.

He heard Chancellor Furia below shout orders to the Shade Guards standing by the gates, their eyes glued to the sky.

"It *is* Draco!" shouted Quintin. "Mother, it's Draco!"

The King of the Shadow Dragons had come home early.

Quintin scanned the foothills beyond the city, looking for the line of torches that meant his father's men were marching home. But he saw nothing.

Was his father still with the Major somewhere? Why would the dragon king return without his father?

The High Beast's flight pattern was strange, tacking this way and that, dipping low and jerking up in a confused, jagged way. Then the dragon screamed, and suddenly he dove for the palace.

No, he *fell*. It was an out-of-control spiral.

Dropping like a stone out of the sky, Draco crashed into the courtyard, his massive tail colliding with the West Tower. The ground shook as the tower crumbled, and every available Shade Guard poured out of the palace, Chancellor Furia shouting directions.

Draco screeched and flapped uselessly, snapping wildly at the men rushing to him, snorting jets of flame. This was not the Draco that had left Dracogart. That Draco was strong, majestic; he welcomed the attention of his people. This dragon, its yellow eyes wild and dilated, looked weak, confused—*frightened*, even.

Then Quintin saw why. Right behind Draco's front leg, thick, black blood slid from a wound between his ribs.

"He's hurt!" yelled Quintin. He leaned way out over the balcony, bellowing to the guards below. "The High Beast is hurt! *Someone fetch the apprentice keeper!*"

But Chancellor Furia and the men couldn't hear him over the wails of the Shadow Dragon and the roar of the fires he'd caused around the courtyard.

Quintin rushed to his mother, quickly making sure the edges of her coverings were tucked in tightly. "Mother, I have to find Keeper Cencius," he said. "I'll be back." He kissed her cold forehead and ran for the courtyard.

Apprentice Keeper Cencius spent much of his time on the observation deck high on Mount Draccus, watching over Umbra and the other hatchlings. He'd be there now, Quintin was sure, too focused on his task to notice the commotion in the courtyard. The deck was only accessible by the Mountain Lift on the east end of the grounds.

But when Quintin emerged into the courtyard, it was impassible: ablaze with dragonfire, choked with rubble, Shade Guards running in every direction trying to douse the flames and get control of Draco. Chains of iron flew over the frightened creature, grinding against his open wound.

"Tie him down," ordered Furia, standing on the steps in front of Quintin.

"Stop!" Quintin told her. "Stop it! He's hurt! You're frightening him!"

Furia turned, surprised to see him, and anger flashed in her eyes. "Do not interfere, young prince. He must be restrained. Look at the damage he's doing."

"But his *ribs*—"

"Tie him down!" Furia called, turning her attention back to the guards.

Looking around for help, Quintin caught sight of two figures by the gates—the round, balding one was Physician Scaleg, but huddled beside him was a red-cloaked stranger. The two cowered as one of Draco's massive wings shot out and collided with the guardhouse, sending bricks flying.

Quintin covered his head, and Draco screamed again, the sound so high-pitched and anguished it stabbed at his heart. The guards had a chain around the dragon's neck now, and it took twenty of them to pull his head to the ground. Other men held a massive scalecoat, waiting to cover the creature's eyes. Shadow Dragons liked the dark. It calmed them.

But no amount of dark would help Draco's wound. Quintin could see a massive pool of black dragon-blood beneath the frightened High Beast.

"Stop!" Quintin screamed, grabbing hold of Furia's arm. "You're hurting him!"

"He's hurting himself!" she snarled, yanking her arm free.

Draco collapsed under the pull of the guards, the impact sending tremors through the ground and up into Quintin's knees. The dragon groaned, shallow breaths escaping through flaring nostrils.

And then, before the Shade Guards had a chance to cover his eyes, Draco's breathing stopped.

The courtyard became silent, save for the crackle of scattered fires around them.

Quintin watched Draco's yellow eyes. The wide, frightened look in them faded like a dying fire. The black pupils that had always absorbed everything with a knowing glare shrank and became unseeing.

Quintin's own eyes burned with tears. The King of Shadow Dragons was dead.

As the Shade Guard began to understand that Draco was no more, Quintin could hear them crying out, horrified that their sacred High Beast had breathed its last in front of them.

The young prince's hands began to tremble, and tears fell down his cheeks. How could this have happened? Did the Ring do this to Draco? Quintin watched the light of the flames flicker off the dragon's obsidian scales, saw them reflected in the pool of sacred black blood. What, then, had the Ring done to his father's armies?

Father. What had happened to him?

A sob shuddered through Quintin, and his hands flew to his mouth. *What will I tell Mother?*

Furia stood on her step, smoothing out her dress, her long black hair. Finally she turned around, seemingly startled to see the boy still behind her. She sighed and placed a hand on his shoulder.

"A tragic loss," she said. And disappeared back inside the palace.

"Young Quintin!"

Quintin turned and saw old Physician Scaleg hurrying as quickly as he could across the ruined courtyard, the red-cloaked figure at his side.

Yes, Quintin told himself. *Mother's tonic. She needs her tonic; it cannot wait.* Not even to mourn Draco.

The boy wiped his eyes and snorted back sobs, doing his best to compose himself. "Physician Scaleg, m-my mother is r-ready for you."

"Yes—yes, of course," gasped the physician, glancing sideways at his mysterious companion. Physician Scaleg had always tended to Quintin's mother alone. Why had he brought someone? "Erhm. My lord, this Oracle has come—"

"An Oracle?" interrupted Quintin. Yes, of course, he recognized the garb now. Fear shot through him. "Is it Mother? Will she die?"

"Not die," said the Oracle, his red eyes blank of emotion. "The mother should not die. Not this night. Not that I've been told."

"Then why have you come? Is it Father?"

"Erhm, my lord," said the Physician. "This Oracle has come with a message that is for you and you alone."

"A message?" said Quintin. "Is it *from* Father, then?"

"I bring with me words from the mouth of a girl so named for the bear," said the Oracle, "and the other so named for the stars."

Quintin looked at the Physician, not sure what the strange man was saying. The Physician offered no explanation, but his mouth was pulled thin in a grim line. "My lord, perhaps it is best to discuss this someplace more private."

"I don't understand," said Quintin. "If not my father, then who could be trying to contact me? Is this to do with Draco or my father at all?"

The Oracle removed his hood. His red eyes seemed to burn in the light of the fires. "The daughters of the Major."

All the children of the House of Hounds stared death in the face that fateful day.

All, except one.

—THE WRITINGS OF RIZLAN,
On the State of the Houses: The Lunar Offensive, *Star Writ*

FIFTEEN

THERE were five sons born to the House of Hounds—five boys, each with different fathers, who shared one mother, Queen Conri.

The brothers stood together in the gamekeeper's shed, the stag they'd spent the best part of the evening hunting hanging on a chain above the floor. It was only half skinned. Murphy, the youngest of the boys, had been doing a fairly clean job under his older brothers' instruction—until an unexpected visit interrupted his work.

A pair of scarlet-cloaked strangers stood by the doors, inquisitive red eyes flicking from brother to brother. The weight of the words they had just spoken hung in the air like lead.

"What does this mean?" Murphy asked. "Is Mama dead?"

His brothers—Arthur, Lorcan, Connall, and Fillan—were quiet.

"Arthur," said Murphy, his small blood-soaked hand grabbing his oldest brother's sleeve. "Mama? Is she dead?"

Arthur's lips set in a grim line.

Lorcan, the second-oldest of the brothers at fourteen, looked over at the small curly-haired boy, the child's big brown eyes wet with worry. "Course not, Murph," he said with a grin.

Connall, the third brother, looked aghast. "Lorc!"

"What? We've no way to know if this message is truthful—"

"It comes from the On-High!" Connall snapped.

"It comes from a *person*," corrected Lorc.

Connall's fists balled at his sides. "Do you honestly think an Oracle would *lie?*"

"Oh, don't be so dramatic, Conall," laughed Lorc. He pointed to the Oracles standing by the door, their heads cocked curiously—not unlike the hounds that lived on the estate. "It's entirely possible someone lied *to* the Oracles, and they're just passing on that lie. Look at them—not exactly the deep-thinking sort, are they?"

A knife flew by Lorc's face, barely missing his nose before pinging off the wall behind him. Fillan's knife. "You're being rude, Lorc," he said.

Lorc scoffed. Fillan was indeed his father's son—his sense of propriety was strong. Even now, while ten-year-old Murphy wiped at his eyes for fear they'd lost their mother, Fillan would not tolerate rudeness. Still, Lorc thought, there was *some* of Mama in him—how else could he be so deadly with his knives?

"My point is that for all we know these Lourdes girls have stolen the Hemoth Bear for themselves. Arthur"—Lorc looked at their oldest brother—"you agree with me, don't you?"

Arthur had been silent ever since the Oracles arrived, and even now, his tight jaw showed no sign of unlocking. He frowned down at Murphy, whose red-stained hand was still gripping his sleeve.

"Lies are to the On-High as oil is to water," said one of the Oracles simply.

"They do not mix."

"No lies," the first agreed.

Lorc laughed, though he felt a cold unease. "Oh, well, if *you* say so, then."

Without a word, Arthur gently removed Murphy's hand from his arm and marched past the Oracles, the heavy wooden doors slamming behind him.

Lorc supposed that left him in charge of saying farewell to their guests. The three younger boys looked to him expectantly.

"Thank you for your message, esteemed Oracle persons," he said with a bow. "That will be all."

The Oracles just stared, seemingly unaware they'd been dismissed. A silly sort, these Oracles. Not at all reliable.

He shook his head and turned to little Murphy. "Stay here and finish up with your stag," he said. "I will speak with Arthur." He left the boys there, the Oracles looking on, and followed his older brother.

Outside, night had fallen. The scents of pine and cedar from the surrounding forest floated on the air, and glowing starflies buzzed above the meadow grasses. Lorc found Arthur standing by the west well, where he was silently watching the Starhounds lounge and roll. Joining his brother, Lorc hopped up and took a seat on the crumbling edge of the well.

Lorc could see the lights of their family estate, a simple manor in the Hundfordian style. He liked the crude stone walls and tiny windows. It was large, but compared to the palaces of the other Heads of Houses, it was rustic. And that was how Lady Conri liked it. It was a home for hunters, filled to bursting with the family's dogs: bloodhounds, foxhounds, wolfhounds, deerhounds, mastiffs, terriers.

But of all the dogs in the manor, the Starhounds ruled, for they were the High Beasts of Hundford. The estate, everyone knew, truly belonged to them.

The sacred animals were enjoying their rest in the meadow after a long day's hunt. Only the pups were here; the rest of the Pack had gone to fight the Ring with Lady Conri, leaving their young behind.

There was no dog like a Starhound. Each of the five pups was big, their heads as high as Lorc's chest. They had a face not unlike a wolfhound, their rough silver beards making them appear older and wiser than they were, and their lean, powerful bodies were covered in a glossy black coat that reminded Lorc of his mother's hair.

Mama, he thought, a lump suddenly rising in his throat.

His ferocious mother, the deadliest warrior in the Highen—the Pack chose her when she was only sixteen. Could she really be gone?

He saw her in his mind, her axe slung over her shoulder, her belt of daggers around her chest, Asterion and the rest of the Pack by her side. Magnificent Asterion, the dominant male. Lorc swallowed hard. What terrible force could stop a team as formidable as Lady Conri and her Starhounds?

Argos, the biggest of the Starhound pups, pawed playfully at a starfly. *He'll be as mighty as Asterion someday,* Mama had told Lorc the morning she left for the war. *Young Argos has taken quite a shine to you, my little monster. You and that pup have a special bond. You must thank the On-High for that blessing.*

Lorc smiled as Argos rolled onto his back, his legs wriggling in the air and his pink tongue flopping happily out the side of his mouth. Argos was nothing like the oh-so-serious Asterion. Argos was a charming fool.

"How can you grin at a time like this?" Arthur's voice was heavy.

Lorc scoffed. "You cannot believe those Oracles' nonsense."

"Oracles are truth-tellers. They have no ability to lie."

"If a person can speak, a person can lie."

"Come now, Lorc. I have just as much trouble believing Mama could be defeated as you do. But this is a holy message—it comes from the On-High's blessed seers. We cannot afford to hang on to childish hopes. We must be realistic."

Lorc looked away from his brother's deadly serious face. *I am being realistic,* he thought but didn't say. Arthur would just try to convince him otherwise.

"Even if we assume the message from Tawnshire is truthful, what business is it of ours what the Minor does to the Major's children? Especially if the Major is dead, as the Lourdes girl claims? I say let Bram Lourdes have them. Two fewer spoiled fools to compete with at the Northern Crowning."

"The Frosmen have the Hemoth Bear. Would you be so willing to let the Minor take control of *that*?"

No, Lorc realized. That would not be beneficial. It was their mother's greatest wish to see one of her sons crowned Major, and if the Minor stole the Hemoth Bear for himself, he could build himself a considerable advantage before the Northern Crowning.

"Don't you understand, Lorc?" Arthur asked, his brow crinkling. "The high king is dead. A *Major* was murdered by a *Minor*. It strikes at the heart of the Highen. If this isn't addressed—if these wrongs aren't righted—the entire realm will fall to chaos."

"Well then," said Lorc, folding his arms across his chest, "what do you want to do?"

Arthur's eyes fell to his hands, picking at the blood that had crusted beneath his fingernails. *"And Tawn saw inside the heart of the human Dov, and found great courage, love, and honor. It glowed inside him, brighter than the North Star herself."*

"And so it was that the Great Lord Tawn chose the human Dov to be protector of all the realm," said Lorc, completing the *Star Writ* quote for his brother. *"So it was that the Highen had their first Major.* I don't need you to quote scripture to me, Arthur. I asked what you want to do."

"Courage, love, and honor," repeated Arthur. "That's what makes a Major. What claim to courage, love, and honor have we if we do nothing to help the Hemoth Bear now?"

"*If*," said Lorc, "the Hemoth Bear does, in fact, need help."

"Don't make me say it again!" Arthur's powerful hand grabbed hold of Lorc's shirt, and he yanked his brother hard. "Oracles are—"

"Truth-tellers!" shouted Lorc, pushing his brother back. "I heard you. But I'm sorry. Mama is the best warrior in the Highen. There is no foe she cannot defeat!"

Arthur scowled, and Lorc could see his mind working out another lecture about *being realistic*.

"But I do agree with you," Lorc said quickly, "that we cannot afford to do nothing. The fact remains that this message has come to us, and it must be addressed, be it truth or fiction. Someone must go to Tawnshire. *You* can call it sending help, but *I* will call it an investigation."

Arthur raised an eyebrow. "You agree we must send someone to Tawnshire?"

"We must send someone to Tawnshire, yes, I agree. When would you like to go?"

Arthur shook his head. "I cannot be the one to go."

"Why not?"

"Have you any idea of the kind of chaos that will erupt when word reaches the kingdom that Mama has been *murdered*?" Arthur asked, his voice low. "Hundford will have no Head of House. *Think*, Lorc. Mama left me and her council in charge, but I'm not yet eighteen—not a man in the eyes of the law. There are those who would try to install themselves as regent over me until a new Head could be chosen at the next Northern Crowning. A very dangerous proposition for us. Anything could happen."

Lorc felt heat rush to his ears. "And who *exactly* do you believe would try something like that?"

Arthur's arms dropped at his sides. Lorc could see his older brother was tired of talking.

"I have to stay here," he said, ignoring the question. "I have to maintain order."

"You're worried about my father, aren't you?" Lorc heard his voice growing louder, felt the anger bubbling inside him. "You think he'll try to take over, don't you?"

Arthur said nothing.

"My father," said Lorc, tremors of rage rippling through him, "has served this kingdom as chief advisor to Mama for *twenty years*! He is a loyal citizen of Hundford, and if he steps up as regent it is because he is the most qualified man to do so!"

"A loyal citizen who tried to poison all four of your brothers."

A dagger of shame pierced Lorc's heart.

He'd felt it ever since that day four and a half years ago. Wolfsbane Day, the kingdom called it. The day all the boys of the House of Hounds were poisoned with wolfsbane. All the boys but Lorc.

The brothers had lingered close to death for weeks, until a physician from Twigate nursed them back to health. Against the odds, all of them survived—a miracle so impressive, Major Jasper Lourdes had declared an annual holiday in the Highen to mark the anniversary. Every year, Lorc and his brothers were forced to remember that it was *he* who was spared the wolfsbane's bite.

"He didn't do it," said Lorc, his eyes on Argos—the dog's perked ears were obviously listening. "You were at the Grand Inquiry. Mama found my father innocent."

Arthur pressed his palms into his eyes with a groan. "I know, Lorc. Please. Let's not do this again."

No, thought Lorc. *Let's not.* After four and a half years, the two brothers had argued enough for Lorc to know exactly what Arthur thought of his father. Arthur was convinced the man was guilty, and that Mama was too blinded by love to accept it.

Because she did love him. Of all the men who had found favor with Lady Conri, Lorc's father was the one she loved best.

Lorc tried to calm himself down with deep breaths. Arthur spoke again: "This is a time for us to be united, little brother. To work together. We can't let past grievances jeopardize what comes next for us. For the boys."

Argos's tail wagged nervously from his spot in the grass. The dog's head cocked to one side, sensing the tension between the brothers.

Finally, Lorc spoke. "So send me."

"What?"

"Send me to Tawnshire to help the Major's daughters."

Arthur was silent, mouth agape.

And Lorc knew why. "You don't trust me. You don't trust me the same way you don't trust my father."

"That's not true, Lorc."

It was, though, Lorc was certain. No matter what Arthur said. To Arthur, Lorc would always be his father's son. The one who escaped the poison.

But if Lorc went to Tawnshire, if he helped the Major's daughters in the name of his brother, in the name of Hundford, then Arthur would see. He would know that Lorc was as much his mother's son as Arthur.

And maybe, finally, he could escape the shadow of Wolfsbane Day.

"Then *send me.*"

Arthur scoffed. "To Tawnshire, where the Minor is slaughtering royalty at will? What do you think he'll do if he finds you?"

"I don't fear the Minor," growled Lorc. "If he truly did something to Mama, then it is the Minor who should fear me."

"Oh, please," said Arthur. "Bram Lourdes is a military man. A soldier. You're a child."

"I'm a better hunter than you."

Arthur straightened; his shoulders squared the way their mother's did when she meant to have the final word. "You are not to go, and that is final."

"You can't tell me what to do. You're not Mama."

"*Mama is dead!*" roared Arthur.

With that word, so short and cold and awful—*dead*—Arthur might as well have struck him. Lorc's breath hitched. He hated the sound of it, the bluntness of it, the finality of it.

Dead.

Lady Conri. Dead.

Lorc's eyes burned with tears. He couldn't believe it. Didn't want to. Didn't want to plan for his life in a world that didn't have her. She was the only person who never looked at him with suspicion, or disdain, or fear. Even little Murph, for all the love they shared, sometimes pushed his cup aside if Lorc sat next to him at table. Mama was the one person who ever saw him, the real him. Saw what was in his heart.

Without her, how long before he lost himself? Before he forgot that he wasn't who everyone else said he was?

"She's dead, Lorcan," Arthur said again, his voice heavy with grief. "We're on our own. I know you know it's true."

The tears fell down Lorc's cheeks, and he felt his strength drain out of him. He did know. Grief rushed in, filling every vein, veins that flowed with the blood she'd given him. Her blood. All he had left of her.

He sank down to the grass, trembling as he cried.

Alone. He felt it like a dark and endless cold. Mama was gone. Taken from him. By the Minor.

Arthur crouched beside his brother, his hands on his shoulders. "We're on our own, brother. We have to be careful now. And rushing off to Tawnshire into the hands of the Minor is reckless."

"But we cannot let him get away with this, Arthur. We must destroy him."

"You never listen." Arthur stood angrily, wiping his tears on his sleeve.

"We must avenge her. I have to go—"

"Enough, Lorc!" said Arthur. "You are not to go to Tawnshire."

Lorc opened his mouth to argue, but Arthur help up his hand. "Lorcan, I forbid it!"

Arthur had never truly *forbidden* him anything before. But with Mama gone, Arthur's word was law, wasn't it?

Too furious to speak, Lorc turned and ran for the house, his brother calling after him. But Lorc couldn't stand any more talk. He couldn't hear any more lectures. If Arthur wouldn't listen, if Arthur wouldn't make the Minor pay for what he'd done to Mama, then Lorc would.

Forbidden or not.

Put Berenice Locks beneath your pillow, and in your dreams the On-High will grant you visions of your future happinesses—whatever they may be.

—TAWNSHIRIAN SUPERSTITION

SIXTEEN

Rizlan.
Rizlan.
Please, show me Rizlan.

DEV saw nothing. No matter how hard he tried, how hard he focused, how tightly he squeezed his eyes shut, he couldn't make visions come.

He tried to remember everything Rizlan had taught him, everything Rizlan had said about clearing his mind and opening himself up to the stars. But nothing worked. He'd been at it for hours, begging the On-High to send him an image, begging for a clue as to whether his old teacher was alive or dead. After trying all morning and for the better part of the afternoon, there was still only black behind his eyelids.

Perhaps he hadn't paid enough attention to Rizlan's lessons. Or maybe…maybe the thing that made a Keeper *see* was a thing Dev just didn't have inside him. Whatever he was doing, he was doing it wrong. He was failing.

A furry muzzle pushed itself beneath Dev's arm. Alcor snorted, practically lifting Dev by the armpit.

"Are you feeling better now, Alcor?" he asked gently.

The bear's nose wiggled back and forth, his lips twitching as he looked hopefully for his dinner. That was good. The poultice Dev had made to treat Alcor's wound must be working.

Dev got up from his spot on the floor and checked the bandage covering the gash in Alcor's flank. The scents of crownseed and bogberry juice wafted out from beneath the cloth, sweet and flowery and clean. Alcor had managed to avoid infection so far. Also good.

With his fingers, Dev gently pressed down. Alcor yelped, jerking away. "It's all right," said Dev. "I just need to see. Stay still." The bear snarled unhappily but allowed the boy to continue. The wound was bright pink and glistening, healing faster than Dev would have expected. He laughed, scratching Alcor playfully behind his right ear. "You can thank the sap of the azure tree for that!"

Dev had never made a poultice with the sap of the azure tree before. It was simply too hard to get—azure trees were native to Twigate, hundreds of miles from Tawnshire. But the Oracles had that sap. Indeed, they had a whole storehouse of rare herbs and flowers and plants and tonics and venoms and powders from across the Highen, all of them useful for curing different ailments. And the Oracles were more than happy to let Dev use what he needed for the Hemoth Bear.

"The Bear is happy."

Dev turned to see an Oracle, short and round, a large silver bowl in her arms. "The skill of his Keeper pleases him."

Dev blushed. "Oh, me? No. I just, I've never used azure sap before. That fixed him, not me."

Alcor's massive head hung over Dev's shoulder, his hungry black nose sniffing at the contents of the Oracle's bowl—a mixture of berries and fleshy pink fish.

The Oracle smiled. "A modest Keeper."

She handed him the bowl, and Alcor shoved his face inside before Dev could even place it on the ground for him. When he looked back, the Oracle had left, disappearing back to the kitchens.

He had the urge to go after her, to tell her no, she was wrong. He wasn't modest. He was just bad at his job. That was all there was to it. What kind of Keeper couldn't have visions? What kind of Keeper would let his High Beast get *stabbed*?

Dev sighed, plunking down beside Alcor's bowl and watching the bear eat.

If I were truly skilled, like Rizlan, he thought, *I would have seen the Minor and his Frosmen before they stormed the Manor.* But he had been too busy sleeping—and letting himself get lost in dreams of his mother. Of home.

The shame of it crashed over him like a wave. Rizlan would be so disappointed.

"*More* flowers!" Aster sat perched on the sill of a great stained-glass window that looked out over the square. It was the only thing that seemed to keep her entertained while they waited for word from the other Houses. "Ursula, come look! I've never seen so many flowers!"

Dev could see Ursula, sitting by the petition candles. They littered the mosaicked floor beneath the great oculus—a massive round opening in the high ceiling of the Oracle House—each one waiting to be seen by the On-High when night fell. Just small, ordinary flames—ordinary fire, representing the wishes of the people who lit them. Ursula had lit one herself, and was so transfixed that she didn't seem to notice her sister calling.

She's praying to the On-High for a miracle, Dev realized.

Ursula wouldn't know if her message reached any of the Heads of Houses' children until nightfall, when the On-High's voices could be heard again. The jars that had glowed with brilliant white starflame the night before were empty in the light of day, just simple glass vessels lining every window in clusters.

All Ursula, Dev, and Aster could do was wait.

Aster sighed, frowning, from her windowsill. She was bored, that much was obvious. There wasn't much for one to do in an Oracle House *besides* pray.

"Can you count all the bouquets?" Dev asked, joining her by the glass. It was a better game than nothing.

"No," Aster said, her earlier excitement gone. "There are far too many." She slipped off the sill to let Dev have a better look outside.

The square was filled with what seemed like every person in Tawnshire Town, all of them come to pay worship to Alcor. The steps of the Oracle House were littered with golden blossoms, glistening in the sun of the afternoon.

"I think it's silly," said Aster. "What sort of an offering is flowers for a bear, anyway?"

Dev smirked. "They're not just any flowers. They're Berenice Locks."

From the scowl on the girl's face, Dev realized the name meant nothing to her. "Berenice Locks?" he said again. "The hair of the Great Lady?"

Aster's nose wrinkled. "Those are *hair* flowers?"

"What? No. They're just the same color as her hair was." He grabbed the *Star Writ* and flipped through its pages. "You *do* know who the Great Lady Berenice is, don't you?"

"Of course," said Aster, rolling her eyes. "She was the wife of the first Major, Dov the Brave."

"That's not all she was." He caught sight of the illustration he'd been looking for and put the book down on the sill for Aster to see. "Look here. Have you seen this before?"

She crowded beside him, inspecting the drawing: a beautiful young woman, with eyes red as fire and hair like the sun, floating among the stars. Dev was surprised to see Aster shake her head. It was only one of the most famous illustrations in the *Star Writ*—he would have thought everyone had seen it. "She was also born of the North Star. She had the blood of the On-High in her veins."

"That's impossible. People aren't stars!"

"Nothing is impossible," said Dev gravely. "The On-High gave us the High Beasts, after all. Look here, read the story. The brightest of the On-High, the North Star, longed for a child to call her own. So she asked her fellow stars to grant her their blessings, and their light combined to create the Great Lady Berenice. And when the Great Lord Tawn chose Dov the Brave to be Major, the Great Lady Berenice saw him from her home in the heavens, and she loved him. With the North Star's blessing, she left the sky and lived her life on earth with her husband. But the On-High were lonesome without her. So they whispered to her, all her life. And the Great Lady Berenice became a link between mankind and the stars. And when she died, the On-High took her home and gave her back her place in the sky."

Dev pressed the three painted stars on the page that made up the Great Lady's image in the sky.

"She was an Oracle?" asked Aster, pointing to the picture's red eyes.

"The very first," said Dev. "All Oracles are born with the mark of Berenice—beautiful red eyes. And they continue to link us with the voice of the heavens. The men and women in this house are very blessed to be chosen by the On-High to continue their daughter's work."

"And what about you?" said Aster.

"What about me?"

"You were chosen too, weren't you? To be a Keeper?"

Dev closed the massive book abruptly. He didn't like to think about that, about the way he'd come to live in Tawnshire. "Yes. The On-High chose me."

Aster sat and folded her legs beneath her. "And how does that work, exactly? It's funny that I never wondered at it before now." She gazed at him. "You must have come from somewhere, mustn't you? Surely you didn't just drop out of the sky and land at the Manor." She laughed at the thought, but Dev was less amused. He hadn't expected this turn in the conversation, and the more she spoke the more uncomfortable it made him. "So tell me, Dev: How is it you came to be our Keeper?"

"It isn't interesting," he assured her, glancing at Alcor, who huffed.

"I'm interested. Come now, I want to know."

He looked back at Aster's eager face. She'd found something new to stave off her boredom, and he could tell she wasn't about to leave it alone.

"When I was born, Rizlan had a vision of it," said Dev, very quickly. "He went to the Oracles and asked them to ask the On-High where to find me. So they told him and he came and brought me to Tawnshire."

Yes. Rizlan came for him, with Hermans. And they took Dev from his mother's arms. He could still remember the sound of her crying, though he wasn't one year old yet.

"You mean you weren't born in Tawnshire?"

He bit his lip. "No."

"So"—she rested her chin in her hands—"where *were* you born?"

He'd hoped his simple explanation would be enough for her. Apparently not. "Erm, Härkädia."

Aster cringed. "Blech, *Härkädia*? The *Ox Kingdom*? Nothing but cattle and peasants and mud! Do you know, Gatch, my nurse, she was from Härkädia. I always imagined the people were all like her—dreadfully dull. But you're not like Gatch at all, are you?"

Heat rushed to Dev's cheeks, and the young Keeper didn't know whether to be embarrassed or angry. "You've never been to Härkädia."

"Certainly not!" laughed Aster. "Who would *want* to go to Härkädia! What would I even do there? Till the fields? Skim the bogs?"

"Skimming bogs is hard, honest work!" he snapped.

Aster's smile faded. She watched him, blinking, as he turned his back.

"Was that what your family did?" she asked quietly.

Dev nodded stiffly. "My mother."

"And your father?"

He shrugged. "I don't remember him. I was just a baby."

"But you remember your mother?"

Dev nodded. Remembered her golden hair, the smell of the bog pines on her skin. He glanced back at Aster. She was still on the floor, leaning forward over her knees, a thoughtful look in her eyes.

"What?" he asked.

"It's strange," she said. "I certainly can't remember anything from when *I* was a baby. But here you are, with memories of your mother."

"So?"

She shook her head. "It's just strange is all."

"You don't believe me?"

"No, no," she said, watching a group of Oracles huddling by the front windows. "I do believe you, actually. You must have an excellent memory."

She thinks I'm a liar, Dev thought bitterly. *But what would she know about it?* Someone like Aster Lourdes. Of course she didn't have memories of her mother from when she was that little. She didn't *have* to remember! Her mother had been with her always. She created new memories every day—she could throw the old ones away the same as she did dresses and dolls. Dev didn't have that luxury. He had to hold on to the few precious ones he had.

And a terrible thought, the one that seeped its way into his mind whenever he felt the most alone, came to him again: *What if they aren't memories?* After all, how could he be sure? What if what he thought was his mother was just some woman he'd dreamed up? Some childish fantasy he'd concocted in his mind?

He rubbed a hand over his hair, trying to rub the thought away.

"Perhaps you're not seeing memories," she said absently. "Perhaps you're seeing like Keeper Rizlan."

"What?"

She looked at him then, a notch between her eyebrows. "You know—*visions*, or whatever you call them. You're a Keeper. Well, you will be. Don't Keepers have visions?"

Aster was right. Keepers were supposed to have visions. The future. The present. The past. Whatever the On-High willed them to see. But the fact remained that Dev had never had one. It had been Rizlan's greatest frustration: no matter how hard Dev tried, visions wouldn't come. And he never had to *try* to see his mother. She was always just there. So it didn't seem likely.

Suddenly, Aster sprang to her feet. There was a commotion by the door. "What's happening?"

Dev could hear voices, lots of them, shouting somewhere outside. Something was happening in the square. Aster climbed onto the windowsill, and Dev was quick to follow. Alcor huffed behind them, his giant head nudging Dev nervously.

"Turds of Tawn!" whispered Aster. "The Frosmen are back."

Below, the people of Tawnshire shouted angrily at men on horseback—there had to be twenty of them, all wearing the familiar uniform of the White Bear.

"Ursula!" Aster shouted. "They're back!"

The older Lourdes sister looked up from her petition candle. Dev was struck by how different she looked sitting there. Humble. Reverent, even. Not like herself at all.

Then she rushed to join them at the window, and Dev noticed her eyes: dark, puffy, sleepless. And her hair: always shining and smooth, now in tangles, her gold barrettes askew. The only thing that looked characteristically opulent was her frost-pearl gown.

"Are they at the door?" she demanded. With a sideways glance, she caught Dev staring. "What?"

"N-n-nothing," he stammered, turning back to the window.

"No, they're not at the door," said Aster.

The Frosmen couldn't even get to the steps of the Oracle House. The people in the square had put themselves between the soldiers and the building.

Aster's nose was pressed to the glass. "The crowd, look at them all. What *are* they doing?"

The Frosmen ducked, arms covering their faces and bodies. The crowd was throwing things at them.

"I think they're trying to protect Alcor," said Dev.

Ursula nodded. "Our people are brave."

A clump of brown, messy mud collided with the lead Frosman's face, and Aster snorted. "Is that horse poo?"

Dev wanted to laugh too. But he had a nervous feeling in his gut.

"Do you see Uncle Bram?" asked Ursula grimly.

"No," said Aster. "No, he's not here with them."

The crowd surged forward, pushing the horses back. Dev saw that some of the people held makeshift weapons—boards and shovels, knives and other tools. Stones flew through the air, and the people of Tawnshire forced the Frosmen into retreat.

"I don't believe it!" laughed Aster. "They're chasing the Frosmen away!"

"For now," said Ursula. "They'll be back. Uncle Bram will come for the bear himself if he has to."

Alcor groaned, and Dev nearly jumped when the young bear nuzzled Ursula's arm. Dev had never seen the bear do that to anyone—except himself, of course. Ursula rubbed the young bear's furry cheek, her sad eyes seeing only what was happening in her head.

"We can't wait for help," she said finally. "We must flee, as soon as we can."

"How?" asked Aster. "Alcor is too big. We'll be seen."

Aster was right. If the Minor's men didn't spot them, the people of Tawnshire would, and then they'd have to stop as everyone touched and prayed to Alcor. It wasn't as though they could just sneak out a back door.

Dev's eyes fell on the little flame of Ursula's petition candle. And an idea began to form in his head. The sun outside had fallen low beyond the buildings of Tawnshire. Night would be here soon.

And so would the starflame.

It is the secret kept only by the Shadow Dragon—the feeling of the clouds.

—THE WRITINGS OF THUBAN,
On Shadow Dragons: The Star Majors, *Star Writ*

SEVENTEEN

QUINTIN sat in the cold cellar dark, the Oracle's red eyes blinking at him. The star priest's words hung on the dank, frigid air like his white breath.

The Minor had betrayed the Major. That was what the Oracle had said. The Major was gone.

Which meant Quintin's father—

The door to the ice larder groaned and scraped along the wet stone floor, and Scaleg slipped inside. The old physician had brought them down to the castle's bowels so that Quintin could receive the Oracle's message in secret. Why, Quintin hadn't been able to understand. If what the Oracle told him was true—that the Major and the King of Dracogart were dead—it wouldn't be long before everyone knew. But still, Scaleg had insisted, and Scaleg's nervousness was beginning to frighten Quintin.

"Furia has ordered the gates to the city closed," Scaleg said, wringing his hands. "No one is allowed in or out, Minor's orders."

Minor's orders. The traitor's reach had come to Dracogart.

And Furia, as steward in his father's absence, was allowing it.

"We have to go to Furia," said Quintin, getting to his feet. "She has to know what the Major's daughters have said!" Then they could work out the best way for Dracogart to respond. The kingdom's army was gone, true, but enough Shade Guards and soldiers remained that they could be sent to Tawnshire.

"I do not think that is wise, my lord," said Scaleg.

"Why not?"

Scaleg cracked his knuckles, his eyes darting warily between the prince and the staring, owl-eyed Oracle. "My lord," began the physician carefully, "don't you find it strange that Furia is enacting orders from the Minor so swiftly? Draco's body lies still warm in the courtyard, and yet our Lady Steward was ready with the Minor's orders before she'd even called the Dracogart council to convene."

Quintin's heart began to race.

Scaleg was right—Draco had descended on the castle so suddenly, so unexpectedly. The city was in chaos, and without this message from the Major's daughters, how could Furia be in anything but a state of utter confusion? How could she even know the Minor's will? And why would she *enact* his will, when King Wyvern might still be alive?

Unless Furia already knew what had happened to Quintin's father.

Unless Furia had been in contact with the Minor before today.

"She is working with the Minor," the young prince said, realization dawning.

Scaleg nodded grimly. "I fear it is so."

Quintin thought of his father then, of his noble brow, his proud face, of him overlooking his kingdom from the balustrade of Mother's bedchamber. His father would destroy Furia for this treason.

Would have. But Drag Wyvern was gone now.

It fell to Quintin.

"S-Scaleg," he said, a tremor of fear working up his spine, "what must I do? If Furia is with the Minor, how am I to answer Ursula Lourdes' call for aid? How can I—"

Scaleg grabbed Quintin's hands in his, forehead creased with crannies as hard and deep as the mountainside. "Stop that, young prince. That is not for you to worry about now."

"Not for me to worry about?" How could Scaleg say that! They

were probably the only two in Dracogart, apart from Furia and this Oracle, who knew what the Minor had done. "I am prince of Dracogart, Physician—"

"That is why you must worry about yourself now!" insisted Scaleg, gripping Quintin tightly by the shoulders. "You are the only heir to your father's throne. We must tread very carefully."

Quintin felt the earth shifting beneath his feet, sensed the root of Scaleg's fears rising up to meet him. "Careful of what, Scaleg?"

His old friend frowned, a grim truth hardening in his cool dark eyes. "You, Quintin Wyvern, are the single greatest threat to Furia's new reign...and to the Minor's hold over Dracogart."

A threat?

Quintin nearly laughed. *A slope mouse*, his father's gamesmaster called him every time he shied from joining them on a grimalkin hunt. Quintin had always been a shadow away from being invisible. The only reason anyone besides his parents ever paid him any attention was because he was expected to be king one day. And now, with his father gone...

Quintin's throat went dry. "You think she means to kill me."

Scaleg nodded. "I fear she does, my lord. That's why we must get you out of here. The castle is no longer safe."

But the castle was his family's home. *His* home. "But Furia can't just kill me. It can't be that simple! I'm the prince!"

"A prince whose father can no longer protect him. You must leave Dracogart before it's too late."

"Dracogart is all I know! And Mother is sicker by the day!" cried Quintin. "You expect me to just leave her?"

Scaleg held a finger to his lips, and then took Quintin's hand in his. "Listen to me, Quintin, listen. Your mother hasn't much time, it's true. But this is bigger than your mother. This is for all of Dracogart. Your father is gone; your mother is too ill to help the people. You are all that is *left* for Dracogart, my boy. You must leave so that you can stand at the Northern Crowning and allow Umbra to choose you."

Umbra. She was just a baby.

"But we don't *want* to stand at the Northern Crowning." Not now. They were still too young. Both of them. He wasn't ready.

"My prince," said Scaleg, "if you do not stand, then Furia will win. You must decide: When they read the *Star Writ* in the centuries to come, will they remember Furia's name? Or yours?"

"I don't *need* to be remembered," whispered Quintin.

The old man smiled. "And that is exactly why the people need you."

And so he must leave? It was unthinkable. This land was in his blood. A thousand years of kingship coursed through his veins.

"Take this." From his robes, Scaleg produced a coin purse. "It isn't much. But it's all the Draccmar and High Coins I have."

"High Coins! Scaleg, I don't want your money!"

"My lord, where will you get any coins now that Furia commands the realm?"

Nowhere. Quintin was a prince. He had never had reason to carry money.

Scaleg placed the little purse firmly in his hands, and Quintin began to feel cold. Could he really be thinking of leaving? Umbra wouldn't understand. And even if he could leave her, he could not leave his mother to face the end alone. His stomach dropped into his feet. "Mother!"

He bolted from the larder, Scaleg calling after him to wait. But he couldn't wait. He'd left his mother alone too long already.

He bounded up winding stairwells, up endless steps, climbing higher into the mountain. He raced through stony halls as fast as his legs would carry him. He only stopped when he reached his mother's door, rich dark scorchwood carved with the image of a nest of Shadow Dragons—he'd closed it for fear of drafts when he left earlier that evening.

But now it was wide open.

He stepped over the threshold and found Furia inside, standing at the foot of his mother's bed, her long nails rapping the bedpost impatiently. His mother lay where he had left her, breath ragged and slow.

"What are you doing here?" he demanded.

Queen Wyvern and Chancellor Furia had never been friends. And Furia had never shown the slightest interest in Queen Wyvern's failing health, except, Quintin was keenly aware, when it appeared to be worsening.

Furia turned slowly, deliberately, a parchment held loosely in her other hand. "Where have you been, little lord?"

We must tread very carefully, Scaleg had said. And indeed, Quintin couldn't help but be aware of how shaky the ground beneath him felt. He stuffed Scaleg's coin purse into his pocket. "My mother needed her tonic," he lied.

Furia cocked one of her eyebrows—eyebrows that had always seemed like little serpents to Quintin. "And yet you are empty-handed. I take it you had trouble locating your physician?"

She was getting at something—did she know about the message from the Oracle?

"What do you want, Lady Steward?"

She grinned, as though she was enjoying whatever game they were playing. "I wanted you to hear it from me," she said, nodding at his mother. "Both of you. Before the kingdom. The Major is gone, little lord, and so is our dear King Wyvern. The Minor has had to assume authority over the Highen, as is his burden."

Burden indeed, Quintin thought.

"And with your father killed by the Ring—Draco keep his

star—and so many of the other Heads of Households similarly fallen, the Minor, naturally, is concerned for your safety."

Quintin balked. "My safety?"

She handed him the parchment, the Minor's decree written there in coiling black ink. "The Minor is well aware that you are all that remains of the proud Wyvern lineage"—she waved a dismissive hand—"what with your father no more, and your mother…" She stepped toward the foot of the bed, her long fingers trailing along the furs that kept Mother warm. "Well, it won't be long till you're an orphan in this world, young Quintin. So alone."

Young Quintin. The quiet hum of her words, even and deliberate, struck him like a blow. Not *prince* or *lord* anymore.

"You must be protected," she said. "That is why I have decided, as Regent of Dracogart, to send you to the Highest Keep. For your protection."

"The Highest Keep?" Quintin could hardly believe she'd said it. The Keep was Dracogart's strongest fortress, built by ancient kings so high on the mountain only dragons could reach it. It had served as a prison—a prison mainly of royals, for the dragons were loath to bear those without Wyvern blood—but it had not been used in decades because it was so hard to get to. Prisoners and their jailers were more likely to die on the journey than reach the fortress alive. "You can't send me to the Keep. My mother—"

"Your mother's condition will not change, whether you are by her side or not," said Furia coolly. "The decision has been made, and the Minor agrees with my judgment."

"You cannot make me," said Quintin, and for once, his voice was steel.

"I see." Furia moved to the head of the bed and brushed a hair from his mother's face. His mother was so helpless, so weak—Quintin wanted to lunge, to slap the chancellor's hand away, but he didn't dare move. Daintily, Furia lifted a jug of water that had been resting on the bedside table. She strode to the hearth, watching him with a darkness in her eyes that stopped Quintin's blood in its veins. "You wish to wait until she's left this world, then..."

She held the jug out toward the fire, threatening to drown out the heat.

He could only stare, outrage and fear filling him up inside so that he couldn't bring himself to speak. The cold would kill his mother. Even if he got another fire started after Furia put this one out, her message was clear—it would be easy enough for her to speed his mother's death.

Finally, he shook his head.

"Very well," said Furia, stepping back from the bed. "Tomorrow, I preside over the funeral of Draco, and you will stand beside me. After that, I have arranged an escort of the finest grimalkin scalers to take you to the Keep."

Scalers—peasants who hunted grimalkin pelts on the mountain's slopes. No Shade Guards. And no dragon to take him up.

She intended him to die on the ascent.

"The mountain is perilous and hungers for souls." Furia drifted past him on her way to the door, her long fingers gripping his shoulder briefly. "Rest well, young Quintin, you will need your strength." And with that, she left.

Quintin's knees gave out, and he dropped beside his mother's bed, tears spilling down his cheeks. Scaleg was right. Furia meant to kill him. Even if by some miracle of the On-High he made it to the Keep, it would be all too easy to bribe the few lonely guards there to poison his food. No one would ever know.

But if he *defied* her...

Sobbing, Quintin reached for his mother's cool, damp hand. "What must I do, Mother?"

She'd been sleeping so long. He was starting to forget the sound of her voice. How he longed for it now!

He returned to a memory, the one he always sought when he thought he might forget. *Hush, baby mine,* he heard his mother's whisper in his memory, *loved by the On-High. Their dragons soar above you, guarding night till day's new....And when you open up your eyes, they'll take you up into the skies....*

He could remember when he was very little, clinging to her after she snuffed out the last candle by his bedside. *Will you stay with me all night, Mum?*

His father laughed from the door. *And leave your poor father all by himself?*

My dragon hearts! she'd said. *Neither of you is brave enough to face the dark alone?*

Quintin shook his head. So did Father.

Come, then, King Wyvern, she'd said. *Prince Quintin. If I must protect you both, then I must.*

She carried him to the royal apartments and tucked him into the great canopied bed there. Then she lay on his one side, and Father lay down on his other side, and the three of them were warm and safe and together.

You'll stay with me forever, won't you, Mum?

Forever.

He watched her now, her weakened body struggling for breath. Forever was a long time, he was starting to realize.

Hopeless, Quintin gave in to his grief, and cried into the bed-clothes. *Please, On-High,* he begged. *Let her speak to me.*

And then she gasped. Deep and long and rasping.

Quintin jumped back, his breath catching in his throat. "Mother?"

But as suddenly as it had come, the breath left her, slowly, painfully, and she settled again—shallow, quiet rasps, her chest barely rising and falling.

No. The On-High would not grant him his wish tonight.

He was alone.

A strong gust of cool night air rushed into the room, threatening to blow out the fire. Quintin leapt to his feet, afraid the chill would be enough to kill his mother, and stopped.

A shadow, big and yellow-eyed, sat hunched on the balustrade. The creature lifted its head and spread wide its wings—a single flap that nearly knocked Quintin down.

And then a chirrup. The happy chirp he knew.

"Umbra," he breathed, hardly believing his eyes. He walked out onto the balcony and glanced over the side, to the city below. There was no way to climb from the mountain to the balustrade. The only way was to fly.

A laugh, sudden and surprising even to Quintin, escaped him, and he grabbed the dragon's stony beak. "When did this happen, Umbra? You're flying already!"

The little dragon must be the youngest in history to fly. Draco himself had been twenty, and everyone thought that made him the strongest Shadow Dragon ever born of Dracogart.

"How proud Draco would be, Umbra!" Tears pricked at Quintin's eyes. *A miracle*, he thought. Was it too much to hope the On-High would grant him one more, show him the way to save himself and his mother from Furia's clutches?

Umbra nuzzled into Quintin's neck, a low purr rattling inside her throat. No, not a purr. It was more like a whine, and she pressed herself against him so hard he worried he might fall over. Umbra was crying, upset.

"I know, girl," he said, patting the sharp scales behind the fins that lined her cheek. "I'm so sorry about your father."

A blast of hot air hissed from her nostrils—a sorrowful sigh—and she rested her head on Quintin's shoulder.

"I lost my father too." Quintin wrapped his arms around the High Beast's neck. "We're the same, you and me. Aren't we?"

With a grunt of agreement from Umbra, Quintin's aching throat overwhelmed him, and the tears blurred his vision. He squeezed her tight. "Furia is sending me to the Highest Keep tomorrow. What am I going to do, Umbra?"

He didn't expect an answer. Just like his mother, what voice did Umbra have to lend him? But answer she did, just the same.

The young dragon's black velvet wings spread open, ready to take to the air. She was magnificent and terrifying like this. Where was the gangly, sweet dragonet he'd spent hours with in the mountains? She barked at him and looked at her back.

Quintin didn't understand. He took a step backward. "Steady, girl."

The dragon huffed, two puffs of gray smoke rising from her nostrils. She looked at her back again, then at Quintin, and flicked her wings.

She was trying to tell him something.

"You want me to climb on your back?"

She grunted, satisfied. But Quintin wasn't so sure. A High Beast was sacred. Riding a Shadow Dragon would be an offense to the On-High, wouldn't it? The only dragonrider in Dracogart was the Head of the House of the Shadow Dragons—and that wasn't him. And not only that—the young dragon had only just learned to fly.

"No, Umbra," he said. "I couldn't possibly—"

And then his mother gasped again. He spun to see her back arched, as if she was trying to rise.

"Mother!" He ran to her side, helpless as she tried to fill her broken lungs. Her mouth bobbed open and shut, a sound like steam escaping her. "Mother, what is it?"

She tried again, her mouth struggling to form whatever she was trying to say. "*Go*," she said, faintly, desperately. "*Now!*"

"Go?" he said, clutching her hand. "I can't leave you."

Her grip on his hand tightened. He wanted her to open her eyes. To see him. But whatever strength had found her, she used it only to speak. "*Go*," she groaned.

She wanted him to leave. She wanted him to escape. Terrified, he glanced back at the young dragon, huffing impatiently on the balcony. She wanted him to leave with Umbra.

The dragon screamed, a shrill, haunting cry that echoed over Mount Draccus.

And voices echoed in the halls—soldiers.

And Furia.

He saw her, through the door, at the end of the hall, Shade Guards at her sides. "I want that dragon in irons!" she shouted.

Quintin's heart thundered in his chest. Chains? For a High Beast? Unthinkable!

"If the beast is fledged," she continued, "we can't have her flying off! She is the future of this kingdom! Young Quintin has gone mad in his grief—seize him!"

The Shade Guards rushed forward.

Umbra screamed, flapping her wings, the wind pushing Quintin onto the bed and knocking the men down.

"*Go*," his mother rasped again.

And as he watched the Shade Guards scramble to their feet, he knew his mother was right. He'd asked the On-High for her voice this night, and the On-High had granted his prayer. She had spoken. It was time to listen.

"Hold on for me, Mum," he said into her ear. "As long as you can."

And he ran for the balustrade. Ran for Umbra. And as soon as he did, the dragon rushed him, her head bowed low as she scooped it between his legs and forced him onto her back. Quintin cried out, clinging to her haunches as he heard Furia and the men shouting, and saw the ground just beyond her tail fall away. Umbra was flying, and Quintin was backward.

But the dragon just kept climbing, the gaping faces of stunned Shade Guards shrinking to nothing but grains of sand, the peaks of Mount Draccus turning to needle points beneath them, Quintin's stomach switching places with his heart. Umbra let out a screech of victory, leveling off just beneath the clouds. Quintin clung to her back, squirming as much as he dared, to turn around and face the right direction. He squeezed his eyes closed, so tight he thought they might fall back inside his skull. He was too afraid to look down.

"Oh please, oh please, oh please don't drop me," he said, again and again, hoping the On-High heard his prayers—and ignored this blasphemy.

But Umbra wasn't worried. She soared through the sky the way a fish moved through water, smooth and relaxed and at peace. Eventually, the sound and feeling of the powerful beat of her wings convinced Quintin to open his eyes. The night spread out ahead of them, black and thick and cool. The wispy clouds veiled the lights of the stars, twinkling through their mists like the windows of a cosmic city. The land below them, hills and valleys and trees and rivers, seemed to bow as they passed over. This was Umbra's world. The sky was her domain. And with her father gone, Umbra was ready to rule over all.

The Queen of Shadow Dragons had made her choice already. She chose Quintin.

But why? A slope mouse, the gamesmaster had called him. And indeed, here he was, clinging to Umbra like a frightened rodent.

But he had to be brave now. Had to keep his wits. Had to figure out where exactly the pair of them were going to go. Difficult, for he had no plan. He'd left in such a rush, he hadn't even had time to confer with Scaleg.

And then the message from the Oracle repeated in his mind. The Major's daughters. They'd asked for his help.

So they'd get it.

"To Tawnshire, Umbra," he told the dragon.

And Quintin couldn't help but wonder about what Scaleg had said to him earlier that night. When they read the *Star Writ* in the centuries to come, would Quintin's name be beside Umbra's in its pages?

The loyalty of the Starhound is difficult to earn.
But once he has chosen to bestow it on him who deserves it, the Starhound
is a friend and guardian for life.

—THE WRITINGS OF BERN,
On Starhounds: The Fore, *Star Writ*

EIGHTEEN

"YOU'RE more morose than usual this evening."

"Things on my mind," Lorc said, trying to keep conversation to a minimum. He had joined his father for supper in his staterooms.

"Heavy things, it seems." His father, graying and dressed in fine green velvet, stared at him intently.

Lorc said nothing, shoveling potatoes into his mouth to keep from talking. The more he spoke, the more likely his clever father would be to sniff out his intention to leave Hundford—despite Arthur expressly forbidding it.

"Something to do with those Oracles today, no doubt."

Lorc straightened, surprised. "You know about that?"

"I know everything that goes on in this castle," his father said. "A little coin placed regularly in the right pockets and a man can have ears wherever he cares to."

It was that kind of talk that made Arthur's fears of Lorc's father hard to argue with.

"So that's why you invited me to dine with you this evening. Because of the Oracles."

"Can't a father simply share a meal with his son?"

To that, Lorc only grunted.

He should have known. His father never requested that they share a dinner unless he was looking for information. Lorc usually ate with his mother and brothers in the great hall, where the entire castle gathered, nobles and servants and even the dogs. But with the queen gone, and Lorc cautious of Arthur, he had hesitantly agreed to his father's invitation.

"Your mother's disappearance," his father went on, "is no doubt the cause of your glumness."

"It doesn't help."

"Well, stop it," his father said. "War is a duty of the Head of Household. And death is a consequence of that duty."

"So you know," Lorc said slowly.

"Of course."

Lorc wasn't all that surprised at his father's lack of sensitivity. The man had always been as cold and hard as granite—that was what made him so unpopular in Mama's court.

"And you'd do well to accept the reality of that," his father continued. "Because with your mother gone, change will come quickly to Hundford."

Lorc raised an eyebrow, surprised to hear his father speak the same sentiment his older brother had voiced by the well. "Arthur thinks so too."

"He does, does he?" His father sniffed, folding his hands over his plate. "Well, no doubt that ungulate Arcas will want to bypass me and push Arthur to the front of the line. He'd *love* to install himself as a regent over his stiff-necked son—and then he'd love to see him king. Major, even."

Lorc pushed his peas around with his fork.

Lord Arcas was Arthur's father, Härkädian royalty from the House of the Ox. When young, Arcas and Conri had been forced to marry by their parents, but she had never liked him. In fact, everyone knew Conri had even resented him, for she had been in love with a handsome young Hundfordian nobleman—Chancellor Tier, Lorc's father. And thus, in turn, Arcas resented Tier. The two had hated each other for as long as Lorc had been alive, and

Lorc knew his father was right: Arcas would not want to see Tier made regent.

"I'll expect you to speak to your brother," his father said, picking venison from his teeth. "Talk some sense into him, erase whatever foolishness the Ox oaf has put into his mind."

Lorc leaned on his elbow, his mother's smiling face filling his head. "*Is* it foolishness? To see Arthur rule in Mother's place?"

His father's face darkened. "You think your arrogant brother or his mud-brained father are more knowledgeable than me to run this kingdom?"

"No," Lorc said calmly. "I just think that…Well, Arthur's almost eighteen. Suppose you were to suggest *him* as regent until the next Crowning. If you did that…perhaps people would think differently of you."

"I see. And how do people think of me, son?"

Lorc sighed, because his father knew exactly how people thought of him. He just wanted to make Lorc say it.

"I don't know," he mumbled. "Wolfsbane Day?"

Lorc watched his father, waiting for a reaction, for him to storm away from the table, hurl his plate against the wall.

They'd never spoken of Wolfsbane Day. Lorc had never wanted to lend the malicious whispers any credence, and his father had never been bothered by gossip. But still, with Mama gone—well, there was no way the two of them could ignore his father's reputation any longer.

To Lorc's surprise, his father only smirked. "Wolfsbane Day," he repeated. "Are you asking me to atone for a crime I never committed?"

Lorc shrugged. "I just think…I just think that if you stepped aside for Arthur, it might make people think again about your involvement."

His father laughed. "Very good, son. Very clever political thinking. That's exactly why *you* will be named Major at the next Northern Crowning."

Lorc rolled his eyes. It would be Arthur who competed for Major; Lorc had no intention of challenging him. He had no doubt his brother would either rule the Highen or rule Hundford. But that wouldn't stop his father from insisting on Lorc contending.

He was suddenly glad to be leaving Hundford. Glad not to have to be around for all the sniping and whispering and struggling for power that would erupt now that a regency was up for the taking. It was not what Mama would want. Would she even be properly mourned, with Arcas and Tier vying for dominance?

"Still," his father went on, "I should like you to speak to Arthur for me, let him know that I am the only qualified person for the position of regent. Emphasize to him that it is the only responsible move for Hundford. He gives you a hard time, I know. But he listens to you, he really does."

Lorc had grown tired of this discussion, tired of this tug-of-war between his brother and father that put him in the middle. "Can we just speak of something else, please?"

"If you wish." His father cocked an eyebrow. "Why don't you tell me about the Oracle's message, then."

"But you already know that Mother...You know everything."

"Let me hear you tell me anyway."

Lorc didn't want to, but he knew Father expected an answer. His fingers tightened on his fork. Arthur wouldn't like him telling Father anything about the message, he was certain. "It's just a ridiculous message sent by the Major's daughter."

"The Major's daughter? Ursula Lourdes, yes?"

"It's nothing, Father," Lorc said. "You know how the Lourdes girls are. Spoiled and silly, everyone knows that. Anyway, I don't think I'm really supposed to talk about it."

"Arthur has instructed you not to tell me?" his father asked, disdain in his voice. "Arthur is giving you orders now, is he?"

"No," Lorc said, even though it was true—Arthur was certainly giving out orders.

"Let me tell you something, son," said his father. "You are just as much a prince as he is. You don't obey commands—you give them."

On that, his father was right. Lorc certainly didn't obey Arthur's commands. But he shoved more potato into his mouth, eager to be done with the whole discussion. He shouldn't have said anything at all.

His father laughed, suddenly amused.

"Oh, that cocky, spineless manure-pusher!" Father loved to make fun of Arthur and Prince Arcas for their Härkädian roots. "So the needle is already threaded. I can see that Arthur is *quite* sure that with your mother gone he and his father will take control of Hundford!"

Lorc's eyes dropped to his plate, his appetite dissolving. Arthur had said his orders were to keep them all safe. He didn't like to think his father might be right, and that Arthur was only acting in his own interests.

He pushed the food away. He had no stomach for politics.

"Well, they can think what they want," Lorc's father said. "What happens next will be beyond the both of them, anyway. I'll make sure of it."

"What happens next?" Lorc asked, uneasy with how pleased his father seemed to be.

"Hundford will seek stability, my son. Just like the rest of the Highen. We will bring them that."

Lorc frowned.

He didn't like that his father was already planning to pit Lorc against his brother.

He didn't like that Arthur didn't trust him enough to go to Tawnshire and answer the call of the Major's daughters.

But mostly, he didn't like Hundford without his mother. It felt colder, darker, the forest that surrounded the estate's gates now stretching, reaching, crawling through every crack and cranny of the manor, ready to pull it all to the ground.

The time to leave was now.

When night fell over Hundford, the shadows cast by the trees so dark not even the starflies could soften them, Lorc waited for the manor to sleep.

Finally, when the only sound to be heard was the chirping of crickets, he left.

He snuck outside easily, dressed in a simple tunic and a cloak pinned with a Starhound cast in silver. Moving quickly, he slid into the stables without being seen, and then saddled up Septimus, Arthur's prized red stallion. Arthur always rode Septimus, and Lorc was usually left with whatever was available. But tonight, Septimus was free for the taking. Arthur would be mad, but, Lorc reasoned, Arthur was going to be mad anyway.

If he was going to defy his brother's orders, he might as well do it atop his brother's horse.

When the guards changed shifts, groggy, hungry, and cold, Lorc passed through the shadowed grounds without being noticed, for the Manor had no curtain wall and was open to the vastness of the forest, protection enough from the world.

He went unseen...except by a single boy carrying fresh goat's milk for the hounds' breakfast.

The boy gaped at Septimus, and Lorc wondered if he'd made a mistake—Septimus was, without a doubt, the finest horse anyone had ever seen. No wonder the child took note. How many other people Lorc passed would stare at his horse?

And then the child's eyes met his, and Lorc saw them bulge with recognition before he stared at the ground and continued on his way.

Lorc dug his heels into Septimus's side. They had to hurry.

When he was well beyond the bounds of the estate, he turned the encounter over in his mind. Whether the boy was loyal to Arcas or to Tier (or to no one), Lorc couldn't be sure—both of them had their spies. He was sure of only one thing: when the sun came up, the boy would tell *someone*. And *someone* would tell *someone else*. And Arthur and Lorc's father would come to learn that he had left. And then it wouldn't be long before they sent someone to drag him home.

Lorc rode as fast as he could for the rest of the night, crossing miles and miles and miles.

He kept to the trees and away from villages and towns, passing through cold-shadowed forest for hours, his hood pulled low over his head. He was grateful for the weight of the thick woolen cloak he'd chosen.

Finally, the cedars began to give way to open sky, and golden fields of wheat stretched out before him, silver by the light of the setting moon. The Härkädian border wouldn't be much farther. Lorc could be there by daybreak. Septimus had never slowed—when other horses would have been slick with sweat, his breathing hadn't even changed.

"Well done, Septimus," Lorc said. "I can see why Arthur likes you best."

The horse gave a snort, and Lorc grinned smugly. After that performance, he needn't worry about Arthur sending anyone after him. No other horse could catch them.

"Thirsty, are you?" Lorc asked. "You must be, after all that."

Septimus whinnied.

So it was settled. They'd stop for a quick rest. A drink. Some breakfast. And then cross through Härkädia to Tawnshire on the other side.

In the distance, Lorc could see the beginnings of the Drakkan Range; on the farthest horizon, its jagged obsidian teeth rose high and scraped the sky. In the nearest foothills, the few lights of a small village were beginning to burn.

That would do. They could find an inn where Septimus could drink at the trough and Lorc could pop inside for an anonymous meal of spiced sausage and barley porridge. His stomach growled. Spiced sausage was a Härkädian specialty.

He clicked his heels, and Septimus waded into the wheat as the red light of dawn seeped into the sky behind the mountains. The air was cool with morning dew, and Lorc felt the chill slide across his neck, raising gooseflesh.

The world was flat here, between the deep forest and the Drakkan peaks. No hills. Barely any trees. Just fields and fields of grasses and grains. A wide, yawning openness that left nothing secret. Growing up in the endless woods of Hundford, he'd never felt so exposed. So naked.

He realized: he was vulnerable here.

Septimus stopped, his head lifted. Lorc watched the horse's floppy ears snap to attention.

Instantly, he understood. They were being followed.

Septimus sidestepped, stomping nervously, and Lorc looked back the way they had come. The white trunks of silver birches at the edge of the cedar forest made shadows easier to see, but still, the thick brush of juniper would cover anything smaller than Septimus.

He hopped off the anxious stallion, drawing his daggers.

And then he heard a whine.

A very familiar whine.

Lorc relaxed, putting away his daggers. "Well, all right then! Come out. No sense hiding anymore—I know you're there!"

Out he came, head low and ears flat against his head.

Argos.

Lorc faced the Starhound, hands on his hips. "You do know Arthur's going to blame me for this, don't you? Go home, before he thinks I told you to come with me!"

Argo's tail swung anxiously as he looked into the trees and back at Lorc. The Starhound's eyes pleaded with him to stay.

"It's not that I'm not happy to see you," Lorc explained. "You know I am. But I really don't need to give Arthur another reason to be mad at me. And if he thinks I made you leave with me, he'll run me through with his sword before he gives me a chance to explain."

Argos's cheeks puffed up and he let out a quiet *woof.*

Well.

The dog had already followed him this far, keeping impressive pace with Septimus. And perhaps it was unwise, sending Argos back alone when they were so far from home. If something happened to the High Beast, Lorc would *really* be in trouble.

He tried not to smile as he patted his leg for Argos. "Oh, come on, you lousy mongrel."

A fat pink tongue flopped out the side of the Starhound's mouth, and he bounded merrily from his spot in the bushes to join Lorc.

Septimus whinnied, decidedly against this new development.

"Settle down, Argos," laughed Lorc. "You're upsetting Septimus."

But Argos didn't care. He weaved between the horse's legs, vaulting out in front to lead the way to the Härkädian village.

You and that pup have a special bond, his mother had said. *You must thank the On-High for that blessing.*

Lorc took hold of Septimus's bridle and looked up at the star-sugared sky. He *was* grateful. Lorc was the black sheep of the Hound brothers. The boy who escaped Wolfsbane Day. He'd grown used to life without friends.

But now, with Argos, Lorc realized he had one.

And he was glad of the Starhound's company.

But still, Argos was a High Beast. And if people didn't, by some miracle, notice Septimus, they would *certainly* notice a Starhound. A Starhound would incite talk, and talk could reach ears Lorc didn't want to reach—Arthur and his father could be the *least* of his problems. In Härkädia, away from home and so close to Tawn-shire, with the Minor overthrowing the Major…They would have to avoid the village.

Stomach growling, Lorc led Septimus and Argos west, away from breakfast and deeper into the sprawling, grassy wilds. He had oats enough for Septimus, and salt boar that would have to do for himself and Argos.

And anyway, it was better they didn't stop. If they kept going, they could be in Tawnshire by the time the sun set again.

...no ordinary fire. For starflame is a thoughtful blaze, with a will of its own, and a desire to please the On-High.

—THE WRITINGS OF THUBAN,
The Mysteries of the On-High: The Star Majors, *Star Writ*

NINETEEN

"Have you gone mad?" Ursula's voice echoed through the rafters of the Oracle House, horrified at the young Keeper's suggestion.

One of the younger Oracles, hands wringing and head shaking, agreed. "No, no, no, it is blasphemy!"

Aster hadn't left her perch by the window all evening, watching the crowds come and go as word of the great Hemoth Bear hiding in the Oracle House spread through Tawnshire. The offerings of Berenice Locks were so thick they carpeted the whole square, smothering the cobblestones. The sun had begun to fall low behind the buildings, and the people knelt among the locks, praying quietly to the On-High.

Ursula was right, Aster knew. If they left with Alcor, the people would swarm him. Whenever they decided to open the doors and step out into Tawnshire, the bear was too big to go unnoticed. Uncle Bram would find them immediately.

But Haven or no, Uncle Bram was coming for them. Escape was the only option.

And it might be possible with the bear boy's plan. A plan that didn't sit well with Ursula or the Oracles.

"It's the only way we can hope to get Alcor out of here without anyone seeing!" cried Dev.

"Burn down the Oracle House?" gasped another Oracle. "On-High, save us!"

To Aster, the Oracles seemed a nervous parliament of owls, hooting and shrieking in horror at the idea of their safe little nest being destroyed.

"There would be smoke, flames—complete chaos!" Dev insisted. "The smokier the better! The Shiver Woods aren't far from here. With enough smoke, we could smuggle Alcor onto a side street, then out of town, then into the forest! No one would even be sure which direction we'd gone!"

Ursula shook her head. "With everything against us already, I can't risk adding the wrath of the On-High to our troubles."

"But Alcor *belongs* to the On-High, don't you see? How could the stars punish us for saving their Highest of Children?"

Aster recognized the two Oracles who had met them the day they had arrived on the steps of the Oracle House. One younger. One older. Standing on either side of Ursula. Both listened thoughtfully before they finally spoke.

"Your plans are confident," said the older. "So sure the will of the On-High is on your side."

"What do you mean?" asked the bear boy.

She shrugged. "Starflame. Not like fire. More volatile. More clever. Each flame is a piece of a star. It *thinks*, young Keeper. How can you be sure it thinks as you do?"

Thinks. Aster glanced at the empty jars and felt a chill run through her.

Dev shifted on his feet, eyes darting between Ursula and the Oracles. Finally, he held out his arms, at a loss, and let them drop uselessly at his sides. "We have to try. Or Bram Lourdes will take Alcor and the Highen for himself." He looked at the rows and rows of glasses, empty in the last red light of sunset pouring through the oculus. "Please, On-High, hear us—hear us and burn this house! Help us save Alcor!"

The rest of the red cloaks flapped and squawked again. But

the two Oracles from the steps, the younger and older, were quiet. Pensive. Considering.

Finally, the younger raised a hand and the others fell quiet. "The Keeper's plan is dangerous," she said.

"Mmm," said the older. "But does danger make a choice the *wrong* choice?"

The Oracles watched the old woman as she rubbed her chin.

"But this house, Favored Ones," said one of the others to the two, "this is all we have."

The old woman's eyebrow rose. "Have it, do we? What do you think we have? The On-High have it. And since the House is had by they, it is only they who can or cannot agree with the Keeper's plan."

Muffled stirrings of the people in the square called Aster's attention back to the window. Those who'd been praying were on their feet now, their backs to the Oracle House as they watched something approach from the direction of the bridge. From the way the people reached for shovels and boards, Aster knew exactly what had upset them.

"Ursula, the Frosmen!"

The Oracle House was silent, eyes on Aster as she pressed her nose to the glass.

Torchlight reflected off the angry faces of the worshippers as horsebacked Frosmen flooded the square. They trampled over the Berenice Locks, blades held at the ready.

One man rode in slowly, confidently, behind the rest, and Aster held her breath. He was small compared to the others, but still he commanded the attention of everyone who watched. She'd always known him as an attention-getter, boisterous and loud, exciting in a way the other nobles who came to the Manor could never be. But this—she'd never seen him like this. Rigid. Tense. A scowl where she was used to seeing a grin.

"Uncle Bram," Aster breathed.

Ursula appeared beside her, the Oracles and Dev all trying to catch a glimpse of the troubling scene behind them.

Her sister's breath trembled. Seeing their father's brother in his battle armor, hard-faced and furious, was surreal. And yet it was more real than anything they'd seen since they left the Manor. He was here, really here. And it made the truth of what he'd done so much more real too.

His voice rose up in the square. "Ursula Lourdes! Come out, by order of the Minor!"

Ursula's hand gripped tight to Aster's. Her eyes were glossy with fright, and her throat bobbed as she swallowed. "This is it."

"What? You're not going out there, are you?"

"He called for me."

Dev shook his head. "No, you have to wait. The starflame's alive, Ursula, and it heard us." He swallowed. "It will burn down this building. And we'll escape."

"We can't wait for starflame," she said as Uncle Bram roared her name again. "He'll storm the House if I don't face him."

"He can't storm *this* House," said one of the Oracles, appalled at the suggestion. "On-High forbid!"

"He can," Ursula said, grimly. "And he will. Nothing is sacred to him."

"Even if you go out there," said Dev, "he'll only kill you. He's here for Alcor."

Kill you. Aster could hardly believe the words.

They were true, she knew that much. Ursula was a direct competitor for the title of Major. Her very breath was a threat to him. But how they'd come to this, she couldn't begin to fathom.

Ursula exhaled. "What would Father do?"

Aster didn't want to tell her what they both knew—Jasper Lourdes would face the Minor. But she also knew that the boy was right—if Ursula went out there, Uncle Bram would kill her and capture the Oracle House anyway. Ursula facing Uncle Bram would only delay the inevitable.

"I know what kind of Major I want to be now," Ursula said. "Do you?"

"Me?" The question struck Aster like a blow to the gut. Of course she did, didn't she? She'd imagined it all her life—a warrior queen, a daring leader—but that was all pretend, just make-believe.

Ursula released Aster's hand and marched to the doors.

"Wait, Ursula!"

But Aster was too late. The massive oak doors burst open, the din of the crowd filling the Oracle House like thunder. Aster leapt down from the window, desperate to run to her sister's side, but the bear boy grabbed her around the waist, pulling her back.

"No!" said Dev. "He'll take you both!"

"We can't let her do this!"

"She's done it, Aster. It's done. You'll only give him what he wants if you go out there."

What he wants. Both daughters of Major Jasper Lourdes. Both threats to his reign.

The old Oracle placed her wrinkled hand on Aster's forehead. "Be still, Daughter of the Major. Where one sister walks, the other is not meant to follow."

"What? I *want* to follow!"

Dev's grip tightened. "Stop, Aster. He'll kill you. Stop."

The old woman's eyes met Aster's, their redness, like dragonfire, blazing. "The sister plays her part this day, as she must. And one day soon, Aster Lourdes, you will have to play yours. But not today."

Aster's eyes began to sting. Uncle Bram had already taken the Manor, had taken her parents. Could she really let Uncle Bram take her sister, too?

"We can still help her, Aster," Dev whispered into her ear. "We just have to wait for the starflame."

The starflame. She glanced at the window. The daylight had almost completely faded. The On-High would come soon. The On-High would set the House ablaze and set them free.

Maybe.

Aster scrambled back to the window, nose pressed against the glass as her sister stepped out before the crowd.

The people who had been throwing things at the Minor's men were still now, eyes fixed on Ursula. Despite her dirty hair and the bloodstains on her gown, she looked magnificent in the glint of the frost pearls that winked to life in the twilight.

Ursula spoke then, her voice muffled by the glass. Frantically, Aster's hands clawed along the seam of the window, desperately searching for the latch. The bear boy's hands reached around her and clicked it open. It would only go a sliver, but it was enough.

Uncle Bram's laugh carried over the crowd. "I've come to take you home, dearest niece."

Ursula raised her chin. "The home you attacked and took for your own, you mean?"

There were murmurs among the people, and Aster watched her uncle. His expression darkened, his shoulders hunching just enough to betray his anger. But he was quick to recover, straightening and smiling in that way Aster had always thought was the most genuine smile she'd ever seen. He'd fooled her.

"Attacked? Lady Ursula, I'm afraid you are mistaken. I never—"

"You attacked my father's estate, Uncle. Your men stormed it and tried to—"

Uncle Bram laughed. "I must apologize, my young niece, if my men frightened you. I suppose, after such a sheltered life, the sight of armed soldiers is not one you are accustomed to. But my Frosmen and I have come here to Tawnshire for your protection."

Aster's eyes flicked to the crowd. They shuffled on their feet, looking from Ursula to Uncle Bram and whispering to one another.

"Dragon spit!" Ursula shouted. "Mizar, like my father, has been murdered. By you! You dare show your face here, before the On-High, before the people of Tawnshire? After you have committed the most heinous of crimes a man can commit? *Astrocide!*"

Uncle Bram ascended the steps, hand on the hilt of his sword, and Aster could feel the blood pumping in her ears. "What's he doing?" she asked. "He won't kill her *here*, will he?"

"He can't," the bear boy assured her. "She's on the steps of Oracle House. The people would riot. She still has sanctuary."

But what good was the protection of sanctuary against a blade swung at her sister's throat? What good was a riot after her sister was already dead? "He'll cut her down!"

"He won't," Dev insisted, a firm hand on her shoulder. "Think. If he hurts her in front of this crowd, he'll make a martyr of her."

"What do you mean?"

"If he hurts Princess Ursula in front of her own people, he'll assert himself as an enemy of Tawnshire. He *needs* the people, Aster. Needs their support if he wants them to accept Bernadine as Major one day."

Aster turned back to the window, eyes roaming over the faces in the crowd. The people of Tawnshire. They were watching. They were listening.

Uncle Bram stood before Ursula. In Aster's memory, he had always seemed rather small beside her bearlike father, but in front of her sister, he was a monster, towering over her with a menacing scowl.

Abruptly, he turned his back on her, arms open to the waiting people of Tawnshire. He was addressing them now. Their opinion—their love—was all that mattered.

"What I have done," Uncle Bram told them, "I have done for the Highen. It is true, the acts I have committed will forever condemn me in the eyes of the On-High. But good people of Tawnshire, know this—it is for you that I have sacrificed my place in the stars. It is for you that I have sacrificed my very soul."

The crowd was silent, fixed on Uncle Bram's words. He was dynamic, Aster knew that much. On his visits to the Manor, he almost rivaled her father in his ability to spin a captivating tale over the dinner table.

"Then you admit to it all," said Ursula. "And the On-High will lock your soul behind the moon with the rest of the damned."

"I have murdered my brother, yes," Uncle Bram went on, ignoring her, "and the Hemoth Bear Mizar. On-High have mercy!"

Aster ground her teeth, looking up at the night sky. She did not know as much about the On-High as her father and Keeper Rizlan would have liked, but she did know this—for Uncle Bram, there would be no mercy.

"But I did it," he continued, "because if I had not, your Major would have delivered to our enemy that which is more valuable than a man's soul—mine or anyone else's—the egg of a Shadow Dragon!"

Aster could barely contain herself. "He did it to trade for the venom from the Prism Scorpion! Because of the firelung in Dracogart! Who could argue with that?"

The bear boy shifted, refusing to meet Aster's eyes.

"What?" she demanded.

The bear boy shook his head.

"No, really, speak your mind!"

Dev shrugged. "Every Shadow Dragon egg is a gift from the On-High. Many felt it was not the Major's to give."

She glanced back out the window, and to her surprise saw nods of agreement among the people. But *why*? Surely they understood that the Major was acting in the best interests of the Highen. He was the Major! His station burdened him with hard choices, and he made the right ones!

Wolves at your back, Mother had warned them. She'd been against the trade with the Ring from the start.

Had Father made a mistake?

"My brother," said Uncle Bram, "took a great many things from this Highen. He bathed himself and his family in the finest luxuries our country had to offer, and expected you all to provide them. Taxes! Reliefs! Grain payments! Even now, you are left with rags, while his daughters are swaddled in the greatest finery. What have they done to earn such extravagance?" Uncle Bram pointed at Ursula, the frost pearls of her gown glowing an eerie white.

Aster looked down at her own clothing—the purple dress that Gatch had brought her. It was only yesterday but now seemed like ages ago. The words of her father's letter, the one Mother read at dinner, sank deeper into her heart like cold stones: *What kind of Major could we hope either of our girls would be?*

"And then," Uncle Bram went on, "he took the egg. Good people, I know, like me, you had your misgivings about delivering something most precious, most sacred to the Ring Highen." More nods of agreement, and Aster felt a churning in her gut. "The On-High entrusted the care of the Shadow Dragons to us! In front of their House, good people of the Bear Highen, I am confident when I say that if the On-High, in their infinite wisdom, wanted the Ring to have the egg of the Shadow Dragon, they would have entrusted the Ring with a flock of their own!"

Aster watched the faces nodding, the ears soaking up everything Uncle Bram was telling them. And she remembered the whispers of the servants in the halls of the Manor. *Betrayed us*, they'd said.

"Who among you have lost the people you love to illness—your mothers, fathers, your children…your wives?" Uncle Bram's voice broke then, and when Aster looked at him, his head was bowed. Uncle Bram had lost his wife, Aunt Gwynlin. But Aster didn't understand. Aunt Gwynlin had been ill. The Heart Frost killed her. Uncle Bram couldn't blame Father for her death, could he? "Is the king of the Ring Highen, our enemy, worth more than they were? I ask you: What has my brother ever sacrificed of his own? Nothing!"

There were shouts of agreement from the crowd.

"Did the Death Chaser chase death from you? Could he keep it from your lives?"

More voices rose up, fists punching air, and Aster's blood ran cold. What was Uncle Bram telling them? That the Death Chaser was no Death Chaser after all? It was written in the pages of the *Star Writ*! It was truth! Aster's father had chased the Nightlocks from the Highen. He'd saved the people from that death.

And yet, with every word from Uncle Bram, they seemed to be forgetting.

"No!" Uncle Bram asserted. "Just as he could not keep it from mine. Now he asks you all to sacrifice the egg of the Shadow Dragon. He wants to give it to the Ring so that *they* may keep death away. Well, it is not his to give! It is yours, good people! He stole it from you!"

Stole it? But Father was Major. It *was* his to give...wasn't it?

"People of Tawnshire," her uncle finished, "I ask not for your forgiveness. My sins are too great, and I am prepared to answer for them when that day comes. What I ask of you is your faith. Faith that the change I will bring to you, the new empire I will build out of the ashes of my brother's reign, will bring you the wealth, the prosperity, the piety, but above all, the *security* you deserve and have always deserved!"

The people were roaring now, every one of them cheering for her traitorous uncle.

Somehow, after all he'd done, he'd made her father out to be the traitor instead. As though the Major had torn the egg from the grip of every person in Tawnshire. How many in the Highen were upset by her father's decision to trade with the Ring to save Dracogart? How many of her father's own men believed he'd betrayed them? But they *couldn't* believe such a thing, could they? Uncle Bram was a liar. Were the people of Tawnshire, her father's people, so unhappy with the deal her father had made that they were willing to follow his murderer?

"Aster." The bear boy's hands were on her shoulders, and gently he turned her away from the window to the jars that lined the walls. A faint white light pulsed at their centers. Small, but growing. "The starflame is coming."

Aster turned back to the window, hope swelling inside her heart. "They're coming, Ursula," she whispered.

Aster watched as Uncle Bram grabbed hold of Ursula's arm and dragged her forward. "People of Tawnshire!" he cried. "I come to the House of the Oracles not for the grace of the On-High. I come to take back the Hemoth Bear. Your Hemoth Bear! Grant me your blessing!"

And voices rang out. But not the voices of the people.

These were the voices of the stars.

Blessed is he who hears the voices of the On-High, for their voices are quiet and often ignored by the ears of man.

—THE WRITINGS OF BERN,
On Oracles: The Fore, *Star Writ*

TWENTY

ASTER leapt down off the windowsill. The sound was growing around them, a resonant, ghostly ringing like singing glass. The jars swelled brighter, the On-High beaming as their voices climbed the walls.

"The On-High have come!" Dev cried to the nearest Oracle. "Quick! Ask their permission, ask that we may use their flame!"

But the Oracles brought their hands to their ears, groaning and wailing from the volume. Aster's hands flew to her own ears, the sound piercing into the meat of her mind, so loud and unrelenting she wanted to run out into Uncle Bram's forces just to get away.

"It is too loud!" the old Oracle shouted. "The voices of the On-High are powerful! We've never had to listen to so many at one time!"

So many. Because of what Uncle Bram had done. All the heavens had come to punish him, because there was no forgiveness for such crimes. No forgiveness for taking her father from her. And now he would try to take her sister?

The On-High wouldn't have it.

And neither would Aster Lourdes.

She stormed over to the closest glowing jar and took it down from the shelf.

"Aster, wait!" Dev shouted.

But there was no more waiting.

She slammed the jar into the floor, Alcor howling with fright as the glass shattered and the ball of white light spilled out onto the stone.

A sudden silence fell over the Oracle House.

Everyone was still, hypnotized by the light spreading around Aster's feet. It was more like glowing smoke than actual fire, reaching outward as if feeling its surroundings. Its light was fiercely hot, and she stepped back, the heat too much for her toes.

It thinks, the Oracle had said. Starflame, Aster could see now, was a thing alive. A living, sentient being. And it was free.

A single, quiet hum rose up from it. A voice.

"What's it saying?" Dev whispered.

The older Oracle held her horn to her ear. She closed her eyes, her head dropping back, and then she righted herself and stared straight at him. "'Release us.'"

Aster didn't need to be told a second time. She hopped over the spreading light and reached for the nearest jar, breaking it on the floor. Another glass crashed to her left—the bear boy, pulling jars down from their ledges. The Oracles wailed with each shatter, others clutching their horns and whispering prayers for forgiveness. More crashing to Aster's right—the older Oracle was breaking jars.

A thrill worked its way through her as the dark Oracle House blazed with the white glow of the stars, smoky pale light whipping and weaving along the ground, climbing for the rafters, eating at the wooden beams. Aster laughed, reaching for the next jar and dropping it, and the next and the next until the cavernous room was so bright she had to shield her eyes.

The singing of the flames was a deafening chorus now, its ghostly pitch echoing up toward the sky. And as the voices rose, so did the smell of burning—not like regular woodsmoke, but something else: melting iron, sugar browned in butter.

And the *heat*. It licked at her skin, burned her nose as she breathed.

She held tight to the jar in her hand, the last one she had grabbed, the little flame begging to be set free. But she didn't break it. The Oracle House was already ablaze. There was no stopping it now—they had to get out. Soon. Before the flames burned them up.

She could hear shouting beyond the doors—the Minor's men. They saw the smoke.

She squinted through the brightness to see the Oracles, light weaving in and around their legs, over their arms, coiling around their necks, reaching up to the rafters. They clutched their horns, reciting prayers. They weren't burning. They didn't seem to feel the heat at all.

"Aster!" The bear boy ran right through the fire, the *Star Writ* clutched to his chest, Alcor stomping nervously behind him. "Aster, we have to go! It's time!"

"Your feet!" Her eyes were wide as she watched the flames encircle the bear boy's boots. "You're not burning!"

Why did Dev not feel the flames? Why did he not burn? Why did the Oracles not burn?

"What? Aster! The On-High are helping us! Now's our chance! We have to leave!"

Leave. Yes, they did. The smoke, the flames—they could sneak away in the chaos. *But Ursula—*

"My sister!" Aster screamed.

"This way!" His hand took a firm hold of her wrist and he pulled her through the flames. They nipped at her heels and singed her skirts, and she shrieked, trying to jump over the streams of starfire.

Alcor was hurrying after them, groaning as he tried to avoid the threads of light. He wasn't agile enough; there was too much starfire for his massive body to avoid. But it encircled him the same way it encircled the Oracles, weaving over and around without burning.

Why was it only Aster who felt the heat of the stars? She looked at the jar she was still carrying, as if the answers were inside. Weren't they? If she could hear the voices of the stars, would the little flame tell her why she burned?

Dev stopped at a small wooden door at the back of the Oracle House, shoving the *Star Writ* into her arms. She nearly dropped the jar trying to balance both objects.

With a loud cry, Dev rammed the door with his shoulder. Aster began to cough, her lungs aching for fresh air. Dev coughed too, stopping between rams to clear his throat. Finally, Alcor pushed them aside, too frightened by the light and the sound to tolerate another second, and plowed the door open with his head, sending splinters flying.

They staggered out into the night, screams and shouts echoing from the front of the Oracle House. Back here, there was nothing but dark, shuttered homes.

"Come on!" Dev coughed. "We have to reach the Shiver Woods!"

He took back the *Star Writ*. Aster glanced down at the jar she was left with, its little flame the only light to be seen.

"Hurry!" Dev said, guiding Alcor forward.

"No!" Aster took off at a run, rounding the side of the Oracle House. "I have to get Ursula!"

Dev yelled at her to stop, but she wouldn't. As she ran, she glanced up at the windows that lined the Oracle House—blazing white with starflame, smoke billowing through the seams. The hum of the stars, a phantom choir celebrating its freedom, was almost louder than the shouts of soldiers and townsmen.

When she came to the edge of the House she stopped and peeked around the side. The square was in chaos, people running and screaming. Some were carrying buckets of water, hurling them onto the House, but it was no use. The flames exploded from every opening, a frightening blaze of celestial light screaming out at the Frosmen. The Frosmen's horses reeled at the chaos, screeching in alarm and rearing on their hind legs. Even Hewitt Pire, the Frosman who had chased them into the Oracle House, was nearly tossed off his frightened mare. He shouted orders, his words swallowed up by the commotion.

Only one soldier at the center of the garrison kept calm—Uncle Bram. He spoke to two men on the ground in front of him, giving orders. Between the two men, Aster saw her—Ursula.

"Urs—"

Before Aster could call out, a hand came down on her mouth, pulling her back around the corner.

"Quiet!" Dev hissed. "Do you want them to capture you, too?"

Aster looked back at the men with her sister. They had her firmly by each arm. No amount of Ursula's struggling could shake them off. She was their prisoner. Aster's heart sank as Ursula was loaded onto one of their horses, a Frosman in the saddle behind her, and carried off into the night. Back to the Manor, no doubt.

"Aster, we have to go." Dev tugged at her arm. "They're coming for us."

He was right. Hewitt Pire had moved his horse up the steps, shouting orders at his men, who had begun ramming the doors to the Oracle House. They wanted Alcor.

Reluctantly, Aster tucked the little jar into the pocket of her skirt and let Dev pull her along, back to the Hemoth Bear. The beast bounced on his front paws—his familiar nervous *bope bope bope* dwarfed by the sounds of the night.

They hurried together through dark alleys and damp byways, the commotion at the center of the city louder than any sound they could make. The fire raged, lighting the night sky red, and men and horses clattered up and down the city's thoroughfares, raising the alarm.

Finally, the three of them passed safely out of Tawnshire Town and into the trees of the Shiver Woods at its edges. The safety of the forest enveloped them, and they paused to watch through the leaves as the starflame ate away at what was left of the Oracle House: they could see its tower smoking, then collapsing, above the rest of the city.

"It *worked*," Dev laughed. "The On-High saved us! We're safe!"

He beamed at Aster, the excitement of escape catching up with him. But Aster couldn't return it. She didn't feel safe. She felt alone.

Ursula was gone. The On-High hadn't saved her.

Uncle Bram had stood on the steps of a holy house—*admitting to astrocide!*—and the On-High hadn't punished him.

Aster pulled the jar from her pocket, looking at the little glowing ball inside. The On-High's fire had burned Aster, and only Aster. Why?

An answer began to form in her head—from where she wasn't sure—but it was there all the same. Her heart, maybe?

Because the On-High hate you.

A sound, long and low and sorrowful, rose from somewhere deep inside Alcor, up through his massive chest and throat, peaking in a wail. It echoed her misery.

"It's all right, Alcor," said Dev, taking the bear's muzzle in his hands. "You're safe now. Everything's all right."

But the bear knew everything wasn't all right, just as surely as Aster did.

The wailing grew louder as Alcor raised his head skyward, a mournful howl sent out to the On-High. The power of it vibrated inside Aster's head, and she knew his cries would call the attention of the Frosmen. "That's too loud!"

"I don't know what's wrong with him!" said Dev. "He's never done this before!" He reached for Alcor's mouth, trying to pull his head down and quiet him, but the bear was too strong.

"Make him stop!" Aster begged.

"I'm trying!"

But there was no stopping it. Alcor's cries echoed on the night air, climbing ever higher into the star-speckled sky.

*And the High Beasts raised their voices to the On-High, as one
they roared mightily into the night. And the On-High heard their cries.*

—THE WRITINGS OF WIP,
The First Battle: The Ring Wars, *Star Writ*

TWENTY-ONE

FLYING was a cold business.

Quintin's fingertips had long ago turned to ice, and his nose was running so much the mucus had frozen to his face. He tried to wiggle his toes, but he wasn't at all sure he could feel them anymore.

He clung to Umbra's neck, resting his head against her hard, cool scales. There was a warmth deep within her he could just make out, and he pressed his cheek to her hide, hoping the heat of her dragonfire would seep into his frigid skin.

They'd been flying for ages now—one sunrise and two sunsets, all of which Quintin had watched on Umbra's back above the world. Everything looked the same from above, but Umbra seemed to fly with purpose, and he hoped that meant she had a better idea than him of her destination. So they flew. On and on and on. They'd break every now and then for Umbra to drink from a stream, but mostly, the Shadow Dragon wanted to be in the air. The clouds were her kingdom. And Quintin wished dearly he were better built to live there with her. For all its cold, it was quiet, and peaceful. A giant expanse of clear, crisp air that asked for nothing. The clouds wrapped around the flying pair, embracing them as they cut through, as though they'd been waiting for them to arrive all along.

But at night, the sky changed. It became an icy, inky emptiness that froze his skin and told him he wasn't welcome. Quintin was no dragon.

It was at night, when the On-High blinked into view, that Quintin thought most about his mother. *I love you, Mum.* Those should have been the last words he said to her. But it hadn't been the last thing he said. *Hold on for me, Mum,* he'd told her. *As long as you can.*

But what if it wasn't long enough? What if she died before Quintin could get back?

He watched the shadows of the clouds pass by through tearstained eyes. She'd been holding on for so long, his mother. He didn't even know when he *could* return.

A hiss, a spurt of smoke, escaped Umbra's nostrils, calling Quintin's attention back from thoughts of home. The dragon's head tilted slightly.

"What is it?" Quintin asked her over the wind.

Her smooth flight faltered. As her wings tipped left, Quintin's legs squeezed instinctively, his grip around her neck tightening. Her body followed her head, twisting left, changing direction.

"What's the matter, girl?"

She spat again. His eyes followed her course, trying to see what had spooked her.

There, rising up toward the stars like a great column of pillowy Härkädian sweet cream.

Smoke.

It rose from the center of a densely packed city. He sat up straighter, excitement swelling inside his chest. "That must be Tawnshire Town!"

He'd been to the capital once or twice, and from above, he recognized it just as he would on a map. There were the broad streets of Brewer's Court and Queen's Lane; there were the wharves on the Tund River; there was the Bridge of Anant. But what was burning?

Umbra brought them soaring around the column of smoke, high enough that no one would notice her black form against the dark of the sky. Quintin glanced over the Shadow Dragon's side, down toward the rooftops, and gasped, the height seizing his stomach. He'd spent all his time in the air avoiding looking down, and now he remembered why. It was frightening being up so high.

Light poked through the smoke—flames. But they were strange. White, not orange the way fire should be. People ran to and from the burning structure, trying to douse the blaze. The building, Quintin could see, was massive, with stained glass and pointed, partially collapsed turrets.

His stomach turned. "That must be the Oracle House." The girls' message had said they were waiting there.

The Shadow Dragon screeched in agreement—a mix of an eagle cry and a thunderclap.

"Umbra!" said Quintin. "I'm not sure you should be calling out like that. We don't want everyone knowing we're here, do we?"

Certainly not, if the Oracle House was under attack. Would the Minor dare order such a thing? And would his men agree to it—firing an Oracle House? Why not declare war on the On-High themselves?

Quintin watched the chaos below, his mind spinning with questions. "What do we do now, Umbra? You don't think they've been captured, do you?"

Umbra snorted. Then, without warning, she banked sharply, Quintin clinging to her scales for dear life.

"Umbra! What are you doing?"

They were descending. Quickly. Umbra was going to land.

"Umbra, don't!" Quintin shouted. "Someone will see you!"

But the dragon didn't listen, and Quintin could only watch as the dark treetops of the Shiver Woods reached up to welcome him.

Septimus snorted, shaking his mane.

"You needn't huff at me," said Lorc, smoothing out the map as he sat atop the horse. "I don't see you helping to figure it out."

Septimus just gave another snort.

"I'm not lost," Lorc insisted, for what felt like the hundredth time. "I'm just...not exactly sure where we are."

The horse tossed his head. Below, Argos was watching Lorc closely, his floppy tongue hidden in his mouth, his eyes worried.

"On-High save us!" cried Lorc. "We're not *that* lost! I said I'd get us there, and I will!"

The trees here were different than in Hundford. Bushy evergreens made it hard for starlight to break through, hard to see beyond the front of his face—and harder still to see the markings on his map. They'd crossed the boundary into Tawnshire, of that he was sure, but how close they were to the capital...he couldn't say. It was a big kingdom. The few times he'd visited, he'd traveled on the main roads with his brothers and mother, an entourage of guards and servants surrounding them. Moving in the shadows now, he'd gotten turned around.

"A little fire, then," he said decisively. "Just for some light. I'm hungry, anyway. I can't be the only one." He looked down at Argos for agreement, but the dog only looked off into the trees with a whimper.

"What about you, Septimus?"

The horse grunted unhappily.

"You're a miserable lot, you two," grumbled Lorc, dismounting. Reaching into the saddlebag for his flint, he set to work building a fire. He'd brought a loaf of bread and a jar of hickory butter-bean sauce, his favorite, and his stomach grumbled as he thought about dipping toast into the hot, spicy mix. "You'll both want to apologize when I get us back on the right track. Now, since neither of you seem to be hungry, I'm going to eat a lovely dinner by myself."

Argos licked his lips.

"Don't expect any handouts," said Lorc, gathering a little pile of sticks and arranging them the way his mother had taught him.

"Not after you doubted me. I expect that from a horse like Septimus, but you, Argos—well, frankly, I'm hurt."

The dog lowered his head, lying down in dirt.

With a couple flashes of the flint, the fire sparked, and Lorc blew until a flame caught the kindling. It worked for him every time. Mama was a very good teacher.

He opened the top on the beans and set the jar in the fire, his bread toasting just off to the side. He wondered what his mother would think about his mission to Tawnshire. He imagined her riding home to Hundford, perfectly unharmed, ready with stories of her great battle against the Ring. She'd ask to see him, and Arthur, still fuming, would tell her where he'd gone, and then she'd smile proudly, pleased with his boldness. That would be nice.

What would she think of the struggle for the regency?

Of his father trying to control Arthur?

He scooped a spoon into the beans and tasted—hot. Carefully he pulled the jar from the fire and broke his bread, smearing beans onto the warm, crispy dough. He missed her. It was a growing ache inside his heart. Neither Arthur nor his father would dare *look* at the throne if his mother were close to home. They wouldn't fight. They'd go on ignoring each other's existence, and that was just how Lorc liked it. Because it was more peaceful that way. His mother kept that peace.

Without her—he didn't like to think of the harm Arthur and his father would do to each other.

He stuffed the last of his bread into his cheeks, the beans nearly gone. He'd devoured that meal quickly. Strange that Argos hadn't begged him for any. He would've shared.

But the dog sat stiff in his spot in the dirt, not looking at Lorc. His attention was on the trees.

"You're really not hungry, are you?"

Argos didn't acknowledge him.

"You want to lick the jar?" He tossed it to the High Beast, but Argos stood, ears perked.

Lorc looked at Septimus. The horse sniffed at the ground, looking for something worth eating. Whatever had spooked Argos wasn't having any effect on him.

"What?" Lorc asked the dog. "Do you hear something?"

Argos began to whine, his tail wagging anxiously.

Lorc stood, watching the trees. He saw nothing. Heard nothing. But still the dog whined.

Unconsciously, Lorc's hand clutched the hilt of his blade. He'd never had to use it before, not in real life—he'd only ever sparred with his brothers, his armsman, and his mother. Still, he knew how to kill if he had to.

Steeling his nerves, he drew the weapon. Would it be the same to kill a man as it was to kill a deer?

Argos barked into the dark, and then, without warning, the High Beast bolted into the trees.

"Argos!" shouted Lorc.

The dog howled somewhere in the distance, and Lorc rushed after him. But away from the fire, the forest was black. He couldn't see anything, only hear—hear Argos' cries growing fainter and fainter.

"Blast it, Argos!" Lorc growled. He raced back to get Septimus, kicking earth on the fire to smother it and swinging up into the saddle. He dug his heels into the horse's side, and Septimus lurched into a gallop, plowing through the forest after the echoes of Argos's barking.

"Argos!" The High Beast was far ahead, his speed nearly better than the stallion's. They rode and rode, so long Lorc worried they were getting farther off course.

And then the barking stopped.

"Argos?" Septimus came to a halt, and Lorc listened intently to the sounds of the woods. "Argos, where are you?"

The dog didn't answer, but now Lorc could make out distant voices shouting in the night. And there was a smell, too, something like burnt caramel and a blacksmith's forge. He looked up, and above the black leaves of the trees he saw smoke. What was burning?

A dark shadow cut through the billowing clouds—too big for a bird.

Dragon?

"What in the name of the On-High...?" He followed the direction the shadow had gone. There! He could see light where the trees began to thin. They'd come to the forest's edge, and Argos was waiting for him in the dark, tail held low, gaze nervous.

Carefully, Lorc guided Septimus between birch and pine until he saw the backs of tightly packed buildings: clay and brick and beam, straw-thatched roofs. Tawnshirian buildings. It was the capital!

Together, the three of them had made it—this far, anyway.

Lorc's throat went dry. Somewhere in there was the Minor. Kinkiller. Usurper.

But the Lourdes girls were in there, too. And so there he had to go.

Mounting Septimus, Lorc raised the hood of his cloak and started into the city. They passed onto Tawnshire's cobbled streets, the same sandy-colored stone he remembered from the last time he'd been there. The streets were deserted, the shops shuttered, the homes silent. But still voices cried out in the dark. Everyone seemed near the city center, which was where the smoke was rising from.

They turned down street after street, heading toward the tumult, and finally they reached a great square, crowded and chaotic and full of screaming. Before him was a building on fire—*strange* fire. The flames glowed white, as though robbed of their true color. And they ate away at what Lorc finally recognized as Tawnshire Town's many-windowed Oracle House.

The Oracle House the Major's daughters had sent their message from.

Men shouted and ran around the burning building, some of them in armor. He recognized it well enough. Frosman garb.

The Minor was *indeed* in Tawnshire.

A whine sounded beneath him; Lorc looked down to see Argos staring up at him with worried eyes. His own worry was rising in kind.

"You don't suppose the Major's daughters are still inside, do you?"

As if in answer, the dog howled, long and low, before tearing toward the blaze.

"Argos! *Stop!*"

Lorc and Septimus charged into the crowd, almost trampling townsfolk and soldiers alike. There was so much panic, so many people running and shouting and trying to control the blaze, that no one seemed to notice the Starhound in their midst.

At the steps to the Oracle House, Argos veered left, rounding the side of the building. When Lorc and Septimus caught up to him, he was crouched low, nose nuzzling the dirt. Smoke billowed out a broken window just above him, thick and black and dark, the sound of crashing beams inside. The Oracle House was about to fall.

"Argos," coughed Lorc, slipping off Septimus's back. "We have to go!" Argo's ears were flat, his hackles up. What was he looking at?

Lorc knelt to look, and then he saw it: impressions in the ash— massive, deep-pressed paw prints. A Hemoth Bear. And here and there a narrow footmark—a girl's. *Aster and Ursula.*

"Well spotted, you," he told Argos. "We'll follow this as far as we can."

He saddled up and rode alongside the prints, and when they disappeared into the cobblestones, he kept going, following Argos in the same general direction as he sniffed the way forward. Behind them the clangor and fire receded, and finally they reached the edge of the city again.

Here, in relative quiet, Lorc became aware of a sound drifting through the trees—it was hard to hear over the distant chaos of the

Oracle House, but it was there, a low, animal moan, repeating again and again.

Argos's ears twitched. He had heard it too. The Starhound whined, feet pawing at the ground as if ready to follow the sound. Lorc wondered: had he heard the moan before, when he ran off so suddenly?

If that was the Hemoth, it wouldn't be long before the Frosmen figured out where he and the Lourdes girls had gone. It was up to Lorc and Argos to reach them first.

He'd found what he was looking for.

"Hurry up!" Aster hissed, pushing deeper into the trees. Her hands were over her ears.

"Please, Alcor," Dev begged, coaxing the High Beast along. "You have to be quiet."

Alcor's *bope*-ing vibrated through his chest: the bear hadn't let up for even a moment. They had to hide him deeper in the Shiver Woods, away from the ears of Tawnshire.

Dev was more than familiar with all of Alcor's different noises, but he'd never heard him make such a sound as this. It wasn't his usual cry—he wasn't angry or lonely or sad. This was something else. It was like he was calling out for something. Dev felt the weight of the *Star Writ* tucked under his arm, and briefly considered consulting it to see if there was anything in its pages that might explain this eerie, mournful *woof*ing. But he doubted Aster would have the patience.

"Oh, what's the use?" asked Aster, arms dropping at her sides. "Surely the Minor knows where we are by now. Maybe the bear *wants* us to be caught."

"He does *not*," Dev said defensively.

"We should just let the Minor find us!" she said. "He already has my mother, my sister. And the On-High don't seem to care!"

"Not care? Aster, they just saved us."

"Us? Us! They saved Alcor and *you*!"

Dev didn't understand. Where was this coming from? "You're here," he insisted, "with us. They saved you, too."

"They *burned* me!"

"What? Burned you? Aster, there was no heat. The flames were harmless."

"No! They weren't harmless to me." Her voice began rising. "I think they must *want* Uncle Bram to succeed! *Hello, out there!* Uncle Bram? Are you listening to this? I'm right here! Come and get me!"

Her shouting was nearly as loud as Alcor's, and it sent a bolt of fear through Dev. "Stop that! Have you gone mad?" He was aghast at her recklessness. Someone would hear. Someone would come.

Something snapped in the thick pine branches overhead, and Dev's breath caught on his ribs.

Aster went silent—she'd heard it too. Alcor nudged closer to Dev, his moaning over.

"Something's up there," Dev whispered, clutching the *Star Writ* to his chest.

Aster moved toward him. "A fisher?"

Another *snap*, and a weighty branch creaked. This was no fisher. It was big, whatever it was. Aster lifted her blade.

And then it fell from the treetops—a wall of shadow, a mass of muscle, hurtling down on them like a Nightlock fresh from the netherworld.

Aster shrieked, and Dev covered himself with the book, his heart begging the On-High to spare them. Someone else cried out—a human voice.

And then there was silence.

Dev dared to peek, and when he did, he could hardly believe the sight before him.

A Shadow Dragon.

The High Beast was crouched low, wings spread wide in an impressive span. Her yellow eyes blinked slowly, and her head tilted inquisitively.

"Turds of Tawn," Aster breathed. Alcor grunted the way he did when he was satisfied with a meal.

Suddenly, the Shadow Dragon's neck snapped around, head swiveling to look at whatever was shimmying down off her back. It fell with a *thunk* and a groan.

A boy.

Dev looked to Aster, whose eyes were already asking him to explain. He could only shrug. Not satisfied, she lifted her chin in that frustratingly regal way she had and stepped forward, her earlier tantrum abandoned.

"Who are you?" she demanded. "Name yourself!"

The boy struggled to his feet, nearly falling back when he saw Alcor. Dev couldn't blame him. Alcor was a frightening sight if you weren't prepared for it. But the boy recovered quickly—after all, he kept a dragon for company.

"P-P-Princess Ursula Lourdes?" he asked, as though he couldn't believe it.

Aster scowled. "No. I am her sister, the Princess Aster Lourdes, and the honorable Keeper Dev. I say again: name yourself."

The boy bowed his head, obviously embarrassed by his mistake and flustered by her tone. "F-f-forgive me," he stammered. "I am Quintin Wyvern, son of Drag Wyvern, King of Dracogart. The On-High gave me your message…that you and your sister were in trouble…."

Dev gaped. It had worked. Their message had made it to the Heads of Houses. *And here was a prince!*

"Indeed we are," said Aster, less impressed than Dev. "My sister is in considerably more peril than we are, I'm afraid. Had you been more prompt in your response, she might have been spared."

The boy—Quintin—looked up, horror on his face. "S-spared?"

"She is the Minor's prisoner as of tonight."

Dev watched as Quintin struggled to digest this bit of information.

"If Dracogart really wanted to help the daughters of the Major," Aster went on, "they might have at least thought to send an army. Or do you have one hidden somewhere?"

"Aster...," Dev said warningly, surprised by her hostility. How were they going to keep this new ally if she insisted on acting like that?

"No. I have no army. Dracogart is under the Minor's control," Quintin said softly.

Dev's stomach sank, and when he looked to Aster, she'd gone a lunar shade of pale.

"He rules it through my father's old advisor, Furia," Quintin explained. "The Minor named her regent because she is sympathetic to his cause. She doesn't know I've come."

So the Minor's evil had spread farther than Tawnshire. How much of the Highen belonged to him already?

"Why *did* you come?" Aster asked.

"To help you, just as you asked. To...to see that the proper Major is restored."

The proper Major.

Before Dev could wonder who that might even be, another beast burst through the brush, and the three children jumped at the intrusion.

The creature barked—a dog. An *enormous* dog. It smiled, pink floppy tongue lolling out the side of its mouth. Alcor grunted, pleased again.

"Where'd he come from?" Aster demanded. Her nose scrunched, as if she found the poor beast mangy. But there was nothing mangy about this dog.

"It's a High Beast," said Dev. "A Starhound!"

The dog's head turned back in the direction he'd come from, and he barked into the darkness.

"Oh, well done," said Aster. "Now *he* can tell the Minor where we are."

Indeed, the beast seemed to have alerted someone—hooves pounded earth, closing in. A horse, a magnificent stallion, broke into the clearing.

But it was a boy astride his back. He looked just as surprised to see *them* as they were to see *him*, and Dev recognized his moppy Hundfordian hairstyle. He was one of the brothers of the House of Hounds.

A smile spread across Dev's face, and he threw his arms around Alcor. The On-High had delivered their message to the other Houses. And Alcor had called the High Beasts to him. Help, it seemed, had finally come—in one form or another.

Woe to him who attracts the mischief of the Nightlocks. For once their mayhem has been completed, they will lead you through the door to death.

—THE WRITINGS OF THUBAN,
The Mysteries of the On-High: The Star Majors, *Star Writ*

TWENTY-TWO

BERNADINE sat on the window bench of Aunt Luella's room, staring out at the front green, black with the shadow of night. Far in the distance, a plume of smoke rose from Tawnshire Town. Something was happening.

Her eyes moved from the plume to the road that approached the Manor. She wanted to see her father on his horse, riding up the path. When she'd first spotted the smoke, she'd run frantically about the Manor, demanding that someone tell her what was going on. Had her father and his men been attacked somehow? Was her father safe? But there was no answer: indeed, the Frosmen left behind to guard the Manor were busy asking questions amongst themselves. The insufferable Neva simply smiled sweetly, trying to stroke Bernadine's hair with a useless "I'm sure all is well, little lady." To escape her new nursemaid, Bernadine locked herself in Aunt Luella's chambers—her chambers, now—and left Neva posted outside the door.

She watched the white column of smoke climbing higher above the trees of the Shiver Woods. The fire, whatever the source, was big. She knew that much. But what burned?

She wished she'd left the Manor more often in all her time living in Tawnshire. Her knowledge of the city was very limited; she and her cousins only really left the estate for the Festival of Tawn, which was held in a great lavender valley deep in the forest. Her father had been headed for the Oracle House when he left, he said. Surely it wasn't the Oracle House that burned?

She swallowed, closing her eyes and calling up the image of her father smiling at her Whitlock clothes. She hadn't worn such garments since before she came to Tawnshire, but she wore them now—a wool kirtle with ermine trim around the cuffs, and a simple, shapeless gray dress over top, a leather belt cinching her waist. Her mother had worn clothes just like this. On Bernadine's shoulders were two wooden brooches, each carved with the image of the White Bear, pinning the dress together. She'd never seen her father look so proud.

Oh, Great Lord Tawn, watch over him.

Her eyes flew open. No, she shouldn't pray. Not to the On-High. *The On-High care nothing for us,* her father had taught her. The On-High were the reason her mother was gone. She couldn't rely on them to bring back her father after they'd let her mother die. Her gaze drifted up to the White Bear in the sky, to her mother's star. *You do it then, Mother,* she thought. *Please. Watch over Father. Keep him safe.*

And she noticed it for the first time that evening—the moon.

Her breath stopped. It was a crescent.

The door to death was fragile tonight. A dangerous time, when the seal on the Nightlocks was weakest.

Glass suddenly shattered in the bedroom, and Bernadine screamed, leaping up from her bench. She could see Aunt Luella's table, the Felisbrook tea set rattling on its tray. Something had disturbed it.

She glanced at the door—hadn't Neva heard her scream? The Frosman should have barged through the door to see what the fuss was about. But the door remained closed. Neva must have left her post.

Cautiously, Bernadine stepped closer to the table, shards of glass strewn around it from a broken sugar bowl. A chattering sound—hollow and babbling—made her freeze. Something was in her chambers.

She listened, the sound somewhere by the bed. Was it *laughter?* If it was, it was the most hideous laughter she'd ever heard, like a cackling rodent that had smoked too much Celeste root.

"Who's there?" Her voice barely rose above a whisper—too frightened and small to command a real answer.

But an answer she got, just the same: the little cackle grew louder, as if Bernadine's fear were a delightful joke. Dread crept up her neck.

The cackling changed to hissing, as if the Something was stifling its laughter. Then the blankets hanging over the edge of Aunt Luella's bed moved side to side as the Something ran its length.

"Pretty Whitlock Princess," the unseen creature whispered, *"you've quite a mischief knack. Lies and deceit, a delicious treat, my favoritest kind of snack. Pretty Whitlock princess, oh pretty princess, please—you've tasty sins inside, and into your soul I'll squeeze!"*

Bernadine clasped her hands over her mouth and pressed her back against the window as the Something laughed hysterically. She knew what it was now—a Nightlock.

It's come for me.

Because of Father. Because of what he's done to Uncle Jasper and the Hemoth Bear and Keeper Rizlan and all the rest. She swallowed, feeling the weight of the bear brooches pinned at her shoulders. *Because of what we mean to do together.*

Because, Bernadine realized, *together, we have forsaken the On-High.*

And then she saw it. A shadowy head peeking out from under the dust ruffle. White glowing eyes. Jagged dark fangs. Knobbly, long-nailed fingers. The sharp lines of a rib cage below a wasted face.

The Nightlock shrieked, charging from its spot beneath the bed, and leapt with a hellish howl for Bernadine's face. She screamed and dove to the floor, covering her mouth and curling into a ball.

If the Nightlock burrowed inside, she wouldn't be Bernadine anymore—she'd be less-than-Bernadine, a shadow of herself. Every bit of her would sour. Each mean thought and secret grudge would grow and grow and grow, until her heart was frozen with anger and contempt. Until it was evil.

The room fell quiet. There was no laughing or hissing, no shuffling or scrabbling. A trick?

Bernadine risked opening one eye.

There was nothing.

A horse whinnied outside; voices rose in the night. The Frosmen were returning. She sat up, her head swiveling from side to side, waiting for the creature to pounce. But it was gone.

"The Minor!" someone outside shouted. "The Minor approaches!"

Frantically, Bernadine scrambled to her feet and pressed her palms against the window. There they were—the Frosmen, on horseback or on foot, marching home along the path. And there he was, her father, riding at their head. And at his side, another rider, a Frosman, with Ursula on his saddle. Bernadine scanned the column for Aster— where there was Ursula, surely there was Aster—but she didn't see her cousin in the party. Nor did she see the Hemoth Bear and his boy. What had happened to them?

Men and women in red cloaks shuffled along behind her father's horse, heads hung low. Prisoners. But Bernadine's skin pimpled as she recognized them.

Oracles. Her father had taken Oracles captive.

She glanced up at the crescent moon, her palms damp. A Nightlock had come for her, the same night her father took prisoner the On-High's sacred ears? It couldn't be coincidence. It was a warning, she was sure.

Bernadine ran out the door, racing along the hallway to the grand banister that overlooked the great hall. Her father and his entourage were marching through to the dining hall.

"Father!"

The ash-covered Minor didn't look up, unable to hear her in all the commotion. She watched him disappear through the dining hall doors, followed by men leading the Oracles. He was in danger—more than he realized. Bernadine was sure of that, and he needed to know before this plan of his got any more out of hand.

Holding to the railing, she hurried down the steps, nearly tripping, to follow him. The dining hall was still a mess of discarded food and overturned chairs and tipped-over casks, and the Frosmen raced about, corralling the frightened Oracles in the center of the room. Aunt Luella was there, too, closely guarded. Bernadine saw her father, seated at the head of Uncle Jasper's table, a stern look on his face as he listened to whatever Hewitt was reporting.

"Father!" she cried again, but it was no use over the din.

"My lady?" Neva stood behind her in the doorway, mouth gaping stupidly. "I thought you were in your chambers?"

"I left," said Bernadine.

Neva took a gentle hold of her arm. "Oh no, my lady, you are not to be down here. It is not proper for such a young lady—"

Bernadine wrenched her arm free. "Don't you dare touch me." She had no patience for Neva and her uselessness, not now, when her father needed her. "I am not a prisoner in this house, I can come and go as I please. It's me who gives the orders here, Frosman, not you."

Neva stepped back, bowing her head. "Yes, m'lady."

The room quieted as her father stepped up onto the table. All eyes, including the Oracles', gazed up at him. Bernadine did not like their eyes—red fiery orbs. When they looked at her father, she wondered, what exactly did they see?

"Sacred Ears," her father addressed them, "it is my great and humble honor to share my house with you in your hour of need. To lose your Holiest of Houses to the very flames you serve can be nothing short of devastating. And I promise you, the villains responsible for your loss will not go unpunished."

"Careful, Minor." An elderly Oracle, the most senior of the group by the looks of her, stepped forward. "The *Star Writ* does not write the words simply because you say them. We here all know the face of this night's true villain."

"A true villain," her father agreed, "who left you homeless in the streets and desecrated your temple to the On-High. You must mean Ursula Lourdes." He raised his chin then, looking to the back of the room, eyes meeting Bernadine's. He paused for a moment, as if surprised to see her, before motioning to someone beside her—a soldier.

Quickly, the soldier pushed open the dining hall doors and revealed two Frosmen, a defiant-looking Ursula bound at the wrists between them.

Aunt Luella struggled against a pair of Frosmen who held her back as her screams of rage echoed through the room. "*May the On-High strike you dead for this, Bram!*"

The Frosmen pushed Ursula forward and she marched, head held high, through the scowling faces of soldiers that watched her. Bernadine was struck at the sight of her cousin, dirty and bloodstained, her loose curls frazzled and her dazzling gown so ripped and soiled it was barely recognizable but for the frost pearls that still glittered as she walked.

Ursula's gaze landed on Bernadine, amber eyes that had always seen Bernadine with a mix of pity and amusement. They looked at her differently now—with contempt. Bernadine's cheeks flushed and she cast her eyes to the floor. Never had her older cousin regarded her in such a way, and it sent a chill through her.

When Ursula stood before the table, Aunt Luella threw her arms around her daughter, smoothing her hair and holding her cheeks. Bernadine thought of her own mother—would she do the same thing for Bernadine if she were here?

Bernadine watched her father reach down and touch Ursula's shoulder gently. He held out a gentlemanly hand, offering to help Ursula up onto the table. Aunt Luella pulled Ursula away, but Ursula patted her mother's hand reassuringly and let Bernadine's father help her up.

"Be assured, Sacred Ears," her father announced, "this villain will be sentenced and justice carried out."

Bernadine watched Ursula. Her cousin's chin never dropped. If Bernadine were in Ursula's shoes, she'd be trembling, weeping. But Ursula was the picture of bravery. *A true Major,* some part of her mind whispered. And Bernadine felt like going back upstairs to hide in Aunt Luella's chambers.

"Lady Lourdes," said the elderly Oracle, "why do you cry?"

Bernadine looked to where her aunt was standing—she was dabbing at her eyes. Bernadine had never seen her aunt cry.

"It is not your sins," the Oracle said, "that the On-High send their servants for tonight. Rest assured, your eldest will sleep soundly while the Nightlocks hunt. It is not *your* daughter they come for."

Bernadine stiffened as the eyes of the Frosmen looked warily in her direction. Her father forgot Ursula altogether, his head snapping in the direction of the Oracle. "What did you say?"

"Don't loose your anger on me, Bram Lourdes," the Oracle warned. "You have only yourself to blame for the trouble that shall soon befall you and your kin. The On-High have passed their judgment, Minor. The true villain in their eyes is you." And then the Oracle turned, all of them did, their red eyes on Bernadine. Bernadine swallowed. "Our sympathies, child," the Oracle said.

"Our sympathies," the rest echoed.

Bernadine's palms began to sweat.

"The actions of your father are his and his alone," the Oracle said. "It is a sad end that it will be you who has to answer for them."

"Hewitt!" her father bellowed. "Get these red-eyed monsters out of my sight! Now!"

Hewitt was quick to obey, rounding up the prisoners, but Bernadine was already shaking. Her father leapt off the table and ran to her, taking her hands in his. "Don't let those daft fools frighten you, my darling girl. That the On-High watch us is a fairy tale, I've told you. They care nothing for the affairs of mortal men." Her father smiled. "No Nightlock would dare come for my Major. Not while I'm around." He hugged her close and kissed her on the head.

But he was wrong. The Nightlocks had already shown themselves—they'd sent one to her bedroom. The old Oracle was right. The On-High were angry. And it was her father's fault. The crimes he'd committed—they were too great.

She opened her mouth to tell him about the Nightlock, but he was already calling for more ale. He wouldn't hear her now—he was too pleased with his capture of Ursula, too focused on his victory over the Highen to let news of a single demon slow him down.

As he took her hand and guided her back to the table where Ursula still stood, amber glare trained on her, Bernadine wondered if it was too late to save her father—save them both from whatever was coming.

True, the High Beasts are all children of the On-High and as such have a great love for one another. But like all siblings, they do disagree.

—THE WRITINGS OF BERN,
On Hemoths: The Age of Tawn, *Star Writ*

TWENTY-THREE

ALCOR groaned, tossing his head to shake off Dev's embrace, but Dev couldn't help clutching him. After everything they'd been through, things were finally going their way.

But the faces that surrounded Dev were not smiling.

The Hundfordian boy, sitting atop his stallion, stared wide-eyed at Alcor, his horse prancing nervously in the company of a bear and a dragon.

"The Hemoth Bear," the boy breathed.

"And who are *you?*" demanded Aster.

The Hundfordian slipped down off the horse, mouth set into a grim line. "Do you know, Aster Lourdes, for someone sending desperate messages for help, you've got a funny way of showing your appreciation when help arrives. And given the way you and yours are blundering through these trees like a herd of mad cows, you clearly need all the help you can get."

Dev noticed Aster's fists clenching, her mouth pursed with rage. Even though it was dark, he was sure her cheeks were flushing.

"I am Lorc Conri," the Hundfordian boy continued, "son of Queen Conri of the House of Hounds. And right now, we need to get as far from here as we can. Those Frosmen won't be long finding your tracks."

Dev's heart began to hammer in his chest. Their tracks. Alcor's would be unmistakable. Why hadn't he thought to cover them up?

Rizlan had never taught him about hiding Hemoth Bears in the woods. "How is it you came to find us first?" he asked, beginning to sweat.

Lorc Conri nodded at the Starhound. "Argos."

Dev glanced back at Alcor, who had sat down on his rump, panting happily. *Thank the On-High.*

"We don't have much time," said Lorc. "Where is your sister, Ursula?"

"Wait just a second," Aster snapped. "Lorc? You're the *second*-born, aren't you?"

"Indeed."

"Hundford sent the *second* son of Conri to help me and my sister?" she asked, the pitch of her voice climbing.

Lorc folded his arms, obviously insulted. "No one sent me. I came on my own."

"Why you? Why not the eldest, Arthur? Didn't he hear the message?"

They didn't have time for this. The Frosmen could discover them at any moment.

"Well, for starters," said the Hound prince coldly, "he considers it a dangerous time for royal blood in the capital, what with your uncle slaughtering every Head of Household he can find. Arthur forbade me to come."

"And you *defied* him?"

"I did."

"Is that supposed to make me feel better?"

Lorc Conri shrugged. "It doesn't much matter to me how you feel. I'm here now, and I intend to make the Minor pay for what he's done to my mother."

"But *you*?" Aster jabbed a finger in his direction. "I've heard about you. You're the one who caused Wolfsbane Day. You're the beast who poisoned his brothers!"

Lorc Conri darkened—a murderous look, hate-filled—but if Aster noticed, it didn't seem to bother her. "They sent us a villain!" she shouted at Dev, as if he'd known this would happen all along. "Are we to defeat my uncle with someone as likely to join him given the chance?"

The Starhound growled, lips curling.

"Aster—!" Dev warned, appalled.

"I told you, Dev! The On-High are against me! And what of you, Dragon prince?" snapped Aster, turning on the boy named Quintin. "I'm sure you've your own dark secrets to answer for. What are they? You poison your sisters?"

Quintin looked confused. "I have no sisters."

"Your mother, then!"

Quintin looked away, pain suddenly on his face. Dev realized Aster had hit some kind of nerve. If she wasn't careful, she'd alienate both princes right here and now.

Dev seized her by the arm. "Aster, *stop it!*"

She ripped herself free, a tiny jar of starflame falling to the dirt. Had it been in her skirts this whole time? "No! What was the point in asking the On-High for help if the only help we get are the *rejects* of the Highen!"

A dry laugh escaped the Hound prince. "That's rich from you."

"What did you say?" Aster's hands fixed firmly on her hips.

"You want to talk about reputations, Lourdes girl? Then let's talk about yours. You have an awful high-and-mighty attitude for a spoiled brat. Everyone knows you spend your time playing make-believe and being waited on in your *palace*—not studying, not training, not reading. You have no respect for the discipline it takes to rule!"

Dev held his breath, waiting for Aster to explode—

But the explosion didn't come.

Her arms dropped to her sides, fists unclenching, and she looked at Quintin Wyvern, searching his face for agreement with the Hound prince. To Quintin's credit, he smiled gently. Then her eyes met Dev's. He looked at the ground.

Because what the Hound prince said was true. Dev had always thought the Lourdes girls *knew* how the Highen saw them—overindulged, idle, vain—and that they were just too self-absorbed to care. But now, after everything, he was starting to realize that they didn't and never had. For all Aster's love of her father's Highen, she had never truly understood that—as the Major's daughter—the whole of the world noticed what she did and didn't do.

"You want the On-High to help you?" Lorc asked. "Why would they? What have you ever done to earn their blessing?"

Again her eyes flicked to Dev, a panic starting to set in. She knew the answer to that as well as him—nothing. She'd barely read the *Star Writ*. But that didn't mean that the Hound prince was right. The On-High had helped them escape the Oracle House. The On-High had brought their High Beasts.

"You're just Ursula Lourdes' little sister," Lorc went on. "The spare. Heir to nothing. A princess without a purpose. A reject, no different from us."

Aster deflated so suddenly Dev felt an ache in his chest for her.

Suddenly, he thought of Rizlan, of the way he counseled Jasper Lourdes when the Major needed help understanding the will of the stars. *It is the Keeper's job to clarify,* Rizlan always said.

"Perhaps," Dev said carefully, "that's exactly who the On-High thinks we need."

The three royal children looked at him, a mixture of confusion and offense on their faces.

"Look at us, Aster," Dev reasoned. "Me, a Keeper who can't have visions. Alcor, a Hemoth Bear too young and frightened to be left alone in the dark. And you—"

"What about me?"

Fixed by her angry glare, Dev almost wished he hadn't said anything. "I'm just saying. Perhaps the On-High see that we all have more in common than we think." He bent, and picked up and held out to her the little jar of starflame. "Perhaps, Aster, it's time you listened to the stars more carefully. And to your friends."

Aster stared into the jar, the light dancing in her honey-brown eyes. She took it, turning it in her hand.

"Where *is* Ursula Lourdes?" the Hound boy asked.

"She is the Minor's prisoner."

The Hound boy looked down at his dog, a tightness in his jaw. "And the Highen's armies? What's happened to them? Have you heard anything at all?"

"We've not heard word from anyone," said Dev. "Not the Major, nor Keeper Rizlan, nor any of the other Heads—"

"My father was killed," the dragon boy said. "I don't know how. Draco, the Shadow Dragon, only barely made it back to Dracogart. He was wounded so badly he died not long after he arrived."

"Died?" The Hound boy looked ill. Of course he did. The death of a High Beast was still a sickening thought for him. Unfortunately for Dev, it was the third time he'd heard of such a loss—first Mizar the Hemoth Bear, then Alurea the White Bear, and now this. He hated to think he was getting used to astrocide.

Lorc Conri opened his mouth to speak again, but a scream and a rush of heat stopped him.

"Oh no," gasped Quintin Wyvern.

The Shadow Dragon had spread her wings and fired the grass by her feet. She snapped at Alcor, who was sniffing the burned ground, and scooped up the smoking body of an unfortunate weasel she'd burned to a crisp. The Starhound bounced around them, barking hungrily.

Bope bope bope bope. Alcor stepped closer, trying to get at Ursula's charred morsel of food. The fins behind the dragon's jaws began to twitch, and she hissed as she slunk back toward the trees.

"She doesn't like to share," said Quintin anxiously.

Blast it all, thought Dev. The Hemoth was probably starving. He hadn't eaten anything since the fish and berries at the Oracle

House, and they'd left in such a hurry Dev hadn't thought to pack food. Without something else to give him, Dev knew Alcor wouldn't give up on that weasel.

The Starhound's barking grew louder, a desperate pitch. "Argos!" said Lorc Conri. "You dumb beast, let the dragon have it!"

But it seemed the Starhound was just as hungry as Alcor. Could no one in this group be good to each other, Dev thought miserably, man or beast?

Both bear and dog stepped closer to the dragon, and with a screech, she turned and tore off into the trees, Alcor and Argos chasing after her.

"Alcor, stop!" Dev shouted. But it was no use. The hungry Hemoth would chase down that dragon until he got a bite of her supper. "Quintin, call the dragon back!"

Quintin held up his hands. "I can't! She's not like a dog!"

"What's that supposed to mean?" snapped Lorc Conri.

"She doesn't listen to me!"

No, indeed—Dev shouldn't have thought so. High Beasts were the children of stars, sublime royalty who answered to no one. Not even a Keeper. The best a Keeper could do was know their Beast as well as they could and appeal to their interests—of which Dev had none available. What he wouldn't give for his kazoo or one of Chef Ingle's lamb shanks. He thought of Rizlan and the other Keepers—Aden of the Shadow Dragons, Callum of the Starhounds. How Dev wished for one of them now. What bags of tricks would they have been ready with?

When no one moved, Aster tucked her starflame into her skirts and stormed over to Lorc Conri's stallion.

"What are you doing?" Dev asked her.

She pulled herself up onto the impressive horse. "We can't have them killing each other!" She kicked the stallion's side and plowed into the trees after the High Beasts, the echoes of screeches and barks and Alcor's moans ringing out in the night.

"Aster!"

Dev ran after her, following the trail of destruction. This was dangerous. They'd bring the Minor and his Frosmen down on them any second with this cacophony.

Lorc Conri appeared in front of him, a faster and vastly more competent runner. "Nether demons take her! That's my brother's horse!"

Quintin was at their heels, calling the dragon's name. "Umbra! Umbra, please!"

The three boys burst free of the trees onto the bank of a wide, raging waterway. Dev recognized it at once: the Great Bear River.

And then his heart stopped.

The Hound prince's horse was on the bank, stomping in a panic, Aster no longer on its back. She was half in the water, pulling at the fur of Alcor's haunches while the Starhound splashed around them, still barking. The Hemoth was wading deeper into the river, his teeth clamped shut on one half of the weasel, the Shadow Dragon flying just above him, refusing to release the other half.

"Aster!" Dev shouted, but the thunder of the river was too loud. He looked at Quintin. "Your dragon is leading them into the river! They'll be swept up!"

Quintin hurried to the river's edge, shouting at the dragon to stop, while Lorc Conri raced to get his frightened horse and lead him away from the frothing water.

Turds of Tawn, thought Dev. This fighting would get them all drowned.

"Trouble with your charge, Keeper?"

Dev spun, his stomach leaping into his throat. Standing at the edge of the wood, broadsword at the ready, was Captain Pire.

Dev glanced back at the thrashing High Beasts, screaming and roaring at one another in the water. No wonder the old soldier had found them. The rest of his Frosmen couldn't be far behind.

"Call the bear, boy," growled Pire.

"C-call him?" stammered Dev. "I—I—I'm his servant. He doesn't answer to me."

Pire stepped farther onto the bank, his heavy sword inching closer. "Try, if you value your life."

Dev gulped. His eyes darted across the treeline as the High Beasts raged. He saw the flicker of movement—Frosmen closing in, advancing through the screen of pines.

Pire lunged, and Dev was too slow: the Frosman seized his arm. He cried out, but Pire's grip was like the Hemoth's jaws—crushing, immovable.

"Dev!" Aster screamed, near hysterics. "Release him, Frosman!" She was soaked and panting—the struggle to control Alcor was draining her—but Dev knew she'd fight anyway if Pire managed to get ahold of her. Alcor was still battling the Shadow Dragon, ignoring the bother of her efforts, oblivious to the danger they were all suddenly in.

"Aster Lourdes," said Pire, pulling Dev against his chest, sword to his throat. "Your little adventure has come to an end, girl. I have the high ground. I have the boy. I have your sister. I have everything."

And then the Frosmen. Twenty in all. Emerging from the trees, arrows nocked and ready. They had come on foot, tracking the Hemoth's path from the city.

Aster watched them, eyes glittering. "You think you can come between a Hemoth and his dinner?" she asked, raising her voice so every man heard.

Dev felt Pire shift. The river was in geysers as the two High Beasts fought. They were a force unto themselves. Ferocious. Untamable. Who would dare come between them?

The air was thick and still.

And then a horse screeched. In a thunder of hooves, blade flashing, Lorc Conri barreled in as if from nowhere, sending Pire and Dev sprawling.

Dev scrambled away as the old soldier roared the command for his men to fire. Crawling through the dirt, he heard arrows whistling overhead. *On-High save us!* he begged.

And then a hand took hold of his. Aster. She had left Alcor to get him.

She hauled him to his feet, plunging with him into the frigid water as arrows splashed around them. The force of the current pulled at his knees, threatening to sweep them both away. And Captain Hewitt Pire, recovering himself, ran after them.

"Grab hold of Alcor!" Aster bellowed, and before Dev could stop her, she slapped the Hemoth Bear's hindquarters.

Alcor gave a mighty roar of outrage. His whole body lurched upward, pulling the clinging Dev and Aster off their feet as he wrapped his front paws around the screaming dragon in a fit of confused anger. Both Beasts hit the water with a massive crash, plunging Dev beneath the waves.

Water overwhelmed his nose, his throat, his lungs. It separated him from the others. His body tumbled head over feet, spiraling in the powerful current. He thrashed out with his arms, his legs—anything to gain purchase, to find the bank, find the surface, find air—and his fingers finally grazed the coarse, shaggy coat of Alcor. He grabbed hold again, pulled himself above water, clung to the High Beast's side.

Arrows flew overhead. Alcor tried to fight the current, but he was losing—the strength of the Great Bear River one of the only forces beneath the On-High that could best the power of a Hemoth. Help-lessly, they tore down the waterway, the river rushing them on.

The Shadow Dragon screamed. Dev saw her just ahead of Alcor, her heavy wings dragging her beneath the foaming water. Quintin Wyvern splashed beside her, just out of reach, fighting to keep his head above water. Had he jumped in after her?

And Aster—

"Aster!" Dev screamed.

He couldn't see her anywhere. Had the river carried her farther away? Had she been pinned against one of the many massive boulders? Had the water swallowed her up completely?

And then a roar—as furious as the Hemoth's, but decidedly human—sounded on the other side of Alcor, and a hand shot onto his back.

Aster. She hoisted herself astride the Hemoth, sputtering and coughing.

"Have you gone mad?!" Dev yelled at her.

"You wanted to stay with the Frosmen?" she shouted back.

On the banks, the soldiers were running, barely able to keep up.. Pire bellowed orders, but none of them were willing to plunge into the waters of Great Bear River themselves.

"Wyvern!" Aster shouted, looking to the Dragon prince, who was losing his battle with the current. "Dev, give me your arm!"

She splashed off Alcor's back beside Dev, hanging on to the Beast's side. Then she grabbed Dev's arm and let go of Alcor's fur, the river trying so hard to carry her away he thought his arm might rip off. She struggled to bridge the distance between them and Quintin.

"Wyvern!" she screamed. "Take my hand!"

The drowning prince reached for Aster and—barely, desperately— took hold. Dev gritted his teeth against the weight, his grip on Alcor nearly ripping fur free. With the greatest effort of his life, he pulled the two back to Alcor's massive body, and the children clung on as the Bear was carried farther and farther downriver.

"Umbra!" Quintin sputtered. "We have to help Umbra!" The dragon's head kept disappearing under the waves, surfacing less and less. "She can't swim!"

But there wasn't anything they could do. They were nothing but leaves in the current, helpless against the power of the rapids. How long could Alcor keep them afloat?

"The Falls!" Aster shouted. "Dev, we're headed for the falls!"

The current was getting worse, the bank flashing by in a blur.

Aster was right. They were barreling toward Great Bear Falls. They'd be thrown over.

"Aster Lourdes!"

Galloping along the banks was Lorc Conri, fresh Frosmen on horseback firing arrows at him. The Hound prince didn't seem to notice his pursuers, too focused on tying a rope to his saddlebag.

"Aster Lourdes!" he screamed over the thundering river. "You'll have to catch it!"

"Help me!" she ordered them, and Dev and Quintin pushed her up out of the water so that she sat astride the struggling Hemoth again.

The Hound prince swung the rope, tossing the bag, but it came up short. The thunder of the river grew louder, the foam and froth at a roiling boil. Dev looked ahead, and he could see where the river stopped abruptly, see the telltale mist rising up from where the water dropped off the earth.

The Hound prince tossed the bag again, and this time, Aster caught it.

"Give it to the Hemoth!" Lorc shouted.

Aster handed the bag to Dev, who reached out to Alcor's face. *On-High, please,* he pled—and Alcor took the bag in his mouth.

No sooner did the Bear begin to pull than Dev saw what was wrong with Lorc Conri's plan. The other end of the rope was tied to his horse—a strong beast, but no match for Alcor. And with one tug from the Hemoth, horse and Hound prince were yanked right off the rocky bank, spinning through the water with the rest of them.

Aster shouted at Dev, but he couldn't hear her over the thunder of the Falls.

And before he could think which star the On-High might grant his soul, the river threw them all into space, water and earth giving away beneath them. Dev's body fell through nothing but air and mist and the memory of his mother before darkness swallowed him up.

Gossip builds the throne of lies; truth paves the way to the stars.

—TAWNSHIRIAN PROVERB

# TWENTY-FOUR

QUINTIN woke with his face in the mud, his legs submerged in water.

He was soaked to the bone, his body bruised, but he was alive. The waterfall of the Great Bear River had spared him. He could hear its rumble behind him.

When he had hit the water, the weight of the falls had pushed him down into the cold, dark deep, and he was sure he'd never come up for air again. But then the river spat him out like a bad taste—the pressure eased, and suddenly, he had surfaced; the current all but gone, the water slow and calm and quiet enough that he drifted gently to shore.

At least the arrows had stopped flying. He was too far downstream for that.

He gripped at the soft earth, his fingers squelching sludge, and he wanted so much to be home, in Dracogart, where the ground was stone—hard and solid and dry, the mountain's inner fire keeping everything warm to the touch. Tawnshire was cold. No fire burned inside. It made Quintin think of death.

Umbra.

She had been drowning.

Quintin struggled up in a panic. Dawn was beginning to break over the forest, and light spilled through the trees, twinkling off the water's surface. He wasn't alone: the Hemoth Bear was farther down the bank, shaking out his thick fur, Aster Lourdes shielding herself from the spray. The bear's Keeper lay flat on his back, staring up at the sky, his chest heaving as he breathed.

But no Umbra. Had the falls taken her?

Quintin plunged into the river up to his knees, looking for her, but she was nowhere. "Umbra? *Umbra!*"

And then a familiar chirrup.

Downriver, the dragon sat in a patch of reeds, coiled around herself, pruning her wings.

"Umbra!" He splashed toward his old friend, throwing his arms around her neck. He buried his face against her scales, stony and solid and warm—*just like home*—as the dragon purred.

Somehow, they'd survived.

The Hound prince, Lorc Conri, was now trudging up the bank, his Starhound loping alongside him. "Septimus!" he called. But the horse didn't come.

The water was empty, its gentle flow drifting by like something out of a dream. No horse. Quintin watched Lorc Conri, saw the way his hands dropped helplessly at his sides as the truth set in. Quintin's grip on Umbra tightened, and the dragon pressed her head to his cheek.

So the river hadn't spared everyone.

But then the Hemoth groaned and chuffed, its wet head nodding toward the far bank.

"Look there!" shouted Aster, pointing.

The Hundford stallion appeared through the alders, shaking off water and bucking, happy to be on dry land.

"Septimus!" laughed Lorc Conri, his Starhound barking. "You're on the wrong side of the river, you dumb beast. Get over here!"

"Where *is* here?" Quintin asked. The river must have carried them for miles. Were they even still in Tawnshire?

"The river flows southeast," said Lorc as his horse sploshed across the water. "So I expect we're halfway to Härkädia by now. The way that Hemoth walks, it will take us near two days to get back to the city."

The young Keeper was on his feet now, tending to the Hemoth. "Back?"

"Of course," said Lorc. "You may not have noticed, but that's where the Minor is."

The Keeper shook his head. "Alcor can't go back."

"Yes," agreed Quintin. "All that matters is the Hemoth Bear. Our duty is to hide him—at all costs."

"Hide him *how?*" laughed Lorc. "He's a Hemoth!"

Quintin couldn't help but agree. Next to Draco, Mizar had been the largest creature he'd ever seen—and Alcor wasn't far behind. Where could a creature like that go unnoticed?

And then the answer exploded in his mind like a Shadow Dragon from the clouds.

"Mount Draccus," he said.

"You want to get the Hemoth to Dracogart... on foot?" asked Lorc scornfully. "That would take weeks! And why *there?* Why not Hundford?"

"You said yourself we must be halfway to Härkädia," said Aster, her voice flat. When Quintin looked over, her eyes were fixed on her jar of starflame—she hadn't lost it in the water. "The Mount Draccus Range connects Härkädia with Dracogart. Most of it is remote, and few dare to pass over it. The Dragon prince is right. No one would find us in the mountains."

She knew this without even glancing at a map. Perhaps Aster Lourdes knew more about her father's Highen than people thought.

"Maybe so," said Lorc Conri, "but the reason few brave the range is because it is dangerous. Rockslides, extreme cold, unpredictable weather. Not to mention *dragons.*"

As if to emphasize his point, Umbra snorted.

Quintin reached back for her, and she moved toward his hand, letting him stroke her beak. "We have Umbra with us. Mount Draccus is her kingdom. As she welcomes us, so will the mountain."

"And how long do you intend to hide there, I wonder?" asked Lorc.

"What do you mean?" said Dev.

"I mean, what happens next? You can't live in the mountains forever! Quintin said Dracogart is under the Minor's control, so little help there, I wager. And anyway, what good is a Hemoth without a Major?"

A wave of sadness passed over Aster's face. "My sister is the next rightful Major," she said, slouching. "She was born for it."

"So what would *you* do, Lorc Conri?" snapped Dev. "Forget the mountains? Waltz into the Minor's den with the Hemoth, swords unsheathed, and risk losing him—and our lives?"

Lorc stewed for a minute. Even he saw the dangers inherent in that idea.

"Well, you can't go to the mountains like that," he said finally, motioning at their sopping-wet clothes. "Even if you *don't* freeze to death, you'll lose your skin to dew-rot if you stay damp too long."

Quintin had never heard of dew-rot. But he had watched Scaleg work with enough patients to know that damp skin could lead to scale-chafe, a fungus that ate away at the skin. He assumed it was similar.

"Lorc's right," agreed Quintin. "We need dryclothes."

The young Keeper nodded. "And food. Unless we want to risk the High Beasts fighting over another meal."

"There should be a town not far from here," said Lorc. "I passed it on my way to find you. I recognize the country."

"Downswift." Aster Lourdes stood, stripping down to her shift. Quintin's cheeks felt warm, and Lorc Conri began to blush. "It would have to be. It's one of the outlying towns of Tawnshire, and it sits near the Great Bear River. The markets will be opening soon. I'll go and get what's needed. Lorc, give me your cloak—I can't wear my dress, it's too rich. I have to look like a peasant girl."

"You'll get what's needed? With what?" asked the young Keeper, apparently unfazed by the Major's daughter wearing nothing but a smock. "You don't have any money."

Quintin cleared his throat. "I do." He pulled Scaleg's change purse wet from his pocket, the High Coins still in place. "My physician gave it to me before I left."

"Your physician?" asked the young Keeper.

Quintin nodded, an ache swelling at the back of his throat. "My friend."

"It doesn't look like much."

Aster Lourdes shrugged. "It will have to do."

So Quintin went with Aster Lourdes to the village of Downswift, leaving Umbra with the young Keeper Dev. Aster Lourdes moved quickly, with purpose, and with no interest in whether or not Quintin could keep up. Every step seemed to trip him over a root or a fallen log or some other obstacle that his feet were not used to navigating.

She finally stopped and looked back, hands on her hips. "Are you quite all right?"

"I'm fine."

"You're *wheezing.*"

He was suddenly aware of his breathing—phlegmy rasps that didn't sound healthy at all.

"Are you ill?" she pressed.

He didn't know. He was short of breath, that much was certain. But was he ill?

He still felt the chill of the river inside his bones. Why hadn't his body warmed up yet? He wore a scalecoat—what better protection against the cold was there? And what was this pressure in his chest? A tightness seemed to be trying to keep each breath from filling his lungs.

"You're *dreadfully* slow," said Aster Lourdes. "Should I continue on my own?"

"No. I'm fine."

"You're sure?"

He wasn't. But he'd come this far: for Mother, for Umbra, for Dracogart.

"Yes, I'm sure," he lied. "I'll be faster, I promise."

"You've probably spent too much time on the back of that dragon of yours. Not enough time with your feet on the ground, getting dirty! Father taught me and my sister the importance of being on your feet, you know. We had a very good sharps master."

That was not at all what Quintin had come to understand about Major Lourdes's daughters. The rumors among the diplomats and ambassadors who came to visit Dracogart, the gossip brought back by chancellors and dignitaries, even the whispers among the people, all had it that the Major's daughters were undisciplined, lazy, extremely spoiled, and generally uninterested in the work it took to make oneself a Major, just as Lorc Conri had said. Indeed, Quintin's own father had shaken his head at the idea of either girl filling their father's shoes.

"Poor Jasper," he'd said after returning home from a visit to Tawn-shire. "How such a strong and confident leader—so commanding, king of a vast realm—could crumble in the face of his own children, I'll never know. Indulgent, that's the problem. Quintin, my son, you may be the only hope the Highen has."

Of course, Quintin had always doubted that. He was a fine rider, if he was honest with himself. But as a fighter he was woefully uncoordinated: he knew he wouldn't stand a chance in half the skills competitions at a Northern Crowning. Besides, becoming Major had never interested him. All he really wanted was to stay in Dracogart.

He clutched a hand to his chest as he breathed, his ribs tight. Could the firelung really have chased him here? He needed Scaleg. Needed the old man to examine him. Scaleg would know. If he lived to become Head of the House of Shadow Dragons, he would continue his studies under the physician. He had a gift for healing, and a good king would care for his mother and anyone else who was sick—perhaps he could found a school for physicians, or build places of healing.

Aster followed the river out of the woods and into a bright landscape of sprawling golden fields. In the near distance, he could see Downswift, gold in the light of the sun. It was walled, smoke rising from little chimneys on the many-colored roofs within, all of them thatched.

"I didn't know the Lourdes went to visit the small townships much," said Quintin, impressed with how confidently she'd led them here.

"We don't," she said. "This is my first time away from Tawnshire Town or the Manor."

"Oh. You just seem to know where you're going."

"I do."

Well, that didn't make much sense. "How is it you know the way to a village you've never seen?"

Aster's eyes, which had been so fixed and determined on the way ahead, suddenly dropped to her feet. He worried he'd said something wrong. Quickly, he tried to remember what his mother had taught him about etiquette—about talking to noble ladies, specifically. Quintin had never much liked talking to people, especially the ones at court, but now he dearly wished he'd taken her lessons more seriously.

"Forgive me," he tried. "I did not mean to pry."

"You did. Or you wouldn't have asked."

He couldn't deny that. So he resigned himself to the fact that their long walk would continue in silence.

"I have a map," Aster said finally. "Of the Highen. I made it myself, you see, bit by bit. Whenever my father had to leave, he would show me on my map where his journey would take him. I'd mark it up—memorize the roads and villages, imagine being there with him. And then, when he'd come home, I'd point out the parts on the map I wanted to hear about. He told the most wonderful stories, my father." Aster went quiet again, and Quintin suspected she was remembering him. Memories of his own father surfaced in his mind, all the times Quintin would stand at his mother's balcony to watch him go wherever his duties as Head of the House of the Shadow Dragons would take him. His father would always stop at the gate and wave.

"Anyway," said Aster. "After poring over the map so much, I suppose I've come to know the Highen by heart."

Quintin nodded. "I'm glad of it. We might never have found Downswift otherwise."

Aster shrugged, but Quintin caught the slightest hint of a smile.

The village of Downswift was a sleepy one, and Quintin was happy to see it didn't keep much in the way of guards at the gate. Just two sleepy white-bearded men who waved pleasantly as they passed.

At the center of the village was a quiet market, with all kinds of crops and breads and cheeses, just as Aster had predicted: shallots, onions, sourdoughs, goat cheese, cottage cheese, cheese curds. The people were busy buying and selling and trading, few of them stopping to notice the girl in the plain cloak and dirtied skirts or the boy wrapped tight in his mantle. They used all of Quintin's High Coins to purchase four linen tunics, some stockings, and a few good wool cloaks that would keep them warm in the mountains, as well as two loaves of bread, a wheel of cheese, and a sack of burst beans.

But knowing Umbra, Quintin wasn't sure those items would make the High Beasts happy.

"We should find some meat," he said, holding up one of the cloaks for Aster to change behind. They stood behind a honey-selling stall, Quintin's cheeks hot as he waited for Aster to get out of her wet things.

"We haven't any more money," she said, her voice muffled by the tunic she was struggling to pull down over her head. Finally dressed, she pulled down the cloak he was holding. "Unless you want to use the Draccmars."

No. He didn't. They'd both agreed that if they were to pass as Tawnshirian peasants, it would be too strange for them to be carrying currency from Dracogart. It could invite questions. And questions could be dangerous.

"What about my smock?" Aster said, holding up the damp clothes she'd just changed out of, tucking her jar of starflame into the pocket of her tunic. "Surely someone would pay for it. It's silk, after all."

"It's damp," said Quintin, doubtful.

Aster frowned. "Do you have a better idea?"

He didn't. So he followed Aster as she marched off in that confident way she had, headed for the stall where they'd bought the tunics.

"What will you give me for this?" she asked the woman without even so much as a hello. "Coins now, I don't need more clothes."

He tried not to grin. The picture painted of Aster Lourdes was always one of a spoiled child, delicate and pampered, incapable of the strength required of a Major. But the girl Quintin was coming to know hardly seemed to fit that description.

The old woman behind the stall inspected the garment, her eyebrows rising with interest. "One High Coin."

Aster waved the offer away. "It's worth at least eleven, but for you I'll settle for five."

"Two, then."

Aster's eyes narrowed. "Four. Or you can forget it."

The old woman grimaced and began to count the coins. It seemed

Aster Lourdes would win this round. And Quintin was getting the sense that Aster Lourdes didn't lose much.

"...burned down the Oracle House, them Lourdes girls. That's what I heard."

Aster whipped around, frowning at a trio of villagers sitting on the steps of the Downswift's humble one-room Oracle House. Not farmers, from the looks of them; they wore rich fabrics and good leathers. Merchants of some kind. A wiry one, a young one, and an old one, all huddled close.

"Ursula Lourdes was taken by the Minor, from the sounds of it," said the wiry one. "Tawn knows if she's still alive."

"Magnificent," said the young one. "Stuck with the little one as Major, are we?"

Quintin watched Aster's eyes go wide. If Ursula Lourdes was gone, that left *Aster* to compete at the Northern Crowning. She would be the Major's only heir.

"No, no, no," said the first, "Aster Lourdes burned up in the blaze, that's what I heard."

The elderly merchant shook his head. "On-High keep her star."

The young merchant laughed grimly. "Good riddance, that's what I say! Those daughters of the Major were a pair of lazy terrors. No one wanted them as Major. And the way those Lourdes act like they own the whole Highen—old Jasper Lourdes takin' that egg and all? It's divine intervention, is what it is. On-High're in a rage, that's what I think. How else do you explain how quickly Jasper was undone? The stars've blessed the Minor—that's what *I* think."

"Blessed, is it? Man committed"—the old merchant lowered his voice, but Quintin could see the word in the way his mouth moved—"*astrocide.*"

The young merchant nodded grimly. "No one said change came without heavy cost."

Quintin glanced at Aster. Her fists trembled at her sides.

The elderly merchant looked aghast. "Come now, Lif, you can't mean you support the Minor after all he's done! He'll be cursed by the stars!"

The wiry man held up his palms for quiet. "It's not good to talk so openly like this, lads. Things being as divided as they are."

"Maybe so," said the young merchant. "But they won't be divided long. The Major dead, his girls as good as gone. Who is it you think the On-High are on the side of, eh? Old Jasper, cold in the ground? Won't be surprised if he and his turn up somewhere as Nightlocks when all is said and done."

Quintin was knocked sideways as Aster stormed off. The old woman chuckled, picking up the abandoned smock and folding it over her arm.

He held out his hand. "The coins?"

She snarled but gave them over, and he pocketed the money. Then he turned to follow Aster, catching her on the far side of the square. "Aster, wait."

"I have to get out of here," she told him tightly.

"People will always gossip, Aster. Don't pay it any mind." He hesitated. "In Dracogart, the people speak in whispers that I was born with a tail."

She looked at him, surprised.

"I wasn't," he said quickly. "But the people always talk. It doesn't mean they know what they are talking about."

She frowned thoughtfully, still walking. Silently, she guided him to a small inn, where they used the last of their coins to buy a dozen roast sausages (the smell making his stomach roar) and left town at last to rejoin the others.

As they walked back across the fields, the shadows grew long and the light faded from brilliant gold to fiery orange. They'd been gone most of the day. He hoped Umbra hadn't gotten into another disagreement with the High Beasts while he was gone.

"What if they're right?"

Quintin nearly bumped into her, she'd stopped so abruptly. "What?"

"The people," she said. She held up her jar of starflame, the light inside beginning to glow as day came to an end. "What if they *do* know what they're talking about?"

Quintin flinched. He'd seen starflame before, certainly. It lined the windows of the Oracle House of Dracogart. But he'd never seen it outside, let alone being held like a pot of fire sap.

"How do you know," she said, the amber of her eyes glowing pale by the white light of the flame, "whose side the On-High are on?"

Quintin didn't know what to say. That was a question for a Keeper or an Oracle. It was a question he'd never thought to ask himself. And just to think on it, for even a moment, sent a tremor through his knees. His father was dead. Draco, too. And his mother, she'd been sick for so long. Had the On-High ever been on his side?

They walked the rest of the way in silence, leaving the fields of the village for the shelter of the woods. The stars blinked to life above the canopy of the Tawnshirian forest, and Quintin felt their gaze as he and Aster made their way back to the river. Her question turned over in his mind, again and again: *How do you know whose side the On-High are on?* The more he tried to come up with the answer, the more frightened he became. Because the truth of it was simple enough—they couldn't know. Not until it was over.

Remember: Where the lake is at its deepest, the water at its coldest, and the shadows at their darkest, the frost pearls glow the brightest.

—WHITLOCK PROVERB

TWENTY-FIVE

WHEN Aster and Quintin returned to camp, the High Beasts nearly knocked him to the ground, smelling the sausages he'd brought back from Downswift. The boys all changed into their fresh clothes, reveling in the dry warmth of their new woollen cloaks. Lorc Conri built a small fire and set to work roasting the burst beans, their skins crackling and popping on the heat until they were a creamy, buttery mess, perfect to sop up with bread. Despite the sweet, nutty smell, Aster couldn't bring herself to eat.

"You really won't come with us?" Quintin was saying to Lorc Conri.

Lorc shook his head. "I came here to make the Minor pay for what he's done to my mother. And to stop him from doing worse."

"What about Alcor?" Dev asked through stuffed cheeks. "You said you came to help the Hemoth Bear."

"And so I have," said Lorc. "But you don't need me to get you to the Drakkans—Wyvern knows the way well enough. Don't you, Wyvern?"

As the boys talked, Aster felt the heat of starflame. Not just in her palm where she held tight to the jar, but everywhere. She could still feel the burn of the On-High—her skin peeling away in the blaze, layer by layer like pages of burning *Star Writ*. *Burned up*, the Downswift man had said.

Abruptly, she got up from the fire and left the boys to their conversation.

The High Beasts looked up from their dinners, their eyes reflecting the light of the starflame as she passed. She felt their gaze as she felt the gaze of the stars—burning through her.

She climbed up onto a fallen log and slid down the other side, sitting on the mossy forest floor with her back against the rotting wood, her knees pulled tight to her chest. Alone in the quiet dark, she held the jar of starflame in her hands and watched it flicker.

The stars were watching her.

They'd always watched her.

The stars had seen her ignore Rizlan's teachings, seen her put off sharps practice and riding lessons and academic studies but still play at being Major in her father's study. *Stuck with the little one.*

Not just the stars—but the Highen. All this time. They'd been watching.

And Aster had never noticed.

Lazy entitled terror.

The fear and shame and embarrassment of it swelled inside her, an ever-growing blaze rising up from her chest and threatening to engulf her. She felt the burn creep into her eyes, and tears spilled down her cheeks. Maybe they were all right about her. The Downswift villagers, Lorc Conri, Uncle Bram. Maybe she was nothing but a spoiled, silly girl who could never follow in her father's footsteps.

Father.

The Death Chaser.

Did he see her the way they all did?

His letter, read by their mother at the dinner table a lifetime ago, echoed through her mind. *The Highen demands a leader worthy of the Hemoth Bear.* Ursula said she knew what kind of Major she wanted to be—she had given herself up to Uncle Bram for the sake of Alcor and the Highen. Ursula was brave. Ursula was worthy. And Aster? It was the last question Ursula had asked before she was taken by the Minor. Aster hadn't been able to answer then, but she had the answer now. What kind of Major did she want to be? No Major. She didn't want to be one at all. She wasn't worthy of it.

Ursula was.

And now Ursula was gone.

Mother was gone.

And Father—

Aster closed her eyes, falling into the darkness behind her lids. Father was gone. Uncle Bram was winning this war he'd started. Ursula was his now. And when the Northern Crowning came, Ursula would be gone and Alcor would be forced to choose whoever Uncle Bram let stand in the ring.

Bernadine. Her cousin. Uncle Bram had taken her, too. Everyone Aster loved, Uncle Bram had taken them.

It wasn't fair.

Aster sat up, wiping her face on her sleeve, and stared into the jar, the white light surging and waning as if it had breath of its own. Lorc Conri was right. She'd done nothing to make herself worthy of the On-High's favor. Was this her punishment? Would the On-High see the Highen burn to teach Aster a lesson? Was all of this, everything that had happened, somehow her fault?

The light flickered in her hand. Could that have been a *yes*?

The light swelled again.

It thinks, the Oracle had said. The starflame burned her. *Chose* to burn her. It didn't have to. It let Dev and the Oracles pass through the flame without feeling anything. Was Dev right? Had the stars been trying to tell her something?

Aster glanced up through the branches of the trees, the inky black of the night sky peeking through. The On-High watched her. The On-High were listening.

Aster swallowed the lump swelling in her throat and spoke, her voice faint and hoarse from crying. "Can I fix it?"

The stars didn't answer.

And then a surge of heat, the flame in the jar growing three times larger.

Aster looked up and addressed the stars again. "If I go to fix it, will you help me?"

The stars flickered and the heat in her palms surged and faded in waves as the flame filled the jar, the sound of singing glass—the voices of the On-High—rising up from somewhere inside it.

Aster clutched the jar close. There was still time to make it right.

"I don't know that this is wise," she heard Quintin Wyvern saying.

She turned back to where the boys had been sitting—they were on their feet now, the beans and bread all gone.

"It's reckless," said Dev.

Lorc Conri was saddling up his stallion. "Reckless or not, I'm going back. Stop trying to talk me out of it."

The Starhound bounced around his legs.

"No, Argos," Lorc said. "You go with the Hemoth. I can't have the Minor getting hold of you. Imagine if he used you to name the next king of Hundford?"

The High Beast's ears flattened, head hung low. The Hound prince took the dog's face in his hands and raised it. "It's for your safety, Argos."

Aster stepped out of the shadows. "I'm going back too."

All three boys jumped, Quintin tripping on the Shadow Dragon's tail and falling on his buttocks.

"I need to save my sister."

Dev released a heavy sigh, and she knew what he would say before he spoke. "Aster, the Minor wants Alcor. If we go back—"

"*We* aren't going anywhere," she said. "Your duty is to Alcor. Not me. But I have a duty to my family. I can't abandon Ursula and Mother to whatever Uncle Bram has in store. And Lorc is right—the Highen needs someone to stop Uncle Bram."

Dev stared at her, his eyes wide and pleading. But her mind was made up. This was how she could make things right. This was how she could be her father's daughter.

Quintin Wyvern frowned. "I will come with you."

"What?"

"You and your sister asked for my help," the Dragon prince said, "and the On-High carried your message to me. Just like you have a responsibility to your sister, the On-High have charged me with a responsibility to the two of you. I will go to help you get your sister back from Minor Lourdes. I'm sure I can be of use somehow."

"But...but you're the last Wyvern," she stammered.

He shrugged. "I am. But I'll never be king as long as the Minor rules the Highen."

Aster felt a warm spot growing in her heart for Quintin Wyvern. She wasn't sure she'd ever know how to thank him—for coming here, for being so willing to help at every turn. The Kingdom of Dracogart would be lucky to have him on their throne—if he lived to take it.

The Hound prince nodded at Umbra. "What about your dragon?"

Lorc Conri was right. Dev couldn't be expected to get Umbra *and* the Starhound *and* Alcor to the Drakkan Range alone.

"Quintin, you know the way through the mountains," Aster said after a moment. "Dev will need your help to keep them safe."

The Shadow Dragon nuzzled the Dragon prince's hand, and he stroked her beak. He nodded, and Aster felt a bit relieved not to be leaving Dev alone.

But Dev was less relieved. "Just what exactly is it you think you're going to do? Storm the Manor? The two of you?"

"No," said Aster simply. "The Manor is my home. I know every way in and out. There are passageways in the walls, built for protection. They all connect and lead to the storm cellar. We used to play in them as little girls, stealing sweets from Mother's quarters. No one knows about them but my family. Not even the servants."

"Forgive me, Princess," said Lorc Conri, "but need I remind you that the Minor is your family?"

"If the rumors in Downswift are any indication," she said, "my uncle thinks I burned up in the Oracle House. He won't be expecting me."

Lorc thought for a moment before nodding. "Do you know where he'd keep your sister?"

"The Manor has a dungeon. She'll be there, and we'll get her," said Aster firmly. "And Mother, too." Because they had to. "And when we do, we'll come and get you in the mountains. Wait for us in the Glow Poppy Valley, between Plowman's Peak and the Sky Reach Mountain. Do you know it?"

Quintin nodded. "I know Glow Poppy Valley."

Dev was quiet. She waited for him to argue further, but he said nothing, his hand on Alcor's mane as the bear began his familiar *bope bope bope.*

"It's settled, then." Lorc Conri pulled sharps from his saddlebag. "I hope you know how to use these."

Aster nodded and tucked them into her cloak.

"What do we do if you don't come and find us?" asked Dev. His eyes were fixed on her. "What do I do if you don't come back?"

"We will come back," said Aster.

He was frightened, she could tell that much—not for himself, but for her. That was Dev's way, she'd come to learn. He worried about Alcor, about Keeper Rizlan, about Ursula, about her. Everyone but himself. And she realized she was going to worry about him, too. After all, in a way, they'd never really been apart—she'd seen Dev every single day of her life. And now they'd been through so much together…and she was leaving him. Sending him into the mountains where the way would be dangerous.

She hugged him, holding on tight. "We *will* come back."

He hugged her back. "But what if?"

"Then disappear," she said. "Hide Alcor. Don't let Uncle Bram find him, no matter what."

But Lorc was more practical. He pulled a ring from his finger, a signet with the image of a hound carved into a gold-flecked green stone. "Wait two weeks, maybe three, and if we don't return, forget the mountains. Risk the journey to Hundford and deliver this to my brother Arthur. He'll know it's from me. If you make it, he'll help you."

And with that it was settled. Without turning back, Aster and Lorc mounted Septimus and disappeared into the trees, bound for the Manor. She could hear a mighty moan from Alcor fading behind her.

No matter what.

Family is one of the On-High's greatest blessings ... or cruelest curses.

—MAJOR OLAN FARR,
The Battle for Skorpios: The Ring War, Act IV

TWENTY-SIX

THOUGH her father's strong arm was around her, Bernadine thought she might faint in the withering presence of Aunt Luella and Ursula.

They sat straight-backed at the Major's table, chins held high, clasping each other's hands. Aunt Luella's stare was all venom, but Ursula refused to look at either Bernadine or her father. And why should she? This was Ursula's father's house. Her father's kingdom. His Highen. And Bernadine's father had stolen it. He'd committed many sins to do it.

"Now," said her father. "Just the family, together. Isn't this nice?"

Aunt Luella *harrumph*ed, but Bernadine's father ignored it. His attention was all for Ursula. He pulled out a chair and sat down beside her.

"I understand that you're angry with me," he told her, "but in time you'll understand. Until then, I won't make you speak to me. But your dear little cousin, my darling Bernadine, she has done nothing wrong. Perhaps you would speak to her? I know Aster is alive. Would you tell Bernadine where she's gone?"

Speak to me? Ursula barely spoke to her when they were living in the same house, before all this happened. Why would she start now?

Ursula's eyes shifted, glancing briefly at Bernadine. There it was again—contempt. Bernadine shifted on her feet.

"You waste your breath, Bram," said Aunt Luella.

"I wasn't speaking to you, woman."

"If you think my daughter would betray her sister to you, you're even denser than I feared. Wherever Aster is, she'll make sure you never get your hands on that bear."

Bernadine's father stood up, throwing back his chair so that Bernadine jumped. "You *will* tell me where Aster has taken the Hemoth!"

Ursula didn't move.

"You throw tantrums like a little child," said Aunt Luella. "It's no wonder Mizar didn't chose you at the Northern Crowning all those years ago. What kind of Major can't control his temper? You can rage all you want, but you know you will never have control of the Highen."

Bernadine watched her father rub a trembling hand over his face. He was shaking with anger, but he breathed deeply, trying to calm himself. Finally, he sat back down, leaning toward Ursula.

"Dear niece," he said, on the edge of control. "What in Tawn's name have you let happen to this fine garment I sent you?"

Bernadine regarded Ursula's bloodied frost-pearl gown: it was ruined, but still the pearls shone.

"Such a brilliant glow," he said. "No matter how much dirt they're dragged through, frost pearls always shine." He looked back at Bernadine. "Like you, my love. A mother taken from you. Forced to grow up in a foreign land. And still you shine."

Ursula shook her head, and Bernadine's father didn't miss it. He smiled coldly.

"I knew it would be the same with this dress. No matter what happened, the pearls would glow, like a beacon in the night. So easy to spot, frost pearls."

Ursula gritted her teeth. "You tried to mark me. You sent the dress to make it easy for your men to find me when they stormed the Manor."

Bernadine looked at her father. Was that why he'd sent Ursula such a lavish gown? He was painting a target on her back?

Her father grinned. "It seems I didn't plan well enough. I should have sent another gown for your sister."

"You won't find her," said Ursula. "Our father taught her well. If she wants to disappear, she can."

Aster? Bernadine had a hard time believing it. When Uncle Jasper was home, he spent most of his time telling stories and laughing with the girls. He wasn't one for rigorous lessons. He left that to the weapons and riding masters, and to Keeper Rizlan. And Bernadine knew Aster took her studies with those old men about as seriously as Bernadine did, which wasn't very seriously at all.

"No one can hide from me in my realm!" her father roared, shooting up again. "Do you imagine I sit idle here in Tawnshire, blind to the workings of the Highen?" He towered over Ursula, and she leaned as far away from him as her chair would allow. "I own eyes in every kingdom, every city, every town. No matter where your sister runs, *I will find her!*"

"My sister is stronger than you know. And she has the On-High on her side," Ursula said through clenched teeth. "They spoke to us through the Oracles. They will protect her. And they will destroy you."

"I'd be the one afraid of destruction if I were you, girl," he growled. "After all, if your sister has the bear, what use do I have for you?"

Ursula's eyes widened, and Aunt Luella wrapped her arms around her daughter protectively. Bernadine swallowed. What did her father mean to do? He wouldn't hurt Ursula, would he?

Ursula straightened. Whatever fear she felt she seemed to push down deep inside. "You have no use for me," she agreed. "Add me to your list of sins, Uncle. The On-High are watching."

The Minor lifted his hand, ready to slap Ursula, and before Bernadine knew she'd made a sound, her voice echoed off the walls. *"She's coming here!"*

Both Ursula and her father stared at her, each looking strangely surprised to see her standing there.

Bernadine swallowed. "A-Aster. She'll come to the Manor."

"What makes you think that, Bernie Doll?" asked her father.

Everything Bernadine knew of her cousin made her think that.

The two girls took their lessons together, spent their leisure time together, rode their horses together, played together, ate together. They'd grown up together. If there was anyone in the whole world that Bernadine knew as well as she knew herself, it was Aster.

"When the Frosmen first took the Manor," said Bernadine, "Ursula wanted to escape, to hide Alcor. But Aster wanted to return for her mother."

Her father watched her, waiting.

"It was Ursula who reigned her in," said Bernadine. "Alone, Aster is reckless."

Ursula's face darkened—this was a betrayal she would never forgive. To Ursula, Bernadine knew, she was the enemy now—a Whitlock girl, daughter of the Minor.

Bernadine took a tiny step back, eyes ever on the floor. "She will come here for Ursula and Aunt Luella. We don't need to go looking for her. She will bring the bear to us."

And so it was decreed by Lev the Quiet that all the children of the Highen should memorize the Star Prayer, to be recited every Festival of Tawn before the Northern Crowning. And the On-High were pleased.

—THE WRITINGS OF THUBAN,
On Faith: The Star Majors, *Star Writ*

TWENTY-SEVEN

LORC Conri and Aster Lourdes rode until they reached the outer border of the Shiver Woods, the forest that lined the city of Tawnshire Town. When night came, they would go to the Manor. For now, they would rest and wait for the cover of darkness.

Lorc left Aster, who looked like she was hurting from the night-and-day journey—they'd covered a great distance, and she probably wasn't used to riding for so long—to look for rabbits. He disliked hunting them—they were fast and stubborn and hard to catch. What he wouldn't give for Argos's help! He hadn't wanted to leave the Starhound, but it was too dangerous; he'd never forgive himself if Argos became the property of the Major, and neither would Arthur.

Though he wasn't sure Arthur would be forgiving him anyway. He tried not to think of his brother—of how angry he must have been to discover Lorc gone, how worried. Even if Lorc managed to succeed here—somehow—he wasn't sure it would be enough for Arthur to forgive him.

By the third brush pile he managed to flush a little cottontail, his thrown dagger finding its mark.

"Here," he said, returning to camp and dropping the dead rabbit into Aster Lourdes' lap.

He handed her one of his daggers, then left to collect whatever other food he could find. The woods here were different than in Hundford, with many plants he didn't recognize, but he managed to forage a good amount of milk beets and luminip—even a patch of felt fungus—that would work well with rabbit.

If the rabbit survived whatever Aster Lourdes was doing to it. By the time he came back, her arms were covered in blood, and she'd hacked up the little creature so badly that she'd carved it right down to the bone, fur clinging to hide in ragged chunks.

"Do you want me to do it?" he asked her, horrified.

"I know how to clean a rabbit!" she snapped.

She didn't, he could tell that much.

He knelt in the dirt across from her and set to work building the fire, trying not to watch as she went back to cutting. His brother Connall hated it when Lorc watched him do any little task, and if Lorc tried to correct him, Connall would leave in a huff. *Just let him sort it out*, Arthur always said.

But eventually, he couldn't take it anymore. If he let her continue this way she'd ruin the meat beyond saving and he'd have to flush out another. "It looks to me like you're making a mess of it."

Aster stopped, eyes narrowing. "You think I don't know how?"

"I'm certain you don't know how."

Aster's scowl deepened and she went back to destroying the rabbit. She was determined, Lorc had to give her that. It was exactly the kind of doggedness his mother found endearing. He knew what Queen Conri would've done—she'd let the Lourdes girl continue this embarrassing display, and when it was over she'd show Aster exactly what she'd done wrong. When Mama was done with Aster Lourdes, Aster would have been able to strip the fillets from a shimmer trout with the heart still working. How was it she didn't know how to use a knife?

Lorc struck his flint and a tiny flame burst to life.

"It isn't true," Aster said haughtily, peeling off a good-sized piece of the rabbit's skin, "what they say about me. I'm not *completely* helpless."

Lorc nursed the flame. "I know."

"Don't humor me, Conri."

He shrugged, piling twigs over the flame. "I'm not. I saw you on the river." Saw her face the Frosman captain without hesitation, saw her save Quintin Wyvern from drowning, saw her catch the line he threw into the water. As the river tried to devour them, Aster Lourdes had fought the hardest. "You didn't seem helpless to me. For what it's worth," he offered, "it isn't true what they say about me, either."

Aster blushed. So she hadn't forgotten the way she'd spoken to him when they first met. "Well. I suppose we would both do well not to listen to gossip."

Lorc poked at the fire. He should have learned that lesson a long time ago. He'd dealt with whispers at his mother's court for years. Why had he believed whispers about Aster Lourdes without meeting her himself?

Without meaning to, he glanced over at the rabbit.

"Then again," she said, looking down at the frightful mess between her hands, "you are good in the woods. A natural huntsman. The rumors about that were true."

Lorc smirked. "I have my talents."

Aster laughed, and he took the knife, finishing up for her. She watched him carefully, paying close attention in a way that reminded him of his youngest brother, Murphy.

"I made a mess. Don't blame the knife," said Aster. "Little point's only following orders."

"What?"

"Something my father used to say," she explained. "If me or my sister ever got frustrated during sharps practice or something. We got frustrated a lot."

"It's a good saying."

Aster smiled. "Did Queen Conri teach you how to clean a rabbit?"

He set the little hare on the fire and checked the vegetables. "Clean a rabbit, skin a deer, butcher a boar. She could have disappeared into the forest and lived out her days there, just her and the wild." He saw her in his memory: a thousand lessons, a thousand afternoons spent with her and his brothers in the shade of the cedars. How many days might she have lived if she *had* just disappeared into the wild?

"I should have rather liked to meet her," said Aster, "your mother. She always seemed so exciting, with her dogs and her furs and her blades. Such a romantic figure."

"Romantic?"

"Of course," said Aster, waving a hand. "A warrior queen! And all those suitors? What must it be like to have so many?"

Lorc frowned. "There weren't *that* many."

"Oh, no...no, of course." She backtracked, flushing. "I only meant...well, never mind." She hesitated, gazing at him. "Have *you* many prospects in Hundford?"

He chuckled, twisting the rabbit on its stick. *"Me?"*

The idea was laughable. Arthur had a bevy of admirers, but that was Arthur. Lorc had never really even thought about marriage. He'd always assumed his mother would make him a match when the time came.

"No," he said finally, amused. And then, "You?"

"Of course not!" she nearly screeched, scandalized.

The hare was crackling now, blistered and browned to Lorc's liking. He pulled it from the flame and hacked off the hind legs. "You know, my mother was right about you lot. *Tough as bloomnuts, those Tawnshirians*, she'd say, *but twice as wooden.* All of you obsessed with pomp and propriety. With the way things *should* be done. Mama never liked doing anything the way it *should* be done."

He looked up, and there was Aster, fuming. "I am *not* a bloomnut.

And I am not *obsessed with the way things should be done*. I am *not* wooden."

"All right, all right," he said, arms raised in surrender at her furious face. "I meant no offense."

"Of course you did."

He sighed, already exhausted. He didn't know much about girls, especially Tawnshirian girls, and he was getting the sense that his ignorance was going to be a problem. "Would saying I'm sorry help, then?"

She shrugged.

Lorc dropped his head and gritted his teeth. *On-High give me strength*. "I'm sorry," he said. "You're not a wooden bloomnut."

Aster didn't say anything.

He cleared his throat. "The rabbit's ready."

They ate in awkward silence, the whispering leaves on the trees nagging him to say something, anything, to fill the quiet.

In the end, it was Aster who spoke first. "We should stay here until my uncle and his men go to supper. With the Oracle House in cinders, the evening bells won't chime in the city, but we'll have the glimmer beetles. They usually come out at the right time, when the sun is gone and the air is cool and men sit down to eat. When we see them we'll know it's time to go."

Lorc nodded. They didn't have glimmer beetles in Hundford, but Tawnshire was Aster's home. He trusted her instincts.

"You can *always* keep time by the glimmer beetles' glow," she continued. "My father taught me that."

"Oh," was all Lorc could think to say. And then, "I can always keep it by Argos's stomach."

Aster smiled. "All our High Beasts seem to have that in common. Hard to believe they're expected to be furious warbeasts someday."

Lorc considered this. Argos had always been so loving. So silly. *Warbeast* was a strange idea. Would he really be like Mama's mighty

Asterion? "I dunno. They've come through rather a lot these last few days, haven't they?"

Aster eyed him, as though he'd told a joke without trying to be funny. "Hardly the glorious battles of the *Star Writ*."

"There's a terrifying thought."

"What?"

"The *Star Writ*," he said with a shrug. "All we've been through. It *will* be in there, Aster. The Minor, the Oracle House, the river. Now Mount Draccus. People will be reading about it for centuries."

Aster stiffened, as though the thought had never occurred to her.

"I wonder," he said. "What will it say about us, you reckon?"

She looked up at the sky, and he could see the rabbit shaking in her hand ever so slightly. Perhaps he shouldn't have said anything.

"Whole paragraphs about my dashing nature and princely good looks, no doubt," he said, trying to make her smile again. "But I'm sure they'll mention you."

Aster glared at him. He really didn't know anything about girls at all.

She took a bite of rabbit and chewed carefully. After she swallowed, she spoke in a quiet voice that was very un–Aster Lourdes. "Do you really think I'm a bloomnut?"

Lorc thought about it. And then shrugged. "No more than I am."

At that, Aster Lourdes did smile.

When the daylight began to fade, Aster and Lorc set out for the Manor, leaving Septimus tied deep in the trees. They moved in silence, and Lorc was impressed at how nimbly Aster made her way through the forest, quiet as a deer. Even Arthur, who'd been hunting longer than Lorc, snapped the odd twig underfoot. Not Aster. Major Jasper Lourdes had managed to teach his daughters one thing, at least.

"How much farther?" he asked.

"Not much," she said. "Six tail-lengths? Seven?"

"Will this bring us out by the front or the back of the Manor?"

"The east edge of the grounds. Where the stables are. They'll provide us cover so we can make our way to the Manor without being seen."

The glimmer beetles began to blink to life, and Lorc marveled at the light and color dappling the trees: a hundred shades of pink and purple glittered, as if trying to mimic the setting sun above. He stopped, watching as the forest lit up like a dream. They had starflies in Hundford, little green flickers in the long grass, but nothing like this.

Aster looked back for him. "They only last till moonrise. Father always said the glimmer beetles wouldn't dare outshine the On-High."

What a shame, Lorc thought, that something so amazing lasted such a short while.

"On-High," Aster said, repeating the word again and again. When Lorc looked over at her, she was patting her pockets frantically. "It's gone. I must have dropped it."

"Dropped what?"

"I have to go back, I have to find it!"

"Aster," said Lorc, "find what?"

Without answering, Aster took off into the trees, back the way they'd come. She crashed through the brush, her earlier care gone. "Aster, wait!" he called after her. This close to the Manor, they couldn't afford to be separated. The Frosmen could be anywhere, patrolling the trees.

"Aster, stop!" he tried.

But she wouldn't. She kicked at the earth and fell to her hands and knees, tossing dirt and leaves.

"Aster," said Lorc, angry now. "Are you mad? What if the Frosmen hear you?"

"I've lost it!" She was near tears. "It's gone, it's gone, it's gone!"

"What?" Lorc hissed.

"My starflame!"

"Starflame?"

She was on her feet, running again. How exactly did she expect to find her jar, running like an angry ox? She wouldn't. Which meant this display wouldn't end anytime soon. Unless Lorc found it first.

Throwing up his arms, he set about retracing their steps. Back to the thicket where the glimmer beetles had first come to light. She'd noticed it missing there. That was the logical place to start. He followed her tracks, gently nudging the earth as he walked. And there it was, her little glass jar, nestled into the root of a tree.

He grabbed it and made his way back, following the sounds of Aster crashing through the forest.

When he found her, she was sitting, leaning back against a stump, staring up at the sky with tearstained cheeks. He held the jar in front of her face. "Is this what all the fuss is about?"

Aster gasped and grabbed the jar like it might run off.

"You're welcome," he said.

Aster dropped her head back against the stump, staring up at the wine and plum hues of sunset shifting and changing above the trees.

"You can't take off like that," he told her. "Do you realize what could have happened if there'd been Frosmen nearby?"

"They burned me," she said suddenly, holding up the jar. Inside, where there had been only air before, a faint light, no bigger than the head of a needle, flitted and fluttered sleepily at its center. Night was nearly upon them.

"The On-High, in the Oracle House," she went on. "Their flames, when we released them, I could feel their heat. It burned."

Lorc waited, not sure what she meant.

"It didn't burn the others," she said.

"What didn't?"

"The fire," she said, handing him the jar. "Can you feel its heat?"

The jar in his hand was cool to the touch, the white light inside emitting nothing but a faint vibration that tickled his fingertips. "It's cold."

She took the jar back, a miserable look on her face. "Not to me. To me it's warm."

He looked up at the sky. When the On-High appeared tonight, would his mother burn bright among them? If she sent her flame to earth, and he found it in the Hundford Oracle House, would he feel her warmth?

"What is that prayer they teach us?" asked Aster Lourdes. "The first one every little child has to learn before their third Festival of Tawn?"

Lorc knew the prayer. Everyone in the Highen knew it as well as they knew their own name. How could it be that Aster Lourdes needed help remembering? Had she asked anyone else in the Highen how to begin the Star prayer, they might have considered her blasphemous. But Lorc only felt a sadness for her.

"*I sleep beneath the starry sky,*" he began, and Aster Lourdes clasped her hands over her heart, "*and wait for morning's sunlit safety. Oh, watchful gaze of bless'd On-High, turn thy sacred eyes on me. For till the dawn I'm all alone, asleep in the deep dark night....*"

"*Watch me from thy heavenly throne, and wrap me in celestial light,*" she finished, a tremor in her voice. Then she saluted the On-High and stood, clearing her throat.

Aster Lourdes kept her eyes on her jar, the starflame burning brighter as the day faded to night.

She was afraid. Lorc could tell that plain enough. And still, she was going to the Manor.

Lorc had only ever seen the Major from afar, on the three occasions when his mother brought him and Arthur to the Festival of Tawn. Both times, as the Major's thunderous voice carried over the assembled crowd to speak about the glory of the Bear Highen, Lorc had been overwhelmed by the power contained in the body of one man.

Looking at Aster, Lorc could see the Major's strength there. If the On-High had favored Major Jasper Lourdes, then surely, Lorc decided, the stars had to favor his daughter just the same.

Memories are hard things to trust—tricky as Nightlocks and slippery as fish.

—THE WRITINGS OF BERN,
On Keepers: The Age of Tawn, *Star Writ*

# TWENTY-EIGHT

THE woman—long golden hair to rival that of the Great Lady Berenice—stood at the edge of the bog, staring up at the stars.

Dev knew her immediately. Knew her from the dreams he had night after night.

Mother.

There was an infant swaddled in her arms, and a boy stood at her side, pulling at her skirts. He often saw her with an infant. Him, he assumed. And the boy—a brother? Where was that brother now?

The woman sang, rocking the quietly fussing baby while the boy joined her song. This was Dev's life. His life before the Keepers came. He hated that he couldn't call up the memories at will. He could only revisit them in his dreams.

His mother glanced up. Right at Dev. He stiffened.

She'd never looked at him before. Not while he watched. She frowned, squinting into the dark. Could she see him? And then she blessed herself with the sign of the On-High and turned her eyes back to the bog.

The boy at her side continued to tug her skirts, insistently, and when she finally acknowledged him, he pointed a chubby arm to the eastern sky.

Dev followed their gaze to where the boy was pointing. In the far distance, beyond the rolling golden fields, beyond the placid fens, toward the distant lights of Tawnshire, a small plume of smoke rose into the sky.

Dev's heart seized. Forgot to pump blood.

Starflame.

The smoke was coming from the Oracle House. The Oracle House they had only just burned down. This was now. Dev was seeing *now*.

Was Aster right? Were these memories not memories at all?

At the thought of her, the stars above him swelled, blinding him, burning the night away. He squeezed his eyes tight, trying to stop the flare, trying to stop his brain searing, but in an instant—it was over.

When he opened his eyes again, he was inside. High ceilings with spiraling columns. Ornate stained-glass windows. Intricate wall hangings.

The dining hall of Lourdes Manor. He was home.

At the head of the table sat a stern-looking Bram Lourdes, his knuckles running along his mouth as Cook Darby shuffled in, led by a silver-haired Frosman. The cook seemed tired, her cheeks sunken, dark circles around her eyes, new wrinkles creasing her face. What had the Minor done to her? Two people sat on either side of him, watching in silence as the cook placed bowls on the table. To his left was a woman, her dark silken hair flowing over black, shimmering armor that looked like scales. To his right was a man, dressed in elegant gold fabrics and a red hunting cape, who pulled a vial from his pocket.

The man in red upended the vial into his gloved palm. It held a powder—crushed purple petals, maybe?—and he dusted it over the steaming bowls from Darby. The Minor nodded, approving.

And then laughter—ghostly and inhuman. The shadows of the trio grew, stretching toward the ceiling, until they each had wide, hideous grins.

Nightlocks.

The shadows dove for Dev, swallowing him in black, and he tried to scream, but no sound came, nor breath, either.

After an eternity, the shadows released their hold, and he felt air in his lungs again.

But it was damp, cold air. Torchlight was flickering off black, leaking stone walls…It was the Manor, he knew that much from the masonry, but not a part he was familiar with.

There was a rattle of chains, and he turned to see figures hunched on the floor in the dark. Carefully, he moved closer, and as he did, he recognized the prisoners, filthy and shivering—Lady Lourdes and Ursula. In their hands, they held Darby's bowls, slurping down the gruel.

A laugh sounded by the cell door. Another Nightlock. It beckoned Dev to follow, and transfixed, he did, stepping through the wood. The hall without was tight and dark, the red glow of torchlight up ahead the only light to see by. The Minor walked toward him with the man in red.

"The poison will be slow," the man in red said.

The Minor nodded. "Good. I want them alive when she gets here."

"How can you be certain she'll come?"

A group of Frosmen materialized, lining the walls by an ancient wooden door. The Minor stuck a key into the door's lock, and when he was done, someone on the other side pulled it open.

Aster.

A chorus of laughter. The cackling of Nightlocks rising as the Frosmen raised their blades. Aster's face, wide with terror.

And then a roar, furious and earthshaking—*Alcor?*

Fire leapt up around Dev in a raging blaze—*dragonfire*, he was sure—engulfing everything in smoke and flame. And a Hemoth, battle-clad and raging, burst through the wet stone walls, all of them crumbling to the ground and burying the Frosmen. Debris rained down, brick and beam and dust.

And above him, Dev saw Aster, sitting astride the Bear.

Before the whole of the Manor came down.

Hands—rough and urgent—shook Dev by the collar. "Keeper! Wake up!"

Dev gasped, blinking into the alarmed dark eyes of Quintin Wyvern.

"Keeper, you were *screaming.*"

Had he been screaming?

Argos, the Starhound, licked Dev's cheek, while Alcor nuzzled his elbow, whining. The Shadow Dragon sat in the middle of the clearing, her head cocked curiously, her neck perked upright, her yellow eyes staring into his.

He was back in the forest. He'd never left.

"Take this," said Quintin. He pressed a wet cloth to Dev's forehead, torn from a piece of the Dragon prince's own cloak. "You gave me a bit of a scare. You were writhing like a Nightlock had taken you! That was some nightmare."

Dev held tight to his heaving chest, trying to catch his breath. "It wasn't a nightmare."

"What do you mean?"

Perhaps you're seeing like Keeper Rizlan. Aster had said that.

A laugh, nervous and tight, burst out of Dev. She was right. Aster Lourdes had been right!

"It was a vision!" said Dev, leaping to his feet. "I saw her—she was looking at the smoke from the fire *we* made! At the Oracle House! It wasn't a memory. It was really her! I saw her!"

"Saw who?"

"My mother!"

"Bad relationship, have you?"

Dev looked down at Quintin, not understanding.

"The screaming," Quintin said.

"Screaming," Dev repeated, remembering Aster, the Frosmen waiting in the dark. "Yes. Yes! I saw her, at the Manor!"

"Your mother?"

"No!" said Dev. "Aster! And the Minor, the Frosmen! They were all there. The Minor, he had Ursula and Lady Lourdes. And—and—" Dev's heart hammered in his chest. What he'd seen was a glimpse from the On-High—it *was* a vision, not a dream. The truth of it made him feel faint, and he leaned on Alcor. "The Frosmen were waiting! Waiting to strike Aster down!"

"Down?" Quintin stood.

Dev nodded.

"Aster Lourdes is dead?"

No. No, the Hemoth had saved her. The On-High sent visions to Keepers as a gift; they'd shown him this as a way to help.

Shown him what would happen.

"The vision was a warning," he said. "The Minor knows she's coming."

"But *how*? How could he know such a thing?"

"I don't know. But the Minor has the passages she spoke of guarded. If she tries to use them, his Frosmen will be waiting for her. We have to help her!"

"Help her?" said Quintin. "But…the Hemoth."

"It's Alcor she needs! And Umbra!" said Dev. "I saw her with the Hemoth, she was sitting on his back! And there was dragonfire over everything!"

"Wait, stop!" Quintin held up his hand, his eyes wide with disbelief. "You're saying you want to bring the High Beasts *back* to the Manor?"

Did he? He'd promised Aster he'd keep Alcor hidden. No matter what.

But he knew this was the right thing to do. "Yes. If Aster is walking into a trap laid by Bram Lourdes, she'll need Alcor to defeat him. Umbra, too. We have to get them there before it's too late!"

"But we're supposed to keep them safe!"

"I know," said Dev. He couldn't blame Quintin for doubting him; this was not the plan. "Quintin, listen. I'm a Keeper, and the On-High are trying tell me something. I need you to trust that what I've seen comes from them."

Quintin was silent. Dev could see in his frown that he wasn't at all sure he could do that.

But then, finally, he nodded. "They must be all the way to Tawnshire Town by now."

"Alcor runs faster than any horse."

Dev turned to Alcor and held his face. Quietly, gently, he asked the Hemoth to carry him once again. When his whispered prayer was over, the bear dropped low, letting Dev climb onto his back.

"I'll fly ahead." Quintin gathered up his things, stuffing them into his sack with what was left of the burst beans. "Alcor may be a fast runner, but flying is quicker. I should be able to find which way they've gone from the sky."

The Starhound barked, pacing by the trees through which Aster and Lorc had left the day before. He was ready to lead the way.

They would all go.

Quintin slung himself onto the dragon's back. "Are you always right, when you interpret these visions?"

Dev swallowed. "This is sort of my first one."

Quintin blinked at him. "Your *first*?"

"At least we know I've never been wrong before," Dev said, straightening on Alcor's back.

Quintin sighed. "We'd better hurry."

Yes. Hurry they must. Aster's life depended on it.

When we die, the On-High bring our souls into the sky, to live beside them as stars. You cannot see most of the stars of the dead, as they are too small, and the On-High outshine them, but make no mistake: they are there. And they are watching.

—A CHILDREN'S GUIDE TO THE ON-HIGH

# TWENTY-NINE

THE many eyes that her father owned arrived at the Manor late
that night.

Bernadine watched from Aunt Luella's chambers as they turned
up on the steps of the Manor. They were a curious mix, some arriving
in lavish carriages signifying their royal status—she knew the polished
lindenwood of the Ox king's coach—others arriving on horseback
with only one or two attendants. After so many feasts and summits
hosted by her uncle, Bernadine had been sure she knew every royal
in the Highen, and many of their nobles besides. But there were faces
here she did not recognize—and they did not belong to kings and
queens. Her father came out to greet them all, welcoming them to
the Manor with a firm handshake and the proud news that Ursula
had finally been captured.

Bernadine rubbed at the chill in her arms. The room was warm—
Neva had built a fire for her—but still…The thought of Ursula
prickled her skin. The way her cousin had looked at her when she'd
told her father Aster would come…it was frigid. But Ursula didn't
understand. Bernadine had been trying to save her.

Though in the end it might have all been for nothing. What
would Father *do* with Ursula?

She tried to push the question from her mind, pacing the room as
if that would help to get rid of it. What was she letting herself worry
for? What her father did, he did because it was necessary—hadn't he

explained that to her? Uncle Jasper was the enemy. He'd let Mother die. He'd bartered with dragons' eggs when and how it pleased him. Her father would fix everything that had been done wrong.

She couldn't be afraid of her own father. Could she?

Under the window, another lavish carriage was pulling up, gilded in silver and gold with a relief of a lynx on the door. Pan Leander.

Aunt Luella would be furious. Though this was no longer a House that cared what angered Aunt Luella. Cared what would frighten her daughters. Cared what would upset the Major.

Her father was the leader of the Highen now. At least until a new Major was crowned.

If her father didn't let Ursula out of the dungeons for the Northern Crowning, Alcor would be forced to choose someone else. Choose Bernadine, her father hoped. She had Lourdes blood, after all.

But Bernadine could hear the laughter of the Nightlock echo in her mind. *Lies and deceit.*

She watched as Frosmen ran out to greet Pan Leander—a tall, thin man cloaked in heavy gray furs. Would the other Heads of Houses, men like Pan Leander, laugh when Bernadine stepped into the ring at the Crowning?

And who else would try for the crown? The Hound boys, of course, but the Ox and Lynx each had children too. Just because her father *wanted* Bernadine to be crowned, it didn't mean she *would* be. Anyone might step into the ring. The laws of Highen decreed that even a commoner could stand before the High Beasts' judgment—it was rare, but with so much turmoil…

The more she let herself imagine it, the more convinced she was that her father had not thought this plan out fully. There were others in the Highen better suited to be Major than she was—many of them. How could he expect her to defeat them all? *There is nothing I have learned that I cannot teach to you, Bernie Doll,* he'd promised. *And when we have the Hemoth, he will come to know you and love you as I do. He'll pick you, you'll see, and the Highen will be better for it. You're going to be Major. I swear.*

But he couldn't swear. Not really. Why would he do all this, bring all this chaos, when there was no guarantee of anything?

This chaos...she thought of Ursula, chained in the dungeons of the Manor. She hated that her cousin was being held there, in the dank and the dark with the rats.

You will be made to pay.

Bernadine chewed at the skin around her nail. Yes, she rather thought she would. Trouble was following her; she could feel it like a shadow. If she *were* crowned Major after all of this, would that mean that the On-High forgave her? She'd saved Ursula, after all, hadn't she? She'd lied to her father to keep him from harming her cousin. And she didn't *know* that Aster was coming—it was a guess, nothing more, so Aster need not even suffer for it. She'd betrayed *Father*, really, not her cousins. Would the On-High consider that?

She watched as Pan Leander went down on one knee and made the sign of the On-High. She held her breath. Such reverence was reserved for the Major.

But she knew it was her father he was bowing to.

Bram Lourdes strode out of the Manor, greeting the Lynx king as he had all the others who had arrived before. But now the Minor seemed...stooped...weighted down, almost, as he took Pan Leander's arm and helped him to his feet.

Bernadine leaned closer to the window, watching her father closely.

He wriggled. No. Something on his back, his neck—*that* wriggled. Writhed.

And Bernadine gasped.

A shadow lifted from her father, stretching and twisting. A warped face turned and looked up at her.

A Nightlock.

She screamed.

But the next moment, there was nothing.

Bernadine stepped back from the window. Had she imagined it? A trick of the light? The gooseflesh on her arms said otherwise. Hadn't she been visited by one herself? They were here. They were at the Manor.

And one was *in* her father, already worked deep into his soul.

The words of the nether demon cackled in her mind: *Lies and deceit, a delicious treat, my favoritest kind of snack.* Everything Father was doing, all his lies, all his deceptions—his soul was blighted with terrible deeds. He'd killed his brother, and a Nightlock—hungry for evil, hungry for rage and sorrow—had finally possessed him.

If Father's plan was so wicked it attracted demons to his body, to his mind, to his soul, so wicked it invited devils to feast on the deepest parts of him, there was nothing redeemable in it.

Unless Bernadine could fix things. Could save her father's soul from being devoured by the Nightlocks, save him from becoming one of them, trapped behind the moon for all time.

"Mother," she whispered, looking up at her star. "How do I save him?"

The stars were silent. They twinkled back, and Bernadine wished she could read the flicker. But there was no message from her mother. Just the gentle glow of her star.

Tears stung Bernadine's eyes. Her father and Pan Leander were still speaking on the steps, Father looking aged and worn. She sat on the window seat and let the tears fall, staring out into the dark of the Manor green—

Where something moved at the edge of the lawn.

Something small.

Two somethings.

Whatever they were, they were too deep in shadow for the

Frosmen or her father to notice. Bernadine held her breath—more demons?

She stared hard, trying to see through the dark. The somethings crept along the edge of the Shiver Woods, just outside the reach of the torchlights on the stables. Bernadine watched as they scurried closer to the house, disappearing into the gardens along the Manor's west wing.

But not before Bernadine caught a glimpse of her cousin's Hemoth-red hair.

Aster had returned to the Manor.

An invitation to Lourdes' Manor is an honor the Major does not give lightly.

—THE WRITINGS OF RIZLAN,
Major Jasper Lourdes: The Lunar Offensive, *Star Writ*

THIRTY

THE lights of the Manor glowed through the trees of the Shiver Woods. Warm and bright, just like always. Aster felt the pull of them, their familiar safety beckoning her home.

But home wasn't safe anymore.

She stepped lightly through the trees, sharps held tight in her sleeves, Lorc Conri close at her heels. She'd brought them to the forest's edge just beyond the Bear Holding, the same place where she'd been forced to leave her life behind. The stable door that Alcor had splintered was gone, replaced with fresh boards and guarded by two Frosmen. Why they would need to guard the Bear Holding without the Hemoth, Aster didn't understand—until she heard the grunting of a massive animal.

"I thought your uncle killed the White Bear," whispered Lorc.

"He did," agreed Aster slowly. "He must have brought Marmoral with him from Whitlock."

"Marmoral?"

"Alurea's cub. A White Bear. She's barely past weaning." Aster listened to the poor beast's cries. How afraid the cub must be: taken to a strange place, its mother gone. Uncle Bram had upended so many lives.

"Why keep her?" Lorc wondered. "What use has he for her now?"

Aster shrugged. "Alurea is dead. I don't think Uncle Bram really even *is* the Minor anymore, not without her. So someone will have to be Minor when the new Major is crowned. Just one more throne under his control, I suppose."

Lorc nudged her, nodding toward the Manor House in the distance. From their spot in the trees they could see the front steps, Frosmen milling about—at least a dozen. "How do we get to your passageway?" he asked.

"Do you see where the ivy climbs the west wall of the Manor? There's a hidden door that opens up there."

As Aster pointed, the Frosmen became excited, hurrying together to the front of the Manor, utterly distracted. A carriage had arrived, an obnoxious ornamented thing that Aster would recognize anywhere.

Pan Leander.

The man who overthrew her mother's family. Welcomed on the steps of her parents' home.

Somewhere inside the Manor, Aster was certain her mother—if she knew—would be burning with rage, and Aster's own blood began to boil. "Keep close," she told the Hound prince.

She crossed the green from the stables as silently and as low as she could, Lorc keeping tight to her heels. When they reached the west gardens, dark in the shadow of the Manor house, the sounds of fountains playing covered their scramble through the herbal hedge. Lorc made for the Manor's ivy-covered wall and began feeling for the door, but Aster pulled him to the ground and put a finger to her lips.

"What are you doing?" he hissed.

"Listen. We can hear them if we're quiet."

It was true: Uncle Bram and Pan Leander were laughing merrily. She dared to creep back into the middle of the garden so she could see them, too, and Lorc followed, the two of them crouched behind a topiary.

"Burned down the Oracle House!" the Lynx king was saying. "No doubt the On-High didn't look too kindly on that."

Uncle Bram laughed again. "Well, they certainly saw fit to deliver Ursula into my hands."

Aster frowned. She hated the sound of her sister's name from that traitor's mouth.

"And how long until you rid us of the girl altogether?"

Aster held her breath.

"Patience, Pan," chuckled her uncle. "Don't cut down the tree until you've harvested all its fruit."

"How much more fruit do you expect this little tree to bear?"

"At least one more, my good friend," said Uncle Bram, patting the Lynx king on the back and walking down the steps to meet another arriving carriage. "The Hemoth."

Alcor.

"And then she dies?" asked Pan, stopping Aster's heart.

"And then she dies," agreed Uncle Bram.

Aster's chest felt tight, her stomach twisting. She needed to find her sister. Fast.

Warm breath on her cheek—Lorc Conri. "Aster, we can't stay out here like this," he whispered. "It's too dangerous. We have to go on."

"You can't go on at all," whispered a voice from the shadows.

Aster jumped, turning to see Dev and Quintin emerge from the darkness under the garden's plum trees. The Starhound grinned between them.

"What are you *doing* here?" she demanded. "How did you find us?"

"I lived here too, you know. I've seen you come out of this ivy a hundred times. I figured this had to be the passage you meant," Dev said, moving to crouch next to her. "Aster, you were right. They weren't memories, when I was seeing my mother. They were visions!"

"You came here to tell me *that*? Where's Alcor?"

"I don't imagine the Keeper ran here on foot," murmured Lorc wryly.

Quintin nodded in the direction of the woods. "The High Beasts are in the forest, waiting for us. They'll be fine as long as the last of the sausages hold out. No one knows they're there, do they? But we need to hurry."

Aster's hands flew at Dev on their own, shoving him hard in the chest. "You brought Alcor *here*? *Are you out of your mind?*"

"I didn't have a choice!" he hissed. "I had to warn you!"

"Warn me about *what*?"

"Aster, I told you: The On-High granted me a vision." He gripped her arms. "Bram knows you're coming."

She stiffened.

"What?" Lorc's voice broke.

"He's posted men in the passageways," explained Dev, deadly serious. "They've set a trap for you."

Aster's heart sank. If Uncle Bram was waiting for her, if the only way into the Manor was guarded by Frosmen, all of this had been for nothing.

But maybe Dev was wrong. He'd never been able to have visions before—how could he be sure he was having them now?

"How would Uncle Bram even know I'm coming?" she said. "How can you be sure you weren't *dreaming*? You said yourself the On-High have never granted you visions!"

"I don't know how Bram knows," said Dev. "But he does. If you walk in there, a dozen Frosmen will be waiting at each passage doorway to kill you. We have to go. Now."

Go. After everything she'd done to get here. If she left, she might never be able to come back. What would happen to her family?

"That's Furia's carriage," whispered Quintin Wyvern, his eyes focused on the front of the Manor.

The Frosmen were stirring again, excited by the arrival of another coach, this one paneled in obsidian scales and glinting in the lights of the Manor. Quintin looked pale, ghostly—but there was something hard in the Dragon prince's eyes that Aster hadn't thought him capable of. Something dark and furious. A hatred that ran deep.

A woman stepped out of the carriage, taking Uncle Bram's hand. She was tall and slender, with long, curling dark locks and brown skin. A beauty, were it not for the scowl on her face.

"Apologies for my late arrival, my lord." She bowed low. "The queen's death caused more of a delay than I anticipated."

A strangled sound escaped Quintin. He clapped a hand over his mouth and nearly bent in half.

"So it's done, then?" asked Uncle Bram.

The Dragon woman nodded. "Dracogart is rid of Wyverns. I am their sovereign now."

"But Wyvern had a son, did he not?" asked Pan Leander.

"Quintin fled the kingdom," she said. "He abandoned his mother to me."

Aster looked back at Lorc and Dev, but they could only stare, shocked. Quintin's mother was dead. His father, too. He was alone now.

Tentatively, Aster reached out for him, placing an awkward hand on his back.

"And he abandoned his people," the woman went on. "Even if he returns, the kingdom will not welcome him. I'll make sure of that."

Uncle Bram nodded approvingly. "And the High Beast?"

The Dragon woman swallowed, her head turning slightly as though she preferred not to look him in the eye. "The Shadow Dragon is also missing."

Uncle Bram's silence was deafening.

"You will find it," he said finally.

She nodded. "I will."

"You will find it and you will bring it to me."

The woman bowed. "Of course, my lord."

Aster's uncle said nothing more, turning on his heel and storming back inside the Manor.

Quintin pressed his hands harder into his mouth, tears spilling down his face.

"Try not to be too hard on yourself, Furia," Pan Leander said. "The Minor is only sore because his Hemoth is still at large."

"And Jasper Lourdes' heir? The older girl?"

"We have that much, at least."

"Keeping her is dangerous. She threatens everything he is working for."

"Patience, Furia," said the Lynx king, echoing Uncle Bram. "Once the Minor gets his Hemoth Bear, there will be no more use for Ursula Lourdes."

Aster's fists clenched at her side as the two disappeared inside the Manor. Leaving without her sister was not an option. No matter what vision the On-High had granted Dev.

Quintin had been trembling beneath the palm she had on his back, but now he straightened and wiped the tears from his eyes. "I can't leave Umbra alone," he whispered, his voice thick. "Not with Furia looking for her. She's all I have left."

The pain behind his eyes was a pain Aster felt in her own heart. The Dragon prince had lost so much—they all had. And it was Uncle Bram who had taken it. But, Aster was determined, he wouldn't take anything more. From any of them.

"Go." Aster nodded. "All of you. Get the High Beasts out of here. I will find Ursula by myself."

Lorc Conri almost laughed. "I'm not leaving."

"Aster," pleaded Dev. "You can't. You don't know what I saw."

"It doesn't matter what you saw, Dev." She turned away. "I'm the only hope she has."

Dev grabbed hold of her wrist, his grip desperate. "Aster, *please*."

"She's my sister, Dev," she told him, holding his gaze. "She needs me."

Before Dev could argue, Quintin gasped suddenly. A figure stood before them, a hood obscuring its face.

The four children froze as the figure pulled down the hood and revealed a familiar face.

Staring back at them was Bernadine Lourdes.

It is the father and mother blessed by the On-High who raise an obe-dient child.

—TWIGATIAN PROVERB

THIRTY-ONE

LORC drew his sword, and Argos gave a low growl. If the girl in the cloak tried to scream for help, they'd be surrounded by Frosmen in an instant.

But she didn't scream. She only stared. Right at Aster Lourdes.

And Aster Lourdes stared back. A tension simmered between them that suggested to Lorc that the girls knew each other well.

"You *did* come back," said the girl.

Aster raised her sharps. "Careful, cousin."

"*Cousin?*" choked Lorc. Then this was the Minor's daughter: Bernadine Lourdes.

"If you so much as breathe too loud," Aster warned her, "I will cut you down here and now."

Bernadine Lourdes trembled, eyes on the blades. "Please, Aster. You don't stand a chance of getting in. My father knew you'd come!"

"I wonder who gave him that idea," growled Aster. She leapt up, grabbed her cousin, and pressed a blade's edge against her neck.

Bernadine swallowed, the point of Aster's sharp pressed dangerously close to the skin. "I can take you to Ursula."

And at the mention of her sister, Aster released Bernadine with a shove.

"How?" she demanded.

"Father grew up here, just like you and me. He knows every secret of the Manor. Every door and passage. Except one."

A light of realization dawned in Aster. "The one we found. In the front."

Bernadine nodded. "The crawlway."

"The front?" said Lorc. "Bad luck there's a posting of Frosmen standing watch by the front door."

"Not watching for me," said Bernadine.

Aster considered this. "You mean to distract them?"

"I do. I can."

"Why are you doing this?" Aster asked, an edge to her voice. "Why help us?"

Indeed, that was the question on Lorc's mind.

"The things Father has done...they're unforgivable," Bernadine said, a tremor in her voice.

"Yes," bit Aster.

"But maybe..." Bernadine swallowed, her eyes glossy. "Maybe I can save him from himself."

Aster opened her mouth, the crease between her brows presaging some vicious response, but the young Keeper placed a hand on her shoulder and she seemed to think again. "All right," she said slowly, accepting her cousin's answer as if that were enough.

It wasn't, not for Lorc—Bernadine Lourdes wanted to *save* the Minor? How could they trust her if her goal was at odds with their own?—but he had to trust that Aster knew what she was doing. She knew her cousin best.

Aster turned to Quintin. The Dragon prince's body was rigid with the pain of grief, his eyes bloodshot. "You'll watch over the High Beasts while we fetch Ursula."

Quintin shook his head. "That's the job of the Keeper."

"No. If Dev is finally having visions, he might have another. I'll need him by me to tell me what he's seeing—and what he's seen. Besides, you're special to Umbra. You know how to care for Beasts."

Reluctantly, Quintin agreed. "All right. I will."

Aster nodded, satisfied, before turning back to her cousin. "After you."

"Wait for my say-so," said Bernadine, and hurried for the wall of the manor. She paused at the wall's edge before she finally rounded the corner, making for the Frosmen standing watch by the entryway.

Lorc's jaw ached, his teeth grinding as he watched the Frosmen greet the Minor's daughter. One word, that was all it would take. A gesture of Bernadine Lourdes' hand, and she could deliver them to her father all but gift-wrapped.

"I don't like this," he told Aster.

Aster didn't say anything. She was barely breathing, eyes focused on the girl and the soldiers. He noted her grip tightening on her sharps.

And then there was movement, the Frosmen shouting at one another. Half ran off down the front green, the remaining three rushing back inside the Manor. Bernadine lingered on the steps, watching whatever was happening just inside the door. And then she motioned them forward.

"Well done, cousin," Aster breathed. "Hurry," she told them, and they followed her to a well-groomed juniper bush that grew against the house. Bernadine joined them, dropping to the dirt and pawing at the bush.

"What did you tell them?" Aster asked Bernadine.

"That Marmoral got loose. I told them I saw her run off down toward the east bothy house, so away they went. The others ran off to alert the grounds and find more men. We haven't much time before they return." She pulled aside a branch and pushed hard against the stone of the Manor, the heavy gray blocks grating inward, revealing an opening barely big enough to squeeze through. The Lourdes girls squeezed themselves inside, one after the other, elbows and knees in the dirt, the young Keeper following dutifully behind. Lorc wasn't at all sure about this—trusting the Minor's own daughter, leaving Quintin to watch over the High Beasts alone. Lorc looked back toward the trees where the Dragon prince had disappeared into the brush. The Dragon boy was defenseless on his own, whether he knew it or not. But still, he'd have a dragon and a Hemoth at his disposal.

And inside Lourdes Manor, the Minor was waiting.

Determined, Lorc crouched down to the little opening in the wall as Argos whimpered behind him. "Go on, Argos," he said, nodding toward the trees. "Go to Quintin. I'll find you later."

But the Starhound only whined.

Lorc glanced into the Manor, the backs of the others disappearing into darkness. He didn't have time to argue.

"All right, then," he whispered, and Argos slunk inside, leaving Lorc the last to follow.

Inside, the hole opened up into a tunnel, barely wide enough for his shoulders. He pulled himself along like a worm through the earth, until the walls widened and he was able to stand at last.

Lorc had imagined the Major's mighty house to be much more open and bright than this dark and leaky little hallway he found himself in.

"We'd better be quick about it," Bernadine said, leading the way out of the hall and down a corridor. "Frosmen are posted by each passageway entry, and they are under strict orders not to leave their posts. We should be free to move through the interior halls as long as we only leave through the crawlway entrance beneath the staircase. Father is busy with the arrival of his guests—each of the kingdoms has sent someone, though Pan Leander is the only true king I've seen. The rest have all been regents, or claim to be, anyway. They're men and women who have aligned themselves with Father. They are all meeting to discuss the Northern Crowning, but he'll soon send someone to check on Ursula."

Regents. Lorc thought of his father, his brother, the struggle for power between them. "The Minor's guests," he asked. "Has someone come from Hundford?"

"Not that I've seen."

Lorc was glad for that.

The hall came to an abrupt dead end. The Minor's daughter crouched down, disappearing again into a tiny hole in the wall like a rabbit into a den, and Aster and Dev dutifully followed. Sighing, Lorc shrunk himself into the tiny opening, and found his nose nearly pressed against Dev's feet.

"What aren't we moving?" Aster demanded somewhere in the dark ahead.

"I'm trying to find it," Bernadine said.

Aster let out a frustrated sigh, and there was a sound of shuffling. "You have to pull down!"

Light split through the dark as Aster slid open a small panel in the wall. When they emerged, Lorc's knees aching and damp, they found themselves standing beneath a massive staircase fit for the On-High themselves. They were in a vast open atrium, adorned with a grand fireplace and dark marble floors, carved wooden columns reaching up to the second-floor balconies.

"Ursula's this way," said Bernadine, heading down a hallway to the left. "Beneath the cellars."

Aster stopped. "Beneath the cellars? Why not in the dungeon?"

"Because *you* know about the dungeon. So he's keeping her in an old storeroom. Father had it cleared out—"

Voices echoed through the atrium. "The Minor doesn't *need* to trust him," said a woman. "He only needs his allegiance."

"We must hurry," whispered Bernadine, continuing on toward the cellars, Aster and Dev following.

But Lorc and Argos lingered behind.

"What are you doing?" Aster hissed.

Lorc waved at her for quiet. "I hear something."

She was beside him in an instant, pulling him away. "Lorc, we can't stay here."

"But someone like *him?*" said a man. "Someone with such an intricate knowledge of poison?"

They watched from the shadows as the Dragon woman and the Lynx king walked together into the middle of the atrium.

"I imagine Lord Tier's knowledge of poisons is exactly what makes him useful to the Minor," said the Dragon woman.

Lorc's heart stopped. *Lord Tier.* They were talking about his father.

Just then, the Minor himself marched into the atrium, storming past the waiting pair. Aster was so close, Lorc felt her stiffen against him.

"Is he here, then?" Bram Lourdes asked.

The Dragon woman and the Lynx king bowed. "He has just arrived, my lord."

The Minor stood in the middle of the great hall, posting himself before the grand front entrance, where Lorc could see the oaken doors of the Manor yawning into the night. And marching up the steps, arms open to the Minor, strode his father.

"Well met, my lord!" his father said with a smile. "You're the man of the hour!"

The Minor embraced him. "And you, the Regent of Hundford!"

Aster looked at Lorc, eyes wide.

Father—regent? But Arthur would never have allowed it.

"I imagine you've brought with you your usual bag of tricks?"

Lorc's father lifted a wooden apothecary case. Poisons. "I live to serve you, my lord."

Aster was seething. "What is your *father*—"

Lorc placed a palm over her mouth, then pressed a finger to his lips, silently begging her to shut up for just a minute.

"I don't need to impress upon you all the importance of the Northern Crowning going exactly as we've planned," the Minor said, leading Lord Tier into the great hall. "We have two months exactly to prepare. Until the Hemoth chooses my Bernadine for Major, my hold over the Highen can be too easily challenged."

"We will defend you, my lord," said Pan Leander.

"Indeed," said the Minor. "But all the same, the wayward children of the Heads of Houses pose a very serious threat to me, and to all of us. The Blue Giraffe is too young to compete at the Northern Crowning, but my nieces—"

"You have Ursula," interrupted the Lynx King.

"Ursula, yes. But Aster is still at large," explained the Dragon woman, and Aster scowled beneath Lorc's hand. "Not to mention Quintin Wyvern. And, Lord Tier, I mean no offense, but Hundford has at least two princes able to compete, and we must weigh what to do with them very carefully."

Two. Arthur and Lorc.

"Babies," laughed Pan Leander. "All of them."

"If those babies show themselves at the Northern Crowning and are chosen by the High Beasts," boomed the Minor, "the Highen could be torn apart. Think, Lynx lord: even if my Bernadine was made Major, imagine Aster Lourdes as Minor, imagine Quintin Wyvern as King of Dracogart. There will be those who follow us, and those who follow them. I cannot have that kind of division. It leads to war."

"You needn't worry about Hundford," said Tier. "There is only one Hound prince who will compete at the Northern Crowning, and he will only do so if I tell him to."

"Your son?" asked the Minor. "Lorcan?"

Lorc's father nodded.

Lorc tried to swallow, but his mouth ran dry. *Only one.* What had happened to Arthur? One word swirled inside his mind again and again and again:

Wolfsbane.

"And where *is* your son?" asked Pan Leander.

"Right now, my Lorc has gone in search of Aster Lourdes and the Hemoth Bear," said Tier, coldly proud.

Lorc shouldn't have been surprised that his father knew where he'd gone. He knew everything—he always had. The boy at the gates when Lorc left home…how long had it taken him to report what he'd seen?

"He is the greatest tracker in Hundford," his father continued. "His mother taught him well. I have no doubt he will locate the girl, and when he does you will have your bear. If the Dragon prince is with them, you will have him and his lizard, too. And our problems are solved."

Lorc held his breath, swallowing the sick rising in his throat. What had his father done? Why was he swearing Lorc's allegiance to this traitor?

Aster ripped Lorc's hand from her mouth and shoved him back, *hard.*

When her eyes met his, she looked at him as though he were a monster. He reached for her, but she backed away, repulsed.

"And the Northern Crowning?" asked the Minor. "How will Lorcan fare there?"

"My son's bond with the lead Starhound is a strong one. I have no doubt the High Beast will choose him should he compete. Do you wish him to?"

Lorc stared at Tier and the Minor, both of them deciding the fates of their children—as if it were all so simple. It took every bit of his strength to keep from running at them, blades out.

"That depends. If he rules Hundford, can you control him?"

"Of course. He is my son."

"And when he discovers what you've done to his brothers?"

"He'll understand that I did it for him."

Lorc's grip on his sword tightened, his body unbearably hot. His father was wrong. Lorc would *never* understand what he had done.

Mother—she would have killed him herself for this. And Aster, what she must think—

"Then let the boy compete for the Starhound. I have no objections, so long as he does not compete for the Hemoth," said the Minor.

Lorc turned, desperate to tell the others he had nothing to do with this, but he saw from the looks on their faces that their minds were made up.

"You *disgusting* liar," Aster hissed, sharps rising. Dev grabbed her and pulled her back, dragging her around the corner and away from the Minor's ears—if he hadn't, Lorc was sure she would have tried to cut him down.

"No," insisted Lorc. "Aster, *they're* lying. I knew nothing about—"

"We can't just leave him," said Bernadine. "He might go back and tell them where we are."

"If I want your opinion," Aster spat at her cousin, "I will ask for it."

"Aster, she has a point," said the Keeper, maintaining a tight grip on the Bear princess. "He could go to them."

"Go to them?" repeated Lorc, bewildered. How could they think that? How could *Aster* think that? "Aster, you know me. You cannot possibly think—"

"You expect me to believe you?" No one had ever looked at him the way she looked at him now. As if she could kill him with nothing but her gaze. "*You?* It's all true what they say about you, isn't it? You *did* poison your brothers on Wolfsbane Day, didn't you?"

Her words tore through him worse than her sharps could. "I told you, I *never*—"

But it was too late. Aster wouldn't hear it. "You're a snake and a liar. And I can't believe I let you fool me."

"Aster," said the Keeper, "I'll stay with him. I'll keep him here, I—"

"You?" she snarled. "And when he tries to overtake you, what will you do? Bore him to death with a *Star Writ* lecture? He's almost twice your size!"

The bear boy shrank, rebuked. Aster looked wild. Like a cornered dog. Lorc could tell she would fight her way out even if it meant tearing down the pack she'd built around her.

Argos drew closer to Lorc, guard hairs raised against the animosity radiating from her. She looked down at the Starhound, realizing that Argos would defend his prince.

"Let go, Dev. You're both right," she said at last. "He can't come with us."

"Aster, please," Lorc begged. "You can't believe this! The Minor killed my *mother*! Why would I ever help him? I want to put him in the ground!"

"We part here, Hound Prince," she said, deadly cold. "Mother, brothers—what's it matter to you?"

"Wait," said Bernadine, "we can't just let him leave!"

"We have no choice. The High Beast is on his side. So go now, Lorc Conri. Go slinking back to your father like the traitor you are," Aster said. "You'll have to hurry if you're to stop us."

And with that, she grabbed her cousin's arm, and she and Bernadine and the Keeper ran for the dungeons.

Leaving Lorc alone in the Manor. Humiliated. Heartbroken. Furious in a way that burned his entire body and set him trembling. He had come here to avenge Mama, to prove to everyone that he was *not* what they said. And now—

He would kill his father himself for this. For his mother. For Arthur and his brothers. For Aster Lourdes, even. He made his way back to the great hall in a blind haste, blade clenched in his fist.

His father was still there, still talking with the Minor. Lorc could rush them. Strike them both down before either of them understood what was happening.

True, the Minor was one of the greatest warriors in the Highen's history, and Lorc was nothing but the boy who was spared on

Wolfsbane Day. But what else was left for him to do? In Hundford, the House of the Hounds sat empty. Everyone was gone.

A pair of Frosmen hurried into the atrium, his father and the Minor turning to face them. Lorc hugged the wall, watching from the shadows. His opportunity had evaporated.

"We can't find her anywhere, my lord," said the first Frosman. "We've searched the grounds, the towers. But we can find no sign of your daughter, Bernadine."

"What?"

"She came to us, reporting that she had seen the White Bear roaming free, but the cub was secure in the Bear Holding. Since then, we haven't been able to locate her."

The Minor darkened. *"Aster,"* he growled. "She's here."

Lorc's heart seized. The Minor knew.

"She'll be after Ursula!" the Minor boomed. "Go now! Alert the men!"

"Hurry, Argos," Lorc whispered, and took off running. They had to warn her.

But as he rounded corridor after corridor, he remembered what Aster had said to him. The Manor was the seat of the Major. It was not like other castles. And with every new hallway, Lorc was more turned around. He was wasting time, searching for a cellar he'd never been to.

He stopped, panic swelling inside him. The Minor was coming for her. How was Lorc supposed to get to her first?

Beside him, Argos whined.

He thought of their conversation by the fire, the rabbit they'd shared between them. *Hardly the glorious battles of the* Star Writ, she'd said.

High Beasts, he realized. If he couldn't find Aster, perhaps he could buy her some time.

The Shadow Dragon is second only to the Hemoth Bear in might. Together, these ferocious High Beasts make a formidable team on the battlefield and are the Highen's greatest defenders. While the White Bear may be the Hemoth's little brother, the Shadow Dragon is, indeed, his best friend.

—THE WRITINGS OF THUBAN,
On the Nature of High Beasts: The Star Majors, *Star Writ*

THIRTY-TWO

QUINTIN pushed his way through the bramble, tears stinging his eyes. She was all he could see—his mother, alone in her room, shivering beneath a pile of scalecoats. Alone. Asking the On-High where he was.

He stopped, his hands on his knees.

She died. And he wasn't there to hold her hand.

Quintin knew what Scaleg would say—that it was necessary, that he had left for the good of Dracogart. But that did nothing to ease the pain in his chest now. Nothing. If his mother had just held on for one week more—

A chirrup sounded beside him.

Umbra. The dragon was all but invisible, save for her yellow eyes watching him from the trees.

He ran to her, throwing his arms around her scaly neck. She was warm and she was familiar and she was all he had left. So he sobbed into her neck, letting the fire that brewed inside her warm him against the cold sting of death.

"It's just you and me now, Umbra," he gasped. "I won't leave you, not ever!" He'd made the mistake of leaving his mother—he would make sure he didn't make the mistake of leaving the Shadow Dragon. He could do that for his parents. For Dracogart. She was Draco's oldest child, the highest of the High Beasts on Mount Draccus, and the kingdom would need her. "I'll take care of you. I promise."

Bope bope bope. The Hemoth groaned behind the dragon, and Quintin could see that Alcor was looking about for Aster and Dev.

"They'll be back soon," Quintin said, drying his eyes on his sleeve. "Come on, let's have another one of those sausages while we wait. And keep quiet, please."

The Hemoth groaned, dropping his hindquarters on the ground in defeat. Quintin moved deeper into a thicket of rowan and white-beam and saw the bag that had held the sausages lying open—and not a sausage in sight.

"Oh," he said stupidly. "You've eaten them all."

He supposed he should have seen that coming. But still, those sausages had not been cheap. And with all their money spent at Downswift, how exactly were they going to afford more food to feed the two massive High Beasts? The Hemoth seemed to be worrying the same thing, because he sniffed hopelessly at the empty bag, repeating his mournful *bope bope bope*.

"It will be all right," Quintin assured them, placing a hand on Umbra's beak as she rested her head on his shoulder. "We'll find you something else to eat soon. We just have to wait for Aster to come back, and that will be any minute now."

"Don't count on it."

Quintin jumped as the Hound prince burst through the trees, Argos at his heels. "What are you doing here, Lorc? What's happened? Are you hurt?"

"The Minor knows Aster's at the Manor. He's coming for her, right now!"

"Coming for her?" Quintin's heart began to race. "Then what are you doing back here? Why isn't she with you? Where's Dev?"

"I'm here for reinforcements." Lorcan pulled down something that had been resting on his shoulder, plunking it on the ground between Umbra and Alcor. Quintin couldn't quite make it out in the dark. "Right, then—have at it, you two!"

Umbra hissed, slinking toward whatever Lorc had left on the ground. Alcor followed, Argos whined nervously, and Quintin had a bad feeling about what was about to happen. "Lorc...what is that?"

"Weasel," said the Hound prince matter-of-factly.

"What!" Quintin grabbed his hair. "You saw what happened last time! You know they'll fight!"

"I did," nodded Lorc Conri. "And I know."

A burst of flame exploded from Umbra, forcing the Hemoth to step back from the weasel—and setting the rowan trees behind him on fire.

Fire that could be seen. Fire that would be noticed.

Quintin looked over at Lorc, horrified. But Lorc seemed satisfied. When he noticed Quintin staring, all he did was shrug. "You were right about her. She doesn't like to share."

"We have to put it out!" Quintin cried.

"No."

"What do you mean, *no*?"

The Hemoth lunged for the singed weasel, but Umbra spread her wings and released another spurt of flame. Lorc Conri whooped as the dragonfire took hold of another patch of brush.

Quintin looked back toward the Manor, watching and listening for the Frosmen. "Lorc! We have to stop this, *now!* Do you want to bring the whole army of Whitlock down on us?"

"Better us with three High Beasts at our disposal than Aster all by her lonesome."

And then Quintin understood.

Lorc was trying to lure the Frosmen from the Manor.

Quintin thought of Dev, of what he'd said about his visions. That Aster needed the High Beasts to defeat the Minor. Was this what he meant? Was this how it was supposed to be done? They would protect her from afar?

And then the Hemoth lunged for the weasel, his massive foot

accidentally stepping on the Shadow Dragon's tail. Umbra screeched, a sound that ripped through Quintin's eardrums and stabbed at the core of his brain.

A sound like that, Quintin was sure, could be heard as far as Twigate.

"This is it," said the Hound prince, unsheathing his sword.

The dragon flame exploded from Umbra's mouth, and the Hemoth Bear leapt sideways, the blast singeing his flank and forcing a roar so loud from the High Beast's throat that Quintin could barely stand.

Lorc Conri had done it. The Shiver Woods were on fire. And voices could be heard, rising up from the Manor.

The Frosmen were coming.

Sometimes you don't find yourself.
Sometimes it finds you first.

—THE WRITINGS OF RIZLAN,
The Crowning of the Fifty-Third Major: The Lunar Offensive, *Star Writ*

 THIRTY-THREE

ASTER had never been down beneath the cellars. The undercroft had been sealed off long before she was born. Making her way through the dank and the cold, she could see why.

Bernadine had led them down a narrow spiral stairwell, its crumbling steps slick, a cool, damp draft blowing up from the depths. Every few feet, a bracketed torch gave off just enough light to see the leaks in the stone. She hated to think of her sister hidden away somewhere in this darkness.

But when her mind wasn't on Ursula, it was seething about Lorc Conri.

How could she have been so stupid as to trust him? After the rumors about him and what had happened on Wolfsbane Day, she should have known he was a traitor from the start. And yet, in the time that she'd spent with the Hound prince, Aster couldn't help but find him...real. Genuine in a way people rarely were. Lorc, she had thought, was Lorc.

But now, she hated to admit, the Lorc he showed her had been a lie. And that hurt her, somewhere deep inside her heart. Somewhere beside the space Uncle Bram had occupied before he betrayed her family.

Dev walked quietly beside her, a comforting presence in the dark. She was glad to have him back with her. Dev, she knew for certain, was exactly who she thought he was. Dev, the bear boy she'd known all her life, was the only true friend she'd ever had. And the only one she could count on.

She bumped into Bernadine, who had suddenly frozen on the step below her. "Bernadine?"

Her cousin just stood there, staring into the darkness.

"Bernadine, what is it?"

"I thought I saw...I thought I...I..." Her cousin trailed off, staring at nothing.

Aster looked back to Dev, who shrugged. She placed a hand on Bernadine's shoulder and felt her trembling. A nervousness wormed in Aster's gut. "What's wrong?"

Her cousin breathed a heavy breath and shook her head. "Nothing. My eyes are playing tricks on me."

Bernadine continued down the steps, and when Aster moved to follow, Dev's hand caught hers.

"Nightlocks," he whispered, so that only Aster could hear.

"What?"

"They're plaguing her."

Aster felt a shiver. "How can you tell?"

"Didn't you see the shadow fall over her face?"

"No."

"Oh," he said, letting go of her hand. "Well, I did."

"Come," said Bernadine, somewhere below them. "Just down here."

Aster glanced at Dev, then continued down into the suffocating darkness. At the bottom of the staircase was a long, leaky chamber, four lit candles barely offering any light at all. The telltale squeak of a rat sounded somewhere in the shadows—On-High only knew how many lived down here.

"That's strange," Bernadine said uneasily. "There should be guards. I thought I could distract them like I did in front of the Manor but...I...."

"Let's just be fast," Dev said, his eyes shifting from shadow to shadow.

Bernadine took some rusting keys from a hook, lifted one of the candles from its ledge, and led the little group forward to a wet wooden door. They all heard the rattle of chains. Pressing heavily on the cold, sticky key, Bernadine turned the lock, shouldering open the heavy door with Aster's help.

"Aster?" whispered a voice, hidden somewhere in the darkness beyond.

Bernadine raised her candle. By the tiny light's flame, Aster saw them—her mother and her sister, squinting against the brightness of the wick. How long had they been down here, that this tiny flame was too bright for their eyes?

"Aster, what are you *doing* here?" rasped Ursula.

Aster dropped to the floor beside her sister, taking her hands in hers. "I came back for you."

"You should not have. Why is Dev here? Where is Alcor?"

"He's safe for now. We need to get you out of here."

"You have the key for the manacles?" asked her mother, hopeful.

"Key? What key?"

Ursula pulled up the skirt of her bloody frost-pearl gown. Clamped around her ankle was an iron shackle. Aster followed the chain to where it split: another shackle was attached to her mother, and beyond that it hooked into the wall.

Lady Lourdes scoffed. "What good is a rescue without a key?"

Aster turned to Bernadine. "Do you know where it is?"

Bernadine shook her head. "I haven't seen it. But…if I had to guess…I would bet my father has it."

"Can you get it from him?"

"I—I don't know. If he has it, he's keeping it close. Probably in his pocket or—"

"Of *course* the girl is no help," Lady Lourdes snarled. "That traitor's blood runs through her veins."

"We need to figure out another way," said Dev, matter-of-fact.

"Ursula, it's not just you the Minor is after, it's all the Houses' children."

Ursula straightened. "What do you mean?"

"We overheard the Minor and some of his regents," Aster explained, pressing Ursula's fingers. "They want to purge any threat to their control over the Highen. Anyone with a legitimate chance of being chosen by the High Beasts. Anyone with the blood of the dead Heads of Houses. The Minor doesn't want us alive to stand at the Northern Crowning."

"Puh!" laughed her mother, disgusted. "So the Hemoth will have no alternative but to choose his little brat."

"I won't stand," said Bernadine. "I won't do it."

The glare Lady Lourdes cut the Minor's daughter was so vicious Aster felt a sudden fear for her cousin. "You say that to our faces," her mother hissed, "but when the power is within your reach, you'll stab all of us in the back to taste it. Just like your father."

"I won't," said Bernadine, near tears. "Aster, you have to believe me. I never wanted—"

"Oh, this is a dream come *true* for you, you little—"

"Mother!" interrupted Ursula. "Enough of this." She squeezed Aster's hand in hers. "You must go."

"Not without you," said Aster.

"There's no time. What matters is keeping Alcor safe—and making sure you are free to stand at the Northern Crowning for him."

"*Me?*"

"Aster?" said Lady Lourdes, incredulous. "Don't be ridiculous."

Her mother was right. The On-High had already decided that Aster was unworthy to stand at the Northern Crowning. They'd burned her. They'd warned her.

"Why do you think we named you Ursula?" Lady Lourdes asked her older daughter. "We named you to honor the Bear. This will be your House, Ursula. Yours. Aster was named for the stars."

"Well, the stars will be honored that their namesake will stand for the Hemoth Bear, won't they?" Ursula snapped.

A rumble sounded somewhere beyond the Manor walls—deep and resonant, like a thunder that could shake the very heavens.

"Alcor," whispered Dev.

Voices echoed from the kitchens above them. Frosmen. Aster and the rest stared up at the dank ceiling.

"What are they saying?" asked Lady Lourdes. "It sounds like they're yelling *fire*."

Fire. The Shadow Dragon.

Ursula pulled her hands back. "You have to go."

Aster shook her head. "No, Ursula, it can't be me. Alcor needs *you* to be Major. He won't choose me."

"He will," said Ursula. "He has to. There's no one else."

Suddenly the weight of the Highen that Aster had watched her sister struggle to carry threatened to crush Aster's bones to pulp.

If she couldn't free Ursula, then Ursula was right: Aster was all that remained of their father's House, the only heir to stand and be claimed by Alcor. But if he didn't—if he chose someone else, someone Bram Lourdes put forward—that would be the end of everything. The Minor would win. The responsibility was too much, too big.

"Ursula," Aster said, swallowing tears. "It's not my place. I'm too—"

Ursula took Aster's face in her hands. "You're all the things I am. Father would tell you as much himself. You can do this, Aster. You *need* to do this."

The shouting grew louder, more voices, and the walls rumbled again. The shriek of the Shadow Dragon joined Alcor's thunder.

"Aster," said Dev, "we've got no way to free them. We have to go."

Aster looked into Ursula's eyes, tears rolling down her cheeks. "But she's my sister."

Ursula kissed her hard on the forehead. "I'll see you at the Northern Crowning." And then she pushed her away, so hard that Aster staggered back into Dev, who caught her and helped her up. "Now go! Get out of here!"

Dev dragged Aster to the stairs, Bernadine clambering behind them. Aster could barely remember how to move her legs. Didn't want to.

But her sister was right. Someone had to stand for Alcor.

And right now, the Hemoth Bear was calling for her.

It is our sacred duty, as parents, to protect our children from our enemies, and to teach them of the threats that face the Highen. For they are young, and cannot know them without our guidance.

—THE WRITINGS OF WOG,
The Threat: The Orion Wars, *Star Writ*

THIRTY-FOUR

EVERY rumbling roar from Alcor tied Dev's stomach in knots. What was happening to him?

Dev threw open the Manor's kitchen door and looked out across the green to where the smoke rose out of the Shiver Woods. The unmistakable orange glow of fire peeked through the trees. And a cacophony of panicked shouts filled the chilled night air.

Another thunderous bellow exploded above the noise.

"Alcor!" cried Dev, hurtling toward the trees.

"*Dev, wait!*" Aster yelped behind him, but there was no time to lose. Dev was the bear's Keeper. Alcor was his High Beast. He should never have left him. Rizlan would never have left him.

Dev threw himself into the forest brush, Aster calling his name close behind. Alcor's cries—Dev knew those cries. The Bear was scared.

The flames came into view, carpeting the forest floor like the spring blooms of Berenice Locks, blossoms of orange fire licking at the trees. Dev made for the center of the blaze, where Alcor's cries and the shouts of men rose with the acrid smoke. He stumbled, ash searing his eyes and stinging his throat—and then slammed hard into the armored shoulder of a Frosman, falling to the ground with a thunk.

"Oi!" the man cried. "What was that, then?"

Dev scrabbled back, frantically trying to get his bearings. Beyond the Frosmen, cloaked in smoke, he could see the Shadow Dragon, wings splayed and fangs bared, hissing at the men advancing on her. Standing behind her protective wingspan were Prince Quintin, Argos the Starhound, and Lorc Conri, his sword at the ready, a Frosman lying in the dirt at his feet.

What was Lorc Conri doing here?

On the other side of the clearing, bellowing and wailing against a garrison of Frosmen, was the Hemoth Bear. They had managed to tie him to the ground with roped hooks.

"Alcor!" screamed Dev. He tried to scramble to his feet, but before he could get up off the ground, the Frosman's foot slammed into his chest.

"Look here!" the soldier shouted. "It's the Keeper, isn't it? Saw him in the city, didn't I?"

"What's the Keeper doin' back here?" sneered a second Frosman. "Got a death wish, boy?"

Hands grabbed Dev by the shoulders from behind, hauling him backward and up onto his feet. Aster Lourdes.

"Brought your friend, have you?" sneered the Frosman.

Aster drew her sharps. "His bodyguard."

Both Frosmen laughed and pulled their blades. Dev held his breath, his heart pounding, his fear sweating out through his pores and dripping down his face.

But not Aster. She glowered back at the Frosmen, poised for a fight, her forehead crinkled in a way that reminded Dev of the Major himself, her fists tightening on her sharps. For the first time in his life, Dev wished he had a weapon too.

And suddenly he felt a swell rise up from his gut and wash over his mind, hot and bright and fast—

He saw her, Aster, hanging over a great abyss. He saw Minor Bram Lourdes raise a jeweled knife above her. With one determined strike, the Minor slashed at her hands, and she fell, swallowed up by the void.

The vision released Dev, and he gasped as if coming up from underwater.

Was that the future? Was he seeing Aster's death?

The Frosmen were advancing. Aster stepped toward the fight—

—and suddenly Lorc Conri was there at her side, bloodied blade glinting in the fire.

"What are you doing here?" Aster growled at the Hound prince. Whatever she and Lorc Conri had shared on the road to Tawnshire—whatever bonds they'd forged, those bonds were broken now. But still, he was here. He hadn't gone back.

"I told you. I am not with my father," said Lorc Conri, and Dev couldn't help wondering if now was really the best time for this conversation.

"Lovers' quarrel, is it?" laughed one of the Frosmen, the pair's blades a hairsbreadth from Aster and Lorc. At any moment, all this steel would meet.

"*Stand down!*"

Bernadine emerged from the trees, putting herself between the soldiers and Dev, Aster, and Lorc.

The Frosmen's amused grins disappeared, replaced by confusion. "My lady," said one, bowing his head.

"I said, *stand down*," Bernadine snapped. "Tell your men to put down their weapons and release the High Beasts."

"But my lady," said the other, "the Minor's orders—"

"I know the Minor's orders! Don't you think I know my own father's wishes? He sent me here to tell you to release them."

The men exchanged dubious glances, and indeed Dev felt his own eyes sliding sideways to Aster. She didn't flinch. If her cousin's attempt at deception failed, she was prepared to fight. Like her father.

"Bernie Doll!" called a voice above the noise.

The soldiers froze, all heads turned toward the speaker. The Minor rode into the smoke on horseback, his advisors beside him—the

Dragon woman, the man from Hundford, Pan Leander, Captain Hewitt Pire.

"What gifts you've brought me, Bernie Doll!" He grinned down at Aster, smug satisfaction on his face. "The threats to our rule *and* the Hemoth Bear himself! You've done your father proud."

Dev watched Bernadine shrink beneath the praise, her eyes on the ground.

"Lorc." The man from Hundford nodded approvingly at the Hound prince. "Well done."

Dev watched Aster. Her grip on her sharps tightened, and she shot Lorc a look of venom.

"Ah, then this is Prince Lorcan?" asked the Minor. "This is your son?"

The Hundford man nodded. "He has led the Lourdes girl and the Wyvern boy here. Did I not promise you?"

The Minor laughed. "Indeed you did, Tier."

The Hound prince fixed a furious gaze on the Hundford man. "Father," he said, his sword still held out, "what have you done? What have you done with Arthur and the boys?"

Lord Tier's face was impassive. "What needed to be done."

"I should *kill you* for this!"

Aster and Dev exchanged glances. Were they wrong about Lorc Conri?

The Minor frowned. "A bit of a rebellious streak in your son, I think."

The Hundford man bristled and narrowed a glare at Lorc. "Enough of this. Show respect in the presence of your Minor."

"I don't bow to traitors," Lorc said. "And I won't stand with a father so greedy for power he would align himself with a killer of High Beasts—and the killer of *my mother*! I came to Tawnshire to stand *against* the Minor. I stand with Aster Lourdes now. And I will see her stand against you all at the Northern Crowning!"

Aster stared at Lorc Conri. Dev could see her doubt about the Hound prince disappearing.

The Minor erupted in booming laughter. "Well, that's all the family squabbling I can handle. However the Bear and children came to be here, they *are* here, and they will be handled. Tonight, we will celebrate the end of our campaign and look to the Highen's future under my daughter's rule."

A puff of air escaped Aster, her mouth opening to argue, but Dev grabbed hold of her arm. He shook his head. After what the On-High had just shown him, Aster was in more danger than ever.

"First," announced the Minor, "let's do away with all these hopefuls, shall we? Guards, kill them."

Bernadine Lourdes screamed.

And Tawn saw inside the heart of the human Dov, and found great courage, love, and honor. It glowed inside him, brighter than the North Star herself.

—THE WRITINGS OF BERN,
The First Major: The Age of Tawn, *Star Writ*

THIRTY-FIVE

ASTER jumped at the shrill wail escaping her cousin. Indeed, everyone in the fiery clearing, even the High Beasts, was startled by Bernadine's scream. The Minor leapt down off his horse, panic in his eyes as he moved for his daughter.

"Bernie Doll!" he said. "Bernie, what's the matter? You don't have to see this. Someone take her away—take her to her rooms."

Aster adjusted her grip on her blades. That was the Uncle Bram she knew—a devoted, caring father. A man who would die for his daughter, and, Aster used to think, his nieces. How could he be that man and this traitor at the same time?

Bernadine pulled away from the Minor, tears streaming down her face. "It's you!" she shouted. "You're what's the matter! Father, why are you doing this?"

The Minor looked confused. "Bernie Doll, you know why. What happened to your mother—"

"She wouldn't want this! Father, you know Mother would never, ever have wanted this. She was a Keeper, for On-High's sake!" Bernadine pointed to Alcor. "Don't you see what you are doing?"

Aster glanced over at the Hemoth Bear, groaning quietly mere feet away under the weight of the ropes. He was making that sound he always made—that sad, fearful *bope bope bope*. She needed to free him.

"Don't you see," Bernadine continued, "how you anger the On-High?"

The Minor's gentle concern for his daughter had given way to something else, something angry, impatient. "We've discussed the stars, Bernadine. I've told you. They don't care what we do."

"That's not true!"

As long as Uncle Bram was focused on Bernadine, there was a chance Aster could make it to Alcor. He was so close. Carefully, she stepped sideways, behind Lorc.

Dev's eyes flicked to Aster, and she saw him shake his head. But the bear boy was wrong. This was their only chance to save the Hemoth.

"Father," cried Bernadine as Aster took another step, "the On-High will send more demons for you if you don't stop this!"

"More?" he laughed. "They haven't come for me yet."

"They *have!*" Bernadine cried. "I've seen them!"

An uncomfortable silence fell over the clearing—and then a rush of murmuring, the Frosmen's faces betraying their fear. After being party to astrocide and the murder of the Major, no doubt they'd all thought about this, all worried about it.

Good, thought Aster. *The more frightened they are, the more they chatter, the more distracted they'll be.*

"You've seen the demons that hide behind the moon?" Pan Leander sat taller on his horse, looking nervously up at the heavens. "Here? In Tawnshire?"

"No!" said Uncle Bram. "She's seen no such thing. She has a bit of an overactive imagination, perhaps, this daughter of mine."

Aster inched closer to Alcor, sliding behind a pair of guards holding the ropes that restrained him. The bear's big round eyes met hers, and she braced herself for more of his crying. But he was silent. Even he seemed to grasp the danger.

"She *has* seen them!" Dev jumped in beside Bernadine, his voice loud, forcing the Minor—and everyone else—to look at him. "I've seen it in her eyes!"

Aster tried to stay hidden behind the Frosmen, crouching close to the ground. She didn't think Uncle Bram could quite see her from where he stood. She had to act fast.

"A Keeper, Bram," said Pan Leander. "A Keeper says there's Night-locks about!"

"This Keeper is a child! An apprentice!"

"A Keeper all the same," said the Dragon woman. She was decidedly calmer than Pan, but her horse sensed her nervousness and began to stomp the ground.

"What are you all afraid of?" roared Uncle Bram.

Bernadine grabbed his arm. "Don't you see, Father? If you don't stop this, the Nightlocks will take you behind the moon forever! If you don't stop this, you'll lose yourself!"

Uncle Bram threw Bernadine off, and she landed hard at Dev's feet. "What are they waiting for, then!"

Aster eyed the ropes closest to her, held by wicked hooks and tying Alcor's neck and shoulders to the ground. The Hemoth's eyes watched her—eyes like Ursan amber, flickering with the fire of his mother. He looked at Aster's sharps, knowing, she was certain, what she meant to do. One strike and she could sever both ties.

"Tell me," the Minor roared at his companions on horseback, "what these demons are waiting for? I've struck down the White Bear. I've dispatched the great Major. Where is the punishment? Where? There will *be* no punishment."

The Minor's arm stretched out, his sword pointing at Alcor, and Aster lay flat against the ground. "I have the Highest of High Beasts. The Hemoth is mine! Why don't they strike?"

The regents were silent.

"It is because the On-High fear me!" he bellowed. "Because they know my quest is just! Because I have remade the Highen! Because I know how indifferent they truly are! My wife's life was taken from me, and I have had my vengeance!" Aster held tight to her sharps, her palms sweaty. "And now," the Minor shouted, "I will have the Highen for my child. Let the On-High's demons come, if they wish. And watch them cower at my blade!"

Aster brought down the paired blades as hard as she could, the razor edges slicing through the ropes like butter.

Alcor was ready. With a mighty roar the Hemoth reared up, as ferocious and awesome in the flames of the Shiver Woods as the legendary Tawn himself. With his razor claws, Alcor swiped at the startled Frosmen nearest him, tearing them down with one swift blow.

The clearing burst into chaos.

The rest of the soldiers were shouting orders, surrounding the Hemoth, trying to secure the lines. Aster kept swinging, her blades slicing at each rope as Alcor felled Frosman after Frosman with his massive paws.

"Aster!" Her name echoed above the chaos, the voice deep and furious. She turned to see Uncle Bram, his sword pointed at her. "You meddlesome little witch!"

The Minor ran, full tilt, across the clearing, frenzied eyes squarely on her. Aster knew her uncle—an elegant warrior, an expert swordsman. She was no match for him.

And Dev's warning outside the Manor—*If Bram catches you, he will kill you.*

She turned on her heels and plunged into the flaming brush, hoping to hide in the forest's growth, her uncle's furious screams behind her.

The Will of the On-High, what is it? Who can say what it is that they Will?

—A PONDERANCE OF STARS,
The Writings of the Great Lady Berenice: The Fore, *Star Writ*

THIRTY-SIX

"Aster!" Dev shouted, his voice swallowed up by the bedlam.

Alcor tore down men in groups, soldiers running and screaming for their lives. Lorc Conri was in the middle of the fray, swinging his blade, his Starhound by his side. Umbra the Shadow Dragon spewed her flames at the Minor's men, driving them back, Quintin hurling rocks behind her. Only Bernadine Lourdes was motionless, gaping and terrified as the bodies of her father's men piled on the ground around her.

Dev ran through the madness, ducking and dodging as he tried to follow Aster. She was alone in the woods with the Minor. He had to get to her, had to help. How, he didn't know, but he couldn't let her die.

"Keeper!" Hewitt Pire appeared before him, his broadsword blocking Dev's path. The old soldier was covered in the blood of his men, his armor a shiny mess of smears and splatter. "Wrangle that bear, *now!*"

"I told you—I'm Alcor's servant!" said Dev, stepping back. "He doesn't listen to me!"

Hewitt Pire puffed like a Härkädian ox and lunged for Dev so fast, Dev barely had time to react. The old soldier's thick arm wrapped around his neck, his sword edge pressed against Dev's throat. "Try."

"Dev!" Quintin had a hand on Umbra.

"That dragon blows one more breath, boy," shouted Pire, "and I run the Keeper through!"

Black smoke billowed from Umbra's nose, Quintin's palm on her flank the only thing keeping her from unleashing an inferno.

Hewitt Pire's grip on Dev's neck tightened. "Now," he growled in Dev's ear, "calm your Hemoth, or make your peace with the On-High."

Dev watched Alcor, a blazing force of raw, celestial power. The cub who cried *bope bope bope* was gone. This bear, fierce and raging in the Shadow Dragon's fire, was a power no one could stop.

"I'd be worried about your own standing with the On-High, Pire," Dev said. "Because when Alcor comes for you, you'll be meeting them soon after."

Hewitt Pire's breath stank of old meat and beer. "Have it your way, then."

Dev closed his eyes, held his breath, and thought of his mother.

But Pire's blade fell away. His grip released Dev so suddenly, Dev fell forward into the singed grass. When he looked back, Hewitt Pire was gripping the back of his knees, stumbling before finally falling sideways.

Behind him, a bloody Frosman sword gripped in both hands, stood Bernadine Lourdes.

"My lady?" grunted Pire.

Bernadine reached down to Dev, and he took her hand, letting her help him to his feet. He saw streaks on her cheeks where tears had fallen.

"Bernie," Pire gasped, "why?"

Dev watched as the Minor's daughter closed her eyes tight, and he wondered if she'd answer. But before she could, Alcor's massive shadow fell over Hewitt Pire, the Hemoth's angry breath disturbing the soldier's silver hair.

What came next—

Dev spun Bernadine around and squeezed her hard.

—Hewitt Pire screamed. And there was nothing.

Dev had tried to warn him.

Who can see what the stars see?
And not cower as they fill
The skies with the fates of men,
Their victories and ends decided…

—A PONDERANCE OF STARS,
The Writings of the Great Lady Berenice: The Fore, *Star Writ*

## THIRTY-SEVEN

LORC'S arms were numb, his knuckles cramping as he swung his sword at Frosman after Frosman. Even with the Hemoth, there were too many to handle. For all his training with his mother, all his skill and study, he was still just a boy. He was no grown warrior.

On his own, the Frosman would have cut him down a dozen times over, but Argos—Argos wouldn't allow it. The Starhound attacked the Frosmen tirelessly, granting Lorc openings to land each strike, protecting his back, protecting his side.

But the one person Lorc most wanted to sink his blade into was Minor Bram Lourdes, and he'd disappeared into the trees, chasing Aster. Lorc tried to cut his way through the throngs of men, tried to get to the trees to go after his mother's killer, but the press was too thick.

A group of five surrounded Lorc and Argos. Argos fought back three at once, leaving the other two for Lorc to handle on his own. He swung as fast as he could, blocking and parrying as his mother had shown him, sweat stinging his eyes, both arms throbbing.

But one of their pommels struck his gut. His breath was forced from his lungs, and he fell to the ground, coughing. The pair of Frosmen kicked him, and Lorc curled into a ball, each blow sending pain tearing through him.

"Stop," he heard his father's voice command, somewhere above the Frosmen.

They did. And when they stepped back, Lorc gritted his teeth against his aching body and looked up at his father, glaring down from atop his fine horse.

"I'm very disappointed in you, Lorc. I always suspected your stubborn streak would be the death of you. So like your mother."

If Lorc could have, he would have cursed his father for daring to insult her. But it was all he could do to breathe through the pain. His face was wet with blood.

"She would never have aligned herself with Bram Lourdes," his father went on, not bothered in the least by his son's obvious suffering. "It would have been impossible for her to understand the power he offers us. She was quite happy for Hundford to remain the backwater it is. She had no vision, no greater ambition. Just like you. If I thought she might have listened to me, she would still be alive."

Lorc growled, using his sword to force himself to his feet. He knew it. Some part of him had always known it. Known his father had something to do with the fate that befell his mother. His eyes burned, his vision blurred by tears.

"But you still have a chance to save yourself, son," his father said. "You can join me and rule Hundford as we should."

"Arthur will rule Hundford," Lorc rasped.

His father sighed, impatient. "Don't be ridiculous, Lorcan. Arthur is dead. I wasn't foolish enough to repeat the mistakes of Wolfsbane Day—I used double the poison. You are all that is left of your mother's sons."

And that was the truth of it. Of who Lorc was. Who his father was. A truth he'd been fighting for so long. Lorc had been spared the poison on Wolfsbane Day because he was his father's son. And now he was alone—alone because he'd left his brothers unprotected from his father.

And his father had taken them all.

"With or without you, Hundford will be mine to rule." Tier

motioned at the Frosmen. "*Without you* will be no burden to me. Perhaps the next son I have will inherit my way of thinking. Men!"

The Frosmen fell on Lorc, their kicks and blows coming harder and faster than before, and Lorc cried out. Between boots, he could see his father watching approvingly—

—before a horn sounded somewhere in the distance. When Lorc caught a glimpse of his father again through the veil of sweat and blood, he was galloping off into the night.

Through the Frosmen's legs, Lorc saw horses. Dozens of them. Another army had joined the fight.

What mortal sees the path ahead, and decides then to defy it?

—A PONDERANCE OF STARS,
Writings of the Great Lady Berenice: The Fore, *Star Writ*

# THIRTY-EIGHT

ASTER fought against branch and plant and thorn, all of them catching on her cloak and threatening to pull her down. And Uncle Bram—she could hear him not far behind.

She tugged at her cloak, suddenly stuck on the limb of a fallen tree. The wool refused to give, and her uncle was closing in. She slashed at the fabric with her sharps, the branch releasing her so suddenly that she tumbled backward, crashing through a bush and landing on hard stone with a yelp.

And the yelp echoed. Her voice carried on the night air and sank behind her, down and down and down.

Trembling, she looked over her shoulder at the steep slope she'd narrowly missed falling down. It was a deep, sheer granite slab, the bottom lost in darkness. A void in the forest.

She was trapped.

"Aster!"

Away. She needed to get away.

Frantically, she searched for somewhere, anywhere to go. Sticking out of the side of the cliff, rooted in a ledge just beneath her, was a tree. Too small to bear Uncle Bram's weight. But for her, it might hold. It just might.

Carefully, she lowered herself onto the ledge, then crawled along the slanted trunk on her hands and knees. Uncle Bram's voice was closer now, shrieking her name in a crazed rage.

On-High, help me.

The time was now to fix it—fix everything. But she couldn't do it alone.

She pulled the little jar from her pocket, the starflame blinking inside. "Please," she whispered to the tiny flame. "I want to save my sister—I want her crowned the same as you. I want to save the Highen. Please, lend me your blessing."

The light swelled. The ringing sound of the On-High's voices rose up from the glass.

Listen to it, Dev had told her.

The Minor burst free of the trees, chest and shoulders heaving furiously. When his eyes fell on her, he let out a deep belly laugh.

"Aster!" he shouted again, triumphantly.

She inched farther back along the tree, dangling over the open drop.

Aster, a different voice echoed quietly.

She glanced at the starflame in her hand.

The Minor jumped down onto the ledge, one foot up on her tree. "You and your sister are all that's left of my brother. I'll be rid of him for good once I'm rid of you."

"Don't take another step!" she warned. "The tree can't hold you—you'll send us both to our deaths!"

"The tree doesn't need to hold me," he snarled. He lifted his sword and began hacking at the trunk.

Aster, the voice sang.

The tree began to bend, her weight forcing it down as Uncle Bram sawed his way through the base.

And then a roar—so thunderous Aster thought the earth itself had opened up—echoed out over the cliff, rattling her bones. The Minor spun, and there, just above him, was the Hemoth Bear.

"Alcor!" shouted Aster. Had he come for her?

The Minor raised his sword.

"No, Alcor!" she cried. "Don't fight him! Get out of here!"

But the Hemoth didn't listen. He slashed out at the Minor, and the Minor—one of the greatest warriors the Highen had ever produced—ducked and stabbed the Hemoth's paw, slicing it open through the center. The bear staggered sideways, shocked.

"Alcor!" screamed Aster. "Stupid beast! Get out of here, he'll kill you!"

But Alcor wasn't running. The bear snapped his mighty jaws, lowering himself onto the ledge—and forcing Uncle Bram up onto the tree.

The trunk bent under the added weight, and Aster slid half-off, fighting to hold her balance.

Aster, the flame in the jar sang.

Alcor roared, his giant head reaching out for Uncle Bram. The Minor stood on shaky legs, balancing on the bowing tree.

"Alcor, stop!" shrieked Aster.

But the bear was focused on his kill. There was no stopping him.

Except Uncle Bram was not afraid. He lifted his blade, ready for the final stroke, ready to plunge his sword into the bear's exposed throat.

And the jar sang louder. *Aster.*

Suddenly, she understood.

Pulling the lid from the jar, she aimed it at her uncle, and the white flame exploded with a blinding light, so bright she leaned back from the force of it.

Uncle Bram screamed. He fell forward as the light struck him, landing hard on the tree, and Aster almost lost her grip completely as the entire thing bent. She slipped farther to the side, began to drop, clawed frantically for something to grab on to.

Her hands caught a branch, and she clutched it, dangling over the precipice.

Uncle Bram was just above her, hanging from the trunk

and growling as he tried to pull himself back up, his sword lost. Above *him*, Alcor began his cry of *bope bope bope*, extending his neck down as far as he could stretch it, but it was still too far for Aster to reach.

The Hemoth whimpered. He placed his front paw down on the tree. Rocks fell away from the ledge under his weight.

"Stop, Alcor!" screamed Aster. "Don't move!"

She had to pull herself up. The longer she hung there, the weaker her arms felt. It was only a matter of time before she fell.

Alcor roared.

She looked up to see Uncle Bram astride the trunk, a jeweled dagger in his hand. *"My brother's rule is over!"*

He lifted the blade to strike at her, and she braced herself for the blow.

"Aster!"

A black shadow swooped in from above, crashing into Uncle Bram and throwing him loose from the tree. With a shriek, the Minor fell—but he fell past Aster, and he grabbed hold of her waist.

The weight was impossible.

She cried out as her uncle's panicked grip on her tightened, and her own grip began to loosen.

"Aster!" There was the shadow, banking around back to her. It was Umbra.

As the High Beast flew closer, she could see Quintin Wyvern on her back, and behind him, calling her name, was Dev.

"Aster!" Dev shouted again. "Hang on!"

She couldn't hang on, not with Uncle Bram's weight. He snarled as he pulled at her, yanked at her hair, tore off her cloak, trying desperately to use her body to climb back up.

Alcor roared above her, and Aster closed her eyes, wishing for her father to save her. But he wouldn't save her. Couldn't. He was gone, there was no changing that.

The On-High wouldn't save her either: they had saved her enough, she knew that now. Starflame, Dragon princes, Hound princes, visions. The On-High had forgiven her. They had always forgiven her. They'd been with her all along.

It was time for Aster to save herself.

She thrashed her legs, kicking and writhing to shake her uncle loose, fighting harder than she'd ever fought before. He held tighter, fiercer, cursing her, and she felt her fingers weakening, straining, almost breaking under the weight.

His arm came up, wrapping around her neck and shoulders, lifting him higher—and she bit, hard, forcing him to scream.

And then she threw back her head, slamming it hard into his chin. Blood spurted from his mouth, and his fingers unlocked.

She felt his hands release her. Felt his bulk lifted from her body. Felt him drop.

With a scream, he fell into the abyss.

And then the shadows came.

They poured over the cavern walls, hundreds of them, speeding down into the dark after him. Shadows that belonged to nothing. Shadows that felt hungry.

And then, all at once, his screaming stopped.

Bernadine was right. The Nightlocks had come for the Minor.

Aster pulled herself back onto the tree trunk, her nails bruised purple. A furry muzzle brushed gently against her cheek. Alcor. He stood with his paws on the ledge just above her, and she grabbed hold of his neck; with ease, he pulled her up to safety, letting her crawl all the way onto his back.

She lay there atop the Hemoth, inhaling his smoky-sweet fur and catching her frightened breath. The Shadow Dragon landed softly beside them.

"Aster!" said Dev, hopping down off the dragon's back and racing for her. "Are you all right?"

She nodded. Miraculously, she was. "You were right," she whispered. "The stars were with me. I just had to listen."

The Starhound and Prince Lorc emerged from the trees, Lorc limping and bruised. A group of Frosmen appeared behind him, and Aster sat up, alarmed. But the Frosmen didn't draw their weapons. Instead, bafflingly, they dropped to their knees, laying down their swords.

"Your mercy, Lady Aster," begged the most decorated of the group.

Mercy?

"It's all right," said Lorc, his face bloodied. "The regents have been captured. Most of the Frosmen have surrendered."

"*Captured?*" Aster repeated. "How?"

The Frosman beside Lorc stepped forward—no, not a Frosman. His armor was different, the image of a Starhound on the breastplate. The young man bowed—a young man who looked so much like Lorc, handsome and proud.

"Hundford stands with you, Lady Aster." Beyond the Conri brothers, rows of Hundford soldiers lined the trees, hundreds of them.

Aster looked at Lorc, confused. "Hundford's men?"

Lorc smirked. "My brother Arthur wasn't pleased to discover I'd left against his orders."

"So he sends an army to collect you?"

"Two," corrected Lorc.

"Apologies, my lady," said Arthur Conri. "We'd have come sooner, but Roarque is a great distance away, and they aren't known for being swift riders."

"Watch yourself, Conri," grunted an old soldier, the image of the Lion on his breast. "We may have come to support Lady Aster together, but now it's done I won't hesitate to shave that ridiculous Hundford hair from your head."

Lorc and his brother laughed, though the old Roarque soldier didn't seem amused. Aster recognized him—he was the uncle of the Head of the House of the Lion.

They'd come. Lorc had said they could count on his brother. And here he was. With the House of the Lion.

And Lorc's father—the anger in Lorc when he'd faced him…

"Lorc, I…" She'd been so awful to him. So hateful. And he hadn't deserved any of it.

"Aw, it's all right," he said. "You're only a bloomnut, after all."

A joke. She wanted to laugh. And cry. Sitting on the back of a Hemoth, the memory of her uncle's screams still fresh, she wasn't sure she could believe there would ever be time for jokes and laughter again. For peace.

"It's over?" she heard herself ask.

"No, my lady," said the old Roarque soldier. "Many Frosmen managed to escape, and still more of the Minor's army are posted throughout the Highen—they were loyal to him beyond all reason, for he was a charismatic man, in his way. There are many who will remain that way, despite the clear will of the stars."

She turned back to Dev. "What is he talking about?"

"The On-High, my lady," said the Frosman. "They favor you."

The On-High, thought Aster. *Favor me?*

Dev smiled. "Of course they do. You bested the Minor."

"Aster," said Lorc with an amused grin. "You're sitting on top of a Hemoth bear. Don't be thick, you're the hero of the Highen."

Aster looked at all the eyes watching her—the dirty, soot-smothered faces of Frosmen—and she suddenly felt uncomfortable. She was no hero. Mercy, they'd asked her. That was granted by kings, by Majors. She was still only Aster.

And she had only wanted to save her sister.

"Ursula," she said to Dev. "I have to get Ursula."

The birth of the first child of Major Jasper Lourdes was greatly antici-
pated by the entire Highen. The blood of the Death Chaser would flow
through new veins.

—THE WRITINGS OF RIZLAN,
Major Jasper Lourdes: The Lunar Offensive, *Star Writ*

 THIRTY-NINE

ASTER burst into the gloom of the undercroft, Dev beside her.

Her mother and sister sat huddled together in the dark, squinting up at the torchlight.

"Aster?" said her sister. "You're back?"

Aster turned back to the pair of Hundford warriors Lorc Conri had ordered to go with her. "Cut them loose," she said.

Ursula and her mother watched, confused, as the Hundford men cut the chains from their ankles.

"I don't understand," said Ursula.

Aster threw her arms around her. "It's over, Ursula. You're safe now."

"The Hemoth?" asked Ursula. "Did you save the Hemoth?"

"Yes, and more," said Dev. "She saved the Highen. The Minor is gone."

Aster, clinging to her sister, flinched at Dev's words. They sounded wrong to her. Too grand and heroic, like something her father would have done. All Aster had done was what she had to. There was nothing heroic about it.

"What happens now?" Aster asked.

"Well," said Ursula, resting her cheek against the top of Aster's head, "I suppose the Highen is in need of a Major."

TWO MONTHS LATER

And so it was at the Northern Crowning, without hesitation or pause, that Alcor, the Great Hemoth Bear, chose the Highen's new Major. A Major who had proven her courage, love, and honor in the battle against the Traitor, Bram. A Major who had already risked her life to save the Highen she loved.

The Major Aster Lourdes.

—THE WRITINGS OF DEV,
The Crowning of the Fifty-Fourth Major: The New Rule, *Star Writ*

Forty

$\mathcal{D}$EV tugged at the tight collar of his new robes, the *Star Writ* weighing heavy in his hand.

He hoped the ink didn't smudge. The last sentence had been written just moments before, but he'd spent months perfecting it, agonizing over every word. It was his first official entry as High Keeper of the Hemoth Bear—and not only that, but the first official entry of the new age. The New Rule, he had named it. It had taken him forever to decide on, and he still wasn't sure he liked it, but it *was* apt. The leaders of the Highen were not only new rulers, but new in their youth. Master Rizlan would have come up with something more poetic, but this would serve well enough.

He hoped Aster would like it when he presented it to her at the end of the night. It was tradition for the High Keeper to present the new Major with their first entry in the *Star Writ* at the Northern Crowning ball.

But nervousness unsettled his stomach. He wanted to show it to her *before* she read it aloud to everyone in attendance. He wanted to know if he needed to fix it. He didn't want to embarrass himself, after all. Or her.

Dev walked into the feast hall of the Manor, filled to bursting with people from all across the Highen. He'd never been to a Northern Crowning ball before—indeed, he hadn't yet been born when the Highen celebrated the crowning of Major Jasper Lourdes—but

Rizlan had told him about it. About the towers of Roarque butter cakes glistening with caramel sauce; about the turning, crackling spits of spiced Härkädian beef; about the twirling, fluttering ribbon of Felisbrook dancers. The ball was an occasion for the grandest and most lavish displays in the Highen.

But this one was different.

Dev made his way through the bustling crowd: red-cloaked Oracles; knights and nobles; city fathers from Tawnshire Town; diplomats from the Ring. The royal courts and religious houses had all sent their representatives, but he couldn't help noticing the more modest dress of many people in attendance—gentleman merchants, minor lords, guild leaders, all wearing the clean and simple clothing of regular Highen folk, for they *were* regular Highen folk. The Lourdes girls had insisted on having them. This was not just a ball for kings—not this year.

The usual piles of gifts given to honor the new Major were nowhere to be seen—the girls hadn't wanted anything. But still, it was a fine ball. The long tables were covered in dishes Dev knew well—including a couple of platters of venison and wild turkey supplied by Lorc of Hundford himself.

Two pedestals had been placed together beneath the jeweled glow of the stained-glass windows lining the room. The left held the egg of the Shadow Dragon, pinpricks of celestial light burning and waning across its obsidian shell. The right held a towering glass vial, shimmering with thick, transparent liquid. Aster would soon be expected to formally exchange the egg for the venom, her first official act as Major.

Dev glanced at the ambassadors from the Ring Highen. Their capes of black fur glittered as if covered in delicate snowflakes, sparkling blue and white. What animal produced such a pelt? Dev couldn't help but hope to see it someday. He found he had a powerful curiosity about the world after surviving so much death.

"Keeper Dev!" Standing off to the side, beneath an elegant

window depicting the Great Lady Berenice, were Lorc and several other boys (who all looked decidedly like him).

"Prince Lorc," Dev said, bowing his head. "I hardly recognized you in your formal wear."

Lorc pulled at the neck of his fine linen shirt, his signet ring flashing. "Truth be told, I don't do well at fancy parties. Not really built for them. You can see why Arthur's king and not me."

No, Dev couldn't see why. Lorc's courage and skill during the fight against the Frosmen had more than proven he was his mother's son. Had he not been too badly injured to compete at the Northern Crowning, he *would* have been chosen—Argos loved him most, after all.

"I feel a bit like an imposter, actually. Still," said Lorc, "just as well, what with my brother being king and all."

Arthur Conri appeared and elbowed him. "That I am." The new Head of the House of Hounds nodded at Dev. "High Keeper."

Dev tried not to blush. He knew what Lorc meant by feeling like an imposter.

"I'm glad to see that you and your brothers are well after…what happened," Dev said, wondering if he shouldn't have brought it up.

"The On-High were watching over us," said Arthur calmly.

Lorc snorted. "Don't let the On-High take all the credit, Arthur. It was *your* sharp eye that noticed the hounds avoiding dinner."

"Dinner?" asked Dev.

"The Starhounds are rotten beggars," explained Lorc. "Normally, you can't get them to leave you alone at dinnertime. But that evening, the dogs weren't interested—they shied away from the tables, from the food. That's how Arthur knew Chancellor Tier had slipped Wolfsbane into the meat."

Chancellor Tier, thought Dev. Lorc refused to refer to him as *Father* anymore.

"Is that the *Star Writ?* Ready for the new Major, is it?" asked Lorc, pointing to the tome in Dev's arms.

Dev clutched it tight to his chest. "Yes. Have you seen Ast—erhm—I mean, the Major?"

Arthur shook his head; Lorc had already turned to greet someone behind Dev. "All hail the brave and honorable King Quintin," he said, grinning, "Head of the House of the Shadow Dragons!"

Quintin Wyvern had shuffled up to them, head low and shoulders hunched, as if he was trying to disappear. All the attention seemed to be more than the Dragon boy could handle. Even at the Northern Crowning, when the crowd cheered his impressive skills on horseback, he had kept his head hung low. And when the Shadow Dragon chose him for Dracogart, the crowd roaring, Quintin had tried to hide himself behind the High Beast's wings.

"Have you seen the ambassadors from the Ring Highen yet?" he asked softly.

Dev pointed to where they stood, the little group conversing jovially.

"Good," Quintin said, though he didn't seem pleased. He seemed anxious. "Dracogart will be grateful for the Heart Frost to come to an end."

"You'll head back to Dracogart today, then?" asked Dev, surprised.

Quintin nodded. "The people need their cure."

"They're lucky to have you, Quintin," said Lorc, serious now. "I can think of no better voice for Dracogart."

"We're not expected to speak today, are we?" Quintin asked, looking strained.

"I don't know about *we*," said Lorc. "But *you* certainly will be, given that your dragons are giving up an egg in exchange for the Prism Scorpion's venom. A lot of pressure...the delicate nature of foreign relations and all."

Quintin paled, and Dev worried he might throw up.

"He's *joking*, Quintin," said Dev, giving his shoulder a squeeze. "Only Aster is expected to give a speech."

Quintin let out a breath of relief. "Poor Aster! No wonder she looked so uncomfortable."

"You saw her?" asked Dev, perking up.

"Where is she?" Lorc asked, his eyes lit.

Quintin pointed. "She was running up the main stairwell."

"I should go find her. Congratulations, again, King Conri, King Wyvern." Dev bowed awkwardly and hurried off, dodging his way through the crowd, back to the great entrance.

More guests were arriving, Ursula Lourdes standing at the door and greeting every one. She wore a simple russet-colored gown—an ancient Tawnshirian dress, beautiful in its simplicity—that the old Ursula would never have been seen in. Dev supposed she'd had her fill of frost pearls, gilded flowers, blue velvet, and other rich things. She was one of the new Major's chief advisors now. A sober dress for a serious role, he guessed. It was strange to see her looking so stately. Not at all how she'd been before…everything. But then, nothing was how it had been, was it?

Dev hurried up the grand staircase, hoping no one would notice him and stop to give their best wishes to the new High Keeper.

It was dark at the top of the stairs, with no sign of the festivities below. A sudden rush of fear filled his body: the image of a furious Lady Lourdes played in his mind. He wasn't supposed to be upstairs at the Manor. At least, he wasn't supposed to back when he was an apprentice. Now he didn't know what the rules were.

A sniffle somewhere in the shadows made him jump. He spun and saw a girl standing in front of a mirror, wiping at her eyes.

"Aster?"

The girl turned, the lights from downstairs illuminating her face. Bernadine Lourdes.

"High Keeper," she said with a little curtsy, the skirts of her splendid pink gown puffing. "What are you doing up here?"

"I was just looking…" Dev was struck by the redness in her

eyes. She must have been crying all day. Maybe longer. "Bernadine, are you all right?"

She shrugged and dabbed a kerchief at her eyes. "I'd just rather not go down there, if it's all the same. I can't imagine what all of them must be saying about me."

"Saying?"

"Of course. Look at me! I'm Bram Lourdes's daughter. They all think I'm a traitor to the Highen."

They shouldn't, though Dev would be lying if he said he hadn't heard the whispers. More than one guest at the ball had wondered why Aster had allowed Bernadine Lourdes to remain at the Manor this fall. "I don't see why they should think that," said Dev very firmly. "Not after the way you stood up to your father."

"The people down there don't know about that."

Dev held up the *Star Writ*, patting its cover. "They will."

Bernadine blinked. "You've written about me in the *Star Writ*?"

Dev almost laughed. How could he write about what happened and leave out Bernadine Lourdes? "Of course. I wrote about how you helped Aster into the Manor to save her sister. I wrote about how you begged your father to stop before the Nightlocks took him. About how you saved me from Pire. *No one* will think you're a traitor after this."

A breath of a smile showed itself on Bernadine's face before it quickly faded.

"I still love him," she said. "My father. Is that wrong?"

"No." Dev was sure of that. Of all the sins Minor Bram Lourdes was guilty of, not loving his daughter was not one them.

"Do you think—do you think the On-High will condemn me to the moon, like him?"

Dev bit his lip. He was High Keeper now. He was expected to understand the will of the stars. But he wasn't at all sure that he did. He could only tell her what he believed.

"You are not your father," he said. "And besides, the White Bear chose you to protect Whitlock. I'd say that means the On-High hold you in pretty high esteem, don't you?"

Her fingers tugged at her handkerchief. "I never wanted to be a Head of Household, you know."

Dev smiled. "That doesn't matter much to the On-High." After all, Dev had never wanted to be a Keeper, but that hadn't stopped the On-High from sending Rizlan to take him from his mother. He thought of her then, his mother, standing on the shores of the bog with the little boy. His brother? Perhaps, now that he was High Keeper, he could go to Härkädia and find them both.

Laughter echoed up the stairs, and Bernadine's reddened eyes snapped toward the staircase as though it might bite her.

"You've nothing to be afraid of, Bernadine," said Dev. "You're a queen now."

She nodded. With a deep breath, she patted her cheeks, smoothed her dress, and headed for the steps. She looked back. "Are you coming?"

"In a minute. I just—have you seen Aster? Quintin said he saw her come up here."

"No," said Bernadine. "But if she is up here, you can probably find her in Uncle Jasper's study." She pointed down the hall on the left. "It's her favorite room in the house."

Bernadine made her way down the stairs, and Dev hurried along the hall, trying every locked door. Finally, he came to one where he saw light glowing in the door's seam.

He knocked twice. "Aster?"

She didn't answer. Dev carefully pushed the door open.

There was Aster, seated at the Major's giant mahogany desk, growling as she tried unsuccessfully to reach the tightly laced strings at the back of her armored dress. The war formals gown was twisted and lopsided, as if she'd tried to claw it off her body.

"Close the door!" she snapped.

Quickly, Dev shut the door behind him. He stepped across the floor, marveling at the detailed Hemoth Bears painted on the tiles.

"This blasted thing is going to kill me!" Aster growled. "The corset is too tight. I can barely breathe. It wasn't like this *before.*"

Dev watched her struggle. He didn't think he'd ever understand royal fashions.

"Don't just stand there!" she snapped. "Help me untie this!"

He hurried over and she turned away from him, showing the intricate weave of lacing and hooks that did up her dress. His cheeks flushed.

"What are you waiting for? Pull the strings! Turds of Tawn!"

With a silent apology to the On-High, Dev closed his eyes and pulled the strings, loosening the gown for her. She gasped and collapsed into the desk's wingback chair, panting. "On-High be praised. I thought I'd suffocate."

The Highen's brave new Major. Dev stifled a laugh.

"What are you doing here?" she asked, fanning herself.

He held up the *Star Writ.* "I wanted to show you what I've written."

"Why? That's not how this is done, you know."

"Because," said Dev, "I wanted to make sure you were happy with what I've written before you have to—you know—read it to the whole Highen."

She sighed. "I'm sure it's fine. I trust you."

As kind as that sounded, it was no great comfort to Dev. "Maybe you should just *practice* reading it, in case—"

At that, Aster let out a loud sound of frustration. Dev jumped back, startled.

The new Major sat up and turned to look at him, her face red. "This is all such a terrible mess, isn't it, Dev?"

"Your Majesty?"

"Don't call me that! Not after everything. Don't talk to me like I'm Major."

Dev was quiet, not sure what to say. Finally, he said, "But you are Major, Aster."

"Yes, I am." She turned away from him, placing her hands on a tattered old map laid open on the desk. "Would you believe I always wanted to be?"

Yes, he could believe it. Lofty goals were very much her way. He would have laughed at such a big ambition not long ago.

"It can't be me, Dev," she said finally. "It wasn't supposed to be me. Ursula was the one. Why didn't Alcor choose Ursula?"

"I don't think anyone can say why a Hemoth chooses a Major. Not really." He thought for a moment, wondering if Rizlan had ever heard the same type of question from Jasper Lourdes. He could ask neither of them now. "It seems to me the Hemoth Bears don't care much for man's plans. After all, didn't everyone think your uncle Bram would be crowned Major? That didn't stop Mizar from choosing your father." He paused. "You're very much alike, you and him."

"Do you really think so?"

He nodded. After everything they'd been through, he really did.

"Then why was it all so hard?"

"I think," said Dev, "that the On-High wanted to get your attention."

Aster thought about that a moment, then nodded to herself. "They certainly got it, didn't they?" She looked down at her map, and Dev noticed wet spots where tears had fallen. "It's too big, Dev. Being Major. How am I supposed to take care of the entire Highen?"

"You won't be alone. You have the privy council, and the Hermans, and your mother. You have Alcor. You have Ursula."

"And you?"

"And me," he agreed. They were bound together, him and her.

Just like Rizlan and Jasper Lourdes. "Come on," he said, holding out his hand to her. "Your subjects await!"

She took his hand and squeezed it gently. "Not just yet, please. I'll go, I just—I'm not ready just yet."

Dev didn't know when a person could be ready to rule the whole of the Highen, but he didn't think waiting a few more minutes would hurt. So he took a seat at the bay window, running his hand over the red velvet cushions. He breathed in the smell of the old books and rich wood furniture and let his eyes roam over the titles on the shelves. He could see why this was Aster's favorite room.

"It's nice in here, isn't it?" she said, as though reading his mind. "It's been the same way all my life. Probably hasn't changed for centuries. Sitting here, you could almost trick yourself into believing nothing's changed, couldn't you?"

Dev smiled, if only to be polite. Because she knew as well as he did that everything had changed. Nothing would ever be the same again.

A loud bang exploded in the quiet as the door to the study was thrown open.

"Jumping Juniper Bears!" Gatch, the nurse, stood in the door, her hands flying to her head. "Miss Aster! What on earth have you done to your formals!"

Aster leapt to her feet. "It's too tight! You shrank it somehow."

"It's the same size it's always been."

"Well, I must have grown."

Gatch rolled her eyes before they fell on Dev and she gasped in horror. "What is the meaning of this, then! You standing here, clothes a mess, and you got a boy looking on?"

Aster rolled her eyes. "I do wish you wouldn't be so dramatic, Gatch. He isn't a boy, he's the High Keeper."

"High Keeper or not," the old woman puffed, grabbing Dev by the arm, "he's got no business being 'round you in yer knickers." She pushed him to the door, shoving him into the hall. "Get on out of here, little Dev, go on and get!" And with that, she slammed the door behind him.

Inside, Dev could still hear Aster and Gatch, shouting at each other over the state of Aster's war formals, and Dev couldn't help but laugh.

It was a small blessing from the On-High, Dev thought, that maybe he was wrong. Maybe not everything had changed.

The Major Aster Lourdes addresses the Highen on her coronation day:

As I stand here, the egg of our mighty Shadow Dragon in my hands, I cannot escape how different our world has become. I was a child when my father left the Manor. I fear I'm not quite now. So much has changed. Dragon eggs. Scorpion milk…Starflame. I knew little of these things before my father's death.

I have learned a lot since then. I have learned that the strength of the Shadow Dragon is in its heart. That a Starhound's loyalty need not be tested. That the cleverness of White Bears lets them divine the good in everyone. And I have learned that Hemoths, while mighty, can be tender.

I've learned that blood and loyalty don't always mix. That friendship is stronger than any blade. And that the stars have lessons for each of us, if we try our best to listen.

I've learned that a Major does not always get things right. That all a Major can do is their best, looking to the stars for guidance. This was the principle that guided my father in his time spent on his throne. The throne I now belong to. And on that throne, my people, I pledge always to learn. To do my utmost to serve you fully. To make my father, and the Highen, proud.

Today I am a Major. Always, I am my father's daughter. And now, I am ready, for what is next.

—THE WRITINGS OF DEV,
The Crowning of the Fifty-Fourth Major: The New Rule, *Star Writ*

ACKNOWLEDGMENTS

A lot of years and a lot of stars had to align for this book to come together, and my wild Highen was very lucky to find such incredible people to bring it to life.

I am eternally grateful to my amazing editor Mora Couch, who, after I lived alone in this bear world for so long, jumped right in with me and saw this world with so much clarity and enthusiasm. I can't express how much stronger and better your talents made this story. Aster and Alcor are so lucky to have you in their corner.

I would also really like to thank Barbara Perris, copy editor extraordinaire; Pam Glauber, awesome proofreader; and everyone at Holiday House, who worked for so long on bringing Aster and her world to readers. And of course, a big thank you to Fiona Hsieh for creating such a beautiful cover!

Thanks to Ali McDonald and the team at The Rights Factory for finding *The Bear House* a home, and big, big thanks to my writing pals and word goddesses, Ainslie Hogarth and Alisha Sevigney, for all your support and encouragement.

And finally, thank you to my patient and understanding family, who let me disappear into Aster's world when I needed to.